THE
JIM BAEN
MEMORIAL
AWARD
THE FIRST DECADE

THE JIM BAEN MEMORIAL AWARD

THE FIRST DECADE

Edited by
WILLIAM LEDBETTER

Jim Baen Memorial Award: The First Decade

STORY COPYRIGHTS

A Baen Books Original

Baen Publishing Enterprises
P.O. Box 1403
Riverdale, NY 10471
www.baen.com

ISBN: 978-1-4814-8281-3

Cover art by Bob Eggleton

First Baen printing, November 2017

Distributed by Simon & Schuster
1230 Avenue of the Americas
New York, NY 10020

Printed in the United States of America

10 9 8 7 6 5 4 3 2 1

ACKNOWLEDGEMENTS

Without help, this contest and anthology would never have happened. I'd like to thank members of the National Space Society of North Texas, former NSS Executive Director George Whitesides, and Lynne Zielinski, NSS Vice President of Public Affairs. The list of people at Baen that help are legion but include Toni Weisskopf, Tony Daniel, Hank Davis, Jim Minz, David Afsharirad, Christopher Ruocchio, David Drake, Walt Boyes, Eric Flint, Mike Resnick, Sharon Lee and Steve Miller. I also owe a huge thanks to my friend Michelle Muenzler who has been the contest first reader since 2013.

TABLE OF CONTENTS

INTRODUCTION

THE JIM BAEN MEMORIAL Short Story Award Contest started because, like so many of you, I wanted to be an astronaut. The imaginations of my generation were primed for such dreams by daring science fiction programs like *Star Trek* and *Lost in Space*, brought right into our living rooms by the technological magic of network TV. Only fiction of course, until that day when it became real. All around the world, people stared in wonder at tiny black and white televisions like mine as Apollo 11 astronauts walked on the moon. That moment changed us, individually and as a civilization. We believed anything was possible and we had just opened a door that would eventually lead to our destiny among the stars.

Fast forward to the twenty-first century where we still didn't have moon or Mars colonies and even though I had "mostly" given up my dreams of walking on another world, I had adopted the space-travel analogs of a long career in the aerospace industry and writing science fiction. In 2006 my local National Space Society chapter won our bid to host the 2007 International Space Development Conference in Dallas, and we were discussing ways to make our ISDC the best ever. Being a science fiction reader and writer, I naturally suggested a short story contest, with the focus being humanity's future in space. The idea was well received by my chapter and the NSS national headquarters. Of course since it was my idea, it was also my project. At that point the contest was supposed to have been a one-time effort, but even for that single event I wanted the best entries I could get. So what was the most effective bait to attract quality writers? A huge cash prize would have been great, but since NSS is a nonprofit organization, money is always tight. The next best thing was professional publication, in a respected magazine. It couldn't hurt to ask, right?

Considering Baen's reputation for hard science fiction, and the fact that I'd recently sold a story to *Jim Baen's Universe,* they were my logical first choice. I sent the idea to Walt Boyes, who had been one of the editors I worked with previously and he sent it up the chain. Much to my surprise I received a reply rather quickly, with approval coming from Jim Baen himself. Sadly, Jim passed away before that first award could be handed out, but since the contest had gone so well and generated a lot of interest, Baen Books asked if NSS and I would be interested in making it an annual effort in his honor. The Jim Baen Memorial Short Story Award Contest was born.

The Grand Prize award is presented by top Baen Books editors like Tony Danial and Jim Minz, or publisher Toni Weisskopf at the International Space Development Conference, which is hosted every year by the National Space Society in cities like Los Angeles, Toronto, San Juan, and Washington, DC. During the years covered by the contest ISDC guests have included commercial space industry luminaries like Elon Musk, Burt Rutan, Richard Branson and Robert Bigelow, and various NASA Directors and astronauts. One year at our award presentation luncheon we even sat with Buzz Aldrin, who is an ISDC regular and a member of the NSS Board of Governors.

The National Space Society's vision is to have "people living and working in thriving communities beyond the Earth, and the use of the vast resources of space for the dramatic betterment of humanity." And our mission is "to promote social, economic, technological, and political change in order to expand civilization beyond Earth, to settle space and to use the resulting resources to build a hopeful and prosperous future for humanity." The Jim Baen Memorial Short Story Award contest and this anthology are just small ways we can help achieve those goals.

Though the contest has changed some over the years, with adjustments in the guidelines, the name and even a new award trophy design, our goal to showcase fiction about mankind's exciting future in space has never wavered. Since the contest's inception, I have read well in excess of a thousand stories and while I'm sure all of those stories were not written specifically for the contest, I know that many of them actually have been. We obviously couldn't publish them all, but those stories are still out there, many appearing in other magazines and anthologies, still spreading our hopeful vision.

Just before writing this, I sent another ten finalist stories off to the judges. It's so hard to believe the contest has been running for eleven years already. The entries come from countries all around the world, from men and women, from seasoned pros and beginners, and they all continue to amaze, educate, excite and entertain. I hope you enjoy this collection of the best stories from those first ten years as much as we did. As for me, the judges, the folks at NSS and Baen, if these stories inspire one boy or girl to become an engineer, or one lawmaker to support a larger space budget, or one entrepreneur to build rockets, or one dreamer to become an astronaut and walk on another world, then this whole endeavor has been worth every minute.

Ad astra!
—Bill Ledbetter

A BETTER SENSE OF DIRECTION

by Mjke Wood

This story by Mjke Wood wasn't at all what I expected when I started this contest, but when I read it I was charmed and my mind expanded. It had a similar impact on the judges and there is a good reason why. Mjke Wood was twelve years old when Neil Armstrong first stepped on the moon. He watched every minute of live TV that came back from each mission. He made balsa wood models of the LEM and Command Module, compiled a folder, mission by mission, with diagrams and notes—the hardware, the astronauts, the mission plans. Then, three years later it all ended with Apollo 17. No man on Mars. No journeys to the stars. Space was just too big and we were too slow. In his disappointment, Mjke had a fantasy about finding a shortcut to the stars and wrote down the spaghetti idea in the back of his Apollo folder. Thirty-five years later the folder was long gone, but the idea remained.

WE RAN OUT OF TINNED spaghetti-in-tomato-sauce less than seven years into the voyage. For my daughter, Stella, it was a crisis. Stella had always hated space rations, but she was okay with tinned spaghetti. It was the only thing she ever seemed to eat. Stella was six years old, and anyone who has ever spent time with a six-year-old will know how fussy they can be with food. Stella's relationship with tinned spaghetti was more a fixation. She didn't just eat the stuff; she didn't just play with it; she *communed* with it.

The spaghetti crisis wasn't the first trauma to follow Stella's unplanned arrival on the crew list, but for Jodie and I, it was probably the most unsettling. Accommodation on a starship is cramped, and privacy is a scarce commodity, so a tantrum under these conditions, let me tell you, is a tantrum on steroids.

Stella was the first true child-of-the-stars. She was conceived on the starship and she was born on the starship. Children had always been part of the mission plan, hence the low average age of the crew (Babes in Space, they called us). But it had never been part of the plan to have the first birth take place only nine months out of Earth orbit.

To be fair, a young crew is an impetuous crew. Me and Jodie, being scientists (of a sort), were drawn to experimentation. Our ship, *Castor*, had been suspended at L2 for the three days that were set aside for crew embarkation and provisioning. Jodie and I were amongst the first to board. We had just three days of weightlessness before the photon engines were due to fire up, hitting us with the point-two gee of thrust that would be our constant companion for the next twenty-odd years; ten years accelerating then ten more to wind it back down.

"Jodie," I said, "have you ever wondered what it might be like in zero gravity?"

"I don't need to wonder. This is zero gravity. It sucks. I've been puking for four hours."

"No, Jodie, you misunderstand. I'm talking about what *it* might be like. You know . . ." I winked. I worked my eyebrows up and down my face in a choreography of suggestiveness.

"Ah."

She got my drift.

"Did you misunderstand what *I* just said, Luke . . . about the puking?"

"Space sickness is in the mind. All you need is something that will take your mind off it."

"And you reckon . . ."

"Undoubtedly."

"Well, okay then."

So we had three days—three days in which to explore the boundaries of science. Well, let me assure you, zero-gee nooky is not up to much. It's tricky, it's horribly messy, and it is *not* a cure for space sickness. Also, it is rife with unexpected dangers. I managed torn ligaments as well as a four-day concussion, while Jodie brought the whole, sorry experience to a close by dislocating her thumb. Then the engines powered up. With the return of gravity the space-sickness sufferers perked up . . . but not Jodie. *Her* space sickness metamorphosed, seamlessly, into morning sickness.

Captain Bligh (her real name's Catherine Blair) was furious when we told her the results of our adventure. She even threatened to turn the ship around and send us home, but the accountants, God bless them, saved us on that call. What the captain *did* insist on, though, was that we share a cabin and assume joint responsibility for the baby's upbringing. This was fine by me; I'd had a thing for Jodie ever since college. Jodie wasn't quite so pleased, though, and she sulked about the arrangement for months afterwards. I put this down to hormonal changes. I knew she would come round eventually, and I was right. She gave up throwing stuff at me a couple of years ago, and we moved to a mutually stress-free and congenial silence. Our relationship did not blossom into what you'd call love, but at least she stopped trying to trick me into the air lock.

I first noticed Jodie at college. It was her walk. She had the action. Jodie's walk could stop traffic, usually in a way that involved broken glass, rolling hubcaps and seeping pools of oil and antifreeze. She didn't seem to realise the effect that she was having on her immediate environment. She would glide through town with those hips all swaying and pulsing to a Caribbean beat, and the traffic accidents would pile up around her. And then I noticed the T-shirts, with slogans printed across her boobs: "Beam me up, Scotty;" ". . . to boldly go"; "Make it so." *She was a Trekkie.*

I tracked down the local branch and joined. I went to all the meetings, the screenings . . . I bought the Spock ears. I learned enough Klingon to get by, and I moved into her inner circle.

But we never spoke. I was one of her entourage; the drooling, pathetic onlookers; the pimply male adolescent no-hopers. I seemed destined to be, forever, a voyeur by day and a fantasist by night.

Then I overheard a conversation. She and a small group of her inner-circle friends had signed up for *Castor* and *Pollux*. Jodie was hard-core Trekkie, and she was heading for the stars. The very next day I signed up myself. I went through the interviews and the preselection training and the medicals . . . I hung in there. The numbers were pared down. Each evening the TV audiences voted, and more fell by the wayside until, at last, the United States of Europe had their four viewer-selected reps: me, Jodie, Jorge and Chantel. Jodie and Jorge drew *Castor*, and I drew *Pollux*, with Chantel. I was supposed to be ecstatic, but I was devastated. The two ships were to fly, side-by-side, for twenty-odd years, and there could be no physical contact between the crews. I never really wanted to even make the trip, I mean, twenty years! I'd faked the psychs; I had motivation but it wasn't space that drove me.

I wrote the email. I was bailing, and my finger was actually hovering over the send button when the news broke; Jorge had concealed a genetic disorder that came about from his tight-fisted father using a back-street baby-designer during his conception, and he was bumped. The reserve, Henri, was French, like Chantel, so they shunted Jodie over to *Castor* with me. Two Brits, two French. There were also four Asians—the rest, thirty-two on each ship, were American.

Jodie and I became a team, sort of. And, well, you know the rest.

So, the spaghetti crop failed, and Stella pouted for a couple of weeks. Things were so desperate I even tried replicating spaghetti by extruding homemade pasta through a spare photon diffuser, then mixing in some tomato paste and boiling the lot to hell and back. Everyone, the whole crew, loved it . . . except Stella. It wasn't the same as tinned. It got me posted in the galley though. I was happier there. My specialty was drive systems, but I'd faked the exams. It made me a bit jumpy when I was poking around in there with my greasy rag when there're so many lives hanging on my imaginary expertise. The engines were sparkling clean, but I knew jack about fixing them if they ever stopped firing. Brad, the cook, on the other hand was a sous-chef, and very frustrated in a culinary world of concentrates, *and* he knew more about photon drive systems than I did. So we swapped, and we were both happier for it.

Stella sleeps through the days, and so, therefore, do Jodie and I. So, when I was dragged from bed by the alarm after only four hours of z's, I felt particularly cheated. I'd only recently reacquainted myself with the luxury of eight straight hours. But it wasn't Stella, this time;

it was Captain Bligh, calling the full crew to the galley, the only room where we could all assemble. Last time we were here was when the weird stuff began with the marker stars, a few years ago.

"Thanks for coming down," she said, as if we had any choice. "We have a problem."

"It's the thrust isn't it?" Jodie said. There were a number of nodding heads. Quite a few had noticed.

"*Pollux* has been pulling away from us for a couple of days. Nothing serious to begin with, but in the last few hours it's become more noticeable."

"I've got greens right across the board," said Brad. "Can't be the engines."

"Unless we're venting for'ard, it can't be much else," said Bligh. "Brad, I want you and Luke to get your heads together and run a full set of diagnostics on the drive. I'll come and help. Anyone else got any ideas?"

There were blank looks.

"Okay, so we need an end-to-end integrity-check . . . everyone. The instruments aren't showing any anomalies, but *they* could be faulty. It's hands-on, I'm afraid. I want every inch of the hull examined."

The gathering broke up amid a sotto-voce chorus of grumbles and curses. An end-to-end was a miserable task, involving hours of crawling and wriggling into the most claustrophobic, cold and inhospitable corners of the ship. I was relieved to have drawn the cerebral option.

It took Captain Bligh five hours to find the cause. She called us all back to the galley. I saw what she had found, and suddenly I developed an overwhelming urge to go end-to-ending; to find one of those cold, cramped corners and hide there.

"Here, in my hand, I have a photon diffuser," she announced. "There are carbon deposits. The resulting hot spots have damaged the machining." And now she raised her voice to an accusatory level. "I was puzzled about the carbon. How could carbon deposits form in this way? The components were installed in ionised white-room conditions."

She scratched some of the black carbon off and rubbed it between her fingers.

"Ladies and gentlemen," she said, "this is pasta."

And she looked straight at me.

Everybody looked straight at me. They looked at their chapped and blistered fingers, the result of five hours of arctic end-to-ending, then they looked, again, at me.

There are times when one longs for a duvet under which to crawl.

The captain wasn't finished.

"What is more," she said, "this is the spare. We had to put the original worn out diffuser back in the engine—the one currently holding us back to just point-eight gee—is in better shape than the spare."

She looked straight at me again, then looked at each of the thirty-five worried faces.

"Questions?"

"What's the bottom line?" This was Anjana, the pilot.

"The bottom line is, at our current loss of acceleration, status quo maintained, we've added about four years to our journey time. On the other hand, my gut feeling is the diffuser will continue to degrade, then . . . who knows?"

"Don't we have more than one spare?"

"There's triple redundancy on all the stressed parts. The diffuser isn't stressed. We have one spare to cover the minimal risk of build flaws. The planners are at fault, they didn't anticipate the additional stresses imposed by cookery."

"How about *Pollux*? Can we use their spare?" said Jodie.

The captain shook her head. "The unstressed parts, the minimal redundancy items, are shared inventory. We carry some of the spares, *Pollux* carries others. This is the one spare diffuser for *Castor and Pollux*. I called Captain Schiffer, just to be sure, and he confirmed—this is the only one."

"Can't we repair it?" I asked. My voice was tiny and unwelcome.

The captain looked at me for a long, silent moment, then said, "No."

"Daddy, why don't people like you any more?" It had only taken Stella a couple of days to pick up the bad vibes.

"What makes you think nobody likes me?" I didn't have a comfortable answer, so I was stalling for time.

"They call you names."

"They're just a bit upset."

"Why?"

"It's going to take us all a bit longer to get to New World, that's all."

"Why?"

"Your daddy made a mistake with the engines, honey. It's nothing more. They're all overreacting." Jodie had leapt to my defence. This was unprecedented. I began to think she was, well, starting to warm towards me a little. Then I realised she was deflecting our daughter away from an associated matter. I had made the pasta to try to appease Stella's long and apocalyptic temper tantrums. Stella had wanted spaghetti.

"If everyone's so upset about us taking longer, Daddy, then why don't we just go straight there?"

"No, honey, we're going slower. It will take us a few more years because we're not gaining speed quite so quickly," said Jodie.

"So why don't we just go the short way?"

I took over trying to explain. "If I want to go from the front of the ship to the back of the ship it will take longer if I walk slower, see?"

Stella exploded in a frustrated storm of tears.

"I *know* that. You *said*. But if you want to get there quicker . . . Why! Not! Go! The *short* way!" She screamed the words. She threw her beaker of juice across the room. It bounced off the holo' and sticky, fluorescent orange liquid exploded onto the front screen and dripped down onto the carpet. Jodie and I looked at each other. We'd seen this sort of thing coming before. We knew the signs.

"I'm not sure what you mean, honey. Explain it to me." I tried to sound patient.

Stella's bottom lip was quivering with frustration or rage or something, but she gathered some control. Then, with a straight arm, she pointed out to her left.

"New World is there," she said. Then she pointed straight up above her head, toward the front of the ship.

"We're going *that* way. We're just going down the *spaghetti!*" she shouted the last word.

I looked over at Jodie and shrugged. I was worried that my daughter was having some kind of a mental crisis. Maybe living in space all her life . . .

Jodie came over and put her hand lightly on my arm.

"Wait," she said. She didn't want me saying any more. Her eyes held a strange, almost wondrous expression. "Explain again, darling, for Mummy."

"We keep going all over the place. Like we're going down the spaghetti. It's stupid. Why can't we just go straight there?"

"What do you mean, honey, down the spaghetti?"

Stella explained. It sounded ridiculous. I smiled to humour her. Jodie smiled, too. But her smile was different. It was almost as if she was taking this nonsense seriously.

We settled Stella down for bed, eventually, and Jodie wanted to talk. We pulled out the sofa bed and relaxed onto it with a glass of wine each. This was great. I'd never felt so close to her, even when we were doing the "science" thing back at L2. I wanted this moment to last. I forced myself to listen; not to rubbish what she was saying to me.

"I think I know what she's trying to tell us, Luke. I think she might know something. I think there is a quicker way."

"Jodie, come on. You used to get lost around college when . . ." I bit my lip. I shouldn't have said it. I'd gone and put my foot in it again. She'd go off in a hissy fit now and storm out.

But she didn't.

Jodie nodded. "Yes. Back home. I admit. I never knew where I was. I could never find my way around town, even. But out *here*, for the last . . . three . . . four years, it's been different. I've felt that I've *known* where I am. But . . . it's felt wrong. *We've* felt wrong. I've had this idea that we've . . . *that we've been going the wrong way!*"

She was so intense. Her eyes were burning. She held my forearm in a talon-like grip. I was loving this, even though I had no idea what she was talking about; even though the two women in my life appeared to be going off their heads.

"I think we should speak to Catherine. I think *Stella* should explain this to Catherine."

"Tell Captain Bligh? She'll lock us up."

"I don't think so."

"Captain Blair, do you mind if I ask, how was your sense of direction back on Earth?"

It was a strange opening. I cringed. Jodie had unusual ideas about how to break into a topic gently. We were sitting around the captain's wardroom table, Jodie, myself and Stella.

The captain gave a half laugh. "It's an odd question, but I suppose it won't harm anything to say, I was pretty hopeless. I was terrible with a map. Why do you ask?"

Jodie smiled. "I have a theory. Stella has something to tell us. It's a little weird but I think *you'll* understand.

"Stella, tell the captain what you told me and Daddy."

Stella began to unfold her bizarre theory again. She was hesitant at first—a little scared of the captain—but she soon got into her stride. She started with the spaghetti. She explained how we were at one end of a piece of spaghetti and New World was at the other end. New World shone down the spaghetti and we could see it shining from the ship, so we followed the light. She said how every star was at the end of a different piece of spaghetti, and how it was silly to follow the light round all the curves and loops and knots, when it would be much quicker and shorter to travel in a straight line and go to New World directly.

Then Jodie took over the narrative.

"Is it possible that some of us can see the shape of space; but that on Earth, where gravity gives everything a top and a bottom, we get confused? Even out here we are confused because after spending our lives living on Earth we're conditioned to straight lines and up and down."

"Go on." The captain wasn't laughing, or shouting, or sneering. In fact she had that same eureka spark in her eye that I had seen in Jodie's the previous evening.

"I know this is a dodgy bit of gender stereotyping, but isn't it widely viewed that women have a poorer sense of direction, even though everyone's scared to say it out loud? But could it be that women have the better sense of direction, that they can see the curves of space-time, but on Earth we are confused because the Earth's surface makes us think two-and-a-bit-dimensionally?"

"Two-and-a-bit?" The captain and I spoke in unison.

"Yeah. We could move around on the surface of the planet. It's hard to go up; it's even harder to go down. If you want to take the quickest way to the shops you don't usually pick up a shovel."

The captain nodded, in a spooky, knowing way. I simply held up my hands with an Oh-my-God-they're-all-nutters kind of expression.

"Stella isn't conditioned," Jodie continued. "She's a child of the stars. She sees what is plain to see, and she believes we are all stupid not to see the obvious."

"But there's gravity on the ship," I said. I had to say something to show that at least *I* wasn't a couple of bricks short of a wall.

But the captain waved an impatient hand at me. "That's thrust," she said. "Nothing to do with gravity."

She leaned over the table and pulled a rolled-up platter screen from a drawer. She tapped her fingers on the desk to activate her implants, then, with rapid finger movements, called up a star map on the screen. It showed Earth and New World connected by a straight dotted line. A small pulsating red dot indicated the depressingly short distance along the line that *Castor* and *Pollux* had travelled in just under seven years. The captain began to explain the map to Stella, but before she had uttered more than a couple of sentences Stella was up on her knees on the stool and pointing at the chart.

"You see!" she shouted. "It's wong! *You all keep getting it wong!* It's the wong shape. It's all straightened out."

Captain Blair reached up into a locker above her head. She brought down an ancient globe of the stars and set it on the table.

"Is this better?" she asked.

Stella stared at it for a long moment. Then she shook her head.

"No. Worse," she said. "There's no inning or outing. There's no . . . through . . . or around. It doesn't even *look* like outside."

Captain Blair clasped her hands together and pressed her index fingers to her lips. She spoke in a quiet voice.

"She's talking about multidimensions, isn't she? She's six years old and she can visualise the universe in multiple dimensions. In one short sentence she has explained the weirdness."

Blair was right. We stared at the globe. It looked just like the sky seen from Earth, albeit inside out. But a few years ago, a year or so into the voyage, the weirdness had started. The stars had begun to shift out of position. The markers—the pulsars—had moved. We lost track of the galactic equator, completely. We'd all met in the galley and worked the problem. We decided that we were seeing some kind of relativistic effect—an optical illusion—but back then we weren't doing relativistic speeds . . . not really. We'd dismissed it. New World was still straight ahead. We could follow our noses. We'd be fine so long as we didn't have to make the return trip. A couple of the crew had decided to do a study of it, but they'd got nowhere. Now, here was a six-year-old girl telling us why. As we'd moved through space our visual perspective had changed. We had moved into a different part of the spaghetti bowl and everything looked wrong to us.

"Stella?" The captain leaned across the table and gently grasped both of Stella's hands. She peered into Stella's eyes, and in a quiet but firm voice she asked the question.

"Stella, would you be able to show us the way to New World? Could you show us which way to turn?"

The captain's tough, but when she announced that she'd been told, by a six-year-old girl, that New World would be much closer if we made an eighty-degree course correction; that it would be the first of many such adjustments; that she couldn't be precise about it because ever since the weirdness had started we didn't even know the direction in which the galactic equator lay; so we would now be guided by the six-year-old, who was to show us the way by pointing . . . When she announced this, there was mayhem. She then added that she would ask all the women in the crew for validation of the directions; but only those women who, on Earth, had displayed a serious lack of spatial awareness. Only those who could not read a map would be consulted.

Mutiny was considered, by the men. But Captain Bligh is one scary person, and mutiny did not happen.

She also explained the plan to Captain Schiffer on *Pollux*. He is a man. His specialty is astral navigation. We only got to hear of his response through gossip and rumour. There was talk of a pirated audio file that started doing the rounds, but it was intercepted and destroyed, so we only had canteen talk as to the range of colourful adjectives that were used. *Pollux* would not be joining us on our fools' errand.

Over the following weeks the crew formed into four distinct groups. Those who could read maps back on Earth—most of the men—became known as the mappies. They sulked. The idea that this strange new way of looking at the universe might have some credibility was an affront to them. They were offended by it. There were some women who were also a little mappy, but they tended to keep quiet about it; they felt a little left out. There were a handful of non-mappy males who probably knew what was going on but stayed clear of it, finding the whole thing to be a challenge to their manhood.

Then there were the non-mappy females. The Stella camp. I tended to hang out with this group, for, although I was one hundred percent mappy, I believed them. Stella was my daughter. I believed her and I was proud of her.

For the Stella camp, a new era had dawned. They were excited and moved by the realisation that *they* had been the true possessors of an innate, accurate sense of direction all along. The scientists among them wanted to explain things, and there developed a small subsect called the Stella Theory Cosmology Group. Catherine Blair, the captain, was a leading light amongst them. It took them a little over three weeks to come up with a credible theory that explained the new universe.

"Dark matter is the key," Catherine explained at one of their lectures. "The shape of the universe that we see: star clusters, galaxies, expansion . . . these are how the universe *used* to be, or *should have* been. We see it this way because we see light as straight lines, whether it *is* straight or not. But then dark matter got in between and wrinkled everything up. The real universe is being contracted; packed into an ever-smaller can of spaghetti by the gravitational pull of dark matter, even though the individual strands, along which we can see, are getting longer, giving the illusion (to the mappies) that we are in an expanding universe."

I put my hand up. I'd been attending STCG lectures right from the start, even though this alienated me from most of the other men on the crew.

"I have a question. If there is all this heavy dark matter between the strands, what's to prevent us plunging into a black hole, or something, as soon as we turn off the star track?"

Blair nodded. "That's a fair point. I think the key is to always head for a star—any star. So long as we can see a star in front of us we are on *a* star track and we can freewheel along between the dark matter.

We just have to avoid heading towards the parts of the sky that are empty."

"So, we have to skip from strand to strand, where the spaghetti meets, and we stay out of the sauce." Stella grabbed my hand and gave it a squeeze. I smiled down at her. I was getting the hang of this non-mappy stuff.

When we made the turn the sky went wild. It was like Guy Fawkes night. There were blueshifts and redshifts, and stars stretched, smeared and splattered all over the sky. The mappies huddled in dark corners of the ship and moaned. Some of them turned to drink, others went to their databases and rediscovered religion.

The women had a party. Five of the non-mappy men came out of the closet and went along. They had a great time. I was with Jodie and Stella, so I had to behave.

It took seven years. We actually did our first flyby of New World after only eighteen months, but we arrived at a fair clip, and had a lot of speed to lose. Stella's good, but she hadn't thought of the dynamics of losing relativistic velocities, so we had to wander around our new star system for a while, decelerating like crazy by sitting on our weakened engines. Once we'd lost enough of our velocity we did a few close passes by some of the system's gas giants, using first their gravity, then later, when we felt we wouldn't be ripped apart, we used their atmospheres for a bit of pants-on-fire aerobraking.

New World's a fine place to call home. A warm, orange sun; oceans, mountains, trees and plenty of wildlife that we cannot eat and that does not want to eat us—the genetic and protein differences are too great—so we are safe from one another.

We sent a message to *Pollux*. Captain Blair told them that we'd put the kettle on for them. They'll get the message in about eight years, but it won't help them, they will have started the deceleration phase of their voyage by now, so shortcuts won't work. They should be with us in about twenty years. They'll be much younger than us of course.

I'll tell you what I like about New World the most, though. I know my way around. I've drawn a few maps, and it's become a bit of a hobby. They're no use to the women, of course. The women haven't a clue . . . forever getting themselves lost, especially Stella. But nobody says anything about this to them, not to their faces, anyway.

Mjke Wood

Mjke Wood was the first winner of the Jim Baen Memorial Writing competition in 2007, followed up a year later by winning the L. Ron Hubbard Writers of the Future Competition. His science fiction and fantasy short stories have appeared in many print and online venues. He has published two novels, the first in his Sphere of Influence series. He is an active member of the Science Fiction and Fantasy Writers of America (SFWA), the Science Fiction and Fantasy Writers of America, as well as the British Science Fiction Association (BSFA) and the British Fantasy Society (BFS). Mjke was born on the Isle of Man and now lives in the Wirral, UK. Find out more at his website: mjkewood.com

LETTING GO

by David Walton

This story had all the classic elements of a winner for this contest. High technology, heroics, new ideas, struggle and most of all, characters we care about. David says he read about the gravity-train concept that Robert Hooke suggested in a letter to Isaac Newton in the Seventeenth century and the story idea bloomed from there. Having a daughter of my own—one that grew up and had to be let go—was probably one of the reasons this story resonated so strongly with me. And since David has five daughters, he'll have to address this "Letting Go" dynamic many times in the years to come.

I NEVER WANTED RACHEL to go into space. Space was my passion, but for my daughter, I wanted a normal American life: Barbie dolls and pony rides, makeup and boys, the senior prom. A good college, a good career, marriage, kids. Only I wasn't there, most of the time, to see it happen. When she played Mary in her Sunday School pageant, I was on the ISS. When she graduated high school, I was on the Moon, already starting the Gravity Train project. But there must be some truth to the argument for nature over nurture, because despite my long absences, she took after me instead of her mother. Joined the academy, earned her pin, and followed me to the Moon.

The morning of the accident, we were all ready to celebrate. We gathered in the control room, Rachel holding my hand, Commander André Gretzsin, Jr., beside her, and the rest of the crew pressed in close behind. On screen, a Herrenknecht Tunnel Boring Machine named Big Betsy churned through the lunar rock at the bottom of the Hole, as it had been doing without stop for almost eight years. Today was different, though. Today, Big Betsy would finally reach the end of her task. No one dared to speak. The only sound was the bass growl of the machine, transmitted back to us through the video feed.

The Hole was two meters wide and more than three thousand kilometers deep, stretching from Mare Serenitatis straight down to the core. On the other side of the Moon, starting at Farside Station and plunging nearly as far, was the dig known affectionately as the Other Hole. The boring machine on that side had been redirected the day before to get it out of the way. As we watched, the last bit of rock tumbled forward in a loose spray as Big Betsy connected the two holes into one long tunnel, the longest ever dug, nearly seven thousand kilometers long.

We broke into cheers. On another video display, the team at Farside danced and hugged each other. It was finished. We'd actually done it.

Four hundred years ago, Robert Hooke proposed the perfect transportation system to Isaac Newton: a straight tunnel through the Earth from any two points on its surface. A frictionless sled dropped down the hole at one end would arrive at the other side forty-two minutes later with perfect conservation of energy. For Hooke and Newton, it was a thought experiment—a puzzle on which to apply the new laws of geometry and gravitation. On the Moon, however, with modern drilling techniques and no atmosphere to cause friction, their idea had become a reality. In a few months, when the train capsules were completed and put into service, a thousand pounds of helium-3 a day would be scooped up from the vast deposits around Farside and transported by gravity train to the near side.

"So there it is," said Rachel. "A really, really deep hole."

I snorted. "That's all we hear from the media." The project had required almost twice the originally planned budget, and most of their news coverage revolved around how much money the government was sinking into a very deep hole. "One of those helium-3 capsules will provide enough fusion energy to power New York for a year. We're going to solve the world's energy crisis, and all they can talk about is the *Guinness Book of World Records*."

Rachel squeezed my hand. "When I was little, I was always out digging holes in the backyard."

I smiled, but it gave me a pang for her to mention her childhood. The childhood I had missed. "Digging a hole to China?"

"Digging a hole to *anywhere,* as long as it wasn't home."

"You wanted to get away that badly?"

"Mostly I just wanted to be with you."

"You and Mom . . ." I began, but she put a finger on my mouth.

"Let it go, Dad. We were too different. Not your fault."

Her blond hair was cropped close, a concession to the hardships of space, and her face showed the fluid swelling typical of long stints in low gravity. She was my height, slender, strong, and independent. She was different than her mother, all right. But she wasn't what I had wanted her to be.

"Dad?"

Her tone worried me. "What's wrong?"

"Nothing. I wanted to pile on some more good news."

Something *was* wrong. Rachel was never hesitant.

"André and I are going to be married."

I pressed my lips together. She knew my opinion of astronauts and marriage. That's why she chose that moment to tell me. "What happened to 'single forever'?"

"I changed my mind."

I glanced around the control room and spotted André at his terminal, watching us.

"What do you want, my blessing or something?"

"I just want you to be happy for us."

"I probably won't make it to the wedding."

"Sure you will. We'll have it as soon as we get home."

"I might have to stay here longer than you, make sure everything keeps running."

"Then we'll wait. You have to come back to Earth eventually."

I shook my head. Against all odds, she'd beaten her mother's influence and made a career for herself. Now she wanted to throw it away for domestic life?

But she knew what I thought; I didn't have to say it. Back to work. Big Betsy had to be redirected to drill into the side of the tunnel, where she would be left forever—it wasn't worth the energy to pull her back to the surface. The other boring machine was already snug in its own little grave, ten meters into the rock.

André must have snuck up behind me, because I heard him say, "I'll take good care of her, Frank."

I wanted to hit him, but I kept my voice soft. "You're on the short list for Mars, André. She's not. What are you going to do, leave her in a Florida apartment with a baby in her belly while you go away for seven years?"

André looked angry, but he didn't snap back.

Rachel said, "Dad . . ."

"Forget it. It's your life. I have work and so do you."

I sat down and ignored them. Eventually they left.

An hour later, I watched her on screen as she worked inside Capsule A. Our command center partially encircled the Hole in a rough U-shape, inside of which were the oxygen tanks for the complex, fuel and extra cutting blades for the Tunnel Boring Machines, construction materials, and in the center, the capsule itself. It was held in place above the chasm of the Hole by the electromagnetic capture system, but for safety, a series of bolts prevented accidental release. She was inside, suited up, spraying the capsule with insulator before its virgin drop the next day. She barely fit; at just shy of two meters wide, the capsule had been designed for cargo, not human passengers.

I watched her work, confident, at ease in a spacesuit, skilled at her task. I had been unfair. André was a talented spacer, a third-generation astronaut whose grandfather had been on the Mir. He was stable, trustworthy, a great commander. He had lost his own father in a training accident when he was young; he knew the risks of space. I knew my reaction had more to do with guilt about my own failed marriage than about him, but I still couldn't see past it. A life in space and a family just didn't fit together. Even so, I owed her an apology. I reached for the comm.

Then it happened. The video feed dropped to static, and I felt a deep vibration in the floor. The moment froze, like a shuttle when the last booster drops away and the battering five-G ascent becomes instantly silent and perfectly still. I ran to the windows, my body sluggish, underwater. My eyes met André's across the room, and we both knew. An explosion. Disaster.

We looked out and saw the impossible: a fire on the Moon. The capsule platform was engulfed in flames. It would be months before we found out what happened—lunar dust had fouled a valve, causing pressure to build up. The resulting explosion had doused the platform with burning fuel and pierced an oxygen tank at the same time, providing the fire with a steady supply of fresh oxygen to keep it alight. At the time, all we knew was that Rachel was in trouble.

Crew members packed the airlock, frantically suiting up for a rescue attempt, but I could see they would be too late. I rushed back to the comm.

"Rachel? Are you there?"

"Roger that, Control," came her calm voice, just as she'd been trained to react in a crisis. "The temperature is rising fast in here. Can I get out the hatch?"

"Negative. Egress is completely blocked."

"Can they put it out?"

The two men who had reached the fire with extinguishers backed away, unable to get any closer.

"Not in time."

My mind raced, trying to keep the horror out so I could think clearly. It wasn't my daughter; it was a problem to be solved. And then the solution was obvious.

"Drop her!"

André turned from the window to stare at me.

"Come on, help me. Release the bolts and drop the capsule."

André shook his head. "Big Betsy hasn't cleared the tunnel yet. She'll die."

"She's dying right now; that fire's going to cook her before anyone can stop it. It's her only chance. Do it!"

We kicked chairs out of the way and grabbed our consoles. It didn't take long. The bolts retracted and the capsule, released, plummeted into the Hole.

André grabbed the comm, thumbed the global override, and bellowed into it. "I need every hand back to Control right now. The capsule is in the Hole. Repeat, everyone back to the control room at once."

He turned back to me. "Big Betsy has twenty minutes to get out of the way."

The Herrenknecht Tunnel Boring Machines were the fastest ever built, advertised to excavate at a rate of a kilometer a day. Their real progress was slower, of course, because worn drill bits had to be changed regularly, and dirt had to be removed. The boring machines used to dig the Chunnel under the English Channel pulled out eight million cubic meters of dirt, which was used to reclaim 90 acres of oceanfront property near Folkestone, creating a public park frequented by children and picnickers. On the Moon, the removed dirt was also thrown into the "sea"—a huge pile at the bottom of Mare Serenitatis.

Under normal circumstances, Big Betsy could have covered two meters well before the falling capsule reached the core, but in this case, it had to turn, and the boring machine did not turn quickly. It tunneled like an earthworm, the back half gripping the rock while the front half pushed forward, then the front half gripping the rock while the back half pulled back in, spraying plasticized concrete on the new walls to help stabilize the tunnel. To change direction, it gripped on only one side, its thrusts altering its attitude by several degrees each time. I didn't know how long it would take, or if it would clear the tunnel in time. There was nothing to do but watch Rachel float weightlessly in freefall inside the capsule, counting down the minutes.

Just days before I had left for the Moon, six months before Rachel graduated high school, I bought her a graduation present: a gold necklace of a bird flying out of an open cage. It was my joke to her, a symbol of freedom from her life at home, a fatherly invitation to go out and do whatever she wanted with her life. Only I'd never given it to her.

I'd come home late that morning from an exhausting all-night training simulation to find a lawyer waiting. He gave me the divorce papers and my wife's message that she would throw out anything I didn't remove from the house before I left.

The necklace didn't seem so funny anymore. I found Rachel at school and kissed her goodbye. I bunked at Kennedy for my last few days on Earth and never went home again.

"Thirty seconds until imp . . . until she passes the core," said André.

The entire team was gathered in the control room, none of them breathing, eyes flicking back and forth between Big Betsy's coordinates and the clock. Ten seconds. Five. Zero.

Nothing. Big Betsy pressed on. The video inside the capsule continued to show Rachel, unharmed. She'd made it through.

I punched the comm for Farside. "Tanager, she's heading your way. Are you ready for the catch?"

Captain Matt Tanager's voice was matter-of-fact, as if this were nothing but a routine drill. "Roger that, Control. The generators are spinning and the magnets are hot. We'll catch her more gently than her own mother."

I thought about Rachel's mother, and hoped for better.

"Just be ready, Farside. I'm counting on you."

"Relax, Papa Bear. She's in good hands."

"Frank!" André called from his terminal.

"What is it?"

"She passed the first sensor."

"And?"

"She was more than two seconds late."

I didn't have to ask why that mattered. Two seconds didn't drop out of a precise gravitational calculation for no reason; something was slowing her down.

"You're sure?"

"I checked it three times."

Then I realized what it must have been. "The dirt."

"What?"

"The dirt dislodged by Big Betsy. In any other tunnel, loose dirt would fall out of harm's way, but in the exact center of the Moon . . ."

". . . the dirt would fall to the center of the tunnel," André finished. "Her capsule plowed right through it."

We were silent for a moment. We both knew a miss would be fatal. If the capsule didn't reach high enough for Farside to catch it, it would oscillate back and forth over a matter of days, slowing gradually and finally coming to a rest at the core of the Moon. Rachel would run out of oxygen long before then.

"Will she make it?" I asked.

André didn't answer. He loaded an analysis tool and started typing furiously. I couldn't wait. I grabbed a pen and a safety manual and started writing equations on the back. The math was complex, but it was also the basis for the project I'd been working on for eight years. The catching mechanism was designed to be extended down into the tunnel to account for slight variations in velocity; the question was, could it extend far enough to catch Rachel? We reached the answer at almost the same moment and looked at each other without speaking, both praying that we were wrong.

Finally, I said, "She'll fall ten meters short."

André nodded.

The comm beeped. I punched it and growled, "What is it?"

"Dad?"

"Rachel! Are you safe? Everything okay?"

"I'm fine, Dad. My air is good, my temp is good. Farside's going to catch me . . . right?"

I didn't hesitate. If there was anything I knew as an astronaut, it was that people do better when they have all the information. "Negative. Repeat, negative. You hit some friction at the core. You won't reach the magnets." I coughed, then said, "We're going to catch you on this side."

She knew as well as I did that the loose dirt would cut her velocity even more on the return trip. Her response was quiet and simple. "How?"

I shook my head. "I don't know."

Rachel's capsule fell short exactly as our calculations predicted and started the long fall back toward the core.

"If there were only some way to speed her up . . ." André tapped a pencil on the screen in nervous frustration.

"Forget about it. No rockets, no means of propulsion, nothing to push out the back. Propulsion means energy, and there's no more energy in the system."

"Could we fire the laser at the capsule, cut a hole in the top?"

"What, and have her jump out?"

André shrugged. "If she jumped just at the top of its rise, in the moment the capsule was completely still, she could prop herself up in the tunnel with her legs and arms until we could pull her out."

"Hold herself up in a sheer concrete tunnel over a several thousand kilometer drop?"

"If it's her only chance, it's better than nothing."

I held up my hands. "I'm sorry. But it won't work. The tunnel is gravitationally straight, but it's not actually *straight*, remember? It has to account for mascons and mountains. You can't reach her with a laser until she's too close to do any good."

We argued for several more minutes, but finally settled on the only possibility. We had no more time to talk if we wanted time to prepare. The only remaining disagreement was who would go down the Hole.

"There's no question, André. You have to work the numbers. They need to be perfect—correct to the centimeter. This isn't something you want me doing on the back of an envelope. If it isn't right . . . well, we'll only get one chance at this."

André nodded. "I'll get it right."

"You do that."

They attached the cable to my spacesuit, the same cable and winch we'd used to lower Big Betsy into the initial hole. It was easily thick enough to handle the strain. I stood, fully suited, at the edge of the Hole. There was no time for second thoughts. I checked my connections and my air, then dove down into blackness.

The cable slowed my descent while above me, another member of the team kept a precise measurement of the length of the cable. At two hundred meters, they slowed me to a stop. On the surface, André was measuring how much the core debris had slowed Rachel's capsule on her second pass. He would make precise measurements of her ascent and adjust his calculations accordingly. I felt the cable vibrate as it was pulled a few feet higher, then lowered by tiny increments, then raised again.

It was dark. I turned on my flashlight and pointed it down the shaft. Living in space had accustomed me to enormous distances, but the sight of that endless tunnel set my heart pounding. I checked my watch, which glowed a faint green. Three minutes.

The cable continued to hum, adjusting my position by small

28   *David Walton*

amounts. Why did it take so much adjustment? Was her acceleration still changing? I thought about hailing André on the comm to ask him what the problem was, but rejected the idea. There was nothing I could do to help now.

Less than two minutes left. I couldn't see it yet, but the capsule was coming. I hefted the hook in my right hand, knowing I would only get one chance. If André's calculations were off, I would get no chance at all—either the capsule would fall short, plummeting back toward the core before I could reach it, or else . . . or else it would rise too high, and two people would die instead of just one.

Where was it? Why couldn't I see it? Had it already reached its peak and fallen back down? I didn't dare look at my watch again, lest the capsule appear in that split second.

Suddenly, there it was, flying up toward me. The lack of reference points made it hard to gauge its speed; one moment it looked too slow, others like it would plow right into me. I shrank back, adrenaline pumping, unable to dodge it or move any higher. Then, just as I braced for the impact, it stopped just inches away. I gaped at it, frozen with shock, and almost didn't move fast enough. I swung out desperately with the hook and wrapped it under a bar on the top of the capsule, just in time. It shrieked and held, jerking the cable with a force that set it thrumming like a bass fiddle. But it did not fall.

When the hatch finally opened and Rachel stumbled out, she ran straight into André's arms. My hands were shaking. During the crisis, there was no time to be afraid for her; now that it was over, the emotions flooded me. At that moment, life seemed so fragile, so fleeting. I watched Rachel and André hold each other and wondered if they could really hold a marriage together. Rachel wasn't her mother, and André wasn't me; maybe they could. Even if they couldn't, what good would I do by standing in the way?

After removing my spacesuit, I retreated to my sleeping quarters, just a closet barely large enough for a narrow bed. I rummaged in my trunk and finally pulled from the bottom a gold necklace, a bird with wings spread wide flying free from a cage. I had kept it long enough.

With special thanks to C.H. "Chas" Hague.

David Walton is the author of the international bestseller *Superposition*, a quantum physics murder mystery, and *Terminal Mind*, which won the 2008 Philip K. Dick Award. His newest novel, *The Genius Plague*, is about a pandemic that is altering the human race.

CATHEDRAL

by Michael Barretta

Amid all the gems given us by Will Rogers, one particular quote has stuck with me through my entire life and has often given a much needed push from time to time: "Even if you're on the right track, you'll get run over if you just sit there." Mike Barretta's winning story applies this wisdom to our struggle to explore space. Sometimes humanity itself needs a not so gentle push and perhaps just a little . . . subterfuge.

I. Conspiracy Theory

"GENTLEMEN . . . for next Monday," said Dave Coyle, the mission director. He tapped a remote and the screen changed to a matrix of potential mishaps and the likelihood of their occurrence. "You have a copy of this operational risk management matrix in your binders along with our first cut on abort options for the revised mission profile. What I need you to do is to flesh out the details."

"This isn't a mission. It's not even footprints and flagpoles," whispered Jerry Beaden to the man sitting to his left. The man snorted and Jerry regretted his whisper. Dave Coyle was not only the mission director but a close and personal friend doing his best to hold the center together and get some hardware into the sky.

"You have to land to plant a flag," snickered the man.

"It's the best we can do, Jerry," said Dave Coyle.

Jerry looked up and felt his face flush with embarrassment. Dave had ears like a cat. The temperature in the room seemed to rise a few degrees. A few muttered agreements indicated he had allies in the room, which didn't mean all that much. Technically, everyone in the room was an ally. No one really liked the mission, but it was the only game in town.

"This is the mission that's economically and politically possible, let's stay focused," said Dave.

"Is a flyby really the best we can do?" Jerry looked around the table. There were more than a few new faces. NASA had lost a lot of talent to industry. One departing senior staffer had remarked to him that if you can't make history then you better make money. The man had departed with a generous offer from Grumman and a lot of sadness.

"This is old ground. You're not the only one that's disappointed. Fortunately, I have a dozen unemployed astronauts to pick from. Do you want the mission or not?"

"Yes, I want it. It's better than nothing," said Jerry. He turned his attention back to the ORM matrix and Dave's somber voice turned into a drone.

"I don't see any abort-to-Mars scenarios," said Jerry.

"The scenario was summarily dismissed. It doesn't make sense to abort to Mars for a flyby mission. It would be a virtual death sentence," said Dave.

"Not necessarily," said Jerry. "After the transit maneuver we are committed to Mars one way or the other. It's too energy intensive for an Earth return."

"You're preaching to the choir," said Dave.

"Well, the next logical place to abort the mission is Mars. The original equipment manifest was designed for in situ survival."

"Agreed, but any abort scenario would maroon a man on Mars indefinitely. We don't have the resources to mount a timely rescue," said Dave.

Heads swiveled back and forth as each man took turns speaking. "Garrison?" said Jerry looking at the pudgy Boeing representative.

"The other two landing vehicles and transit boosters are in deep preservation in the Huntsville facility. The launch boosters have been in sheltered storage at Boeing since the contract was cancelled."

"That's certainly enough hardware," said Jerry.

"The sticking point is reconstituting the technical expertise to bring the hardware out of preservation and build the stack," said the Boeing representative. "It's all been laid off or reassigned, but then again, in this economy, you would be amazed at what can be done if you throw enough money at the problem."

"The sticking point is the financial resources and political will," corrected Dave.

"Hardware is the easy part."

"How long would an astronaut be marooned for?" asked a support engineer.

"Three years minimum provided the decision is even made to rescue him," said Dave. He checked his watch. "Let's cut to the chase. Are we in agreement that an abort-to-Mars is a viable though not necessarily politically plausible scenario?"

Jerry watched the group nod in agreement. "It's consistent with astronaut safety," said Jerry. The magic words. With high-profile mishaps part of NASA's history, nearly anything could be done if it was in the best interests of safety.

"Then let's design for it. What I need is fully developed risk scenarios and resolution options regarding the proposed abort-to-Mars option. Thank you for attending." Notebooks folded shut and chairs shuffled. People filed out of the room.

Jerry waited till the room was clear. "Dave, I'm sorry about my sarcasm. I didn't mean anything by it."

"I know. Forget about it"

"I have an idea," said Jerry.

"Close the door."

II. Willing Accomplice

The gin and tonic went down smooth. Jerry placed the glass down on the coaster. It was his third one and he was feeling mellow. The waves rolled into the beach in no discernable pattern. A few teenage surfers practiced their skills in the confused surf. He laughed as one amateur took an unexpected header off his short board. Allegra Perricone-Beaden, his wife smiled back at him. By her smile he could tell she didn't mind his drinking. He did it so rarely. Her two glasses of Zinfindel qualified as a knock-down drag-out rave for her.

He felt her hand wrap itself around his and he was surprised at the sudden warmth. He turned to the bartender. "Bobby, I got a question for you."

"Another?"

He hoisted his glass, inspected it, and swirled the half-melted cubes. "No, I'm good."

"Watcha need Jerry?"

"Who was the first American in space?"

"John Glenn." Bobby dragged a damp cloth across the mahogany bar and smirked. "Dumb-ass astronaut, you're supposed to know that," he muttered. Bobby turned and tucked the damp cloth into the rear pocket of his Levi's. He walked to the other side of the bar and leaned in close to the two female office workers that were the vanguard of the after-work crowd.

"My point exactly," said Jerry to his wife. No one would remember a flyby mission.

"I'll remember," said Allegra. "You'll be gone for eight months. Actually now that I think about it, that might be a good thing. I mean you still have direct deposit. I have power of attorney. I just might get that beach house and matching cabana boy to take care of the pool."

"A cabana boy? I've got three empty seats on that ship. I just might take you along as part of my personal allotment."

She twirled a lock of hair and sipped some more wine. Her face was slightly flushed. "What could we possibly do for eight months cooped up in that cozy capsule of yours? I know. We could do what has never been done."

"Oh, it's been done before," said Jerry.

"Really now. You've never told me that astronaut story."

"You'll have to read about it in my memoirs."

"If it was you, you won't live long enough to write any memoirs. I have three Sicilian brothers."

"I know . . . you're from a small but influential crime family." It was a standing joke. Her father was an engineer for Alenia Aeronautica and immigrated to work for Lockheed-Martin. Her brothers were all doctors or lawyers. He turned around to face the gray-blue Atlantic.

"I think I'm going to do it," he said suddenly. Over the past month he had dropped hints knowing that she would be able to put the pieces together on her own.

"I know," she said.

She sat up straighter changing from wife to engineer before his eyes.

"What about the supply manifest?"

"Substantially unchanged from the original mission, it's been redesignated as emergency supplies," said Jerry.

"Rover?"

"No. Dave didn't think that he could possibly slip that by the suits."

"I thought so." She opened up her purse and took out a folded drawing and handed it too him.

He unfolded it. "What is it?"

"An early birthday present. You can use parts on your manifest, reconfigure them, and make yourself a bicycle. I think it would work. See how broad the seat is; it would easily fit a space-suited butt."

"All the other astronauts married beauty queens and TV reporters. I had to marry an engineer." He leaned into her and kissed her. "Thank you."

"You need to come home to me," said Allegra. Her eyes began to tear.

He reached over and wiped the corners of her eyes. "Write your congressmen."

III. Abort-to-Mars

Allegra stood outside Dave Coyle's office. She thought about walking away and waiting for the news but then changed her mind. She knocked.

"Come in."

Dave sat at his oak desk watching the high-definition monitor that displayed the mission control floor and operational parameters of the *Barsoom Express*, the unofficial nickname of the Mars ship. The volume had been turned down and the normal mission chatter was a dull murmur. He stood.

"Do you have a few minutes?" asked Allegra.

"Yeah, Allegra, of course," said Dave.

"Can I sit?"

"You don't have to ask."

"I'm nervous that's all." In three hours the possibility of an abort-to-Mars scenario would expire and the ship would be committed to a return to Earth. The *Barsoom Express* would not be able to shed enough velocity to capture Mars orbit. She half hoped that her husband would give up on history and come home, but that would be out of character for the man she married.

"If he is going to do it, he will do it soon to give the engineers down here time to recommend the option." On cue, mission control erupted into controlled chaos. Supervisors stood and leaned over technicians' shoulders. His phone rang. He answered and listened for a moment. "Verify that the pressure drop is genuine and not a sensor or indicator malfunction and convene the crisis team. I'll be there in a moment." He hung up the phone and turned to Allegra.

"He's made his decision."

She nodded and took a deep breath.

Dave got up rounded his desk to leave. He touched her shoulder gently as he walked to the door. Her husband would either die on Mars or force the United States to spend billions to bring him home.

IV. The Great Man Theory

The landing module had been optimized for the flyby. The engines that would have lifted the return portion of the ship had been removed for additional living space and weight savings. The ship could theoretically land but it could never lift from the surface of Mars. The fuel and oxidizer tanks were left in place and filled with cryogenic hydrogen ostensibly to be used as contingency fuel for the flyby or as raw material to manufacture water, oxygen, and methane on Mars.

Jerry sat in the pilot seat gazing at the thirty-six-inch flat-panel monitor that had been set such that it seemed to be a cockpit window. Six smaller multipurpose screens and a few backup analog gauges were mounted below. The oxygen reserve tanks still indicated full. A secondary screen displayed the false data relayed to mission control.

He could imagine what was going on back at mission control.

Engineers were trying to interpret the data, decide if it was glitched or not. The crisis team was halfway assembled and soon they would contact him and he would have to corroborate the lie.

Does it matter to be the first? In the grand scheme of things it probably didn't. Sooner or later, Mars would be explored and perhaps even colonized.

"*Barsoom,* this is Houston. We have indications of a breach in your primary O2 tank. We need to know what you're seeing and have you take a direct tank reading."

Three years alone. No, not really alone. He had routine mission communications, private calls with his family, and his public blog. He had thousands of hours of entertainment and books electronically stored. He would be able to stay involved with the Earth so it wasn't exactly the man-in-the-lifeboat situation that was described in scenario-development meetings.

"Houston, this is *Barsoom.* I've taken direct readings. The primary storage tank has vented. I'm standing by for recommendations." He was amazed at how easy it was to lie.

Is this sacrifice or selfishness? The boundaries blurred. Does it really matter who is first?

Yes it matters, he answered himself.

It matters to me and maybe, just maybe, everyone else.

V. Done Deal

Allegra took a seat next to Dave. She knew her presence in the room was unprecedented and unwelcomed. She didn't care. If they were going to make her leave they were going to have to tell her and the only person who would do that was Dave.

"Maybe she shouldn't be here," said the flight supervisor. The man fidgeted uncomfortably. It was an unspoken rule that astronaut family was royalty.

"She's his wife," said Dave. "If anyone has a right to be here, it's her."

"I didn't mean . . . it's just . . ." stammered the flight supervisor.

"It's okay. What are you recommending?"

"We are recommending an abort-to-Mars. We need a four-minute engine burn at full throttle." He checked his watch. "And we need it in twenty-three minutes to capture orbit in six weeks."

"Or," said Dave.

"No other real option given the data we have. Primary O2 tank is completely depleted. We have sufficient reserves and scrubbers to reach Mars where we can keep him alive for about three and half years or we can get a corpse back in three months."

Allegra winced at the man's blunt statement. As an engineer she appreciated the no-nonsense purpose behind it; as the wife of the subject at hand it was a dagger in her heart.

"Hydrogen boil off?" asked Dave.

"Within expected parameters. We have sufficient quantities to manufacture oxygen and water in situ."

"That's good. Then the abort option is a consensus decision?"

Heads nodded around the room.

He turned to Allegra. "Allegra, we need to reschedule your private communication time until the burn is complete."

She nodded. Anxiety warmed her. She felt her breathing quicken and she hoped no one would notice. The last thing these people needed was a distraction. They were all acting in good faith. She needed to play her part, but she didn't know what her part was: anxious wife or sly accomplice.

"Let's get to work. We have twenty-one minutes to make this happen," said Dave. "And I have to call the administrator."

The crisis team broke up to coordinate the abort-to-Mars.

"I'm going to sit here a moment, Dave," said Allegra. The room emptied quickly and quietly as people returned to their work stations to address the crisis. She took another deep calming breath. When her husband had deployed in the navy she was a cruise widow, left behind by the needs of the navy, now she was a Mars widow, left behind by choice.

"Here, drink this."

She turned and a ponytailed man with the look of tech support about him handed her a glass of water. "Thank you."

"I've been a data analyst for twelve years," said ponytail man.

The man wore a NASA standard uniform circa 1970s: white short-sleeve button-down, black pants, paisley tie, and a no-fooling pocket protector. She couldn't help but smile.

He pulled out a chair one removed from her and sat down. "They think that just because you're into computers you're socially stupid, but I watch people. I can read between the lines. I've seen you and your husband around. He wouldn't leave you for so long without letting you know."

"What are you suggesting?" she said quietly.

"I'm suggesting that everyone here is looking at processed data, just what the screen says. You and Dave seem like you've had a while to prepare for this or you're both really cool cucumbers. Oh yeah, and the raw data stream that I monitor indicates the oxygen tank is full."

"What do you want?" It was the obvious question. Was she being set up for blackmail?

"Nothing, I've altered the archived raw data files. His tank is empty like it should be and no one will ever be able to prove otherwise unless they go to Mars. Maybe this NASA thing will last long enough that I can work my way up to the big table." He rapped the faux-wood table top with his knuckles. He pulled black-rimmed glasses from his pocket and put them on his face. They slid down the bridge of his nose and he pushed them back up. He blinked to focus.

"Thank you," he said. "I would have hated to go into game design when real life is so much more interesting."

VI. Trickle-Up Effect

Barlowe DiFate, NASA administrator, paced outside the Oval Office. His Armani suit caressed his skin like a lover. It didn't comfort him. He had never felt out of control before. Powerful forces jerked other people around, not him. He was a career bureaucrat, one step below politician, but far more lucrative with half the risk. He had fewer constituents to please and most of the time he only had one constituent to please. His constituent was going to be pissed.

The door opened and the President's chief of staff, Gabrielle Hernandez glared at him. "The President will see you now."

He crossed the threshold into the room

"Barlowe," said the President. "I've heard rumors. What's happening?"

Presidents don't hear rumors, thought Barlowe. They receive

intelligence. Hernandez had probably poisoned the well. "We've had trouble with the Mars mission."

"What sort?"

"A rupture in an oxygen tank."

"What is the plan? Bring 'em home early?"

"That is not possible, Mr. President. The ship is committed to landing on the planet."

"So we have an accidental Mars landing. Barlowe, when you screw up you screw up big. Okay, don't get me wrong here but what does that mean to the astronaut . . . and me?"

"It means that this country commits billions to rescuing the man or he dies. The political fallout is beyond my purview," said Barlowe.

"I'll make it your purview, Barlowe. I am beginning to regret I ever appointed you."

Now he was down by one constituent. "I'll have a more comprehensive brief for you tomorrow morning."

The President nodded indicated he was dismissed.

VII. Smiles Across the Miles

Mars loomed. The angry red planet filled the viewer. It filled the viewer ominously. How could it fill the viewer any way but ominously? Jerry's initial fascination turned to fatalism. The planet's reflected light filled the cockpit with its redness and at the moment it felt like a march down a dim prison corridor. Soon he would land and the door would slam shut and it just might never open again. He pushed regrets away. They were pointless now.

Mars vanished and his wife's face appeared on the monitor window. She smiled three minutes ago and the image just reached him. He stretched his hand out across the millions of miles and touched her face. He felt better.

VIII. Cathedrals in Space

"One hundred sixty billion dollars? You want me to go to Congress and request an additional one hundred sixty billion dollars? Have you been watching C-SPAN lately, David? Have you been watching CNN? I am getting raked over the coals for losing a man. I am up to my ass in inquiries and panels, all of them trying to figure out where I screwed up," said Barlowe.

"I'm sorry. It's not your fault, but it is your job," said Dave. "And he isn't lost. We know exactly where he is."

"Don't tell me what my damn job is," grumbled Barlowe.

"And that's one hundred sixty billion dollars plus the inevitable cost overruns and delays. Sell it as a welfare program for engineers. They have to eat, too, you know."

"Sarcasm. That's exactly what I need right now. That's going to go over great on the Hill."

"Why shouldn't it? Congress has bailed out every other business enterprise in this country. Why shouldn't scientists and engineers get a helping hand? At least they're making something instead of just consuming. We're building cathedrals," said Dave.

"I wish I knew what the hell you are talking about," said Barlowe.

"Medieval Europeans would build cathedrals to house relics of saints. The cathedrals would employ thousands of craftsmen, merchants, and farmers for decades. Do you know how many pizza shops, laundromats, and used-car dealerships depend upon NASA facilities?"

"Okay, I get it. I'm just pissed," said Barlowe.

"Barlowe, pull out the stops. If they don't appropriate the funds make him a martyr, make his wife a widow, and make her unborn son fatherless."

"Oh my God, you're kidding me. She's pregnant."

"She got pregnant just before the launch, last night on Earth kind of thing."

"This is starting to sound like a conspiracy," said Barlowe.

You have no idea, thought David.

IX. A Reason to Live

Olympus Mons rose in the eastern horizon like an immense frozen wave. The *Barsoom* had landed in a field of odd vertical wind sculpted stones that turned out to be remnants of igneous rock. They peppered the landscape like bizarre chess pieces. The Martian sands in their infinite graduations flowed like slow-motion water around the base of the stones. It was a natural Zen garden and the marks of his presence were polished smooth within a day. An American flag fluttered in the carbon dioxide breeze. Footprints and flagpoles after all, thought Jerry.

He walked back from his modest power farm in his filthy Mars-stained spacesuit with his daily survival chores more or less complete. Power was life and to that end he had cleaned dust from solar fabric stretched out over aluminum poles and lubricated the three lightweight wind turbines. His power farm augmented the ship's thermal decay reactor that kept the *Barsoom*'s lithium batteries charged. He entered the lock and brushed himself off. He turned on the vacuum filters that pulled the air downward as he swept himself clean. Satisfied, he shut down the vacuum and cycled breathable air into the lock. He undressed in the chill utility room and climbed the ladder to the main deck. He stopped for a drink of Mars-flavored water and then continued his climb to the flight deck.

He waited for the monitor to come to life.

"Jerry, I have a surprise for you," said Allegra. "Please don't get upset."

Her image blurred and the screen turned blue with momentary signal loss. She reappeared frozen in time and then the image skipped. His private fear was that she would grow weary of waiting, whereas he had no choice but to wait. Her image came back.

"Why would I get upset?"

He waited for the reply and looked around in mild disgust. The ship looked like a college dorm room. He was becoming increasingly sloppy with his work schedule, less fastidious about his appearance, and short-tempered with surface ops staff. His pointless unscheduled bike rides on Mars were a constant source of frustration for staff members responsible for his every movement.

"You're going to be a father." She stood up and showed her belly. "I found out four weeks after the launch."

"Why didn't you tell me?"

"I didn't want you distracted. Are you happy?"

"Yeah, I'm happy. Well, I don't know how to feel. I wish I was home with you."

"I wish you were home too. Jerry, you need to pull yourself together and do things right. This is bigger than you. This is bigger than Mars. You're going to have a son."

"That's wonderful." How many NASA shrinks had gamed out this conversation with her? No one wanted to freak out the marooned astronaut. He silently admitted it was mostly his fault that a lot of the conversations he had with Earth personnel other than his wife were as tense as a hostage negotiation.

"I testified before Congress and was interviewed on *Good Morning America*. I think they are going to pass the appropriations bill."

"Awesome."

"And the Europeans are sending you a care package. Their rover mission was replaced by a dumb capsule."

"Out of the goodness of their hearts?"

"You are famous, but not that famous. NASA cut a data-sharing deal with them. They get access to all raw data you generate and a seat at Mission Control to observe surface operations. You get twenty pounds personal allotment so think about what you want. You should get it by Christmas."

"I love you, Allegra. Take care of my son."

"I will. I love you too, Jerry."

IX. Pigs in Space

"Your bacon should be arriving in four days," said Dave.

"Good. I miss it almost as much as sex," said Jerry.

"The French had a hard time believing that you wanted twenty pounds of bacon."

"It's not that turkey bacon, is it? Real bacon comes from pigs," said Jerry.

"It's the real deal. The NASA dieticians had conniption fits and I am up to my ass in protest letters from PETA."

"Tell them I grow my own alfalfa sprouts." Indeed, the lower deck was a riot of food plants rooted in pale amber gel. He grew enough to have a salad every two days or so.

"The damage has been done. We've already exported meat eaters to other worlds. Anyway, Allegra is doing a wonderful job on the talk show and political circuits. She knows how to keep the pressure on the powerful without alienating them. She is a great public speaker. I swear, I think they're a little bit afraid of her."

"Good, I've always been a bit afraid of her," said Jerry.

"The mission design for your rescue has been finalized. The first launch will have a four-man crew including a French geologist. It is payback for the care package. The second will be an unmanned mission with high-endurance facilities. Belkow Aerospace has sold NASA three inflatable structures. We're pulling out all the stops down here but the earliest window is four months away. We're working hard to make it, but I don't want to make any promises at this point."

"I know you're doing your best."

X. Dehydrated Water: Just Add Water

They can put a man on Mars, but they can't make self-cleaning underwear, thought Jerry. The washing machine had washed its last and the nearest laundromat was a long way away. Martian grit had scoured the seals such that the machine would no longer hold water. Anyway, it was a travesty to even compare the microwave-sized machine to the earthbound behemoths that handily managed sixteen pairs of blue jeans at a time. He found it mildly disturbing to be scrubbing stains out of his skivvies in his kitchen sink knowing that he would drink the very same water next week. Some things didn't get mentioned in astronaut school.

The care package had arrived on target. The French had sent him a bottle of champagne. The Italians sent extra-virgin olive oil, tomato sauce, and pasta. In all, he received about sixty pounds of gifts from various nations. The most precious thing was a lock of hair from his son's first haircut.

NASA was completely pragmatic and sent various gaskets and seals, tubes of epoxy that looked suspiciously like JB Weld, rolls of Mars-resistant duct tape, spheres of hydrogen, and various gaskets, filters, back-up software, and other consumables. Even the packing material could be used. It was made from vitamin- and mineral-laced rice pressed into cardboard. He hoped it wouldn't get bad enough to eat the boxes.

He squeezed out his underwear and draped it over a length of fiber-optic cable stretched between bulkhead fittings, sighed in disgust, and contemplated the work he needed to do. He was behind in his public relations blog and the "Ask the astronaut" email account. Earthbound geologists had been debating a green streak in a rock formation and wanted him to take yet another sample. He sat down as heavily as he could in the light gravity and looked at the ruddy dust on the floor. He was behind in his housekeeping and that had potentially dangerous consequences. What would all the other astronauts think of him when they came in twelve weeks?

He sneezed explosively and wiped his nose on his sleeve and became conscious of the subtle ache in his bones and the tickle in the back of his throat.

XI. Sick of Mars

"Dave, we need to know what he has," said Trang Nyugen, Director of Surface Operations for the second mission.

"We don't know yet," said Dave. "All we can do is rely upon his reports."

"His symptoms are consistent with the flu or a very bad cold. It doesn't appear to be life threatening, just oddly persistent," said the flight surgeon. "I don't think it is that serious."

"Your medical opinion aside, it is dangerously serious. To survive for so long he has had to do everything perfect every day and now he is sick. There is no redundancy in the human component of this mission," said Dave.

"I understand the gravity of the situation. I really do. What I meant to say is that it is my opinion that he has a biosphere syndrome."

"What do you mean?"

"Basically, his personal ecology is out of whack. The biosphere experiments were the first large-scale experiments in closed ecologies. The general consensus is that the effort was flawed, but we did learn that closed systems are hard to regulate. The biosphere was plagued by insect swarms, and out-of-control molds and fungi. My point is: Jerry didn't go to Mars alone. His entire body is home to a multitude of bacteria, prions, viruses, and mites. The system is closed and his body is having a more difficult time adjusting to imbalances. Additionally, he is under an immense amount of stress, which has compromised his immune system. My best guess is that a simple rhinovirus finally got a toehold."

"What if it's not? What if it's some alien virus lying dormant in Martian soil just waiting to colonize a warm wet human body," said Nguyen.

"Yeah, the Andromeda-strain theory. Highly unlikely. The odds are astronomical that an alien organism would be compatible with our physiology," said the flight surgeon.

"No matter," said Dave. "We can't take the chance of contaminating the other astronauts with whatever he has. In three weeks we are putting four more men on Mars. We'll take a wait and see approach. If he doesn't get better by landing day we will revisit the matter."

XII. Home Stretch

The wind howled. At least it howled as much as a Martian wind could howl. He found the sound and the rasp of sand on the hull oddly reassuring. He rolled and felt the chill of Mars through the hull and it nearly aroused him from the thin state between wakefulness and sleep. He dreamed of a field of baroque stone rockets festooned with balconies, sharply chined spires, and parapets all held to the pale-yellow Martian sky by flying buttresses. He tossed his sweat-soaked blanket aside and shivered in the cold. He dragged himself to full consciousness and tried to open his eyes but they seemed to be glued shut. He felt around and found his NASA approved self-balancing sippy cup and drank water flavored with grit and iron. He felt his way to the small sink, wet a facecloth, and began to clean his eyes till he could open them. He was immediately aware that he felt better, just the slightest bit achy and ravenously hungry. He stopped the sink and filled it with warm water. He stripped off his clothes and pulled off the telemetry leads that NASA insisted he wear. An alarm chimed softly and he silenced it. He began to sponge himself clean. With a reasonably fresh uniform on, he went into the main cabin and noticed immediately that the mission clock indicated two days later than the last time he remembered. He climbed the ladder to the flight deck and sat heavily in the pilot's chair. The camera eye was on.

"Good morning, Jerry," said Dave. "We've been waiting for you. You have no idea how relieved we are."

"Good morning."

"The flight surgeon tells me they lost biomedical telemetry. Is there anything wrong?"

"No. I broke telemetry when I washed off. I feel much better."

"Allegra is here with Alex. They've been camped out in my office."

The screen filled with his wife and son. Her smile lit up the dim light inside the capsule flight deck.

"Hey baby, good morning. I miss you. Do you feel better?" said Allegra. "You look so much better. We were worried about you. Say hi to daddy." She waved her son's hand at the camera. Alex grinned at the screen.

"I feel a lot better. How is Alex the Great doing?"

"He had a cold just like you, but he is feeling better now. He can almost hold himself up. "

"Allegra, I'm so tired. I want to come home."

"Soon. You'll be home soon. Dave needs to talk to you about changes to the meeting protocols."

"I love you."

"I love you too."

Dave's face appeared on the screen. "The *Tsiolkovski* is in orbit and they've locked onto the beacon you planted. After their landing checks, Dr. Carroway is going to disembark and make his way to you. You need to transfer over your sample swabs and then he is going to take some new ones. He will give you a broad spectrum antiviral and antibacterial. He won't be removing his spacesuit. It should take a couple of days for him to culture the samples and identify what you had. If it's garden-variety cold or flu then you guys can share environments."

"What if it's not, Dave?"

"We'll cross that bridge when we come to it. In the mean time keep an eye out at about 13:35. They should be commencing their descent."

"I will, thanks, Dave."

"Houston, out."

The monitor defaulted to its exterior panoramic image of the strange vertical stones and the flowing sands.

XIII. *Tsiolkovski* Descending

The *Tsiolkovski* fell like an angel, an incandescent streak, racing across the sky becoming brighter and closer. Massive white parachutes blossomed and the ship slowed. At three hundred feet the parachutes separated and the engines ignited. For a moment, the ship was obscured in a roiling cloud of exhaust and dust. Dust devils swirled up and wheeled away from the ship. He saw a flash of silver hull through the cloud. He could feel the roar of engines and the vibration in the soles of his boots. The engines cut off and he could hear the squeal of metal on metal as the ship settled. The light wind carried away the plume of dust. Though they would be eager, it would be a few hours before they were ready to disembark. With nothing to do, he mounted his bicycle and pedaled to the parachutes before they got too far away. Nothing was thrown away on Mars.

XIV. Cleared for Contact

Three days had passed since his first meeting with Dr. Carroway and now he watched Captain Nathan Nesius and Michael Carroll approach in their clean white Mars excursion suits. They splashed through one of the many puddles of fine talcum powderlike dust. They disappeared from view as they left the camera's field of vision. He heard the airlock cycle as he waited impatiently at the inner door. It cycled open.

Both of the suited astronauts faced each other and unfastened the neck-ring latches on each other's helmets.

Captain Nathan Nesius lifted his helmet off and hung it on a wall peg. "Jerry Beaden, I presume?"

"Captain, it is good to see you," said Jerry.

Nesius took off his gloves with a twist of his wrist, careful not to touch the frigid metal wrist rings with unprotected hands. He peeled of his under gloves and then offered his hand to Jerry.

Jerry shook Michael Carroll's hand next. They had been in the same astronaut class.

"Jerry, my brother, I like what you've done with the place and what the hell is that smell," said Michael. "We should have brought a fifty-five-gallon drum of Febreeze."

"I've been recycling my sweat for two years," said Jerry. "You'll get used to it. What did the Doc say?"

"Martian fever, you're doomed," said Michael.

"Common cold in an uncommon place," corrected Captain Nesius. "Jerry, you've received your orders from Houston. Do we need to clarify any points?"

Nesius was more senior than Jerry and should have been assigned to a Mars mission. He dropped out to take care of his ailing mother. Jerry imagined that ordeal had been resolved. "No, you're in charge."

"Good. Michael is your new roommate until the resupply module lands and the inflatables are set up." He took an appraising look around but restrained from commenting. "He'll help you clean up a bit and do some maintenance. You've ranged pretty far from the *Barsoom* and I won't allow that anymore. Everyone stays on mission and no one goes anywhere alone. First orders are to suit up. We're going back to *Tsio* for a party. It's surf and turf."

XV. Freefalling

Jerry pressed his forehead against an insulated window of the International Space Station. At one time the window offered an unobstructed view of Earth but now the planet was partially obscured by trusses and panels.

"Jerry, it's time," said Colonel Makarov. "The Soyuz has been prepped and you should be in your own bed in twenty-four hours." The Russian colonel tucked his legs and gently kicked off the wall. Jerry followed much less elegantly through a gauntlet of the sixteen crewmembers of the ISS. Captain Nesius floated at the Soyuz hatch.

"Safe landing," said Captain Nesius. "When the rest of us get down we'll go to that beach bar you like so much."

XVI. Fallout

"Have you seen this book?" asked the President.

"Yes, sir, but I haven't read it," said Barlowe DiFate, NASA administrator.

"I haven't read it either, but I've been briefed. It's a *New York Times* bestseller and it makes me look like an idiot." He picked up the hardback copy of *The Martian Conspiracy* and waved it in Barlowe's face. He turned to Dave. "Is there anything to this?" He held his finger under a jacket cover blurb that read, "Based on a true story!"

"It's a techno-thriller, sir, the technician who wrote it has published a few science fiction stories. It seems credible only because the man has insider knowledge. I've read it and it's just entertainment," said Dave.

"Maybe because you come off as one of the sneaky little heroes," said the President. "There are going to be inquiries."

"Because of a fiction book?" said Barlowe incredulously.

"Yes, because of the damn book. It reads too well," said the President. "Or so I've been told. Is there any way to shoot holes in this guy's scenario? Maybe we can smother this baby in the cradle."

"Well, yes," said Dave. "Send a team to Mars and do an engineering analysis of the *Barsoom*. We know the quantity of consumables he used. We just need to see what is left. The calculations should be straightforward."

"Another one hundred sixty billion to send a mission to Mars just to find out we never should have gone in the first place. Are you crazy?"

"We could ask the Russians and Chinese to do it for us. They're sending a mission and their planned landing site is within a kilometer of ours," said Dave.

"What the hell?"

"It makes perfect sense. They have a ready-made base and a supply of resources if something goes wrong with their landing. They'll have access to the *Barsoom,* the *Tsiolkovski,* the resupply module, and the inflatables. They're even using some of our suppliers for fittings to ensure compatibility."

"Didn't your genius astronauts lock the front doors?"

"No, sir, they are no locks on the doors. Our space treaties and common decency require us to render aid to a distressed astronaut whatever the circumstances. If you want to keep the Russians and Chinese at arm's distance then we need to beat them to the site or we can internationalize the mission."

"That last idea might have some merit," said the President. "All right, I'll talk to you when I need to." He waved his hand in dismissal.

Barlowe and Dave got up from the chairs and left the office.

"Why do I think you and Jerry are building this cathedral out of lies? I've got half a mind to believe that book," said Barlowe.

You've got half a mind, thought Dave. "Sometimes, the desperately faithful would cling to a few finger bones or wishful lies and they would surround these things with gorgeous stone monuments that were the height of engineering technology for the time. Centuries later we marvel at their audacity and scarcely care if the relics are genuine or not." He remembered seeing the Ares V stack rising from early morning fog the day of the launch. The machine speared the sky like a cathedral's spire. "Do you want to build a cathedral or tear one down?"

XVII. Reentry

Arkalyk, Kazakstan; Moscow, Russia; London, England; Cape Kennedy, United States. Jerry stepped onto the boarding stairs of the extended-range Sukoi Superjet and saw his wife for the first time in nearly three years. He squinted in the late morning light and willed himself to breath slower. He stepped down as fast as he could, which he had to admit was not very fast. He felt as if his heart would explode out of his chest from fatigue and excitement. His knees and lower back ached.

He saw her.

Her hair was longer and she seemed a bit thinner. Alex the Great wore a NASA baseball cap with the *Barsoom* mission patch stitched on. She broke away from the small crowd of perhaps twenty people that were too important to deny and met him halfway up the ramp.

He took them both into his arms and the crowd clapped.

"I missed you," said Allegra.

"I missed you too," said Jerry. He kissed her.

"Alex, this is your daddy."

Alex the Great looked at his father for the first time in real life, sleepy eyed in the gathering warmth, and yawned.

"I don't think he's that impressed."

"He will be one day," said Allegra.

They descended the remaining steps together, inseparable.

"Welcome home," said Dave as he offered his hand.

"It is so good to be back," said Jerry.

A profusion of hands clasped his hand and clapped him on the back.

"Thank you," said Jerry to everyone that came into his field of view.

After what seemed an eternity under a tent set up for the arrival, Dave stood on a chair.

"Ladies and gentlemen, thank you for coming. As you can imagine Jerry is eager to spend some time with his family. All of you have received tickets for the formal reception next week. I'm going to let his wife take him home now." The crowd applauded as Dave stepped down from the chair and steered Jerry and Allegra away.

"She has your schedule. You have seven days and then it's back to the grind," said Dave.

"Dave, I have about ninety days accumulated leave."

"Earning leave is your right, taking it is a privilege. You have physical therapy, grip-and-grin meetings, and inquiries into the cause of your accident. NASA has some momentum here and I am not about to lose it. We have a narrow window of opportunity to internationalize the Mars missions and you have a role to play. For now, let Allegra take you home. You have lot of catching up to do."

"Take your son," said Allegra.

He took him and placed the sleeping boy on his shoulder. He could smell the sun in his dirty-blond hair and feel the rapid patter of his heartbeat. Allegra took his hand and they walked to the parking lot. She led him to her silver Audi A-6 hybrid turbo-diesel. She opened the rear door so he could put his son in the car seat and the smell of fine leather and exquisite luxury engineering wafted out. The car oozed extreme comfort and power. He strapped his son in and opened his own door.

"How can we afford this thing?" He slid into the passenger seat and let it cradle him. He sighed in extreme comfort. "Never mind, we're keeping it."

"You have sixteen messages from mother-in-law," said the sedan. She touched a button on the steering wheel to silence the car's messages.

"You're mine for the rest of the day, honey. Our family will be flying in later in the week," said Allegra. She started the car and all he heard was a slight purr. As they drove he reached over and took her hand.

"You're going the wrong way."

"No, I'm not."

The roadway was lined with signs and well-wishers hoping to glimpse the astronaut. After four miles the crowd thinned out and he watched the world roll by. It rained briefly, a typical afternoon shower in Florida, and he marveled at the sight of water falling from the sky.

She pulled into a driveway that wrapped around a sand dune. "Surprise, this is where we live now."

"How?"

"We're commodities. I've written two books and I give speeches all over the country. I have a fashion line for crying out loud and you . . . you're an action figure."

"I never should have given you power of attorney."

"Best investment you ever made." She parked the car underneath the beach house's pilings.

"I'll get Alex. Here's the key. The alarm code is 2024."

"The year we were married." He climbed the steps to the porch and put the key in the door, feeling like an intruder. He opened the door and stepped inside the foyer. He silenced the alarm chime and walked into his unfamiliar living room.

"Jerry, sit down," said Allegra. She closed the front door with a nudge from her heel and let the baby's bag slide off her shoulder to the granite countertop. "I'll put Alex to bed and get you . . . ?"

"Water, please."

She disappeared into a bedroom.

Jerry opened up French doors overlooking the beach. Three-foot Atlantic breakers crashed onto the sandy shore and retreated with a foamy hiss. Sea oats waved in the dunes. He sank into a cushioned wicker chair. He was surrounded by miracles.

He heard the clank of ice cubes and then the sound of running water from the faucet. It ran for what seemed an unusually long time and he felt a bubbling flush of panic. On Mars that much water would keep him alive for two days, maybe three.

She crossed the room, handed him the glass, and pulled a chair to sit in front of him.

"You're home," she said.

He had forgotten how blue her eyes were. He had never even considered how much she had sacrificed for his navy and then his NASA career. It was time to stop and build something beautiful and earthbound with her. He felt a twinge in his lower back. Earth gravity was cruel. "When does my physical therapy begin?"

She leaned close and whispered in his ear. "Right after you finish your glass of water."

⇒

Mike Barretta is a retired U.S. Naval Aviator having deployed across the world flying the SH-60B Seahawk helicopter. He currently works for a defense contractor as a maintenance test pilot. He is married to Mary Jane Player and they have five children. He holds a Master's degree in Strategic Planning and International Negotiation from the Naval Post-Graduate School, and a Master's in English from the University of West Florida. When the obligations of the day are over, he writes. His stories have appeared in *Baen's Universe, Redstone, New Scientist, Orson Scott Card's InterGalactic Medicine Show* and various anthologies such as *War Stories: New Military Science Fiction, The Year's Best Military SF and Space Opera, Apex,* and the *Young Explorer's Adventure Guide.*

SPACE HERO

by Patrick Lundrigan

Pat's winning story from 2010 is a testament to persistence and determination. He won second place in the contest the year before, with an excellent tale called "Burst Mode," but he wanted to win the Grand Prize, so he carefully crafted a new story. Unfortunately, once the story was finished and polished and ready to submit to the contest, he realized there was little actual life in those words—it did nothing for him. He knew if it didn't work for him, it wouldn't work for the contest judges and readers, so with less than two weeks before the contest deadline he started over with a blank piece of paper. The result was a touching story that not only worked, but did so by turning the "Space Hero" stereotype totally upside down.

THE SPACE HERO came out of the old Soyuz docking ring in a flight suit that looked so new you could have cut titanium with the creases.

"Just call me Rob," he said as an introduction, pocketing his sunglasses and shaking Jake's hand in a firm Naval Academy grip. Jake would remind him later about the bone loss the longtimers suffered.

Jake had the orbital shuttle ready to go, but the hero had to update his blogs and establish a downlink. "For the folks downstairs," he said, doing a tight half gainer over to the communication console.

Jake waited as Rob, or Robert Danforth, NASA astronaut and self-appointed ambassador of good will and public relations, downloaded a pocket cam full of videos from his launch and then set up for a live Q&A session with a class of third graders in Ohio. He answered the usual questions (how close are the stars, what does the Earth look like, can you see Ohio, how do you go potty) like he'd spent his whole life teaching kids about space. Jake wondered if NASA had a training program for that, since most of the current astronauts spent all their time on the ground. Jake hadn't done much PR in the past three years, with the business of space and keeping the manufactories running the sum total of his time, both working and free.

"We don't get many of you blue suiters up here," Jake said after the sendoff from Rob admonishing the kids to do well in school and pray.

"That'll change soon," he said, stowing his assorted com gear. "Once they pick the first crew." He gave a wink, as if he knew already who would make the cut for the first manned Mars mission. "I can't wait to see the ship."

"Let's see if our launch window is still open," Jake said, and led him though the hub, toward *Freedom*'s main docking pod.

Wrangling a visiting NASA astronaut made for a difficult assignment. The old days of steely-eyed fighter jocks had gone the way of blank checks from the government and grand presidential visions of space conquest. Everybody upstairs these days had *work* to do, with some science thrown in if they had the time. He turned back, taking another look at the space hero. A few years back, when those third graders from Ohio were just future plans for their farmstead parents, Robert Danforth turned a shuttle launch disaster into a miraculous landing, bringing his damaged orbiter back with all hands. He put the American space program back in the news for a year or two, and launched his current career.

But he must've spent all his time doing the PR shuffle, or else he'd have known the first Mars ship and the "scheduled" first mission would remain a plan for a very long time. Jake's own manufactories had multiyear contracts that had to be completed before they'd have the robot-hours to get back to working on the Mars ships. The deep space tracking network didn't have a hertz of bandwidth to spare, with all the rovers and orbiters and the belt miners out exploring the solar system. And robots and computers could explore the universe for a lot less cash than a tin can full of men.

Jake and Rob floated into the docking pod. Jake introduced Rob to the duty crew, and within minutes the old astronaut had them under his spell, telling stories, asking questions, handing out commemorative pins. He knew some of them from their days at NASA, before they'd "gone commercial." Jake turned to the main terminal as Holly broke from Rob's orbit.

"Sorry, we got a load of tourists coming in," she said, "you'll have to wait until they dock."

"Good news for you," Jake said, "more time with Mr. Right Stuff."

Holly swung around, one arm on the terminal. She tucked her loose hair back and looked toward Rob. "I dunno. Nice to have a real astronaut visiting and not another zero-g robot jock."

"Well, if he gets tired of shaking robot claws over at Tri-Star, I'll send him back early."

Holly gave him a hip check, nudging him away from the terminal. "Let me make sure the Love Boat hasn't gotten lost," she said, calling up a panorama of navigation screens. "Two hours late, right on schedule. You'd think Astro-Disney would run a better operation." She picked up a headset and put on her official voice. "*Astro Princess*, this is *Freedom* traffic control. Docking cleared on port seven."

Updated telemetry came in, and Holly juggled the transit lanes, a dozen ships in transit, seventeen commercial habitats, a swarm of satellites, and the usual cloud of junk and debris that filled low Earth orbit these days. Nothing got past her watchful eyes.

"Damn, a five-hour layover," she said. "Remind me to tell the eggheads to lock up the labs or someone'll grab a mouse to take home."

Jake did a flip, moved in closer to her ear. "Trade ya," he said.

"No way," she said, rotating away. "I got two days downtime next week—you free?"

Jake sighed. If he got the space hero squared away, if his robot crews made the weekly quota, if the Russians made the next delivery . . .

"I can find a day," he said.

Holly gave him her best pout. "Maybe Rob will have some time," she said. "He could show me his medals and I could show him the stars."

"A day and half! I'll make the time."

Holly gave him a wink and turned back to the terminal. Soon the station shuddered as the tourist ship made hard dock, and within minutes of a good seal a dozen tourists floated into the hub, bouncing off each other and the bulkheads. Jake realized then he should have gotten Rob on the shuttle first.

"Welcome to space," he thundered, shooting toward them. They circled around him, the usual mix of enthusiastic, rich, older people, and Rob started his standard meet-and-greet. Like the crew, most of them knew him, and before long the stories started and the autograph pen came out.

"I may never get back," Jake said.

Rob settled into the pilot's chair with an uncanny ease. He pulled the checklist from the slot and flipped to the first page. Jake hovered behind him.

"As much as the world recognizes your piloting skills, sadly, the owners of this beat-up orbital shuttle, Tri-Star Industries, and their numerous insurance policy providers, don't. So I have to fly us over."

"C'mon, Jake. I've flown these in the simulators a thousand times. A quick trip, no one will know." He beamed his thousand-watt smile, gave a thumbs-up. "Wheels-up in ten minutes."

Jake debated arguing. He wished for failsafes and lockouts and an advanced computer interface, something to keep Rob's hands off the controls. Instead he rolled into the copilot's seat, strapped in. "You can't deviate from the flight plan," he said. "Or else you'll screw up Holly's traffic control."

Rob looked up from the checklist, one hand over a switch. "Can't we swing out to Hubble, for few photos?"

Jake opened his mouth, ready to scream. Every tourist ship boosted to the high-parking orbit, but they'd have to burn all the shuttle's reserves to get there and back.

"Just kidding, sport. Man, you should see your face. Now make sure I don't make a mistake." He went back to the preflight, and Jake slowly calmed down. At least Rob, turning serious and professional, did have the time in the simulators, because he knew his way around the shuttle cockpit.

After getting final clearance from Holly, they undocked. Rob held his hand on the joystick, but the autopilot pulled them away cleanly, spun them to the right vector, and ignited the main engine. Rob kept alert, eyes on the viewscreen, ready for anything.

"Have you done any work on *Mars One*?" Rob said after they had cleared the station.

"Way back," Jake said. "I did the chassis assembly. My robots, actually."

"Outstanding. I can see you take pride in your work—and your robots."

"At least I don't worry about strikes or sick days. But a solar flare can send the entire production line off their rails."

Rob gave a quick laugh, then turned quiet as they crossed the terminator. He looked poised for action, as if about to make a night landing on a carrier. But the shuttle plodded on, with no need for any input from her crew.

"This mission means a lot to me. Even if I don't get selected, I'll support it one hundred and ten percent."

Rob might be a dinosaur, an old stick-and-rudder man who could fly an automated ship, but didn't look happy doing it. He came from a previous age, and the next age of exploration wouldn't come around for a dozen years, or whenever the orbital factories caught up with demand. And he'd never get selected then. Jake hoped his enthusiasm would cover the disappointment of seeing *Mars One*.

"You don't have to go to Mars," Jake said. "We have a booming economy right here in Earth orbit. With your NASA training, you'd fit right in. A dozen observatories, manufactories—"

Rob held up his hand. "I know. Work like that, and I know it takes work, would drive me crazy. I can't even . . . never mind." He flexed his hand around the joystick, eyes back on the instruments. "Let's just concentrate on the flight."

Jake watched the nightside for the rest of the trip, until Tri-Star station came into view. It reminded him of an erector set gone crazy, docking hubs sticking out at odd angles, solar panels flying atop a two-hundred-meter boom, pinpricks of light from a dozen welding robots around the main module. Rob looked too, but his eyes searched until they found *Mars One* and never left. Jake reached over and switched off the autopilot.

"We just cleared the transit lane," he said, "and sometimes the docking sequence goes haywire. Why don't you take us in?"

Rob smiled, and if he knew that an autodocking sequence hadn't gone haywire in six and a half years he didn't say anything. He already had the docking ring on the heads-up, and his approach and capture felt as smooth and solid as any the shuttle computers ever performed. Together they went through the shutdown sequence.

"We got about three hours before dinner," Jake said. "We got a downlink ready for you, so you can catch up." Tri-Star kept shifts running 24/7, but most everyone came together for one meal a day. And they'd all look forward to a new face.

"Can we see *Mars One* first? She looks good on the outside. I can't wait to see the inside."

Jake had cargo coming in, and a bunch of robots to check on. He guessed Rob could find his way around, and charm anyone he met along the way.

"Why don't you take the self-guided tour? I'll answer any questions later."

Out of habit and tradition long established before Jake ever arrived, the galley module maintained an Earthside ambience, complete with faux-wood paneling and incandescent lighting. The tables met in a single plane, providing space for everyone on-station to sit at one time—although sitting only required bellying up to the table and Velcroing in. Station etiquette also meant sitting while eating. Jake came late, grabbed a loaded tray and floated over. He found a spot next to Dan, who had a pancake in one hand and a squeeze tube of syrup in the other. Dan had the next shift in Jake's production area, station morning for those who kept track.

"So did you lose the cargo," he asked.

"Half a ton light, but the Russians got it here," Jake said. "If you get the time, have it unloaded."

Dan took a shot of syrup, caught a sticky drop before it got away. "No, the other cargo, the dead weight from NASA."

Jake looked around the table. He should have known by the volume of conversation. Just the usual table chatter, and some heated debate on the other end of the table about the World Cup.

"I left him at the ship," Jake said.

"Well, when he gets tired of nosing around, I could use some help."

Jake pulled open a pouch, squeezed out a mouthful. "NASA paid for his trip."

"Yeah, just so he can look around, and ask questions, and get in everyone's way."

Some of the others at the table joined in the conversation, wondering when the space hero would show up. After a few months on the station, everyone got to know everyone else well enough to get along, but they all seemed hostile to Rob. A stranger on board made for a distraction, an outsider, someone to vent on. But Jake knew Rob could charm anybody. He pushed off, dinner half finished, and stowed the tray.

Shooting down the main corridor, he stopped twice on his way to the docking ring to make sure his robot crews hadn't crashed or rebooted. Both bays had the usual hum of activity, forges running and the mills rolling. He hit the junction feet first and bounced off, redirecting himself toward the ship-building hub. Not much activity down this way, orders for ship frames and modules having fallen off in the last year. Lights in the transfer tube led him in, but inside *Mars One* all the lights remained off. He kicked off toward the cockpit.

Rob sat in the pilot's seat, with a pocket cam Velcroed to the bulkhead aimed at him. The instrument panel, a duplicate of the one in the shuttle, showed a few systems powered on, the rest dark and lifeless.

"Oh," Jake said, "I didn't mean to interrupt a taping."

Rob looked over, the shadows across his face hiding his expression. "I'll wait for sunrise," he said. "Quite a ship you've built."

Jake anchored to the back of the flight engineer's seat, took a look around. Most of the panels had mock-ups installed, colorful decals in place of actual equipment. *Mars One* could fly, if she had to, but she'd never leave Earth orbit. "We still have some work to do," he mumbled.

"I know the plans and schedules, but I had to see it for myself. See the plumbing and tankage. Feel the fabric. Flip a few switches."

"We just need a few more deliveries," Jake said, suddenly defensive. *Mars One* would work. Nothing exotic about her design. Just a matter of putting the pieces together.

Rob shook his head. "Yeah, I know. But the Mars mission needs a lander too, and a hab module for the surface, and the refinery. Just putting the command ship together doesn't make the entire mission."

"It'll happen, Rob. NASA has put up the money, more or less, and the schedules will work out."

Rob looked out the viewscreen. An arc of Earth, glowing in sunlight, appeared behind the framework of the station.

"Back on *Discovery*'s last flight," he said, talking slower now, in a half-whisper, "when the hydraulics started to go halfway over the Atlantic, you could measure my life in minutes. I had one thing to do. One path to follow. No options. And I did it."

He shook his shoulders, like he fought back a laugh. "I made it look easy, but I never did anything so hard. And now my life has expanded, and I have years and years ahead of me, but nothing as hard or as easy as those few minutes."

The station crossed the terminator, sunlight playing on the framework outside, reflecting into the cockpit. Without the shadows, *Mars One* looked more real, less like a shell. Rob smiled now, as if the light had washed away his memories. He put his sunglasses on. "Time to get the video show on the road," he said. "Hit the record button for me."

Jake took welder number seven off-line and stowed it in the shop. When ever he got some time he'd crack it open and try to figure out what made the damn thing reboot ten times a day. His daily checkout of the hardware done, he floated over to the terminal to check the paperwork. He had to get a dozen certs out, and make sure they had enough inventory for the next week, and get started on the quarterly report. Instead, he dug into the archives, checking into the old *Mars One* contracts and specs. The design looked good, no technological leaps required. But the mission plan required support ships, and landers, and habitation modules. All in the appropriation stage. But it could happen. Could happen soon, with money and juggling the schedules. If anyone would pay for it.

The station gave a shudder as something undocked. He didn't know Dan had the cargo unloaded already. He called up his schedules, ready to get back to work, but couldn't concentrate.

Dreams. Did Rob come up here to sell a dream? A dream only he believed in? Too much business these days, Jake guessed, too much profit/loss, too much cost/benefit. They could send a boatload of robots to Mars right now, but who'd do the video shows? And what if the things rebooted during re-entry?

Dan's face broke onto his screen, his brows knitted together. "Jake, just what the hell is wrong with your flyboy?"

"I haven't seen him today," Jake said.

"Then *Mars One* just undocked all by itself?"

Jake kicked off from the console toward the nearest window. At the other side of the station, *Mars One* pulled away from the docking ring and the loose transfer tube. She started to roll, then the aft thrusters fired, moving her away.

Jake didn't reply to Dan on the screen. He pushed off from the window and headed out of the manufactory toward Central as fast as he could move.

The Central hub had all Tri-Star's communications and control, and by the time Jake shot in, bouncing hard off a bulkhead, everyone else had gotten there first.

All the screens flashed warnings, and a looped clip of Holly played in one corner, declaring an emergency. All flight plans rescinded, all stations to maintain alert.

"What has he done?" Jake asked. Dan hovered over to him. "This has nothing to do with the space cowboy," he said. "The Astro-Disney boat hit a solar panel fragment an hour ago and lost control."

Jake let out a breath. Just the usual over-caution when any mishap occurred. There would always exist a danger of an expanding debris field after a collision, and space tracking would take a while to count all the pieces. He saw the tourist ship on the radar screen, looking to be in one piece, but tumbling.

Dan pointed to the rest of the crew. "If we get him back in time, they might not even notice," he said. "He hasn't gotten far."

Jake grabbed a headset and turned back toward the main communication console. The emergency looked under control; Astro-Disney ground control had good telemetry from the tourist ship, and although they had lost navigation, life support remained online. He found the com freqs for *Mars One*, and switched on the transmitter.

"Rob, you couldn't have picked a worse time for a joyride," he said. "We got an emergency and everyone has to stay put."

The station handshook with the ship and data flowed back and forth. Half the displays stayed dark, with the ship waiting for most of its major systems.

"Rob, I know you can hear me. Listen, you've only got a hour or two of air at best, and we don't have time to mess around. Come back right now."

"Jake, good to hear you." Rob's voice came over the headphones with his usual bright attitude. "She flies better than I hoped."

The ship had cleared the solar panel boom, heading for the transit lane. "Look, Rob, this will be your career. We don't have any flight clearance, and even if we did, you don't want to fly around when a debris field could expand into your orbit."

"We have a bigger problem than that," Rob said. "I got in touch with NORAD as soon as the tourist ship went off-line. I have to program my burn, talk to you in a minute."

Dan moved in closer, picking up a headset. "Has he started the Mars mission by himself?"

Jake paid no attention. He signaled to *Freedom*, trying to get Holly on the line. After a long moment, her face came up.

"I don't have time to chat," she said. "Astro-Disney's got a rescue ship prepped. They should launch in an hour, and I have to clear traffic."

"We have an unscheduled launch," he said. They'd never hide Rob's joyride once he entered the transit lane. "We will attempt to recall."

"Attempt? Negative, Tri-Star station. You will recall all ships." With a jab at her console, she closed the screen. Jake switched channels.

"Rob, listen, you got to get back now."

"Jake, I'm almost ready to burn," he said. "You know what the difference between a government contract and a commercial contract?"

"Rob, please, no jokes."

"A government contract goes to the lowest bidder, a commercial contract goes to court. You should hear from NORAD soon."

Dan shrugged his shoulders when Jake shot him a look. "He must have gone crazy," he said. The rest of the Tri-Star crew had somehow assembled around his console, watching. They all looked to Jake, as if he had launched *Mars One*.

Then Holly's screen popped up. "Tri-Star, NORAD has requested your assistance."

The alert screens shifted as the tracking updated. The circles expanded, encompassing more of low Earth orbit. Tri-star and *Freedom* hung on the outskirts, and the tourist ship flew above them.

"NORAD casts a wider net," she said, highlighting a dozen orbits that intersected LEO. "Once the tourist ship lost thrust, it put them right in line with an old booster. Can you render assistance? We've got no ships in the transit lanes."

The telemetry from *Mars One* had the interception course plotted.

"Affirmative," Jake said, feeling like he had arrived in the middle of a movie. "We will assist."

Jake stayed at the terminal as the rescue unfolded in slow motion. Rob still had an hour to match orbits with *Astro Princess* and dock, and just a nudge from his thrusters would pull them both out of the path of the booster. Some of the Tri-Star crew filtered out, back to the production areas.

Still, something didn't look right. *Mars One* had most of its parts, could fly, but a lot of pieces had never been installed or tested out.

"Looks like you got yourself another mission," Jake said. He had the schematics out, and kept checking the telemetry. He worried that something wouldn't work, and unlike wrangling a dozen welding robots, lives hung in the balance.

"This one might have to last me for awhile," Rob said.

Then Jake saw it, right on the schematics. "Rob, confirm your O2 reading."

"You know what I read."

"Rob, you have to come back."

"Negative."

"Rob, you saw it yourself when you went on board. You don't have an autodocking module. You'll never mate with the tourist ship, and you don't have enough O2 for a return trip."

"I got a mission to last me a lifetime," he said.

"Rob," Jake said. But Holly's screen came up, interrupting him.

"Jake, what's going on? Rob's changed course."

Mars One veered away from an interception with the tourist ship. "Rob, speak to me," he said, switching channels.

"I knew about the docking module," he said. "But I won't need it to hard dock with the booster. I'll just take it out of harm's way, and the rescue ship can bring the tourists back home."

Jake punched up the orbit of the booster. "Rob, that's an eccentric orbit. You'll never get back in time."

"I know. But I have to do this."

"Rob, you still have the fuel. Turn back now. The booster might not even hit."

"I can't take that chance," he said.

"What about Mars? You could still go to Mars."

"That's a long way off, my friend, even if everything falls into place. To tell you the truth, I just can't wait that long."

Slowly the ship diverged from *Astro Princess*, toward the booster.

"Getting kind of stuffy in here," Rob said. "Two minutes to rendezvous."

He made a neat hard dock, grappling the front end of the booster on the first try. The two jittered as thrusters stabilized them.

"I'm going to let the autopilot take over from here," he said.

Mars One's main engine fired.

"Mainly," Rob said, his words starting to slur, "I didn't want people to forget. You'll remember me, won't you, Jake?"

"Sure, Rob. No one can forget you."

Holly stood watch on the docking hub alone when Jake arrived. Dan and the rest of the contingent from Tri-Star headed over to the observation deck for the memorial service. *Freedom* had shuttles from every station docked, and an honor guard had come up from Houston.

Jake floated over to Holly. She closed down her terminal, plucked a data chip from the console.

"Wait," she said. "We have to talk."

Jake anchored himself. "I know this has been hard on you. I liked Rob, too."

"Not that," she said. She held up the data chip. "Telemetry."

"So Rob left before you actually requested assistance. No big deal, he had *Mars One* ready, so what if he entered the transit lane early?"

Holly ran her hand through her hair. "Not that either."

Jake took her hand, closed her fingers around the chip. He waited.

"The news people keep hounding me, asking for more details. They want to know everything."

"So tell them. Rob would've wanted that."

She opened her hand. "The booster never would have hit the *Princess*," she said. "I've gone over the numbers again and again. Nothing more than a near miss. NORAD's numbers weren't as good as mine."

Jake closed his eyes. "I think he knew. And he would have went either way." He took the chip from her hand. "NASA contacted Tri-Star this morning. They want us to finish *Mars One*. I can find a place for this on board."

Holly kicked away from the console. "We'll let the news guys make up the story," she said. "They'll do a better job."

⟨⟩

Born in Brooklyn before the hipsters invaded, Pat now lives in New Jersey with his lovely wife, who continues to read his first drafts with undiminished enthusiasm. He's been a part-time writer since the fifth grade, when he first started turning English composition homework into science fiction stories. His other current job is in the aerospace industry, where he uses his engineering problem solving abilities to make Power Point slides. In addition to the Jim Baen Memorial Short Story Award, Pat's story "Hangar Queen" was a first place winner in the L. Ron Hubbard's Writers of the Future Contest, and has been reprinted by Digital Science Fiction (https://books.pronoun.com/hangar-queen/). His stories have also appeared in *Space and Time Magazine* and *Flash Fiction Online*.

THAT UNDISCOVERED COUNTRY

by Nancy Fulda

Nancy's story about a group of plucky octogenarians, who refused to be filed away or pushed around, has always been one of my favorites. Using her own grandparents for models, she created a cast of believable characters who were the perfect long-term residents of an orbital station because they didn't need to worry about issues like dangerous pregnancies, bone loss or cumulative radiation effects. Her attention to scientific accuracy and engineering detail add a whole new level of believability to life aboard a rotating space station. We see subtle nods to the Coriolis effect, large agricultural biomes, cockroaches that won't stay put, and her use of space tethers is a real concept explored by NASA as a way of lifting payloads into higher orbits. Hudson Exospheric is named for space-flight entrepreneur and renowned engineer Gary Hudson, and after the story's publication his wife contacted Nancy to express her delight with the tale, and tell her that Hudson was also a longevity enthusiast, making his name even more appropriate to the story!

THE GARY HUDSON EXOSPHERIC LABORATORY rotated lazily against an expanse of brilliant stars. Sunlight glinted off its blockish airlock, accentuating the trellises that joined its three concentric rings.

Norma Jean Goodwyn, cofounder of the laboratory and currently its chief administrator, stood with her back to the habitat's medical office and glared into the star-spattered void.

She was not usually one to gawk at viewports. She'd been alive for twelve decades and spent three of them in orbit; by now, the scenery was routine. Comfortable. Like the feel of a socket wrench between her fingers, or the sound of laughter from a nearby room.

Like a friend who hasn't betrayed you yet.

An amused voice drifted over her shoulder: "I see you've spoken with Akash."

"I am *not*," Norma said without turning from the window, "letting him put some glitchy mechanical contraption into my chest."

Boney knuckles nudged her aside, and Nkiruka Azikiwe joined her at the railing. Wiry and wizened, but far from frail, Nkiruka moved with sprightly precision. She cast a calculating glance toward Norma. "A mechanical heart isn't the end of the world, you know."

"The things aren't reliable."

"Admit it. You're scared."

"Of course not! I just—it's just. . . "

Norma faltered. How could she explain? Artificial hearts were common enough, nowadays, but they were still sadly lacking. They seemed somehow a desperate woman's ploy—weak fingers snagging to hang onto life, any sort of life, for just a few moments longer. She knew where that path led, and she refused to follow it.

Norma's hands, withered and leopard-spotted with the passage of time, kneaded the support rail set into the window. "I suppose Akash has already placed the order?"

Nkiruka hesitated, as though party to a secret and uncertain whether to reveal it. "It's coming up on an emergency payload tomorrow."

"*What?*" Norma's head spun around. Gravity seemed to evaporate, and she was grateful for the support rail beneath her palms. "He can't . . . That idiot!" Nkiruka was watching her with thinly veiled amusement. Norma took a rigid breath. "Do you have any idea how much it *costs* to expedite a payload through the space tether?"

"I don't, actually. I prefer to concentrate on my microorganisms and leave the finances to you administrative types." Nkiruka's grin faded. "But I know Akash, and if he says your heart won't last until the next scheduled payload, then it won't."

"He didn't say it won't last. He said it *might* not last."

"He said you need a new one, and speaking for myself, if getting it here causes a little negative publicity, that's a price I'm willing to pay."

"*Negative publicity* is all those fools on Earth need to snatch this laboratory out from under us." Norma gripped the cool security of the railing. It was her imagination, surely, that made her breath seem to come in such desperate bursts.

Nkiruka's brows drew down in concern. "Norma, is there something you haven't told us?"

"Yes. No. I don't know . . . Now that the lunar activists have agreed on a schematic, a moon base is looking like a real possibility. And Hudson Exospheric is perfectly situated to serve as a way station."

Nkiruka cocked an eyebrow. "You think the lunies want to steal our habitat?"

"Why not? It's sturdy, self-sufficient, and commercially viable." Norma's fingers drummed the railing. "Remember the scuffle over the International Space Station? Everyone knows the lunies bribed at least two officials."

"Well, yes, but that was an abandoned piece of junk. The lunies may not have been legally entitled to it, but nobody else wanted it. *This* station is United Earth's leading institution on space biology and zero-gee manufacturing."

Norma leaned toward Nkiruka. "*You* know that. And *I* know that, and so do a handful of university professors who follow research in those fields. But to the masses on Earth, this place is nothing but a big cemetery in the sky."

"Now you're being paranoid."

"I'm being realistic. It takes more than money to build a space habitat. Chad and I worked for ten years to get Hudson Exospheric's structural diagrams approved, and that was after we had funding. If the lunies can cut corners by snatching someone else's accomplishments, believe me, they'll try."

Nkiruka's grunt was skeptical, but Norma felt the familiar, cold weight of certainty in her gut. Public support for Hudson Exospheric had never been strong. Politicians may have seen the logic of permitting senior citizens to establish mankind's first permanent settlement in space—how better to avoid the perils of low-gravity conception and a generation of children who could never return to Earth?—but the typical man on the street still had reservations about allowing the elderly to handle such a delicate task.

Norma had no doubt that the lunies could peddle her expensive heart delivery into a fiasco of public scrutiny and inevitable inquiries: How had Norma's deteriorating heart tissue gone undetected for so long? When had Hudson Exospheric's technicians last been evaluated by an accredited source? Might the colony's residents be growing—dare one say it—dangerously decrepit in their waning years?

Norma leaned into the window's indentation, her pale eyes studying the stars. "To the folks on Earth, we're nothing but a bunch of doddering cripples. Old people waiting to die."

"That's nonsense. We built this place, rivet by rivet—and those EVA suits get awfully sweaty after a while, I must say. If anybody's qualified to keep Hudson Exospheric up and running, it's us."

Us. The e-generation. That group of citizens who'd ridden the wave of technical innovation ever since biomeds boomed in the 2030s, and who as a consequence had spent half their lives pushing against other people's expectations of age.

Norma's late husband, Chad, had said it best. "Face it," he'd growled after being forced into retirement for the third time. "We're the oldest generation on the planet, and it's going to stay that way until we die. It doesn't matter how good our résumés are. As long as we're mired in a bureaucracy run by people younger than we are, we're going to have to prove and re-prove our worth every decade."

That had been the beginning of Hudson Exospheric. The idea had been a joke, at first: a way to show those uppity mid-lifers that being a senior citizen didn't automatically render you incompetent. They used to laugh about it with their friends, evenings, and then—

Then the space tether finally got up and running, and the idea didn't sound so ludicrous after all.

Norma's fingers continued to drum against the support rail. The speckled backs of her hands rose and fell with the rhythm of her thoughts.

This emergency heart shipment might be precisely the break the lunies had been waiting for. The image of a multibillion-dollar space habitat squandered in the name of geriatric sovereignty raised hackles all across Earth. The lunies need only build on that fear to wrest Hudson Exospheric from her.

And if the lunar activists won, Norma and every other member of her generation would be branded as senile old coots, unfit to build a space station, unfit even to live on it. They would be back fighting uphill battles every time they applied for a job, back arguing with relatives over whether they could safely live alone in a house. No one would entrust them with anything, ever again.

Norma's hands froze, clamped like ice around the railing. A stubborn, uneven line formed at her lips.

So help her, she was not going to let it happen.

Norma arrived in her office to discover five urgent messages from Earth. The first was a letter of inquiry from her insurance company, requesting confirmation of her physician's current standing with his nation's medical association.

The second was a courtesy call from the adjoint secretary of the United Earth Assembly, notifying her that Hudson Exospheric's colonization charter had been called for review according to section 12, paragraph 14 of the United Earth Constitution, the inquiry to be directed by the Department of Public Health.

The third, fourth, and fifth messages were automated notifications of newsworthy events related to Hudson Exospheric. Norma's expression hardened as she read.

"Of all the—Maximilian!" she shouted, startling workers up and down the corridor. Living constraints aboard an orbital habitat being what they were, Norma's "office" was actually a cubbyhole along a heavily crowded walkway that served both as the colony's administrative headquarters and as a convenient shortcut between the drop chutes and the cafeteria.

Maximilian appeared from the spinward direction, head ducked in deference to the shallow ceiling. His hair hovered about his skull in a wispy halo. A resonant thump sounded each time the base of his gnarled hickory walking stick struck the floor.

"That's it," he grunted, propping his elbow on the back of Norma's chair. "I want the legal offices moved closer to the doorway. I'm too old for all this stooping."

"Blame the engineers," Norma said. "On second thought, thank them for making the industrial levels, at least, higher than two meters. Take a look at this." She gestured towards her work screen. "Can they *do* this?"

Maximilian scanned the open message, then reached past Norma's shoulder to scroll through the others.

"Hmph," he said finally. "That happened fast." He stretched his vertebrae, and his voice took on a professional timbre. "Yes, they can do this. The United Earth Assembly may review—and revoke, if necessary—any charter for orbital habitation granted by that body."

"I know all that," Norma said irritably. "But they can't possibly have amassed enough evidence for a charter hearing so quickly. I expected public outcry, or a call for independent auditors to inspect the station. Not . . ."

Not . . . whatever this was.

Norma had the unpleasant feeling of being outmaneuvered. She'd walked into her office ready to begin an aggressive public relations campaign: interviews, press releases . . . enough bravado to convince the public that one expedited payload did not constitute a health crisis. Instead, the rug of public opinion had been swept out from under her, to be replaced by the far more dubious soil of political repartee.

Norma disliked the new playing field. Public opinion could be swayed. *Political* opinion, now . . . Political opinion could only be purchased, and Hudson Exospheric didn't deal in the right currency. They didn't even have a voice in the United Assembly.

"If United Earth revokes our charter," Norma said slowly, "then Hudson Exospheric and all its equipment becomes unclaimed territory, which United Earth can reapportion as it chooses."

"Yes, that was one of the provisions of the initial research grant. Although the habitat rings have been expanded since then. We might be able to contest a reapportionment on the basis that the colony is partially privately owned."

"Not good enough."

Norma's mind raced. She'd been blindsided, robbed of any political leverage. Oh, she had friends in the United Assembly, good ones, even. But they couldn't push her cause effectively without a few days to prepare, and the hearing was scheduled to begin in five hours.

Rushing into a hearing was, Norma conceded, a brilliant decision on her opponents' part. The hideous logic of it made her want to weep. Or fume. Or something.

She rose and began to pace.

"How do we fight this, Max?"

"There's nothing to fight yet. They've scheduled a closed hearing, we've no way to access the meeting's minutes or even know which consultants they've called in."

In other words, they were blind and deaf.

And outgunned.

Norma's pacing grew vigorous. In the narrow confines of the corridor, the effect was much like a tiger prowling its cage. "Our opponents' game hinges on demonstrating that we've violated our charter. Since the inquiry is being conducted by the Board of Public Health, they'll have to show that medical care in this colony does not meet United Earth standards."

"Which it *does*. Akash is the most competent doctor I've ever met. And I've known quite a few. When will those fools on Earth stop doubting our intelligence just because we're *old*?"

Norma's heart was pattering. She placed a hand on the back of her chair and paused to catch her breath.

Maximilian watched gravely. "Norma," he said. "About your heart... "

"Oh for—is there anyone on this habitat who *doesn't* know about that yet?"

Maximilian's wrinkles deepened. "There may be a few fellows on sanitation duty who haven't gotten word." He sobered and arched his eyebrows in an authoritative expression. "Now, young lady—and I'm allowed to call you that, seeing as I'm twelve years older than you are—you listen to me. You couldn't have stopped this. No one could have. So don't you go chewing on Akash because he ordered that heart without consulting you first."

"Who says I'm going to?"

Maximilian held up a hand to forestall further protest. "He's a doctor. He did what was best for his patient, and politics be damned. It's one of the reasons I like him. But even if he hadn't ordered the heart, our charter would have been called into question soon enough. There are too many space agencies jostling for power right now. One of them would have found an excuse. Or made one."

Norma exhaled heavily. With a slight grunt, she settled into her chair and swiveled it to face Maximilian. "You know what's ironic about all this? I don't even want the heart."

"You'd better rethink that."

For a moment, Norma thought she hadn't heard right.

"Beg pardon?"

"I'm not talking about your personal preferences," Maximilian continued. "Heaven knows, we've all got a line, and I'll not fault anyone for refusing to cross it. But if this hearing comes out badly, we're going to spend up to two years mired in appeals process." He rested his weight on the cane and leaned inward. "I don't pretend our chances are good. But without you, we've no chance at all."

"Don't be silly. I'm not the only person capable of running a habitat."

"I'm not suggesting that you are. But you have thirty years of experience in this position, plus a hefty set of political connections. I'm not asking you this as a friend. I'm asking as a member of this colony. Take the heart. Don't make us fight this battle without a leader."

Norma stared, dumbstruck, as he turned around and left.

The tap of Maximilian's walking stick receded down the hallway.

With nothing to fight until the results of the hearing were announced, Norma was forced into a waiting game. Once she'd placed calls to her contacts in United Earth and set Maximilian working on a formal appeal—just in case—the day vanished in a flurry of trivia. Messages, staff meetings, and local disputes all required attention. Nkiruka stopped by to report a case of patent infringement. A chemical spill in the synthetics laboratory threw off work schedules station-wide.

That evening, long after the other office workers retired to their beds, Norma flipped off her screen and stood to water the spider plants crammed around her work area. Her vision blurred as soon as she left her chair. Heart hammering, lips compressed against a sudden rushing breathlessness, she placed a wrinkled hand against the doorframe for support as she completed her evening chores.

Dizzy spells had plagued her throughout the day, a continuation of the pattern which had driven her, finally, to Akash's office for that long-overdue checkup. Now, traveling alone along the darkened corridor, Norma was forced to consider that Maximilian might be right: If she intended to aid Hudson Exospheric through the current crisis, she was going to need a mechanical heart.

The thought disturbed her. Norma had spent much of her childhood at her grandmother's bedside, watching nurses scurry in and out of the room, listening to the labored breathing of a woman who'd once had more gumption than the rest of the family combined. Near the end, Grandmama was not even allowed to get out of bed; the nurses were afraid she'd slip and break a bone.

Norma had sworn, all those long decades ago, that she'd never go *that* way: propped up on a heavily pillowed mattress, forbidden to lift anything heavier than an orange juice tumbler; dependent on others not because her body was too frail, but because their fear was too strong. Made smaller than she should be by their well-intentioned stifling.

It was late, and the hallways were deserted. In the faint glow of the floor lights, the ivy was nothing but shadows dangling from wall alcoves. Norma's feet whispered against the floor on the way to her sleeping cubby.

Snugly in bed, Norma stared for a long time into the dimness. Eventually she tabbed the laboratory's intercom and left two messages: One to the colony's workforce coordinator, offering to join the volunteer crews preparing for tomorrow's emergency payload.

The other message was to Akash, telling him she'd report for heart surgery the next evening.

"Ready!" Norma called.

With a grating scrape, the man clinging to the ceiling unhinged the safety clamps and let the cutting torch drop.

Its descent was more amble than plummet; acceleration here on the inner ring was barely a quarter of Earth standard. Norma adjusted for the coriolis effect, careful not to overexert herself, and intercepted it before it reached the floor. Her dizzy spells were a bit worse this morning, but she wasn't going to let that stop her from doing her share of the work. It was *her* heart that today's payload capsule would deliver, after all.

She loaded the cutter onto the transport cart and dusted her work gloves on her overalls. It felt good, moving around, working with her hands instead of sitting trapped at her desk. Like changing brake pads in her father's auto shop on Earth or welding heat radiators onto the habitat rings. Good, honest work, without political scuffling.

The next tool dropped—a massive metal-bender. Norma stowed it with the others. "That's it," the man on the ceiling called. "Be sure to bring 'em back when you're done."

Norma waved a polite farewell and pushed the cart into the drop chute. She clipped the gloves onto her tool belt and rode to the outer ring, ignoring the queasiness that plagued her stomach whenever she shifted acceleration levels.

The drop chute opened. Norma pushed the cart into the cramped corridor. Windows rolled past as she trundled along, mere centimeters bridging the space between the cart's edge and the wall. The ceiling, too, seemed to press against her.

Maximilian had once called these hallways claustrophobic, an appellation she had never agreed with. "Claustrophobic" to Norma Jean would always mean cramped hospital rooms and the smell of antiseptic, and your grandmother's frail hands clutching yours so tightly that your fingers go numb, because you're the only one in that whole bubbly, doting, Southern-bred family who knows your Grandmama isn't helpless, and so you're the only one she dares rely on for support.

And Grandmama died anyway, dammit.

Yet the tragedy hadn't been the death itself. Chad had died, too, and Norma had never resented it. He'd died on his feet, in an EVA accident helping add a new module to the habitat, not smothered to nonexistence by relatives desperate to shield him from every possible injury.

Norma was panting by the time she reached the airlock. She locked the cart's brakes into place and rested against the handle while she waited for the world to stop spinning.

Across the room, volunteers were sliding potted plants away from the airlock doors, cautious not to scuff the paneling. The windows here were floor-to-ceiling, made of transparent ceramic. Through them, Norma watched colonists in EVA suits inspect the free-flying grapple that would match momentum with the payload and maneuver it to the airlock.

"There you are!" Nkiruka waved a cheery hello and rested both forearms against a massive peace-lily planter. Her face crinkled in a well-accustomed smile. "I forgot to bring the extension cables, so I sent Akash to fetch them. I mean, it's *possible* to dismantle a capsule without them, but—having tried once to get a good angle for the cutting torch with only five feet of cable—I can tell you it's really not worth the trouble."

Norma smiled at the decades-old complaint. "Perhaps we should have built the drop chutes large enough to cart payload capsules down to the machine shop wholesale. The metal would be just as useful, and we'd save the trouble of cutting it up."

"*I* say we just start chucking the things down to low Earth orbit. This colony doesn't need to get any bigger."

"Costs too much fuel," Norma said automatically. Hudson Exospheric had, occasionally, sent a pod back, when there had been handwritten letters or other physical gifts to be delivered to the residents' relatives. The amount of fuel needed to get a capsule down to low Earth orbit just wasn't economical in most cases.

Nkiruka brushed the grit from her hands. "Not really. Fuel's only costly if you have to ship it from Earth. *We're* sitting on five tons of liquid hydrogen that every resident in the colony would rather die than use."

Norma opened her mouth to object, but thought better of it. Nkiruka had a point. In Hudson Exospheric's early days, it had seemed prudent to have an evacuation plan in place lest the bioregenerative systems fail and leave the inhabitants literally gasping for air. Rather than weighing down the habitat with emergency transport pods, they had elected to make the colony its own lifeboat, stocked with enough fuel to shift all three rings to near-Earth orbit for rescue and salvage.

Apparently deciding she'd won the argument, Nkiruka moved to the next planter in need of repositioning. "What's the latest from Earth?"

Norma shook her head. "Nothing. They haven't said a word."

Nkiruka frowned, a sentiment Norma agreed with. The charter hearings had concluded hours ago, but the Assembly had not yet announced the results. Could this strange silence be a positive sign?

"We've confirmed that the lunies are behind it, though?" Nkiruka asked.

"We think so. Maximilian traced three money trails to their organization. Not that it particularly matters."

Norma's gaze drew inescapably to the windows, and to the delicate globe hanging in the darkness. Somewhere down there, too thin and fragile to see, the space tether whirled like a bolo, snatching payloads as they breached the atmosphere and flinging them into higher orbits. Right about now, if Norma made her guess, it was transferring momentum to the capsule that would deliver her artificial heart.

"Well," Nkiruka said philosophically, "If it's gonna blow, then it's gonna blow. I suppose they'll get around to telling us what they think eventually. Give me a hand with this rhododendron, will you?"

Norma complied, a decision she regretted when, a moment later, Akash entered the far door with a handful of cable. His physician's eye took on a critical gleam as he watched Norma straining to move the hip-high pot.

"Norma. . ."

"Don't coddle me, Akash," she said testily. "We're replacing this heart tonight, so there's no point squabbling over whether I'm mistreating it. I'm *fine*."

Norma's body gave the lie to her words. She couldn't keep herself from snatching extra breaths between each sentence.

Akash's gaze grew, if possible, even more stern, but he either decided this wasn't a fight he was likely to win, or his mind was distracted by more pressing matters. "You should come over to the observatory," he said abruptly. "Bernadette has a line of sight on the payload capsule."

"And . . . ?" Norma prompted, mystified. She wasn't in the habit of viewing payloads through freefall telescopes.

"Just come see."

Hudson Exospheric's observatory resembled nothing so much as an overfilled computer cubicle. The telescopes themselves drifted *out there*, stably situated at Lagrangian orbits respectively ahead of and behind the habitat. The data they broadcast was displayed at a cramped tangle of screens and keyboards shared by Bernadette and three other astronomers in a space large enough for only two people at a time. Indeed, the observatory was affectionately referred to as the "broom closet," and on one memorable April Fool's Day someone had gone so far as to stuff it with mops and dustpans. Bernadette had been livid, Norma recalled.

Bernadette seemed more perplexed than livid this morning, however. Her stout fingers skimmed across the keyboard with alacrity that defied their arthritic knobbiness. "There," she said, a few moments after Norma, Nkiruka, and Akash had crowded behind her in the observatory's doorway. "That's the best view I can get; any more magnification and the optimization subroutines will break down."

The dull oblong of the payload capsule hung near the center of the observatory's largest view screen. Even accounting for the pixilated haze of algorithmic magnification, Norma could tell that it looked . . . wrong. The smooth outer shell of the capsule was broken at three points by nodes that looked very much like thrusters, and an array of antennas clustered near the nose suggested that . . .

"That's a Human-Transport module," she said suddenly.

Unlike the usual payload capsules, H-T modules were equipped with thrusters for the return to low Earth orbit and a communications relay for passengers traveling inside.

"Of all the. . ." Nkiruka's voice was appalled. "Why didn't they notify us?"

Akash said, "Perhaps they were afraid we'd reject the passenger. So they sent the capsule without asking."

"Well, they can send him or her straight back," Norma said firmly. "Those modules carry enough air for a round-trip. If we don't send the grappler to pick it up, they'll have no choice but to head home."

"And take your artificial heart with them," Akash pointed out.

Norma hesitated.

"How many people could fit in a capsule that size?" Nkiruka asked. Her voice was thoughtful. "Because it wouldn't take more than five or six armed men to seize control of the entire habitat."

"They wouldn't dare," Akash said.

They'd better not, Norma thought. Because Nkiruka was right. The colony had no firearms and no trained security personnel. She and Chad had discussed the possibility, in the early days, but in all the years they'd lived in orbit, their handpicked, peaceable senior citizens had never proved to need a police force. Crime, it turned out, was for the young.

Or at least, Norma amended to herself, violent crime was. Hudson Exospheric had hosted its share of research fraud, to her regret, and one particularly nasty embezzlement case that had resulted in the perpetrator being sent back to Earth.

Bernadette was tapping at her keyboard again. "Based on the acceleration records . . . there can't be more than one or two people aboard. Otherwise it would have picked up less speed coming through the tether."

"Two SWAT officers would do well enough," Nkiruka muttered.

"They couldn't," Norma said firmly. "It would be illegal entry— assault if they harmed anyone—and would start a political and public relations tangle that I can guarantee you *no one* in the United Earth bureaucracy wants." She thought about it some more. "We'll seal the receiving area from the outside, just in case."

No one seemed satisfied with that half solution, but nobody offered any better ideas, either. Norma stared at the payload capsule, growing imperceptibly larger against the sleek blackness of the computer screen, and frowned.

The Asian man who exited the capsule was . . . *young*, was the first thing Norma noticed. Hardly more than forty, his black hair showing the merest speckle of gray. He stumbled slightly as he pulled his girth over the capsule's edge, clearly disoriented by the station's simulated gravity, and nearly knocked his head against the low ceiling of the airlock chamber.

Norma, Akash, and Nkiruka waited for him in the corridor. The rest of the colony's residents were watching the exchange by video feed, safely ensconced behind the sealed bulkheads at either end of the hallway. Safely, Norma decided wryly, but perhaps unnecessarily. The man edging his way through the narrow space between the wall and the capsule had a distinctly bureaucratic figure, and the heavy manila package tucked in the crook of his arm bore little resemblance to a weapon.

He reached the corridor, still looking off-balance, and straightened his spine for a formal greeting. "Mrs. Norma Jean Goodwyn?"

"Yes, that's me."

"Joseph Hwang, UE Medical. I've been assigned to evaluate conditions here on Hudson Exospheric, and to deliver some rather important correspondence from United Earth."

Norma ignored his proffered handshake.

"You are trespassing, Mr. Hwang," she said coldly. "This habitat is private property, and you have not been invited aboard."

Hwang's congenial expression faded. "I'm afraid the documents I carry change that situation, Mrs. Goodwyn. United Earth has rescinded Hudson Exospheric's charter. As of yesterday, this laboratory is no longer approved for habitation. I'm sorry"—to his credit, his contrition seemed sincere—"but you'll need to maneuver the station down to low Earth orbit. From there, United Earth will arrange transportation to the surface."

In the silence that followed this statement, Norma Jean became acutely aware of the gentle thrum of the ventilation system, the rustle of rhododendron fronds, the reflected glare of the sun through the corridor's windows.

"That's . . . a very serious set of claims," she said finally.

Hwang hefted the manila bundle with both hands. "I assure you, the documents are all here, with all the proper signatures. United Earth's administrative offices are prepared to corroborate every statement. Under the circumstances, they felt it was better if I delivered the news first, in person."

"Spineless, sneaking, *mid-lifers*," Norma growled. "They knew if they told us any earlier, we'd never have let you aboard."

Hwang almost smiled. "Probably. Look, I know this must be hard for you. For all of you. But please realize that I'm not the one who made the decision, and I don't have any power to change it. I'm just here to—"

"Snoop around in our business," Nkiruka cut in. "Study our medical records, nitpick about whether we've all been given proper medical care . . ."

"And especially, to look for evidence to justify United Earth's decision ex post facto," Norma added softly. "They know they're on shaky ground, and they want you to find reasons why this habitat's residents aren't fit to operate it. Isn't that right?"

Hwang looked uncomfortable.

Norma was tempted to send him back into his capsule that instant, but sanity prevailed. Hudson Exospheric wasn't properly situated to launch a capsule back toward Earth, and it would be inhumane to make him wait in cramped confinement until the next launch window.

She sighed.

"Well, come along then, but don't expect to be given access to anything private. We'll review your paperwork and get back to you."

At Norma's signal, the residents on the far side of the bulkheads released the seals. Hwang followed Norma through the crowded corridor, clearly uneasy at edging past so many bodies in the narrow hallway. Akash gestured for his attention.

"What about Norma's heart?" Akash said. "Is it still in the payload capsule?"

Hwang's discomfiture increased. "United Earth didn't send it," he said after an awkward pause. "They felt it would be better for you to have your surgery at the recreational space station in low Earth orbit. Where it would be easier to provide follow-up treatment, if necessary."

It seemed to Norma as though time froze for an instant before slowly thawing back to its normal rhythm.

"Of all the sick manipulations," Nkiruka whispered. "They're holding your heart hostage to make sure we leave the habitat."

Norma delegated Akash to show Hwang to the cafeteria and after that, if he wanted to stretch his muscles, to the gym. He gave her a concerned physician's glance as they departed. She gave him a glare.

As soon as they were out of sight, she leaned against the support rail and let her panting lungs catch up with her heart's insistent demands for more oxygen. Beside her, Nkiruka hefted the manila bundle she had collected from Hwang. "I'll take this to Maximilian. If there are loopholes in the paperwork, he'll find them."

"I doubt he'll find anything," Norma said. "Whoever's behind this will have made sure it's all official and proper. They've probably had the paperwork drawn up for months, waiting for the right opportunity to pounce."

Hwang's arrival had changed everything. Norma had expected United Earth to revoke the charter, but she'd presumed there would be formal announcements, a chance to contest the decision . . . not this steel-plated eviction notice.

With a sinking sensation, she realized she had been outmaneuvered again.

"We can still fight this," Nkiruka said, sounding almost vicious in her determination. "Appeals procedures, lawsuits . . ." Her voice trailed off as she thought it through. Any recourse they took would cost them time.

And time, right now, was Norma's enemy.

Norma would have fought anyway—and damn her heart and damn anyone who tried to tell her otherwise—if she'd thought Hudson Exospheric would come out victorious. But she and her colonists were trapped between hopeless choices: surrender, or be defeated.

This isn't fair, Norma thought bitterly. *This isn't how it should work. I don't want to fight and lose.*

I need a way to win.

Nkiruka adjusted the package in her grip, seemed to be searching for something more to say, gave up the attempt, and headed off at a brisk walk.

Alone at last, Norma headed—not towards the drop chutes and the community areas where everyone else seemed to be congregating, but spinward, toward the agricultural ramp. The slope seemed to drag against her feet as she ascended. She stepped off the ramp, passed through the humidity lock, and entered the wheat fields.

Vast, Norma reflected, could be a surprisingly relative term. Like the colony's other agricultural areas, the wheat spanned the full width of the ring—nearly four meters from one wall to the other—and was hemmed by a ceiling of trellised, semiopaque panels that left barely enough room for Norma to stand. But the field ran spinward and antispinward for nearly half a kilometer, far enough that the rippling grasses vanished into the curvature of the ring.

The ripening seed heads rustled pleasantly as Norma traversed the footpath, and the sunlight, redirected by an array of external mirrors, warmed her shoulders through the ceramics.

What would it be like, she wondered, to walk on native soil again? To wander through fields that stretched farther than the eye's capacity for sight?

Not worth the price.

There was no point in deluding herself. There would be no cheerful walks through sun-drenched fields, no daring hikes up steeply sloping mountainsides; not when thirty years of orbital living had reduced her bones to half their previous density. Earth had nothing to offer her— nothing to offer anyone on Hudson Exospheric—except hospital beds and dinner trays and potted Begonias viewed through window panes.

Norma's jaw grew tighter. Her hip pained her, and she was beginning to wish she'd taken time to fetch a walking cane from the tool rack next to the humidity lock. Yet she would not turn back.

Five minutes of exertion brought her to the edge of the wheat. Beyond, tomatoes and peppers sprouted in ordered rows, followed by soya and lettuce farther down the ring. Here and there between the lines, agriculturalists knelt to spread their fingers in moist soil, or inspected stalks for signs of malaise, or measured acidity levels. Norma greeted them as she passed, exchanging cheery pleasantries that, on this day of uncertainty, were likely as feigned on their part as they were on hers.

Norma was proud of this colony. She was especially proud of the bioregenerative system. Hudson Exospheric replenished its own air, recycled waste into biomass, produced its own food. . . it had been decades since they'd required supplements from Earth.

Because, of course, Hudson Exospheric had always been intended as a one-way trip. That was one of the reasons they'd limited residence to postoctogenarians in the first place. Dragging this marvel of self-sufficiency back into the stifling gravity of earth seemed a most hideous betrayal.

And yet—what else could she do? Norma might be able to stall United Earth for a month, or even a year. But they were outmatched in this little game of politics, as her opponents had already demonstrated twice.

She could refuse to comply with United Earth's edict, she supposed. But that would only bring peacekeeping forces to breach the habitat and compel the residents to leave.

She was halfway through the soya now. In the quiet warmth of the biome, Norma imagined she could hear the soft scrabbling of harvester ants as they traversed fresh stalks and delicate white blossoms. Something skittered between the rows. Norma glimpsed a sturdy, inch-long carapace, and smiled.

As she approached the next humidity lock, to her surprise, she encountered Akash and Hwang coming from the other direction.

"Yes," Hwang was saying, "but *cockroaches*?"

"They're hardy, nutritious, and easy to breed," Norma interjected by way of greeting. "And they snuck out of the tropical biome again. Pierre's going to be furious."

"You saw one, too?" Akash's relief was apparent. "Mr. Hwang and I aren't the ones who let it through the humidity lock, then. Or at least," he amended, "not the *only* ones."

"Touring the habitat?" Norma asked with polite effort. She did not wish to converse with Hwang, but reminded herself firmly that *he* was as much a pawn in this power scuffle as the rest of them.

"Yes. Akash said it would take the local lawyer a while to finish reviewing the documents, so I asked to be shown around. I confess, Hudson Exospheric isn't . . . anything like what I expected."

"Most things aren't, once you look closely."

Hwang cocked his head in acknowledgement. "I . . . hope you understand. I was assigned to this investigation because United Earth needed my skill set. I didn't ask for it. I don't necessarily approve of it." He paused, a hint of iron creeping into his voice. "But I *will* carry it out."

Norma sighed. "No one expects any different from you." She glanced sidelong. "Are you required to report your private conversations to your superiors?"

"Are you kidding? At United Earth, if it's not on paper, it didn't happen."

Norma chuckled. "I take it that means 'no.'"

She joined Hwang and Akash in walking back along the route she had come. Hwang studied everything—the crops, the soil, the ventilation system, the overhead trellis—with the air of a man who'd expected to enter a police box, and walked into a garden instead.

His astonishment did not surprise her. Space habitats had a reputation as sterile, metallic structures, but Hudson Exospheric was dominated by organics. Two-thirds of the walkspace was devoted to bioregeneration, and in the residence regions, wood and wallpaper made far more pragmatic paneling, given the cost of shipping heavy materials up from Earth, than steel.

"Do you know what convinced me to join the colony?" Akash said conversationally. He spread his hand to indicate the crop fields. "These. The plants. The engineering diagrams were of interest, but the biomass projections . . . When I saw that men could live, untethered from the nourishment of Earth . . . That is when I knew I must come into space."

"Interesting choice of words," Hwang said quietly. "Because it's the space tether that shackles you. If it wasn't so easy to lob payloads up here, no one on Earth could afford to enforce the evacuation order."

Norma stopped walking.

"Akash," she said slowly. "How far *can* the tether fling payloads?"

Akash shrugged. "The original plan was to launch payloads to Mars. But the funding floundered and the project remains incomplete."

"That's what I remember, too. Given the current length and speed of the tether . . ."

Norma glanced at Hwang. Was it safe to discuss this in front of him?

Too late. He'd already caught the drift of her thought. "Hudson Exospheric marks the edge of its range," he said with an enlightened expression. "At least for payloads of any significant weight."

"Akash," Norma said urgently, "this habitat stores over five tons of combustible fuel. Instead of using it to take us to near Earth orbit, let's go *farther out*."

"To the Earth/Moon Lagrangian?"

"Why not? We'd have built the station there in the first place if we'd known how to get materials out that far. Easier access to asteroids, and to the Moon, too, someday."

"Norma—it won't work. The space tether's not the only way to launch a military force into high orbit."

Norma waved a disparaging hand. "I know, I know . . . But: If we use most of our fuel getting out there, how are they going to bring us back *in*, hm? And we can use electromagnetic tethers to maintain position there."

"That's no good," Hwang said suddenly. He cringed under Norma and Akash's combined stares. "Earth's magnetosphere is too weak at the L4/L5 orbits. You won't get enough drag for orbital adjustments."

"I was thinking of the L1 orbit, at the gravitational balance point between Earth and the Moon," Norma said. Her gaze on Hwang intensified. "But that was a very astute observation."

Hwang shrugged. "United Earth made a point of assigning this job to someone with a basic education in astrodynamics."

"Hm." Norma began, despite herself, to raise her opinion of their unwelcome guest.

Akash was ticking out more objections on his fingers. "No way to build new solar panels, no manufacturing capacity for silicon chips, no backup support if we collide with an asteroid."

"No earthquakes, no tsunamis, no flooding . . ." Norma smiled wryly. "Natural disasters happen everywhere. Our risks aren't so much worse than any other domicile. We can mine silicates from passing asteroids; carbon, too. At least one or two will pass close enough for the grappler to intercept, over the next few years."

Hwang added, eagerly, "And the tethers could provide supplemental energy when they're not being used for orbit adjustments." He hesitated, seemed to remember his official capacity, and glanced at the dirt. "Um. Not that I support this idea, or anything."

Norma nodded in approval. "And if anyone comes after us, we'll disrupt the orbit and slingshot out past the Moon."

"It's . . . not the worst idea you've ever had," Akash said diplomatically.

"It's pure genius and you know it. Besides . . . "Norma's voice softened. "We've nowhere else to go."

"The recreational space station in low Earth orbit . . ."

"Doesn't have the capacity to take all of us. Most of our people would end up on Earth. In wheelchairs."

From Akash's pained expression, she knew he agreed with this analysis.

"I suppose," he said finally, "that only leaves the matter of your heart."

An uncomfortable silence settled over the trio.

"My heart . . ." Norma said slowly. "Will take care of itself. Or not. The colony comes first."

She paused for breath. "Mr. Hwang. Hudson Exospheric will give you access to our medical records, our personnel, whatever you require to complete your investigation. However, what we choose to do after you leave the habitat is our own business."

Hwang nodded, looking far more comfortable than he had when he'd boarded the residence ring.

Norma grew breathless on the long trek back to the habitation areas, during which she and the others bantered, plotted, and nearly trod on three cockroaches. As they neared the habitat ramp, Akash strode ahead to fetch her a walking cane.

Norma contemplated the burnished chestnut of the cane's handle, extended from Akash's hand. She had always been afraid of crutches. Always feared that to accept aid was to lose a piece of oneself.

Perhaps, she thought, extending a gnarled palm to accept the gift, it wasn't necessarily so.

Perhaps one might find a piece of oneself, instead.

Norma called for a vote, of course. The colony's residents professed her scheme to be everything from utter madness to sheer brilliance, but when they finally cast the ballots, although nearly a quarter of the colony abstained, not a single voice was opposed.

By the time she and Maximilian had completed the text of Hudson Exospheric's formal secession from United Earth, Hwang had completed his official inquiries. Norma's cane thumped against the hardwood as she escorted him back to his Human-Transport module.

"I'm sending you home to an unpleasant greeting," she said. "I do apologize for that. I trust United Earth will understand that there was no way you could have stopped us."

"I've been in worse situations," Hwang said dryly. "Any news on your mechanical heart?"

Norma hesitated. Should she tell him? He looked so hopeful . . .

"There won't be a heart, Joseph," she said slowly. "United Earth announced a trade embargo two hours after we seceded. Earthbound companies are no longer authorized to send us supplies."

Hwang seemed taken aback. "That . . . seems rather drastic."

"They were afraid some of the other orbital facilities might follow our example."

"Ah." Hwang's distress increased. "There's, um . . . room in this transport module for one more."

"No," Norma said gently. "There's not."

Hwang glanced in confusion at the capsule, which was equipped for up to three passengers. A blank-stared moment later he seemed to catch her meaning.

Her soul could not squeeze into that capsule, nor into any of the fancy wheelchairs that awaited her on Earth. Something would break if she tried.

Hwang accepted this with a nod. He swung his legs into the capsule and glanced once more along the corridor. "I'm going to miss this place. To be honest, if I didn't have a wife and kids back home . . . well . . . It's a beautiful station you've built up here. You all have a right to be proud of it."

He vanished into the opening. Norma abandoned her cane long enough to help seal the capsule from the outside and bang on the shell by way of parting. Supported again, she watched with a strange, unfamiliar sensation in her gut as two teams of residents closed the airlock.

The floor rumbled; the outer door popped open. Hwang's capsule drifted into view beyond the windows. It receded rapidly, flung toward Earth by the habitat's rotation.

"All readouts clear," Hwang's voice carried over the tinny radio from his communications array. "I'll start the burn for Earth once you're under way."

Norma nodded. Within minutes, she felt the soft vibration of the station's propulsion mechanisms beginning the long, slow process of expanding its orbit. Hwang's capsule, now almost too small to be visible, ignited its thrusters as if in a final salute.

On the planet below them, the Aurora Australis flared to life in the solar wind. Somewhat closer, but too delicate to see, circled the whirling bolo of the space tether. And far beneath both, amid the bustle and lights on the dark side of the globe, a roomful of stuffy politicians was in for a surprise.

Norma smiled grimly. On impulse, she keyed the wall switch that activated transmission. "Mr. Hwang? Check back with us in a few decades. We may have openings for immigrants."

A puff of laughter crackled through the speaker. "I may do that. Any last messages for Earth? Something I should relay to your families, perhaps?"

"Yes," Norma said. "Tell them . . ." She hesitated, groping for the right words. "Tell them we're not afraid to die. No, more than that: We're not afraid to *live*."

—◆—

Nancy Fulda is a Phobos Award winner, a Jim Baen Memorial Award recipient, and a Hugo and Nebula nominee. During her graduate work at Brigham Young University she studied artificial intelligence, machine learning, and quantum computing. In the years since, she has grappled with the far more complex process of raising four children. All these experiences sometimes infiltrate her writing.

TAKING THE HIGH ROAD

by R.P.L. Johnson

Richard's story of an ill-fated Mars mission has everything we were looking for in this contest, but primarily he has people who refuse to give up. Through pure determination, pluck and resourcefulness, they build a future for themselves and give the rest of us a tantalizing glimpse at what it might take to gain a permanent foothold in space.

Personal Log: Lori Childs - Senior Planetary Scientist
Date: 12/04/2037 (+4 Months, 7 days)
Distance From Earth: 1.19AU

THEY WAITED TWO WEEKS to tell us about the accident.

I guess they had to be sure. There was no point in making us worry unnecessarily. But it meant that when the announcement came, it seemed there was no way out: no wiggle room, no chance of a second opinion.

I was in the Deck 3 Lab when the call came through to meet in the storm shelter. Beth Young was behind me, almost back to back in the small compartment. She was checking the readouts for the solar array: something to do with a power drain in the aeroponics lamps. Anyway, she was looking right at the data. If there was some kind of solar storm, some unpredicted event that could force us into the storm shelter she would have seen it in the data. She just looked at me and shrugged.

I was never a very good astronaut. Don't get me wrong, I love Mars: I have done ever since I can remember. I used to dream about walking on that red dirt, and my whole career has been about making that dream a reality.

But *getting* to the red planet takes a different set of skills. I never triggered any red flags that would have seen me bounced me from the mission, but neither was I comfortable in space.

We were two decks down from the storm shelter. Not far, not in a ship like the *Liberty*, but far enough when you're expecting radiation or pressure alarms to start sounding any second.

Some people say they can feel the difference in gravity between decks, but I think they're just fooling themselves. The *Liberty* looked like two grain silos connected by a tether five hundred metres long that was essentially one huge carbon molecule. One silo was the crew compartment, the other housed the reactor. And the whole thing was spinning through space to give us the illusion of gravity as we hurtled between Earth and Mars. At the centre of rotation was a small unmanned module that housed the communication gear and solar array mounted on gimbals so that they always pointed where they were supposed to despite our rotation. On that scale, the three-metre difference between decks means next to nothing.

Commander Campbell looked like hell, as if he hadn't slept for two nights although I had seen him at breakfast and he'd been fine then. He didn't say much, he just played the message that had come through at the start of the morning shift.

I don't remember much of it, just snippets like how the file was marked MC+ meaning it was for the mission commander's eyes only. I remember wondering if Campbell was going to get into trouble for showing it to us. That was before I realised that rebukes from Mission Control were the last of our worries.

There had been an accident on Mars: an 'Unexpected Environmental Event' in the Agency's typically understated parlance. Even two weeks later they were still working out exactly what had happened, but the best guess was that higher than expected winds had forced enough dust inside a joint on the fuel farm to clog a pressure valve. Shortly after that initial fault an explosion had devastated the site. All telemetry from the fuel farm ceased and reports from other systems all pointed to a massive systemic failure. Now, two weeks later, the only data they were still getting were temperature readings and they were showing Mars ambient.

The fuel farm was dead, and with it had gone all the other modules intended to support us during our time on Mars.

I don't think I realised at first what that meant. I remember turning to Beth and seeing tears in her eyes. The *Liberty* had finally spun down to Martian gravity three weeks ago, and great globes of one-third-gravity teardrops clung to Beth's lashes until she blinked them away.

The fuel farm was our ticket home. It was a self-contained chemical plant that mixed hydrogen with carbon dioxide from the Martian atmosphere to produce methane. It had been sent to Mars on an unmanned probe along with the habitation modules twenty-six months ago during the last launch window. Making fuel on site spared us from hauling that mass all the way from Earth. The fuel farm was what had made a manned mission to Mars a reality and now it was gone.

There was not so much panic as anger. Less shouting than I thought the situation warranted, but what there was echoed off the aluminium walls. Campbell held up his hands for quiet which was a long time coming. Eventually he said, "As of now, I am activating the emergency response plan. Now I realise it's been a while since you've read it but it's in your kits and it's on the network so dig it out and get to know it. There will be a meeting of section heads in five minutes. For everyone else, remember that there is no immediate danger. Our biggest enemy at the moment is panic, so I expect to see everyone at their stations. That is all."

You are going to die, but don't panic and go back to work. That is all.

The shouting started up again even before he had finished speaking. He let us carry on, like an angler letting out line for the fish to tire itself out before reeling it back in.

"I know this looks bad," he said eventually. "But we've got months of consumables, more if we're strict about it, and I'll be damned if I'm going to spend that time with my thumb up my ass watching the O2 gauge and waiting to die.

"We have a ship full of PhDs. Everyone here is a certified genius and I'm going to ask you to prove it. We'll find a work-around: something they've missed. Section heads, you now have two minutes."

Eventually, we did go back to our stations. For one thing, although the storm shelter was big enough to hold the entire crew, it didn't do so in much comfort and I found that comfort was what I needed right now more than anything. I needed my seat in the lab, my music: the consolations of the familiar.

We were all in shock I suppose. There was a note blinking on my terminal when I got back to my workstation: something about grief counsellors being on standby back on Earth in case we wanted to pour out our hearts in an e-mail. But the twenty-minute round-trip for messages didn't seem appropriate. In the end we were alone.

"There must be something they can do," Beth said. "A new orbit, slingshot around Mars and build up speed for a fast trip back—that sort of thing."

"I don't think so. If there was, they would have told us."

Fumi Mashimo and Claire O'Brian had followed us back from the storm shelter and we sat together, knee to knee in the cramped compartment.

Beth tried again. "Perhaps they could send a rescue mission," she said. "It wouldn't have to be manned, just a heavy-lift rocket with a care package of consumables. That might be enough to last until a window opens up for a return orbit."

Fumi shook his head, long locks of snow-white hair swaying in the reduced gravity like a slow-mo video from a shampoo commercial.

"It would take too long," he said. My youthful years watching old kung-fu movies imbued his accented words with a wisdom they probably didn't merit. Fumi was a palaeobiologist, not flight crew. He knew as much about Hohmann transfer orbits and Oberth manoeuvres as I did, i.e., not much.

"If it wasn't manned they could send it at higher acceleration," Claire O'Brian said. "That must open up some new orbits."

"Unless it is on the launchpad now, it won't get here in time. And if it was, they would have told us." Fumi shook his head again. "There will be no rescue from Earth."

"Then it's up to us," Claire said sounding almost chipper. "Like Campbell said, we have a ship full of geniuses. We just have to figure out a way to harness that."

"Unfortunately," Fumi said, "gravity is not swayed by academic credentials. There are realities that we must face."

"Realities, yes, but not certainties. Beth, how long would it be until we could harvest crops from aeroponics?"

Beth looked shocked. "We're not set up for that. The aeroponics labs are basically just keeping the seedlings alive until we reach Mars. We don't have the capacity to start farming on board ship."

"What if we made capacity? We're carrying spare parts and lamps ready to be set up on Mars. What if we doubled or tripled the capacity of the labs? What then? We could supplement the food stores and the extra plants would take the load off the CO_2 scrubbers."

"That won't get us home," I said.

"No, but it enlarges the window for a rescue mission."

"Water," Beth said. "The recyclers aren't perfect, and the more water we use to grow plants, the less we have for ourselves. I'd have to do the numbers, but if we doubled our crop my guess is that we'd all die of thirst before we saw a harvest."

Claire was undaunted. "Then we'll just have to increase the efficiency of the recyclers. Come on, we have to try!" She looked around the small group. Beth was quiet, probably doing the calculations in her head. Fumi was typically inscrutable, but he was the type to dress for dinner and go down with the ship rather than fight for survival. And me? I just wanted to go home.

Personal Log: Lori Childs - Senior Planetary Scientist
Date: 23/04/2037 (+4 Months, 18 days)
Distance From Earth: 1.201AU

Just when I thought we were beginning to accept our situation, our little community started to tear itself apart.

Our mission plan included a flyby of comet 10P/Tempel. We were never going to get closer than five hundred kilometres, but that would have been close enough to view it with the naked eye. There had been robotic missions to comets before: even impacters and landers, but this was to have been a first for the manned space programme.

The problem was, the manoeuvre would use fuel.

"I don't see why we should stick to the mission plan when it's going

to dramatically reduce our options later." By virtue of having the
loudest voice, Ed Carradine had become the unofficial spokesperson
for the ditch-the-mission-plan faction.

Craig Rowe took a deep breath. As pilot and second-in-command,
he was responsible for internal ship matters including quelling a
nascent mutiny.

"Our trajectory has been locked in since we left Earth. Yes, there
will be a course correction both to finalise the flyby and also to put us
back in the groove for orbital insertion at Mars. But changing the
trajectory to avoid the comet will also cost fuel."

"But it will save some."

"You don't know that."

"Where exactly do you want to go?" Tom Barischoff, the chief
engineer said, "We can forget both burns if you like. Just carry on the
way we're headed now. It won't mean anything. We'll die with full
fuel tanks, that's all."

There it was: the "d" word. Up until now everyone had been talking
about efficiency, optimum use of resources, avoiding the obvious
objection to all these plans which was that none of them would get us
back to Earth.

We were in the storm shelter again. It was even more crowded than
usual now that a third of the space had been given over to Beth's
expanded aeroponics racks. The crew had split right down the middle.
From day one there had been two distinct groups on the mission.
Mission Control had even fostered the split with friendly, morale-
building softball matches on the Antarctic tundra during our training.

On one side were the scientists: the guys who were going to study
Mars. We were not so much payload specialists (as we would have been
called in the shuttle era), but payload. We were the reason for the
mission: to get our hands and eyes and brains to the surface of Mars.

On the other side were the flight crew and engineers, professional
astronauts whose job it was to deliver us safely to Mars and keep us
alive when we got there.

By a few days after we were told about the accident, you could run
your finger down the roster and by looking at each person's job
description you could tell which side of the debate they would come
down on.

The flight crew argued that we would best honour our memories by following our mission plan to the last breath. A few even argued for an attempted landing on Mars. The arguments had started with the hope that enough of the base would be salvageable to allow the mission to continue. Later some expressed a wish to at least stand on the red planet before they died.

But there were difficulties even in dying. Along with the fuel farm, the habitat and all the solar panels, we had also lost the transponder that would guide the lander in. Finding a nice spot on Mars to sit down and just let your air run out had a certain tragic beauty to it. A forced march across the landscape with a broken collarbone and a ruptured suit because the unassisted landing was a bit too hard was less attractive.

But the scientists didn't have the same response to authority as the flight crew. Absolute obedience to the chain of command wasn't drummed into us the way it was into them. We had all had years of training, but we were still scientists first and astronauts second. And guys like Ed objected to following the plan, not because they had any particular notion of what to do instead, but out of a more general inertia.

With every gram of fuel and litre of air being precious, the reluctance to utilise any of it was paralysing.

And Claire? Despite being one of the most vocal of the science department, she never aligned with either camp and instead attacked all ideas equally. Tom joked that talking to her for five minutes was like a stress test for ideas. She probed every problem from multiple, simultaneous fronts. Some of the things she threw into the discussion were fanciful to say the least, but they were always novel and her scientific knowledge was prodigious extending well outside her specialty in geophysics.

I had spent hours in deep discussion with Claire. Indeed, in the days following Campbell's announcement it seemed that everyone on board had spent hours with her.

Our predicament seemed to instil in her a fervent energy. For most of us the adrenaline produced by fear was a short-lived reaction. In the face of such a gradual catastrophe as ours, no one could sustain the flight-or-fight reaction for long.

No one except Claire.

I remember that we had talked about the concept of functional immortality: the idea that if you could increase the functional life of something, be that an engine part or a human being, by just a small amount, even as small as one day. And if you could keep doing that day in day out, then the part would never wear out. It would perpetually be one day away from failure, but if that day could be pushed ever further into the future then it would never come, and immortality of a sort could be achieved.

Claire was convinced that the concept could be applied to our situation. If we could solve the problems of the day, and keep doing that day after day, then the final collapse would never come. To that end she worked tirelessly. She helped to increase the efficiency of the waste recyclers, she brainstormed with Tom and Beth and together they managed to increase the yield from aeroponics. At her insistence we even started eating together, all fifteen of us in one large sitting in the storm shelter, so that the sharing of food became easier and less was wasted. Everything she did helped to push that final day a little further into the future.

Her refusal to align with either camp made her something of a lonely figure, and her manic energy had gained her the reputation of a bit of a kook. But we all ate together anyway. And when she spoke, dissenting voices on both sides of the argument yielded the floor.

"Could we match orbit?" I asked. Fourteen pairs of eyes turned in my direction.

"I mean, it's ice isn't it? That's what we need."

Claire was beaming at me. Oh crap! Whatever faction Claire was in, it looked like I was in it too!

"Lori's right," Claire said. "The question is not whether we should go look at the comet; it's what we do when we get there. Do we just watch as it flies past the window or do we try and use it?"

"Now hang on," I said. "I wasn't—" but I was drowned out as the chamber exploded in furious debate.

"We're headed away from Earth like a bat outta hell and you want us to accelerate?" said Ed Carradine.

I didn't want that, I didn't even know if catching up to the comet was possible, I just knew that Beth needed water for the crops and we were going to pass within a few hundred kilometres of megatonnes of the stuff. Like Claire said: solve a day's problems and keep doing that every day and you can live forever.

Craig Rowe hadn't stopped staring at me since I'd first spoken. It was like he'd just seen a hamster whistle "The Star-Spangled Banner" and was wondering if it would do it again. Then he smiled and started making some calculations on his pad.

"Look at it this way," Claire said. "We're victims of a shipwreck and a lifeboat is floating right past us. It's heading away from shore, but if we don't climb aboard we're going to drown."

"Tempel has a period of what, five years?" said Ed Carradine. "You're signing us up for a five-year joyride out of the solar system."

"Better that than choking on carbon dioxide within five months," someone said from behind me.

"More than five years," Tom said. "The next orbit won't bring us any nearer to Earth. But she's right. The one thing we need right now is water. With water, ice and sunlight we can make all the atmosphere we need. With water and dry ice we can make fuel. We have enough phosphates and nitrates to grow food for years. All we need is ice and time. If we can catch that comet we'll have both."

The vote was carried eleven to three with one abstention, mine. I left as soon as the result was announced. That night as I lay in my crib, I turned the noisy little air fans up as high as they would go so that no one would hear me cry.

Personal Log: Lori Childs - Ice Miner
Date: 2/08/2037 (+7 Months, 28 days)
Distance From Earth: 0.87AU

I'm becoming a pretty good welder. There's not much to it, ice is a much more forgiving material than steel and the new welding lances and hot knives coming out of engineering are much easier to use than the clunky first generation tools.

The *Liberty* is starting to look more like a snow-capped mountain than a ship. We used the Mars Lander as a kind of manned grappling hook for the initial contact with the comet and then brought the bulk of the *Liberty* in by reeling in the tether. Soon after the ship was secured to the surface, we started to clad it with ice.

The ice was Claire's idea. Not only does it act as shielding against cosmic rays, but it also protects against micrometeorites. With this extra armour we're less reliant on the storm shelter. The whole ship has become as safe as the shelter—safer even.

In the original layout, the storm shelter was an additional pressure hull inside the ship: an air-tight cylinder shielded both by our limited supply of heavy metals and also by the water tanks that encircled it. By adding the ice we have essentially taken our water stores, frozen them and fixed them externally to the hull. That's freed up a lot of internal space. There is already talk of cannibalising the storm shelter's metals and its triple-redundant, self-contained life support. It was supposed to be our last resort in an emergency, but as Claire pointed out in the last Union, every day is an emergency.

The extra space is mostly given over to aeroponics. Living in the *Liberty* now feels like living inside a greenhouse. The loss of gravity has allowed Beth and Chris Mendenhall to start farming the walls and ceilings. Sometimes you float into a chamber and it's like being on the inside of a kind of biological geode. All around you are the tendrils of soya plants and the broad leaves of ferns.

At Union last week, Beth and Chris announced that they were engaged. Commander Campbell ordered that the last of the chocolate pudding be served and joked that he was saving the ice cream for the birth of the first child in space. At least I think he was joking.

Tom and the engineering crew are working around the clock taking the sensors, vents, antennae and all the *Liberty*'s other external hardware and extending them out on a forest of ducts and conduits, metres long. Then we grunts come along with our lances and the ice blocks as big as pool tables and make with the igloo building before the engineers reattach the hardware on the new ice.

It's hard work. At close to absolute zero, ice is as hard as steel. And even in microgravity the big blocks of ice still have mass and inertia. Getting them going is hard work and manoeuvring them into position even harder. We've had a few injuries. Muscle strains and one nasty crushing. Fumi was only saved from a broken ankle by the bulk of his suit. Even then his foot swelled up like the pulp of a blood orange.

God, I miss blood oranges!

When I go to sleep at night, my forearms are burning with fatigue and I sleep like the dead. There is talk of modifying some thruster units to help manoeuvre the ice, but it was voted down at Union. We need the exercise.

I'm glad of the work. This week marks the closest approach of Earth as its tighter orbit means it catches up with Tempel. Soon we will leave the plane of the ecliptic and start our journey out into the black. When we failed to make the orbital correction burn that would take us away from the comet, we started on a whole new mission. One that I am responsible for. Even though Commander Campbell is still nominally in charge, this joyride was my idea. Fifteen people's lives bet on my blurted out suggestion.

Personal Log: Lori Childs - Ice Miner
Date: 17/06/2038 (+1 year, 6 months, 12 days)
Distance From Earth: 4.265AU

Some of us make more sacrifices than others.

I saw Tom Barischoff in the flight deck today. With no need for course corrections or any hope of landing on Mars, the compartment is now given over completely to storage. The only instrument of any worth is the radio, which is the only reason the space is not given up to the wet warmth of aeroponics. I sometimes go there to escape the pervasive heat. Tom, it seemed, was there for different reasons.

"Talking to my wife," he said. His eyes were raw like wounds. In his hands he clutched a scrap of something that glittered even in the low cabin illumination. He caught my stare. "I coated it with some of the diamond monofilm we were supposed to test on Mars," he said. "I was worried it would fade."

It was a small photograph of a size easily tucked into a wallet. As he turned it in his hands I saw the faces of a woman and a child pressed together in a shared hug and smiling at the camera.

I felt instantly ashamed, both for intruding on his privacy (and God knows that's hard to come by on board ship) and also for forgetting that Tom was married.

Back when the vote was taken to hitch our fate to a speeding comet, it was Tom's vote that had settled it. Tom with the unofficial voting block of his engineering team, and his affable matter-of-factness that brought along many more. Tom with his casual competence that comes from years of getting real machinery to work in a real world that cared nothing for appearances and politics. Tom and his selfless action against interest.

I realised then that although I had forgotten about Tom's wife and child, others had not. They saw this man with so much to go home for vote to take a ride out of the plane of the ecliptic and they figured that was the only way to go.

And so here he was . . . weeping in front of a radio while his words made the thirty-five-minute trip back to Earth. Plating family photos with abrasion-resistant film and looking in vain in his engineer's tool kit for a tool capable of mending the broken jagged lump in his chest.

The speaker crackled with a woman's voice as raw as Tom's eyes. I left them to it.

Personal Log: Lori Childs - Engineer's Mate 2 Class
Date: 12/02/2039 (+2 years, 2 months, 7 days)
Distance From Earth: 3.486AU

I'd almost forgotten what gravity feels like. We're spinning up slowly: barely half a revolution per minute at the moment on a five-hundred-metre tether. That's enough for about 0.15G. But after acclimatising to Mars gravity and then spending nearly eighteen months weightless, believe me, fifteen percent is plenty.

The halls of the *Liberty* ring with curses as all manner of stumbles, trips, drops, and falls have painted us all in a palette of bruise-purple.

But it had to be done: Diana is pregnant.

She told us at Union two weeks ago. She was concerned about the effect of weightlessness on the unborn child and so petitioned the group for the construction of a centrifugal exercise chamber.

Claire suggested one better. She announced that she had been studying the mineralogical maps of the comet and had found what she called a possible counterweight: a large mass of ice that was thoroughly marbled with useful minerals that she believed could be cut free relatively easily.

Claire proposed freeing the mass and using it as a counterweight to set the *Liberty* spinning again. It would mean free flight and so we would have to use fuel to hold station with Tempel. But that wasn't so much of a problem. We're now producing kilogrammes of methane and free hydrogen every few days. Barely enough to coat the inside of the fuel tanks and not nearly enough to take us home, but more than enough for station keeping.

And so it was back on the lances. More detailed work this time, and more dangerous. The counterweight massed close to half a million tonnes. Over a period of weeks we cut away at the surrounding ice and placed shaped charges around its remaining supports.

We were all aboard ship and in pressure suits, helmets on but visors raised when Tom Barischoff fired the charges. It was a supreme anticlimax: the explosion, buffered by half a million tonnes of ice was little more than a ripple to bend the fronds of our aeroponic walls.

Amy DeLuca never got to fly her lander down to the Martian surface, but she did get to pilot a comet, or at least a fragment of one. The explosion had set us moving away from Tempel at the rate of a few centimetres a second. The *Liberty*—never a sportster at the best of times—was a sluggish tugboat hauling a half a million tonne barge. It took hours to rise clear of Tempel.

Over the next few weeks we slowly started to set the giant mass spinning. We used mirrors to vaporise chunks of the surface, forming a fog of out-gassing volatiles that slowly became a mini comet's tail as the counterweight started to move.

We were aiming for 0.52RPM: enough to give us our 0.15G at full tether extension. 0.52RPM was not much. It equated to a speed on the surface of about nine kilometres per hour.

Once that magic number was achieved, we gathered again in the storm shelter. Everyone except Claire was in spacesuits. She had opted for comfort and wore shorts and a T-shirt with the NASA logo that read, STOP THE WORLD, I WANT TO GET OFF!

We all listened in on the intercom as Craig Rowe took the left-hand jumpseat in our underused bridge and slowly let out the tether, leaving the lander attached to the counterweight while the bulk of the ice-clad *Liberty* eased away at low thrust. We must have looked like a spider extending on a gossamer thread from a slowly spinning globe of muddy ice.

There was an embarrassing flatulent chorus as our internal organs negotiated for space inside our bodies. And with that fanfare, gravity returned.

Personal Log: Lori Rowe - Engineer's Mate
Date: 21/08/2042 (+5 years, 8 months, 16 days)
Distance From Earth: 0.835AU

Today we had the first death in the manned space programme since *Columbia* and it was all my fault.

It was a routine operation. My team was on the counterweight, mining a particularly rich seam of aluminium oxide dust. Grunt work, nothing that we hadn't done a score of times before. Fumi was helping secure the power cables for my lance. One minute he was fine, the next I turned round to look at him and saw the inside of his visor splattered with vomit. A light blinked on his chest plate, low oxygen.

It took us forty minutes to get him back to the *Liberty*. His body was limp: limbs splayed out like a human starfish by the internal pressure of his suit. We had to manhandle him inside the small airlock like we were bringing in a chunk of ice, which in a way we were.

Fumi was dead.

Diana read out the autopsy at Union that evening. He died peacefully, she said. A bad regulator in his suit slowly asphyxiated him. So slowly, he never even realised there was a problem. He would have just felt a bit light-headed and fainted inside his suit. The vomit I saw was just a reflex, he was probably past saving even then. There was nothing we could have done, but Tom suggested a thorough overhaul of all the suits to make sure it wouldn't happen again.

There is an unspoken convention at Union: everyone attends and everyone stays until the end. Dinner is a politics-free zone, but after that comes a town hall meeting. If someone is criticizing you or your department, tough. You get the right of reply, but no one dodges the issue. Everyone gets a chance to be heard. It's worked pretty well so far.

This time, I just couldn't do it. There were other people crying, but what I felt was more than just sadness. It was as if everyone was looking at me. I was the one who had dragged us out here. If I hadn't suggested catching the comet, Fumi would never have had to make a single spacewalk. I remember nothing of the eulogy, I just remember a rising sensation of smothering and cloying warmth as if my regulator had malfunctioned and I was the one who was asphyxiating.

I fled.

Claire found me in the ready room where the suits were kept between shifts. The casing on Fumi's suit was open, the faulty regulator exposed. I was staring at it.

"It wasn't your fault," Claire said. "These suits were never designed for the kind of punishment we put them through."

"If we hadn't landed on the comet, we wouldn't have needed to use them at all."

Claire took my hands. With a maternal gesture that I found at once intensely invasive but also reassuring, she smoothed a lock of my hair back behind my ear. The look in her eyes was one of almost beatific kindliness and calm.

"Then his death was as much my fault as it was yours. I pushed for this just as much as you: more even."

"Don't you ever worry that it was the wrong thing to do?" I saw in her eyes that she didn't.

"We're five years into an eight-month trip," she said. "If we hadn't landed on Tempel, Fumi would probably have died long ago along with the rest of us."

She hugged me and her voice was a whisper against my ear.

"Don't think about one death. Remember his life and the fourteen other lives you saved."

She said it with such conviction, such assured passion that for a moment I almost believed it.

Personal Log: Lori Rowe - Assistant Astrogator
Date: 7/03/2054 (+17 years, 3 months, 2 days)
Distance From Earth: 3.022AU

Jessica was almost uncontrollable today. The pressure testing of the new habitat wasn't even complete and she already wanted to move in. I tried to reason with her, but the confidence of teenagers, along with the mass of the electron and the speed of light, seems to be as constant out here as it was on the Earth of my youth.

"Oh Mum!" she said. "We don't have to wait. If the ice held the overpressure during mining, then it's bound to hold up under one lousy atmo. Even if there is a pip-squeak leak, we can just find-and-fix after we've moved in!"

A pip-squeak leak! She was talking about a hull breach. It was the kind of thing that would have sent the engineers at Mission Control into paroxysms of activity and my fourteen-year-old daughter talked about it as if she was discussing the colour of the drapes.

We were one of the last families to move over. The counterweight already held the new aeroponics garden, the pool, sick bay and suites for four families. A warren of chambers had been melted into the muddy ice and lined and clad and lit and pressurised. There was more enclosed volume over there now than there was in old *Liberty*.

Our ship now resembled a flying barbell of glittering ice. I'm sorry that I haven't chronicled this better, but Tom will have catalogued the changes in exhaustive technical detail. Where once we were an ice-armoured tin can being spun around at the end of a tether from the spinning ball, years of mining, building and tunnelling had distributed the mass almost evenly. The tether that once connected us was still there, but its carbon nanotubes were mostly used for data cables now. The structural work was taken up by the shaft, a fifty-metre-thick column of reinforced ice enclosing the transfer tunnel. At the barycentre a slight thickening held not only the old comms array and sensors, but also the zero-Gym and sort of parish hall-come-nightclub where Aaron Rhodes traded his home-brewed beer and which the youngsters had named the *Centrey-Bar*.

We didn't eat together anymore, but we still held Union once a week. Sometimes we premiered new movies beamed straight from Earth. Other weeks were taken up by ship business or celebrations.

We had shed a lot of mass: sloughed off the looser, friable material and sent it back to the main body of the comet where we could pick it up any time. The *Liberty* was now a sprightly twenty-five hundred tonnes, five times her launch mass and more massive even than the orbital shipyard where she had been built.

Now each family had a suite of rooms to itself and the tunnelling was still ongoing. Maria Cosatti, Diana and Frank's daughter, was nearly sixteen and she had been going steady with one of the Mendenhall twins for nearly two years. This first generation of born spacefarers had grown up quickly. The smart money was on a marriage as soon as the next apartment was ready and a third generation soon after that despite the protestations of Diana, the soon-to-be first grandma in space.

Personal Log: Lori Rowe - Assistant Astrogator
Date: 7/01/2059 (+22 years, 1 month, 2 days)
Distance From Earth: 2.36AU

Claire's will left specific instructions on how to deal with her remains.

We'd had a couple of deaths so far, Fumi's accident and Kristen Bradfield's tragic death during childbirth, but Claire's was the first death that we had time to prepare for.

I read out her instructions at Union and tried to remember when she first told us about the cancer. It was about six months ago. This letter was dated two years prior to that—handwritten on pages from a NASA notepad a quarter-century old. She had known for some time, but had kept it from everyone.

I have transcribed it here in its entirety:

Do not grieve. That's the first thing. Death itself is nothing—only a cessation of things, an end to pain. The anticipation of death is only somewhat more frightening, but only because of what I fear for my loved ones. I do not fear the end, but I do tremble at the thought of being the cause of sadness. So do not grieve, I could not bear it.

I would like my body to be placed in the biome for recycling. By the time you read this, I will have gone. All that remains are chemicals pressed into my form. If that is too much for you, then let the children do it. They understand. They see this final sacrament for the gift that it is and are not encumbered by the mawkish sentimentality of what once was. Their mythology is one born of looking forward. They tell tales of what will be. No campfire yarns of the deeds of ancient heroes for them. Their heroes are yet to come and indeed may be closer than any of you realise.

I don't want to say I told you so.

So do not grieve for me. I, out of all of us, gained the most from our prolonged detour. I signed on for a three-year mission, thinking that was the closest I would ever get to life lived among the stars. I sometimes feel guilt. Guilt at having enjoyed my life so much. It was almost as if the accident was my fault: an act of karmic sabotage to bring about what I wanted more than anything else.

Look at us now. Comet riders and spacefarers: a pocket-sized nation of citizen scientists with a unity of purpose not seen since we left behind the subsistence farming of medieval village life and yet with all of space before us. No longer limited to our fields, our herds and the banks of our river—we can now take these things with us and there is no limit to our wanderings.

So do not grieve. Pick me apart and set every molecule to work. This ship is my dream and I have worked all my life to see it come to fruition and I'll be damned if I let a little thing like death intervene.

Ad Astra
Claire

Personal Log: Lori Rowe - Assistant Astrogator (retired)
Date: 24/06/2062 (+25 years, 6 months, 19 days)
Distance From Earth: 0.01AU and closing!

There it is, our first view of our home planet in twenty-five years. A few of us gathered in the observation bubble once word got around that Earth was now a recognisable sphere rather than just a cluster of blue-green pixels.

It looks odd. No, that's not right. It looks exactly as it should look, exactly as it has always looked from this distance. It looks like it looked from the Moon in Apollo, like it looked from the *Liberty* during those first days. It looked exactly the same as it had always looked: it is my perception of it that has changed.

At one time I would have given everything I had to see that old ball again and to know that I was coasting towards it. All I ever wanted was to go home. And now, faced with the planet of my birth, I realise that I will never again call it home.

It has not changed, but I have. My parents are gone and I never had much of an extended family or even friends outside of my career. My family is here now.

Maria Cosatti is commander now and she has a shopping list as long as the tether. We can do a lot on board ship, but some things need manufacturing clout or technical expertise that we just don't have in our potted population of twenty-seven souls.

Although we don't have money, we're not short of things to barter with. We have a hold full of magnesium and titanium. Nothing too spectacular, no asteroid-sized diamonds or alien artefacts. But every tonne of mass we leave in orbit is a tonne less to be lifted out of Earth's gravity well. Factoring in that markup, we are all returning Earth as billionaires.

There is an ulterior motive too. Every plate and pressure vessel, every kilo of water ice we leave in orbit is an invitation. Like a cookie held out to a wary child, it says come on, we won't bite. Come and play.

The fact is that we've had a hell of a run of luck. We set out in a fragile tin can hurled like a *bolas* at the blackness but we are coming back in a glittering spaceship under our own power and with fuel to take us anywhere in the solar system.

But we're lonely. Our little community can't last forever. Parts wear out, people too.

Along with the refined metals, the premanufactured solar cells and tonnes of water and methane ice, we are also returning to Earth with a lifetime of experience. This you can have for free. Along with these excerpts from personal logs, all the technical specs of the *Liberty* along with all the other manuals, drawings, routines and algorithms that we've used to turn the old girl into the ship she really wanted to be will be transmitted to the net . . . Probably they seem a bit old-fashioned to you. Sure, we've had twenty-five years of hands-on experience in spacefaring, but our materials science and sensor and propulsion tech is now a quarter century out of date. I'm sure you can do better.

We'll be swinging by just long enough to drop off Tom and a few sightseers and arrange for the trade of those items we need. After that who knows? Perhaps a few months in a pole-to-pole orbit mapping Venus, or a trip to the Jovian system if we can work the bugs out of the magnetic shielding.

We'll be back in a few years. No one fancies another quarter century between refills of chocolate, steak, penicillin and morphine. But it will be as visitors, traders. We are not Earthlings, not anymore.

And space is too interesting to watch from the bottom of a planetary gravity well.

I thought I was coming home, but this is my home now as one day it could be yours.

That's about all I have to say. No doubt as well as my humble account, you'll want to read the logs of some of the other crew members. I understand that Claire's video diary has already gone viral. Some of you may even be interested in Craig's mystery trilogy that he insists on including in the upload. But don't spend too much time reading. It's a big system out here. Enough for thousands of ships, millions even.

Come on up . . . We'll be waiting for you.

Richard Johnson is an award-winning short story writer having won the Gold Award at Writers of the Future in 2011 and the Jim Baen Memorial Award in 2012. He lives in Melbourne, Australia, with his wife and two young sons where he works as a structural engineer.

THE LAMPLIGHTER LEGACY

by Patrick O'Sullivan

In 1969, Patrick's dad brought home a handful of golden coins. They weren't gold bullion, but something better. Hard-anodized aluminum "Moon Money" from the local savings and loan, guaranteed redeemable for a $1,500 insured account at any branch location . . . on the Moon. That's roughly $10,000 per coin in today's terms, a king's ransom for a blue-collar kid in 1969. Patrick wondered how the bankers could afford to be so generous. Because he firmly believed he'd be there one day, on the Moon, to open that account and that's the sort of feeling he wanted to put into this story. Of course that savings and loan company is long gone, but the moon is still there, the stars are still there, and Patrick still has one of those golden coins, in his pocket, bright and shiny as the day it was minted.

September 15, 2021
Earth

THE ASTRONAUT gripped Ernesto's wrist. "Look, kid, you want to put the phone down and look around?" He had to shout to be heard over the helicopter's deafening noise. "This is a once in a lifetime experience."

Ernesto adjusted the gain on his aviation headset. "Yes, sir." He reluctantly pocketed his cloudnode and leaned back in the plush leather seat. He peered out the helicopter's canopy at the broad, open ocean off the coast of Ecuador. They'd passed over the shrouded mass of the Galápagos an hour ago. Now the ocean looked the same as it had ten minutes earlier, and ten minutes before that; wet, and choppy, and indistinguishable from the ocean he could see any day at home in San Diego. It was a wild and memorable experience meeting an astronaut, but that was yesterday. When the astronaut had to shout over the thumping of helicopter rotors it reminded Ernesto not of Captain Weber, a real American hero, but of Ernesto's dad after half a bottle of Captain Morgan.

Shouting and astronauting did not go together. Ernesto would write a blog post on that topic later tonight. He would also mention that too much dollar-store aftershave and astronauting didn't go together either, at least not in the confined cabin of a trillionaire's ramjet helicopter. Ernesto was mortified at his mistake but man enough to admit the truth for once; that he was more enthusiastic than experienced when it came to both astronauting and shaving.

Cosmicgrrl wouldn't have made such an egregious error. She would have consulted an expert. She had once messaged to ernesto2003 that admitting ignorance was a virtue, not a weakness. That exposing oneself was the first step to understanding. Then she'd ruined everything by making a joke about his screen name. That was nearly four years ago and Ernesto's face still burned whenever he thought about her message.

Last month, when cosmicgrrl discovered that ernesto2003 had won the Lamplighter Prize for Best Amateur Space Blog, she'd been shocked, shocked, shocked. Ernesto was convinced he'd admitted to cosmicgrrl that *Blogespacial!* was his creation. Even if he hadn't boasted so baldly, it said "moderator" under his screen name in all his posts. What did she think, he was just some high-school slacker with nothing but time on his hands? That just because he wasn't a NASA engineer like her he had all day to pontificate on some else's blog?

The astronaut shouted. "Something bugging you, kid?"

Yeah, there was. Ernesto had blown all the money he'd saved waiting tables on a worldwide data plan. "No, sir," Ernesto said.

The problem with virtual keyboards was that you had to look at them to type. Ernesto could touch type sixty words a minute on an old-school keyboard, in the dark, with the covers pulled over his head. He couldn't input a word here without insulting the astronaut and Mr. James Lamplighter, whose generous award had funded *Blogespacial!* for as long as Ernesto cared to continue posting, and who had invited Ernesto to witness, in person, the launch of Lamplighter's latest satellite. The launch would take place from a floating platform positioned on the equator, somewhere up ahead. Ernesto clutched his cloudnode powerlessly and gazed out at the broad, empty ocean.

One wave looked just like another.

In pictures Lamplighter seemed bigger, more imposing. He was the richest man on Earth, and when the newsblogs ran posts with his photo they were inevitably shot from below, as if Lamplighter was a rocket set to blast off and the photographer a mere mortal like Ernesto, so much extra payload crowding the launching pad.

Ernesto's voice quivered when he said, "Pleased to meet you, sir," but he looked Lamplighter in the eye and managed to shake hands without sweating all over Lamplighter's manicured nails.

"Call me Jim," Lamplighter said. His voice was an average voice, his eyes average eyes, neither blue, nor green, nor brown. He was in his late fifties and dressed in a white guayabera shirt, jeans, and sandals. Ernesto might have waited on Lamplighter a thousand times at Casa Suarez without noticing him, if not for one thing. Lamplighter quivered with energy, like Hidalgo, Mr. Calderón's golden retriever, after Ernesto had thrown the ball but still had a grip on Hidalgo's collar.

The astronaut had passed Ernesto off to Lamplighter on the command vessel's helicopter landing deck. The helicopter had circled the launch vessel so that Ernesto could photograph from above and up close. It was a bit of a letdown. The platform was huge, a converted North Sea oil rig, but there was no launch vehicle in sight. Ernesto wanted to ask the astronaut what the deal was but he didn't fancy shouting at a real American hero over a helicopter's thumping racket. Instead he took shot after shot of what he could see, camera clicking in bracketing exposures, more shots of an empty launch deck than he felt necessary, but his activity seemed to please the astronaut, and Ernesto had no end of image storage on his cloudnode.

The command vessel was big but not huge, like a cruise ship, but

empty. Lamplighter said that there was the ship's crew of forty on
board, but the people involved in the launch numbered a total of only
eight, including Captain Weber, who was acting as a technical advisor.

Ernesto asked how many people were on the launch vessel and
Lamplighter told him there wasn't anyone on the launch vessel but
the ship's crew of twelve. Not yet. There'd been a change of plans.

Mr. Lamplighter asked if Ernesto would like to get the personal
interview over with. As part of the Lamplighter Prize, Ernesto had
won the right to an exclusive interview with the richest man on Earth.
Mr. Lamplighter said that things would get hectic later and now was
as good a time as any. Ernesto must have looked worried because Mr.
Lamplighter asked if Ernesto was feeling okay.

Ernesto pasted a confident grin on his face. "Never better, sir." It
was a good thing that Mr. Lamplighter was paying for *Blogespacial!*'s
bandwidth fees going forward, because an interview with Mr.
Lamplighter was like gold, and traffic to Ernesto's site would explode.
It wouldn't just be regulars like cosmicgrrl, and lucky_yellow_dragon,
and cornelius_simeon, and vikenti_123 who would argue back and
forth on *Blogespacial!* Lots of people were interested in Mr.
Lamplighter for all sorts of reasons, most of them having nothing to
do with his space projects.

"Tell you what," Lamplighter said. "Why don't you get your kit
settled, and get freshened up, and meet me on the fantail?"

"I don't know what a fantail is," Ernesto said. "Let alone where it
is."

Lamplighter grinned. "You're the real deal, aren't you,
ernesto2003?"

Ernesto started to look at his feet before he forced himself to meet
Mr. Lamplighter's gaze. "Sir?"

"Many young men would have said, 'Sure,' and then wandered
around for half an hour in ignorance, wasting their time. And mine."

"Maybe they'd already know what a fantail was, and where it was."
Cosmicgrrl certainly would. Her family had a boat. A yacht. Until
today the closest Ernesto had ever gotten to a boat was on Sundays,
when he helped his mom load the minivan with fresh dorado from
the fish market.

"Tell you what." Lamplighter subtly tapped the cloudnode
implanted behind his right ear, an Hermés Executive II, certifiably

uncrackable, nearly invisible, and more costly than the helicopter Ernesto had arrived in. "I'll squirt you my id addy. Ring me when you're ready."

Ernesto stared at the cloudnode in his hands. On its display was the address of the richest man on Earth. The temporal cloud address of the richest man on Earth. This was unreal. He flicked to his friendnet glyph. There was a message waiting, one from cosmicgrrl.

Well? What's it like?

Ernesto typed madly. *Exciting. I've met him, and he's calm, just like you. There's been a delay in the launch, but he doesn't seem perturbed. Very collected, like sending a payload into orbit is an everyday occurrence. Like it's normal.* Ernesto pressed the send glyph and waited.

He didn't have to wait long. *Wouldn't that be fantastic? If it was?*

Ernesto stared at the display projection and contemplated the implications. *I'm not so sure. Maybe then no one would view my blog. Not if space missions were normal.*

The satellite time lag was minimal. *I would.*

No, she wouldn't. Not if she realized just how close she'd cut when she'd joked about his screen name. He'd never replied to her message. *2003? Is that your birth year or something?*

Like cosmicgrrl would even look at him twice. Ernesto Suarez, heir to the great Suarez restaurant fortune. Ernesto went into the tiny ship's bathroom and splashed water on his face. He stared at the boy in the mirror. He was about as far from a great American hero as they came.

His fingers worked the keyboard projection. *Got to go. Can't keep the big man waiting.* He hammered the send glyph and went to search his suitcase for a shirt that didn't reek of astro-shave.

It turned out that the fantail was the rear of the command vessel. The stern.

Mr. Lamplighter leaned against the rail. He looked like a king, or a god. "I imagine you have some prepared questions."

The command vessel was underway. An apparent wind blew from behind Ernesto, battling the cross breeze that had begun to whip up whitecaps on the dark waves of the Pacific. The deck vibrated and water churned, pale and foam-flecked, salty spray thrown up by massive, unseen propellers far below. Ernesto's hands shook. This was so bizarre. He, Ernesto Suarez, was on the deck of a wet-launch command vessel, chatting with the richest man on Earth. Chatting like they were buddies.

Ernesto's voice quivered but didn't crack. "A couple, sir."

"Here's the agreement. For every question you ask I get to ask one. If you ask a boneheaded question I get to ask a boneheaded question. Anything I say gets reported word for word. Anything you say gets reported word for word."

Ernesto shifted his feet. He'd interviewed a number of NASA, CNSA, and ROSCOSMOS experts for his blog. "Verbatim transcriptions can be boring, sir. People tend to wander, and . . . um . . . do that a lot."

"I don't. And you won't. Those are my requirements. Take them or leave them."

"I'll take them, sir."

"Then shoot, ernesto2003."

"Yes, sir." Ernesto flicked the recording app on his cloudnode alive. He'd scoured the cloud for every interview of James Lamplighter in existence. He'd never interviewed anyone but scientists and engineers and they couldn't stop talking once Ernesto got them started on the subjects his friends cared about. With Lamplighter he didn't know where to begin. Lamplighter was a money man, not a scientist, and notoriously secretive. Plus, it wouldn't just be *Blogespacial!* regulars reading this interview. Millions of people would read Ernesto's words simply because the subject was James Lamplighter.

Ernesto decided to begin where every other interviewer began. "What's it feel like to be the richest man on Earth?"

"It feels like dirt. And that's a boneheaded question. I was born the tenth richest man on Earth. When I die I'll still be the richest man on Earth. And that will feel like dirt squared." Lamplighter glared at Ernesto. "My turn. What's it feel like to be born a nothing?"

Ernesto felt his face burn. "What?"

"You heard me."

"I'm not a nothing."

"Then prove it. Next question."

"You want me to post . . . that? Without editing?"

"I don't want it. I demand it. Now next question, son."

"I'm not your son."

"That's not a question."

Ernesto was so angry he couldn't see straight. He knew he was that angry because the idea that he couldn't see straight was a cliché, and Ernesto hated clichés with a passion. "You're the richest man on Earth. You can have anything you want."

"And you were born a nothing. And you can't. That's still not a question. Is this all you've brought, ernesto2003? Because I have a score of questions, and you're going to answer every single one of them."

Ernesto rubbed his forehead. His guts churned. "Why are you doing this?"

"Now that's a question, and it's not a boneheaded one. Do you want to film this?"

"Why?"

"Because no one's ever asked me that question. It's good copy."

"No, I don't want to *film* this."

"Fair enough," Lamplighter said. "I imagine, in your mind, 'Why are you doing this' pertains to why I am beating up on a seventeen-year-old kid, whose parents aren't even legal residents, and who would be entering college next year if he could scrape together the coin, but instead is wasting his talents waiting tables at the family restaurant, which will one day be his, and which he will hate with all the passion in the world because it isn't what he wants. He will hate it, not because he couldn't imagine better for himself, but because he can.

"Now, in my mind, your question, 'Why are you doing this,' pertains, not merely to this conversation and your precious feelings, but to everything I've brought you here to witness, and everything I've done in my life up to this moment. Do you, perhaps, see a difference in these two questions, and in the nature of our perspectives?"

Ernesto's face burned. He glanced down at the recorder in his hand. He could switch it off and go home. He didn't have to do this. He didn't like it when his dad got angry, and he didn't like it when he got angry. Anger made him stupid, and maybe he wasn't much, but he wasn't stupid. Ernesto took a deep breath and looked Lamplighter in the eye. "I see it."

"Well, I don't. They are faces of the same coin. So I will give you the same answer to both questions. I'm 'doing this' because I want to. And because I can."

"What? That's your excuse?"

"You don't get a follow-up. And for the record, that was an explanation, not an excuse."

"That's . . . cold."

"My deck, my rules. Now I get a question."

Ernesto tore his gaze away from Lamplighter. He glanced out to sea, where the wind had begun to whip the white-capped waves higher. Ernesto could feel his nostrils flare as he sucked in great gulps of salt air. Lamplighter would probably ask if Ernesto had any socks without holes in them, or what it feels like when your parents can't make a mortgage payment. "Go ahead."

Lamplighter leaned against the rail, stretching his legs. His gaze never left Ernesto's face. "What, ernesto2003, do you want more than anything in the world?"

"What?"

"You heard me."

Ernesto couldn't speak the truth. Not in a thousand years could he speak the truth. Not without messaging cosmicgrrl first. In private. "I haven't given that as much thought as it deserves."

"Give it some." Lamplighter lounged against the fantail railing. He crossed his tanned ankles and pursed his lips, examining Ernesto like some unidentifiable, alien stain discovered lurking on his freshly pressed tablecloth. "While we wait, maybe you'd like to ask the obvious follow-up question."

Maybe, right after Ernesto finished stuffing his fist up Lamplighter's posh aristocratic nose. Some things never changed, no matter how much you wanted them to. Ernesto took three deep breaths and counted to ten. "Umm . . . What do you want more than anything in the world?"

Lamplighter grinned like an imbecile. "I thought you'd never ask. I *have* given this as much thought as it deserves. I've thought about it every night since I learned to read, and since I learned to think for myself. I wish to be the richest man—"

"But you already are!"

"Hear me out, son."

"I'm not your son."

"You think not?"

"I wouldn't want to be."

"I don't blame you for feeling that way. It changes nothing. Now stow it, and let me say what I want to say. For the record."

Ernesto jammed his cloudnode in front of Lamplighter's face so the microphone wouldn't miss the man's gloating words, and so that later he could transcribe every arrogant, elitist inflection of Lamplighter's boarding-school voice. "Go on."

"You'll laugh, ernesto2003."

"I promise you, Mr. Lamplighter, I find none of this amusing."

"I wish to be the richest man on Mars."

Ernesto snorted. "What?"

"You heard me. And you laughed."

"That's impossible."

"I heard you laugh, son."

"No, the other thing. Being the richest man on Mars. That's impossible."

"That doesn't stop me from wanting it."

"But you can't have that." Even the richest man on Earth couldn't have that. No one could.

Lamplighter's gaze locked with Ernesto's, and it was like when Ernesto was eight, and crouching in the basement of his Aunt Vera's house the day before Christmas, peering into the firebox of the furnace, trying to figure out why the house didn't burn down, and Ernesto felt for an instant that the fire saw him watching, and all it was waiting for was for Ernesto to turn his back and run.

"Are you a writer, ernesto2003?"

"Trying to be."

"Then surely someone, sometime, has told you how writing is like eating an elephant. That there's only one way to do it."

"One bite at a time."

"Exactly."

"So?"

"One small bite for a man is still too much for mankind to swallow. At least too much for mankind's politicians and their hidebound masters."

Lamplighter's gaze shifted from Ernesto to the sky, tracking something that probably wasn't invisible to Lamplighter's augmented eyesight but was far too small for Ernesto's naked eye to see, watching it soaring, up, up, and away.

"Too much until now."

The viewfinder of Ernesto's cloudnode had grown very steady. Very still. He realized he'd been holding his breath. Shouting and astronauting didn't go together. He needed to be cool as mission control. Cool as cosmicgrrl. Ernesto took a deep breath and let it out slowly.

"How do you intend to get to Mars?"

"I'm following your plan, ernesto2003. With slight modifications to the budget."

"What?"

"You'd do me a great favor if you'd stop shouting after every question I ask."

"That was a statement. That I shouted after."

"So it was. Let's try this again. Are you sure you don't want to film this?"

Ernesto felt his face twist into an imbecilic grin. "That's a boneheaded question."

"Then get your gear. And meet me in the assembly bay."

"I will, sir. Umm . . ."

"Ring me when you're ready."

"I will, sir." Right after he messaged cosmicgrrl.

Safe in his stateroom, Ernesto tried to keep from hyperventilating. *You are not going to believe this.* Ernesto messaged cosmicgrrl everything he'd learned; that Lamplighter intended to go to Mars using a plan cosmicgrrl and Ernesto's other friends had worked out on *Blogespacial!*

Cosmicgrrl's reply was nearly instantaneous. *I am shocked, shocked, shocked. Tell me more.*

Later. When I know more. First, Ernesto had to do something he'd been putting off. There were a pair of elephants stomping around on his guts now, and if he wanted a good night's sleep ever again he couldn't ignore either one. His pulse raced as he typed rapidly, pressing the send glyph before he ran out of courage. *Do you ever get out to San Diego?*

It cost a small fortune, but Ernesto's international data plan was worth every penny. Cosmicgrrl's reply rocketed back instantly. *All the time. Why do you ask?*

Ernesto's palms wept sweat. His cloudnode squirted from his fingers. He scooped it up off the pristine bedspread and took the coward's way out. *Tell you later. Gotta go.*

The camera rattled in Ernesto's hands. It had image stabilization, but that wasn't enough. Stretched the length of the command ship's assembly bay was the great bulk of a multistage lift vehicle. Three engineers were stripping the payload. Captain Weber and a lady engineer were working on another payload package in a distant corner of the shipboard high bay. Sodium light bathed every inch in uncompromising detail. It took Ernesto a minute to adjust the white balance of his camera before he was satisfied with the results. Ernesto panned the camera the length of the bay. He wished it could capture everything, not just the way shadows fell across titanium and steel, but the scents, of machine oil, of ozone and hot metal, of salt air, and copper, and the sweat of honest work, scents so thick he could taste them; sights, and sounds, and smells that if distilled and condensed could fuel his imagination for a thousand years.

Lamplighter shifted so that he was in the frame. "Recognize that bird, ernesto2003?"

"Yes, sir." It was one of the old Zenits.

"Care to read off the specs for your online amigos?"

"I'll add them in a voice-over, sir. If I get any of the details wrong my friends will ream me a new . . . I mean, I'll lose a significant amount of credibility, sir."

"Recognize the payload they're removing?"

"I think it's one of your communications satellites, sir."

"Right. What about the new payload Captain Marine Band and his shapely sidekick are working on?"

"I can't tell from here, sir."

"Let's take a walk."

"I'll have to stop recording." Ernesto couldn't afford to trip and break his camera.

"Do what you need to, son. Lamplighter's first and only rule."

"Yes, sir." Ernesto clicked the camera off and stepped over a thick black power cable, following along in Lamplighter's wake.

Lamplighter paused as they passed the three engineers wrenching on the payload at warp speed. "Would you like to take a break, gentlemen?"

"Thought you'd never ask," a compact man said. He wiped a red bandana across his face. He eyed Ernesto up and down. "This the new guy, chief?"

"That remains to be seen."

The man stuck out his hand. "Well, either way, glad to meet you. I'm—"

"No names." Lamplighter glanced at Ernesto and for the first time he looked uncomfortable. "They're on loan from NASA. An off-the-books deal."

"Temporary Duty Assignment," the first engineer said. "About as temporary as it gets, if this bird doesn't fly. Either way, we're all qualified for early out if we want it."

"Volunteers," the second engineer said. He'd wandered over, sipping a Diet Coke. "True believers, ernesto2003. Maybe these old coots are ready for retirement but I'm not."

"I shouldn't be recording any of this," Ernesto said. "If you'll get in trouble I—"

"Screw it," the third engineer said.

"Easy for you to say, beatlestix69." The second engineer sipped his diet cola.

"Listen, wiseacre, stony1632 said my screen name needed numbers in it."

"Did he now?" The engineer glanced at his coworker and chuckled.

"I might have, duckman."

"It's mandrake, compadre." He wiped his hands on a shop towel and looked Ernesto up and down. He turned to Lamplighter and grinned. "*Ab ove maiori discit arare minor.*"

"We'll see," Lamplighter said.

"Hey, wait a minute." Ernesto looked from face to face. "Are you guys saying you're posters on *Blogespacial!*?"

"That's why we're here," the third engineer said. "Even then, it took some conniving. Uncle Sugar is unusually tight-fisted now that he's broke."

The first engineer grinned at Ernesto. "We're all grownups. We know what we signed up for. Even if the *Federales* don't. Officially."

"Like I said. You do what you need to, son. It's better to ask for forgiveness than permission."

"Try telling that to my dad."

"When I meet him, I will." Lamplighter smiled at Ernesto, a devil's smile, all teeth. "It takes three days to transfer this bird to the launch vessel and fuel her with LOX and RP-1. Until then no one's going anywhere. No one, including you."

Ernesto tried to keep the look of terror off his face. His dad would murder him. There was a wedding reception scheduled for Saturday night and Ernesto had promised to work the private room. "I need to make a call."

"First you need to see the new payload. The one you and your transnational, net-dwelling coconspirators designed."

"I didn't do anything." Ernesto said. "I just made a place where people could share ideas."

"You're right, kid, that's nothing."

"I think he's a little too overwhelmed for irony right now, stony."

"Is that so, kid? Are you a little overwhelmed?"

"No, sir." Ernesto was a lot overwhelmed.

Lamplighter gripped Ernesto's elbow and hauled him away. The engineers went back to their feverish wrenching.

"You've met Captain Weber," Lamplighter said. "Or should I say hohnerman?"

"That was a typo," the astronaut said. "There's no way to edit your screen name."

"It's off-the-shelf software," Ernesto said. He'd tried to edit his own screen name a thousand times.

"That's what the chief's little princess claimed."

Ernesto wasn't listening. He was trying to check out the NASA lady without her noticing. Maybe she was cosmicgrrl. Maybe that's why cosmicgrrl's replies were coming back so quickly. She was on board the command vessel.

"And this is—"

The astronaut grinned. "She goes by butterbug_babe. Online."

Ernesto stared at the engineer. "Oh. I mean, wow. Really?"

She smiled at Ernesto. "Really."

"Your posts are brilliant. And your Spanish is outstanding."

"I paid attention in class."

"Yes, ma'am." Ernesto spent most of his time online cleaning up typos and grammatical errors. Half the people posting on *Blogespacial!* lately weren't native speakers. He'd tried writing a program to clean up the common English-to-Spanish translation errors but it hadn't worked out. He'd had to read and edit every post manually. Ernesto couldn't keep his eyes off butterbug_babe, who looked like he'd imagined cosmicgrrl would. Brainy, and competent, and calm under pressure. Everything Ernesto wasn't.

"You know what the greatest benefactor to space exploration is, Ernesto?" The astronaut grinned.

"War." That's what cosmicgrrl said. Ernesto had tried to argue with her but it was like a stone trying to argue with the wind.

Butterbug_babe crossed her arms and frowned. "Reasonable people might disagree."

Ernesto glanced from face to face.

"War," Captain Weber said. "The mother of invention. Take a look at this bad boy."

Ernesto followed the astronaut to a workbench where a mottled brown-and-tan box hunched atop a vacuum clamp. "Recognize it?"

"It looks like a Miller-Lee 3D printer. A Mark Four. With some sort of adjunct processor and one big-a . . . I mean, some sort of large external power supply, sir."

"Like a remotely controlled Millie Tri-Delta. A Mike Five Roger. EMP hardened. Sealed and jacketed for desert use. Hydrogen fueled. We started using these puppies in the second Syrian War and—"

"Police action," butterbug_babe said. "Technically."

"Call it what you like," Captain Weber said. "It smelled like war to me. Anyway, it's heavy duty, and this one's special. One of a kind."

Ernesto's stomach felt like it was filled with broken glass. "The first of its kind."

"Right. It's self-replicating."

This was all beginning to make sense. Lamplighter wasn't going to Mars. He had other plans. Plans that were all Ernesto's fault.

Lamplighter leaned over Ernesto's shoulder. "You don't look so good, son."

Ernesto didn't feel so good. The timing all made sense now. It was September 15th, 2021. In two weeks Ernesto would turn eighteen.

He'd be called up for the draft. By December he could be frying in a sunbaked, 3D-printed sand hut, waiting to die. If he was still breathing he could search the desert sky and witness nothing. The asteroid 4660 Nereus would pass within 3.9 million kilometers of Earth. Close, but too distant to perceive with the naked eye.

"On *Blogespacial!* I was just . . . thinking out loud."

Ernesto had trained with milspec 3D printers in citizenship class, trained with them so often that he dreamed about them, and about what they could do. Not just what they were born to do, but what they could do, if they were free to choose. When his number came up and Ernesto went to war he'd vowed to do it on the front lines, sweating over a Seabee's shovel if he had to. He wasn't made to lounge in a safe, air-conditioned room, twitching a joystick from ten thousand miles away. That didn't make him a fool, regardless of what anyone said.

"I was just trying to get a discussion started."

Lamplighter rested his palm on Ernesto's shoulder. "Well, you did that, son."

Ernesto swept his gaze the length of the assembly bay.

"You still want to make that call?"

"I have to, sir." His dad was counting on him for Saturday. He deserved to know that Ernesto was going to disappoint him. Again.

Ernesto flicked his cloudnode off. That hadn't gone well. The less he thought about the shouting the better. He rubbed his thumb across the cloudnode's controls. He flicked it alive and typed out a message.

Maybe next time you're in San Diego you'd like to have lunch. I know this great Mexican joint. They'll treat you like family.

Ernesto stared at the blinking cursor, heart pounding, index finger hovering over the send glyph. He stared at the virtual display for the longest time before he switched off and pocketed his cloudnode. Who was he kidding? He couldn't make any promises. Especially not that one. Not after talking to his dad. Not anymore.

Lamplighter leaned against the fantail rail. The ocean churned white behind him.

Ernesto zoomed in on Lamplighter's face.

Lamplighter frowned. "Power that down. We need to talk. Off the record."

"But you said—"

"Turn it off."

"Yes, sir."

"What's eating you?"

"Sir?"

"You heard me."

"It's nothing."

"Earlier, I asked you a question. You danced around it." Lamplighter pinned Ernesto to the deck with his gaze.

Ernesto shuffled his feet. "I wouldn't say that, sir. I said that I hadn't given the topic enough thought."

"Have you now?"

"Umm . . . Too much, probably."

"Well, let me make this easier for you. In three days, maybe five if the seas don't lay, we're going to launch a mission to 4660 Nereus. On it will be a payload a bunch of space-crazy kids designed. Kids on *Space Blog*."

"*Blogespacial!*, sir."

"Whatever. You kids dreamed it up."

"We had help."

"Nevertheless, it's your project. Your mission."

"With some modifications to the budget, sir."

"Of course." Lamplighter leaned forward. "By December that payload will begin to dig in, and it will begin to replicate itself. Every two years—"

"One point eight two years, sir."

"Okay. Anyway, that asteroid will pass close enough to Earth that we can reprogram the payload, and the factory it's built, reprogram it on every pass, adjusting as we need to, so that in forty years—"

"Thirty-nine, sir."

"Will you stop interrupting?"

"Yes, sir."

"In thirty-nine years, when 4660 Nereus passes within . . ." Lamplighter glared at Ernesto.

"One point two million kilometers."

"Right. The nearest approach in six hundred years, and we'll have everything we need. Everything, ernesto2003, that we need to get to Mars, will be there waiting, a handsbreadth away, cosmically speaking. Everything needed to get to Mars in style, and free for the taking." Lamplighter smiled. "Free, to whoever can lay off their boneheaded squabbling and get there first."

"Yes, sir." Ernesto glanced at his shoes. "But you'll be . . . umm."

"Dead, son. But you won't. Ernesto. 2003."

"I hope not, sir. I'd like to see what happens."

"I expect you will do more than see it, son. And I'd like to ask a favor."

"Anything, sir."

"Take me with you. Take me with you, if only in your fevered imagination and your mad, improbable dreams."

Ernesto gazed far, far out to sea. He looked anywhere, everywhere, anywhere but at Lamplighter's shadowed face. "Yes, sir."

"Now I'll ask you one more time, and I expect a straight answer. What, ernesto2003, do you want more than anything in the world?"

"Hang on." Ernesto fished in his pocket for his cloudnode. He closed his eyes and pressed the send glyph. It wasn't ten seconds before the device twitched in his fingers. It took twice as long for Ernesto to screw up the courage to look. He stared at cosmicgrrl's reply.

It's a date. I absolutely love, love, love Mexican.

"Well, son?"

Ernesto's heart felt as if it might leap out onto the deck and race away on a trail of burning fire. When Ernesto glanced up he found Lamplighter watching, the sun pressing low against the western sky, close enough to touch, the broad waters of the Pacific churning behind Lamplighter, a long trail of foam, sun-kissed and endless in his wake.

"I, Ernesto Suarez, wish to be the richest man on Mars."

"Truly?"

"Or the poorest. It doesn't really matter."

Lamplighter turned and gazed toward some unseen, farthest shore. The last rays of the sun lit the parting clouds as the stars began to rise.

"It wouldn't to me either, son."

Ernesto pressed his eyes closed, not fighting the tears, but letting this singular moment, this calm, pregnant moment unfold gently around him, like wind embracing stone.

"I know. Sir."

September 15, 2081
Mars

Diego Suarez clasped the cinerary urn to his chest. It was ugly, and crude, and until this morning, the most precious thing in all the world.

"That's an impressive show-and-tell," Mrs. Singh, his fourth grade teacher, said.

"That's the tell. This is the show." Diego held the urn out at arm's length.

"It's a nice urn, Diego."

"My granddad printed it, on 4660 Nereus. Right before he died. Died saving people he'd never even met. Grandma Suarez says they were people he didn't even like. That's the story."

"You must be very proud."

"I'm supposed to be. But I'm not. Look." Diego upturned the urn on the teacher's desk. A thin dusting of ash trickled out, not enough for one man let alone for two. "It's all a lie. Everything everyone ever told me was a lie." He had to stare at the bulletin board because if he didn't he'd choke on the nasty lump swelling in his chest, swelling exactly where a Lamplighter's heart was supposed to be. And wasn't.

Mrs. Singh held out her hand. "May I see that?"

Diego handed her the urn. Mrs. Singh took it, cupping it in her hands like it was a fresh oxygen charge and she was just back from a long walk. She closed her eyes, and ran her fingers up and down the ugly, lying pot, touching, feeling, searching its surface for something Diego couldn't see. A single tear ran down her cheek.

She spoke without opening her eyes. "Tomorrow we'll take a field trip. To hydroponics. Tonight, I'd like you all to look up calcium phosphate, and be ready to discuss. Class dismissed." She ran her fingers over the urn one last time before she opened her eyes and handed it back to Diego. "You won't believe me, Diego, but this was the best show-and-tell. Ever."

Diego's grandmother scowled when he handed her Grandpa's and Mr. Lamplighter's urn. Not that he believed that anymore. It was just a nasty fabber pot, the sort Diego could crank out in half an hour on a bad day. It was a lie. He never should have taken it without asking permission but he'd forgotten about show-and-tell until the last minute and he was desperate to show up Chandra Patel for once.

"She really said that?" His grandmother watched Diego's face like she'd never noticed it before. "Padma Singh said that?"

"Yeah."

"And she cried?"

"Not crying, really. Just a tear. It wasn't a big deal."

His grandmother glanced out the viewport. Diego couldn't see what she was looking at. Everything looked red, and sharp, and normal.

"Well." His grandmother shifted in her chair. "I don't mind telling you, Diego." His grandma cradled the urn like a baby. She closed her eyes and Diego began to worry that she'd fallen asleep, or worse.

"Grandma?"

His grandmother cracked one eye open, then the other, pinning Diego to the carpet with what his dad called "that damned Lamplighter look."

Diego shifted from foot to foot. "Don't mind telling me what?"

"That I am shocked, shocked, shocked." Grandma Suarez held out the urn for Diego. "Now go put this back where it belongs."

Patrick O'Sullivan is a writer and engineer living and working in the United States and Ireland. O'Sullivan's stories have won additional awards (1st Place, Writers of the Future), appear in several short story anthologies, and can be found in print and electronic form most places books are sold. For more information see O'Sullivan's web site, patrickosullivan.com.

LOW ARC

by Sean Monaghan

"Low Arc" had its seed in an article from the winter 2013 issue of Ad Astra, *which is the magazine published by the National Space Society. The article, titled "Choosing for Science: The Farside of the Moon," by Marianne J. Dyson is about the Schrödinger Basin on the moon's farside and made Sean wonder about the resources that were there and how we might exploit them. This winning story was born when Sean became ever more intrigued about what kind of infrastructure might be needed to enable human occupation of the farside without the benefit of line-of-sight communications with Earth.*

WHEN COLIN BERTELLI heard Johnston's scream over the comms he dropped the pyroprobe and headed back up the small gray scarp.

"Randy?" Bertelli said. "Status?"

Silence.

Schröedinger was vast. Now he was going to be in trouble for straying too far. He was a hundred and eighty meters from the ridge.

Four minutes walk.

"Randy? Come in."

Bertelli far preferred the science secondment over his old job. But the suits were flimsier. You couldn't afford to fall down. Not at a full run.

He'd lived at the moon's south pole for three years. Ice mining.
That was where he'd picked up bad habits.

Running his suit empty. Pushing tools beyond their rating. Running across the mare or up crater walls.

Valerie was glad he wasn't doing that anymore.

He called for Johnston again.

Still no response.

Johnston wasn't where he was supposed to be. Bertelli should be able to see him from here.

"Orion?" he said. Suze Baldwin, up in the module, should have been monitoring all their comms. "Come in Suze."

Ahead Bertelli saw a smooth area. He jumped across. Another bad habit.

Clearing fifteen meters he stumbled when he landed. He kept his legs going.

"Copy you," Suze said.

"Randy's gone silent."

"I heard him yell. I was pushing cycles on the scrubber."

The Orion capsule had been running on a gammy CO_2 system since they'd broken Earth orbit. That was the trouble with old technology.

NASA really needed to retire the Orion and figure out the next thing.

"Can you spot him?"

"I'm just over the rim. I'll run the scopes."

"Just pull the video."

"His feed's offline."

Bertelli kept running. The capsule was in a high elliptical orbit. It ran out long and slow over Schröedinger so they had maximum contact time.

When she whipped around the other side—facing Earth—she was so low she practically stirred up dust. If there'd been an atmosphere.

Suze joked that on pericynthion she had to aim between the mountains.

"Where are you?" she said.

"I'm getting there." His knee twinged. He'd rubbed in liniment before they'd come out. Randy had complained about the stink. *Surety* was a pretty confined space.

Suze swore. "Are you offtable again?"

"I saw some likely rocks."

"And this is the kind of thing that happens when you do that."

"It would have happened no matter where I was."

Randy was on a different grid. They wouldn't have been near each other even if Bertelli had stayed on the grid.

Still, Randy Johnston did some stuff on his own. Liked to think he was the one in charge. The one who knew everything.

On the flight up, Bertelli had woken to find Randy running fuel system checks. Bertelli's responsibility. Another time Randy had checked and corrected Suze's flight vectors. Without asking.

No, Bertelli didn't feel bad for stretching out what he got up to.

"I am never flying with you again," Suze said.

Bertelli came up over the ridge. He saw the landing site and realized no one was ever flying with him again.

The *Surety* pointed at the wrong part of the sky.

One of her three legs had failed. She was leaning at a twenty-degree angle. Maybe twenty-five.

Very bad.

Bertelli started down the slope. He called Suze again. Gave her the news.

"The leg failed?"

"Are you getting my video?"

"Gimme a second."

As he drew in he could see the leg hadn't failed completely.

The grid work had collapsed in on itself. Part of the lower section had jammed into the upper frame.

It looked like it was barely holding.

"That's bad," Suze said.

Understatement, Bertelli thought.

The *Surety* was stuck.

Her maximum takeoff angle was a shade over nine degrees. Not much wiggle room.

And as he closed the distance he could see that it was even greater than twenty-five.

Running in he passed the broken rover. The new one. A real example of why not to go with the lowest bidder.

On the first day they'd driven it a half mile before one of the wheels had frozen. Bertelli had tried going back and forth to dislodge it. He succeeded only in digging a shallow trench.

"Reminds me of that Mars rover," Johnston had said. "*Spirit*. That little guy still did a lot of good science."

"Well, we're not doing any good science with this piece of—"

"Sure we can. Let me debug the system."

"Great. You debug." Bertelli had clambered out. "I'm hitting it with a hammer."

Johnston hadn't replied.

The hammer hadn't worked. Neither had the debugging. Now the rover was just another piece of abandoned hardware stuck on the lunar surface.

A three hundred million dollar piece of junk.

"Gotta call Houston," Suze said.

"Make it quick," he said. "Then start running scenarios."

"What do you mean 'scenarios'?"

"I mean figuring out how to get us out of here."

He knew it was out of reach.

The moon was developing fast. There were plenty of people working up here now. But they were all an awful long way off.

With a surface area more than four times that of the continental United States there was a lot of ground to cover.

There were probably two hundred people up here. Half of them were on the near side—facing Earth. And most of the rest were at the poles.

Commercial mining.

Exactly what he'd been doing.

That was supposed to be the high-risk stuff. Eighteen lunar fatalities in thirty years of continuous occupation.

Seventeen of those in the mines.

The other had been an ESA suicide. Afterwards they'd all looked at her psych profile and scratched their heads.

The moon was unpredictable.

Bertelli had pulled two of the miners out himself. A burst hydraulic line had flicked a stay cable like a whip.

One man had been almost cut in half. The other had gotten just a cracked helmet.

And a crack was all it took up here.

That was when he'd given mining away. But he couldn't give up the moon.

More than once there had been talk of linking up all the various commercial and government installations in a kind of mutual rescue web. Nothing ever came of it.

It always came back to money. The mines had plenty, but siphoned it all back to Earth. The science installations had none.

"Colin? Are you still there?"

"Yes. I mean figure out who's closest to us. Has anyone got a working rover? Or maybe a lander? See if there's anyone about to land and can divert to our location."

"That's going to take a while."

"Then get to it."

"Copy that."

The *Surety* was less than fifty meters away. With every step he took the damage seemed worse. The lower tips of the landing nacelles had touched the dusty regolith. Cables connecting the ship to solar gatherers had ripped out.

He still couldn't raise Johnston.

"Suze? Any luck?"

"Houston's sending us alternates."

Protocols, he thought. "Nothing from your end."

"I'm waking people up. Working through the list. Sirius haven't got anything ready to fly."

"Too far away anyway."

"Likewise ModCon and ESA. The Virgin Hotel's got gear, but they're plum in the middle of nearside."

"What about something in orbit?" Bertelli stopped and looked over the *Surety*'s exterior.

Parts of the outer skin had buckled. Right around the leg frame. It was just the landing base—the part that got abandoned—but it was still concerning.

Surety was basically just an overscaled Apollo LEM. A crew module and a disposable rocket base with legs, just twice the size.

The base became the upper module's launch platform for departure.

Assuming the base stayed level.

He walked around and couldn't see any sign of why this had happened. Except for the leg, everything seemed nominal.

The suit air was getting hot. He could hear the dim whine of the regulators trying to keep up with his exertion.

Completely different to a mining suit. With some of those you had to keep moving or freeze to death. The moon was cold, but mining ice at the poles made Antarctica seem balmy.

"Sorry, Colin," Suze said. "There are five vessels in orbit. None of them has landing capacity."

"Okay. I'm going to have to climb on board and see what's up with Randy."

The most recent footsteps led right to the access ladder. Randy had gone back?

The internal comms might have broken down when the ship went over. Maybe he'd just stumbled and busted his radio.

There were redundancies though.

Bertelli didn't like to think of any reasons why Randy didn't use the alternatives.

"Are you sure you want to do that?" Suze said.

"Got to find him."

"What if it tips right over? With you on it."

"Risk I've got to take." He started doing the sums in his head. If they had to leave, there was spare oxygen on board. They could refill their tanks.

Once.

The supply was built into the *Surety*. If he could bring that with him he could just about walk to a rendezvous point.

On a single tank his range was no more than fifteen kilometers. Maybe twenty.

Assuming he wouldn't be walking back.

The capsule itself was very low volume. Cramped. Like the Orion, it didn't have an airlock.

They'd taken two excursions so far. It was rated for fifteen swap-outs. But if they stayed in there they had a couple of weeks of breathable air. Without counting the scrubbers.

It would be stinking inside by then.

Still, technically they could wait it out.

Bertelli put his hand on the ladder.

He didn't want to spend two weeks inside. Not with it at that angle. Suze was right; it could tip over at any time.

He put some weight on the ladder. It seemed firm.

They needed another solution.

He started climbing.

The ladder shook under his foot.

"Are you on?" Suze said.

"Two rungs up. Seems stable now."

He kept moving up. The normally level rungs angled down at the right and his boots slipped against the upright. He could feel the crushing.

"How's your oh-two?" Suze said.

"You tell me. I'm concentrating here."

"Your telemetry says seven point five liters. Nominal."

"Twenty minutes then."

"You shouldn't go out so far."

Bertelli sighed. He was almost at the top. "Tell you what. Why don't you give me the dressing down when I'm safely back on Orion?"

Silence for a moment, then, "Copy that."

At the top of the ladder he nestled his feet into the exit step. There was nothing there to brace the side of his foot against. He gripped the vertical rungs beside the hatch.

There was a dinner-plate-sized viewport in the hatch. Bertelli peered in.

And jerked back.

His feet slipped.

As he scrabbled for balance one of his hands came loose.

He got it on the other rung. With some pulling he managed to get himself on again.

"All right?" Suze said. "Heard you yelp."

"Got a fright. That's all." He wasn't going to tell her just yet.

Peering in the window again, he saw Randy.

He lay against the sample return locker. In the narrow space only his head and torso were visible. He was in his suit, but his helmet was off.

He wasn't moving.

Unconscious. Or worse.

Bertelli swore.

"Language," Suze said.

"Problem down here."

"I know that."

"What's your telemetry on Randy? Has he still got his medical sensors on?" A holdover from old NASA. Voluntary now, but Randy was a stickler for it. Liked to contribute every bit of science he could.

"Everything's nominal," Suze said. "Heart rate, breathing. BP's a bit low. Like he's sleeping."

Unconscious then.

Bertelli tapped on the window. With his glove on it would be as loud as a butterfly kiss.

Taking the rock hammer from his waist he knocked it on the hatch.

Silent to him, but it should ring through the capsule like a gong.

Randy didn't stir.

Trying a couple of times more, Bertelli figured what had happened.

Randy had been standing at the download console when the leg failed. He'd stumbled back, maybe hit his head.

But why did he have his helmet off?

Why was he even inside?

Where he was supposed to be was halfway between Bertelli's waypoint and *Surety*.

Protocols.

"He's down," Bertelli said. "Like maybe he's hit his head or something."

Suze didn't reply.

Bertelli tapped again. "I think he's not coming to."

What had Randy been doing in the module at all?

Activating the dumb door panel, Bertelli tried to query the system. It didn't give a lot of information. The interior was pressurized. Seals were good. Power was good. Gyros were shot.

That was all he could get.

"I can't get inside," he told Suze. He wondered what he'd do if Randy had already been dead. Depressurizing the module and opening the door wouldn't make any difference.

Remembering what Suze had said about Randy's low BP, Bertelli looked in again.

Yes. There was some blood on the locker.

Randy needed medical assistance. Someone had to get in there. Fast.

The only way in, without subjecting him to vacuum, was to dock with the Orion.

But there was no way to launch from this angle.

And no way for Orion to come down to them.

If Randy was going to survive they had to get *Surety* back up to orbit.

Bertelli realized that applied to him too. Just that there was no way to get inside. No way to tend to Randy. To open the hatch was to kill him.

"Suze?"

"Yeah."

"I need you to pass something on to Valerie."

"No you don't. You'll be seeing her in a couple of days."

"Sure. And if I don't, you can tell her from me that I'm sorry."

"Okay. And I've got a message for you from Valerie."

"Huh?" How was that possible?

"She says that you need to make sure you come home. Whatever it takes."

"Johnston's got kids." Jaimee was three and Samuel was nine months. On the way up both Bertelli and Suze had gotten sick of seeing the photos. Cute kids sure, but who needed to see the seven hundredth photo of the baby asleep? Suze did better with that than he did.

"Yeah. Valerie's pregnant."

Bertelli smiled. "You were doing okay until then."

"Well, she could be."

He let his smile fade. There weren't going to be any kids for them. Plumbing problems on both sides. There was only Valerie.

Bertelli sucked in his breath.

Valerie.

He focused back on his task. Licking his dry lips, he stepped back down. Standing on the moon's surface again he took another sip of water.

If he had power tools and six hours, he could cut the other two legs off. The whole thing would settle down onto the open landing nacelles. Nice and level.

If he had those kinds of tools.

And if he had the luck of that lottery winner from a couple of years back.

Two billion dollars. With a ticket bought on the spur of the moment. Minutes before the cutoff for the draw. And the ticket was lost for a month. And went through the laundry.

When she went to get the prize—just before the money would have been declared unclaimed—the ticket was barely legible.

That kind of luck.

Bertelli wasn't going to be setting *Surety* back upright. Not with the best will in the world.

"Suze? Except for the angle, *Surety*'s still in good shape, right?"

"You can't launch. If the landing section collapses further you're going to turn into a fireball."

"But everything's in reasonable shape, right?"

Hesitation, then a curt, "Yes."

"Okay. Can you launch her on remote?"

"Yes." The same curt tone.

"Start the procedure."

"I've got four minutes left in line of sight. Then you're going to lose me."

"Route the signal." Surely there was a lunar satellite she could bounce off.

Suze *tsked*. "Bad coincidence there. Nothing to route from. Schröedinger's in a bad spot. Those satellites I guess you're thinking about? Nothing high or local."

Bertelli thought fast. He needed to get her to send him control.

He could fly it out himself using the suit's command systems. They were pretty primitive, but it was just launching. Suze could chase them down in Orion later.

That's what the command ship was built for.

"Also," she said. "I've run launch scenarios. Assuming the landing section actually doesn't collapse under you, the *Surety* will burn too much fuel trying to compensate for the angle. Even if you didn't rip out the gimbals, you're not going to have enough fuel after that to make orbit."

"This is the moon we're talking about." The escape delta-v was only 2400 meters per second.

But of course the module only carried enough fuel for that and some maneuvering.

Bertelli whacked his hammer against the side of the lander. There was still plenty of extra fuel in there. Randy had made a pinpoint-perfect landing. Not a drop wasted.

Of course there was no way to get it siphoned over into *Surety*.

"Sit tight until I come around again," Suze said. He could hear the concern in her voice. Worried that they wouldn't live long enough.

"Sit tight," he said.

"I'm still working with Houston on alternatives. We're bound to come up with something."

"I bet. Listen. Download the remote control system to my suit." He would figure this out.

"Can't do it."

"Start now. I'm in charge here."

"I mean it'll take three minutes to just sync. I don't even know if your suit's got enough memory for it anyway."

"Start. Just start."

Suze sighed. Bertelli saw a telltale light on his helmet's inner rim. The download had started.

"What are you going to do with it? You can't launch."

"See if I can scramble something from the code."

"I don't follow."

"Don't worry. Now get me a link to Cooper P mine. I need to talk to someone."

"The Australians?"

"You've got a minute and a half."

"All right."

Bertelli unrolled his palm screen and started deleting data. Geology. Temperature. Lux.

Gigabytes of stuff.

He hoped it made space for the remote console.

If that rover had been working he could have driven a few hundred miles in it. Maybe. If the battery held out.

That might have put him within walking distance of one of the bases.

With lunar gravity he could easily cover a hundred miles on foot. Probably more. Even with the suit.

Perhaps it was just as well the rover was frozen. It meant he didn't have to make that difficult choice of abandoning Johnston.

There were just thirty seconds left before silence when Suze came back.

"Colin?"

"Go."

"All right. I've got a link to the Aussies."

"Thanks. Who's there?"

"Colin Bertelli!" He recognized the voice right away. Brian Thorpe. One of the old-timers. He'd been at the south pole for years before Bertelli had even arrived.

"Brian. Can you—"

"So," Thorpe said. "What's the news? I hear you're still single. I—"

"Listen," Bertelli said. "I've got a situation here. I'm about to lose my contact."

"I'm listening."

"I'm at Schröedinger. Busted launch vehicle."

"Copy that. Got nothing can reach you."

"Yeah. Can you get something to . . ."

Static hissed at him. Faded.

Suze had gone over the horizon.

Bertelli cursed. He was on his own.

Once, communications would have been continuous. Lunar excursions were just too routine now.

Bad luck for him.

He looked up at *Surety* again. Her white faceted cone glinted back at him. The sun's stark white light could be blinding.

At least that was something that was going to be reliable. With 360 hours of continuous daylight the moon was tough. Well lit, but harsh.

He would be dead long before the intensity of light was a problem. He moved into the *Surety*'s shadow anyway.

Taking out his slate display, he looked at the data Suze had sent. Reading through the download, he saw there was crucial information missing.

Her download was incomplete.

He had start and ignition sequences. Unlatching. Gyro and gimbal control. Load balance.

No attitude retros.

All this data was just a couple of meters away. Locked up inside *Surety*'s computer. Inaccessible from here.

With what he had he could launch *Surety* and have a fair shot at keeping her upright. But without those retros—which were really only for docking maneuvering, not a launch at all—he would struggle.

Really struggle.

This was going to take a physical mod.

He looked up at *Surety*'s external locker. Their stupid rover had been stored in there.

Quickly he got back up the ladder. The rover's locker had been designed to take return samples and some of the science packs that had arrived on the base.

Plenty of space for him to squeeze in and find the internal connections.

Or not plenty of space. He found that out as he attempted to get inside.

Too narrow.

The rover locker was never meant to accommodate an astronaut.

He was going to have to remove his backpack. Slim as it was, the life-support system added too much width.

Working fast, he sealed and uncoupled the main tube. The system was integrated into the suit. It took two people to get it off. But it did have an emergency release. Just in case one member of the crew had become incapacitated. Designed to be used inside the main cabin. Pressurized.

Not in the vacuum of the moon's surface.

Bertelli got it shucked off. The internal reservoir gave him about fifteen minutes. Enough time to get hooked up again.

He stuffed the pack into the locker. Right away he followed. It took some shimmying. He had to slide along into the space. His faceplate bumped against the top.

That would confuse them, he thought. If it cracked and he depressurized, the whole situation would confound the investigators.

He needed to concentrate. The suit was starting to stink of his own exhalations.

Getting the hoses back in place was tough. He had to work by feel. He was used to gloves. Thick, stiff. No feedback.

He got the oxygen tube in first.

Nothing flowed.

With his left arm crushing against his neck, he adjusted the connection. The electronics synced. His headset gave a quiet bleep.

Cool air washed in.

He still had red lights at the helmet rim. Disconnecting the pack had cost him radio and main telemetry.

Worry about that later. At least he had oxygen. He needed to focus on getting the ship out of here.

Just as well Suze was behind the moon. Nothing in the manuals sanctioned what he was about to do.

With the rock hammer he chipped at one of the aluminum joins. There wasn't much reach. He couldn't get anything like a good swing. It took about fifty blows.

The join split.

He wedged the chisel end in. Twisted.

The hammer vibrated in his hand as the aluminum tore.

Just as well he couldn't hear it.

Bertelli kept tearing. Wires and conduits inside. He caught a couple of cables with the hammer's tip and stopped.

What he needed was a USB port.

But that would be far too convenient.

He was just going to have to look for a data cable.

Taking care not to snag wires, he kept tearing. The aluminum folded out of the way.

Reaching in he felt around the wires. The internal hull was just inches away. He reminded himself to be real careful not to puncture that.

The whole reason to do this was to give Randy a chance. If he wasn't dead already.

Bertelli reminded himself that Suze had seen Randy's bio telemetry. He'd been alive twenty minutes ago.

If he could just find something useful, Bertelli knew he might be able to get them both out of here.

Back in training they'd been over the whole schematic. Theoretically he'd seen every part of *Surety* diagrammed out. Every connection, every switch.

He knew there was something somewhere here.

He kept on tearing.

The suit bleeped again. Oxygen level.

Breathing too hard. Too fast.

Sweating too.

If their situations had been reversed he was sure Randy would have had some Zen calming technique to extend out his air. To focus on the task.

Bertelli was far too practical for that. He wondered if Randy would have ripped holes in a spacecraft looking for a way to override the system.

Bertelli laughed.

Sweat dripped into his eyes.

"Valerie," he said. "Sorry. I tried."

The suit bleeped again.

"I really tried."

He blinked, but more sweat just came. Spacesuits weren't designed for horizontal work.

All he needed to do was wipe his forehead. Too bad about the faceplate.

There. He saw a data cable.

A black plastic sheath. Thicker than the others.

He grabbed it.

Quickly he traced it through the maze of others.

Followed it all the way to its plug.

Not compatible with his slate. Well, he hadn't expected that, but he could wire it up. At least he knew the order of the pins.

When he pulled the plug it didn't budge.

He twisted around, tried again.

The suit gave a double bleep. He needed to replace his tanks.

Soon.

Another go at yanking the plug.

"Valerie," he whispered. He needed some kind of motivation.

Sticking the hammer's chisel in against the plug, he wrenched.

Nothing.

Great, he thought, something with a quality build. Kind of reassuring, really.

Too bad the landing struts hadn't had the same kind of attention.

Three bleeps.

He flipped the hammer around and hit the plug with the striking face.

The hammer bounced back.

With a grunt he hit it again.

He was going to die here. Ignominious. Stuck on his back in the rover locker.

Better to die out on the surface. Kicking at the regolith. Stamping his boot prints into the dust. Looking up at the stars.

That was how.

He slithered out a foot.

With a smile he thought he could write Valerie's name in the dust. She knew anyway, but then she would really know.

Valerie.

She was the reason he couldn't get out and do that. He owed it to her to try everything. Not just Valerie, he thought. He owed it to Randy as well.

Twisting, he swung at the plug again.

It shattered. Plastic shards shot around the space.

The cable dropped down.

Bertelli grinned. Great workmanship succumbs to geology hammer.

He grabbed the cable.

The plug had completely shattered. The pins were bent and twisted. Some had sheared off entirely.

This was going to take some work.

Holding the slate beside his faceplate he prized the casing open. The bezel flapped away.

Don't crack the screen, he told himself.

He slipped the multitool from his belt and opened the pliers. With a squeeze the cable gave up its sheathing. He splayed the wires out.

Guesswork, he thought.

And years of experience jury-rigging equipment in the mines.

Using the corner tip of the hammer's chisel again, he eased some wires out from the docking jack.

That was easier.

The suit's bleeping had become continuous now. He tried to shut it out.

Fifteen wires.

Four connections in the slate's socket.

Almost like a lottery. He hoped he didn't fry everything on his first attempt.

It was tough work. His heavy gloves were okay for working with wrenches and hammers. Not so great for delicate electronics.

Using the pliers he got the first connection made. Twisted them together.

Second connection. Third.

When he got the fourth connection in, the first one came apart.

Cursing, he tried again.

When he got it back on again he tried the slate. The deframed screen came on all right. No sign of the external connection.

He pulled one wire and connected the next.

This was no way to fly a spacecraft.

Still nothing.

Breaking and making new connections, the screen stayed blank. He wondered how many possible combinations there were.

Something like thirty thousand possible connection variations?

"Really a lottery," he said.

The air stank now. Hot and humid.

What he was counting on was that the systems were more fluid than that. So long as one connection was right, he hoped, the whole thing would work.

He pulled off one wire, connected the next.

Rinse and repeat.

On his twelfth try the *Surety*'s system came up on the slate. He would have whooped but the air was like treacle.

Careful not to damage his connections he worked through the access levels. He found the launch controls quickly.

Very limited.

Nothing like the helm inside.

With this he had no gimbal control. No retro-rocket control. No throttle.

Ignition. Shutdown.

That was it.

"Just one break," he told the ship.

Bertelli knew the ship would manage its own gimbals. It was

programmed to fly upright. Assuming they made it clear of the lander, the *Surety* would swing its way upright and aim for space.

The problem was, if she did that her fuel reserves might deplete much too fast. And she would know. The ship would fly an abort course and attempt a soft landing. She was flat-based enough to probably stay upright. Her center of gravity was lower than the landing stack, the framework was strong enough to hold.

It was an emergency protocol only. It assumed that all other options were exhausted. Land with a reasonable degree of safety. Sit tight and wait for rescue.

The protocol assumed that the crew were safely on board.

There were sufficient supplies to wait it out. Rescue might take a couple of days. Might take a week.

Only he wasn't in the crew compartment. He couldn't access any of that. Life support. Food. Water.

He was stuck here in this little compartment, hacking his way into her.

With next to no air.

He was tempted to try another combination of wires. Maybe if he got it right he could access the whole system and override those contingencies. Actually fly the thing.

He sighed. He could feel his vision blurring. His breathing rate increasing.

Sure, he could fly it like this. Lying on his back in an eighteen-inch-high gap. With a slate spliced into *Surety* with twisted wires.

And if he did nothing, at least Randy might survive. The air circulation in the cabin would continue. Someone might get to him in a day or so.

Bertelli looked at the slate.

Ignition. Shutdown.

Or, he thought, *ignore.*

That's it. Good luck, Randy.

Good luck, Valerie.

"I'll miss you," he whispered. He felt sleepy.

As he went to pull out the wires, Bertelli remembered the maps. His old mining set. Back from the south pole.

Those were the days.

Roughnecking and being real makeshift.

The guys would be proud of his attempt here. He hoped someone told them.

The maps. Something about the maps.

Almost unconsciously he opened up the set.

The south pole. Schröedinger. Aitken. Zeeman. Such a beautiful landscape.

That's right, he thought. He didn't want to die stuck inside the can like this. He wanted to look up at the stars.

Staring at the map, he felt his concentration going.

The south pole was only five hundred kilometers away.

Lunar escape velocity was 2400 meters per second. He wasn't going to get that out of her.

But what if he didn't try to escape?

Ignition. Shutdown.

He tapped back up two menus. Found navigation.

Destination.

Locked out. It only wanted to get to orbit.

"I'll fix you," he said. His voice sounded like a wheeze.

He pulled up the map overlays and some old mining data.

Bertelli grinned.

The old systems didn't have the formal niceties of NASA.

Worth a shot.

With a couple of taps the map loaded through the destination system. *Surety* didn't like it, but she accepted the data.

Destination: south pole.

This was, he thought, the last time anyone would ever be able to do that. NASA would plug that software hole with fifteen hundred lines of code. And cover that with another fifteen hundred lines.

As he felt himself blacking out, he squinted at the slate.

Destination: south pole.

Ignition. Shutdown.

His finger wavered. He felt punch-drunk. This is what it's like to die, he thought.

He tapped *Ignition.*

Surety shuddered. Light blazed around him and he thought of Valerie.

Smiling. Laughing.

"Valerie," he said. "I did my best."

The light faded. He wasn't sure if it was from lifting off or from dying.

Probably dying.

He didn't feel heavy at all. He felt light.

Airless or weightless.

The world shimmered around him. He hoped Randy made it.

He hoped Valerie did okay.

Haze.

Black.

Haze.

That was surprising.

He could feel the shuddering again. But it wasn't *Surety*.

There were lights overhead.

The air felt cool and crisp. He smelled pineapples. Weird.

Someone speaking.

"Got him," they said.

Male. An Australian accent.

Bertelli blinked. He wasn't in his suit anymore. But he was still lying on his back. Moving. They were carrying him. More voices, jabbering and yelling. Something about cutting into the capsule.

His vision felt constricted, like he was looking through a dark tube. He bent his head up and someone pushed it back down.

Taking another breath of the sweet air, he let them. After a moment they set him down. He was in a small room with a poster of the Sydney Opera House and SuperSpire on the wall.

Aussies.

Someone looked down at him. Brian Thorpe. "Sheesh. Did you come screaming in at us?"

"You look older," Bertelli said.

"Back at you." Thorpe grinned. Toothy.

"Thanks. How's Randy?"

"Alive. We're getting him out, don't worry. Put a bubble over the hatch and we'll get a helmet on him. Are you going to tell me how and why you pulled that?"

Bertelli frowned. "Pulled what?"

Thorpe shook his head. His raggedy blonde hair shivered. "So. Here's what I know. You called me up. Some problem. So I start figuring your location. You were close but not that close. Comms went down, but I knew you had a busted ship. We were going to send Scooter over in a wagon but then you took off. The monitors tracked you coming in. You'll want to see the footage."

"Footage?" Bertelli was only half listening. He was glad it had worked. Glad he would see Valerie again.

"Video," Thorpe said. "You came in fast. On a low arc. Not even trying for orbit. And you swung the ship around somehow. Landed on her engines. Like she was always built to do that."

"How about that?" Bertelli said.

"And we found you in the sample locker. Gutsy. NASA's been on the horn to us. I think they're going to give you a medal and fire you."

Bertelli laughed. "Did you talk to Suze?"

"Sure. She wants to punch you then take you out for a drink."

"Well," he said. "I'll let her hit me, but I've already got someone who might take me out for a drink." A drink and a meal and a walk on the beach. In the moonlight.

"You?"

Bertelli sighed. "Yes me. Her name's Valerie. And actually if you let me use a radio I'd like to give her a call. Tell her that I'm coming home."

Sean Monaghan studied at the University of Queensland and now makes his home in New Zealand, where he works in a busy public library. Sean's stories litter the internet and the pages of magazines, from *Takahe* and *Landfall* to *Asimov's* and *Amazing Stories*. Web: seanmonaghan.com.

WE FLY

by K.B. Rylander

K.B.'s unusual story about a human mind uploaded into an interstellar probe artfully shows us the terror and loneliness of being totally alone when you are light-years away from the help and support of other humans. Though unique in setting, the story perfectly captures the spirit of this contest when something goes wrong and our protagonist refuses to give up despite the odds being against her.

AT 18:27 input received. <Unidentified Error detected.>
Get me out. Let me breathe.

The carbon-steel hull lies a scant half centimeter from my face, but I can't dwell on that. It's what started me into panic in the first place.

I crawled to my spot next to Matthew James in the back of Dad's two-door classic Chevy, trying to keep my bare legs from burning on the peeling vinyl. Dad rolled down the window in an attempt to cool things off, but I resigned myself to sucking it up and breathing the soupy hot air. As the engine puttered to life and the radio blared "Summer in the City," I scowled at Mom and Dad's delight in the ancient song. In the rearview mirror Dad's bushy eyebrows crinkled as he laughed.

He tossed back a hard candy. "Hang in there, Natasha."

❖ ❖ ❖

In deep orbit around Alpha Centauri AB.4, encapsulated in a coffin-sized hunk of metal, I'm surrounded by nothingness—silence and cold and dark. The ship pings, announcing the return of the first Little Guy probe. Cool peppermint lingers on my phantom lips from the memory.

My robotic eyes open, but see only darkness. The metal shell around me clunks and there's a mechanical whine as the beach ball-sized Little Guy docks with the ship and silence again while its data uploads. *Please let the planet be habitable. I came all this way, give me something.*

While I wait, I check with the comm-bots on the Beacon construction and try to ignore the itching. My skin is a synthetic polymer covered in forty two-thousand sensors that were overkill in training, but now, inside the capsule, they're worse than useless. They pick up every tiny dust particle. My mind-construct interprets these as itches and somewhere during my malfunctions I've lost the ability to turn the sensors off.

My biggest complaint is the choking. I know I'm not *actually* choking. I'm not crazy. But it's the same sensation, a tightening as if a hand grips my nonexistent throat.

I think back, trying to figure where I went wrong. It makes no sense. Everything was normal before I shut down for the journey—months of training, psychological assessments, and self-diagnostics came back with flying colors. Upon arrival three days ago I awoke to panic and malfunctions. Sure, fifty-two years passed back home but it felt like a blink of an eye for me. I remember with perfect clarity the day they mapped my brain and uploaded me into the probe, how afterward I said goodbye to my old self, that human Natasha, and watched her go on her way.

The data from the Little Guy finishes uploading. This is it. I can't get the files open fast enough.

The first several photos show a dense atmosphere of swirling browns. A few manipulations give me access to surface images of a gray crust filled with rocky gullies like the wrinkles of a massive elephant.

As the rest of the Little Guys return and fill me in on the data they've collected, the choking in my throat gets worse.

Alpha Centauri AB.4 is a lump of rock. Six thousand kilometers in radius, dense carbon dioxide rich atmosphere. No chance of sustaining life. In other words, Venus but warmer. All of this, my life's work and traveling 4.3 light-years to find the twin of our nearest neighbor.

The rain pattered against the windows as Grandma pulled chocolate chip cookies out of the oven and I watched from the kid-safe distance of the kitchen table. Grandma hummed absently and I took a deep, cookie-scented breath. Warmth filled me all the way to my toes. Just as my mouth started watering, shadows fall over the memory, swallowing Grandma and her kitchen, and I resist a tug pulling me into the darkness.

Vivid, perfect memory is one of the perks of upload technology, but with my malfunctions I can't even get those right.

I jerk free of the shadows and end up on the road beside the airfield. This isn't a memory I'd choose. When I was thirteen, not long after Sophia died, my parents took me all sorts of places trying to cheer me up. During one of those attempts we stopped at Luke Air Force Base. Mom, Dad, Matthew James, and I stood beside the chain-link fence with the Arizona sun beating down on us as it leached the sky a dull blue. The air smelled of rain without a cloud in sight. The necklace I wore that day feels too tight now and I want nothing more than to take it off, but the memory doesn't work that way. Mom and Dad stood close to me, but all I could think about was the terrible inside-twisty feeling of everything being so wrong.

Sophia would never grow up and fly. She'd never even get to see a plane.

My eyes prickled as a jet engine roared, the ground beneath our feet rumbling. Matthew James, ten years old at the time, let out a whoop and jumped against the chain-link fence. "This is more like it!" he yelled. The rest of his words were swallowed by the roar of the plane.

A whoosh of adrenaline surged through me as the jet zoomed off—a childlike excitement I don't remember having felt. Some of the pressure lifts from my chest.

Dad sighed and squeezed my shoulder. "We can take you someplace else if you'd rather?"

I don't mind watching a few more, but I said, "Yes, please."
Matthew James scowled.

The files from Earth include forty-eight years of updates sent to me at the speed of light while I slept. In those files was the discovery of another rocky planet, AB.6—this one looking even less promising than AB.4, so they didn't send me there right away.

It's taken me two months at my reduced speeds, but AB.6 is within spitting distance. During that time I've been awake, malfunctioning, and staving off panic by reliving memories and avoiding shadows. I can watch my video library thousands of times per hour, but somehow memories take longer.

Once again the ship's cameras fail to respond, so I'm blind as the ship settles into high orbit around the planet. Metal clunks within the capsule as the bay doors open to release the five Little Guys that will take pictures and run analysis of the planet below.

I reboot and run another self-diagnostic which tells me the same thing as the others:

<Unidentified Error detected.>

Great. As if I didn't know that before running the tests. The least it could do is give me an idea of where my processing went haywire.

Only seconds after the bay doors close the comm-bots ping me. The Beacon relay ship beat me here by weeks.

<Beacon construction complete. Spooling commenced.>

The "Beacon" is a misnomer really. It's not setting up an actual beacon so much as connecting two points in space, allowing instant transfer of data four light-years away. It's revolutionized our ability to work with the Mars teams, but this beacon is the farthest out by far. Some of the pressure on my chest lets up with anticipation of communication with Earth.

Another ping, call it a virtual knock on the door, this time from a human-controlled computer back on Earth.

The Beacon works.

As the systems connect—thank God they connect—I pull up my avatar file, look it over, and decide my face doesn't look quite right. I sharpen the features and add a different hairstyle. I remove my once-beautiful braids and give avatar-Natasha short hair.

I'm done in nanoseconds and wait a few more before the channel opens and two video feeds of Mission Control come into view, one an overview of the room, the other near ground level.

In fifty-two years Mission Control's design has changed little. A redesign with dark wood paneling and comfortable-looking leather desk chairs gives the room a warmth it never had before. Three rows of desks have given way to a more spacious two and the room is packed with people smiling at the camera in anticipation. In a couple of seconds their visual feed kicks in and they break out in applause and cheers and clinking champagne glasses.

I send a smile to my avatar face and their cheers grow louder. *Don't act crazy, don't act crazy.*

"Can you hear us, Natasha?" says a man's voice.

<Loud and clear,> I send back and hear it spoken in Mission Control. "Nice to see the human race hasn't changed much."

They all laugh in delight even though it wasn't funny and I search the crowd for familiar faces, albeit much older ones. Three individuals stand in front of the up-close camera: a man and woman in lime-green uniforms with United American Space Agency splashed garishly in neon orange and a young woman in a tan business suit. It looks like something my mother would have worn.

"I'm Commander John Cook," the man in the garish uniform says. He reads from the palm of his hand and clears his throat. "I see you're sending us your data already, that's excellent. Have you already reached AB.4?"

"Yes, sir, but I'm afraid the news isn't as we hoped."

Cook looks at his companion. The crowd murmurs.

Halfway through briefing them on AB.4 and AB.6 there's a hiccup in my processors so I restart and reconnect.

When the cameras come back online Cook stands frowning at me, his arms folded. "Did you go offline for a second?"

So much for hoping they wouldn't notice. I feel remarkably like a child standing in front of the class. "I'm back now," I say, sending a toothy grin to avatar-Natasha.

"You were telling us about AB.6," he prompts. "You're in orbit now and there was some reason you couldn't send us pictures. Something about the ship's cameras?"

"Not functioning," I say. My throat clenches and avatar-Natasha brushes her neck without me directing it to do so.

"But you've deployed the probes."

"My communication with them is down. I have to wait for their return."

"Damage during the journey?"

"Diagnostics tell me it's not a physical problem." Avatar-Natasha runs her hand over her throat again, as if trying to remove something that's not there. *Get a grip.*

The faces in the crowd are all too young to be anyone I know. They stare up at their screens with rapt attention. No one seems to have noticed that my cartoon avatar has a nervous tick.

"Care to explain in more detail?" Cook says.

"Can I talk to Howard?" My voice comes out sounding too high pitched.

Cook glances at the people around him for clues. "Howard?" He shifts from foot to foot and reads something on his palm. "Howard Vine? The lead compu-psychologist in your training?"

The uniformed woman at his side turns and addresses the crowd. "Can we clear the room of all nonessential personnel, please?"

In the minute it takes the people to file out I run through video files of hang-gliding to calm my nerves.

Cook straightens his uniform and speaks slowly, as if I'm a nut job. "Natasha, you understand you slept fifty-two years, right?"

I go through my defensive excuses in nanoseconds, discard the childish ones and settle on the mature response. "Actually, the compu-psychological team might be of some help."

Cook nods to the woman in the business suit who steps forward. "Hi, Natasha, I'm Dr. Najim, the lead psychologist for your team and a theoretical compu-psychologist."

I get her caught up on the basics, trying not to sound too crazy: the panic when I awoke, the choking sensation, the problems communicating with the Little Guys.

She stares at my avatar.

My avatar clears her throat. "This problem can't be new to you. Sure, the technology was cutting edge when I left but—"

"Uploading was banned over forty years ago. This was for political reasons, not because there was something wrong with the technology, Natasha. A problem like the one you describe was never reported. Before the ban, we had scientists volunteer to have themselves copied for upload and sent on space missions within our solar system, and others who were shut off for long periods of time, as you were. None have reported problems."

"What are you saying?" Cook asks.

"I don't know how to help," she says.

I stood at our dining table back home in Phoenix, with friends crowding around me as I prepared to blow out six tall candles on a princess cake. Mom's perfume made my eyes water and I felt her close behind me, leading everyone's singing in her off-key way. Dad stood across from me, taking pictures with his phone and grinning like a fool. Matthew James looked at me with sad eyes and I wondered why. I wore a pink frilly dress that I had always loved before, but now it feels wrong and my cheeks flush in embarrassment.

On the real day I didn't dislike the dress, did I? I wore it for years afterward. The others at the party must see that I look ridiculous wearing this. They'll make fun of me for being a girl.

No one seems to notice.

AB.6 is a thing of beauty. The first pictures from the Little Guys show all whites and blues and a deep purple I can't help but speculate is plant life. Its atmosphere is eighty percent nitrogen and nineteen percent oxygen. The surface temperatures estimated in fifty locations range between negative twenty Celsius near the winter pole and a max of positive forty. It's roughly three-quarters the size of Earth, with slightly more landmass. It is, in other words, just right.

I call it Goldilocks.

"So how ya feeling?" Whitaker asks with his deep, ninety-year-old vibrato. He's a colleague from my team back before takeoff and the only person I've met who was alive when I lived on Earth. His sagging eyes water with thinly veiled emotion at being allowed the visit. I didn't anticipate how good it would feel to see someone I know, even someone I didn't know well. I've wondered about the other Natasha, how she's doing and if she'd be able to tell me what's wrong with my memories.

Despite the tears, there's laughter in Whitaker's eyes and in those around him. Everyone is in a better mood today after the news about Goldilocks.

I smile. "I'm ready to get out of this metal box and down to that damn fine planet."

More chuckles.

Dr. Najim says, "All in due time. Protocol, after all."

While I have the ability to run the mission on my own, protocol dictates that Mission Control authorizes the landing. They say they're waiting for the Little Guys to finish their flybys and perform preliminary safety tests, find a suitable landing site, what have you. Easy for them to say. They're not suffocating in this box.

I send over a friendly but exasperated expression.

"Follow your heart, kiddo," Whitaker says.

Dr. Najim shoots him a look.

"She's anxious to get down there, of course," he says.

"I'd prefer if you didn't refer to me as 'she' actually," I say.

"Pardon?" Najim asks.

I don't want to tell them it feels like nails on a chalkboard being referred to as the wrong gender so I say, "I'm a machine. 'It' is more accurate."

UASA folks try to usher Whitaker away, but he plants his feet and grips the armrests of his chair.

Dr. Najim looks at the others, opens her mouth, and closes it again. "Okay? If that makes you more comfortable, we'd be happy to refer to you as an 'it' rather than a 'she.'" She nods slowly and leans back from the camera as if trying to distance herself while she thinks things through. "It" is not a pronoun for a human. She's probably mentally adding that to her long list of "problems."

But she's an idiot and I couldn't care less if I confuse them, I just want out of this ship and down on the planet. They sent a computer out to space and a computer is what they're going to get. Maybe they'll authorize my trip sooner.

On the southeast hemisphere of Goldilocks there's this mountain range that puts the Himalayas to shame. The desert stretching out on its leeward side ends with rolling violet plains. Beyond that is the planet's equivalent of a forest, with white-barked trees and brilliantly hued leaves the size and shape of dinner plates. These same trees, a taller variety with pink leaves rather than purple, are also found on a continent five thousand kilometers to the north.

I revel in every new piece of information the Little Guys bring back. Their high-res telescopic cameras take detailed pictures from orbit, but I'm itching to get down there and see it for myself, analyze the air and determine if it's truly habitable for a human colony.

There's no evidence of animal life yet, but the place teems with plantlike organisms. Xenobiology was my first PhD and remains my passion. I've found my landing site without Mission Control's help—a high plain on the edge of several ecosystems. Nearing the ocean is a three-thousand-foot-high cliff with incredible rock formations at its base.

It's been weeks and they still won't authorize my landing. In that time I've gleaned clues about Earth they neglected to send me in the official updates. Parts of the planet are getting worse. The Indian Space Agency sent generation ships this direction in the blind hope habitable planets would be found. With their speeds I won't get visitors for decades, but I might create the groundwork to save their lives.

I enter my landing site into the ship's navigation.

<Initiate landing.>

<Error.>

I reboot and try again.

<Unidentified Error detected.>

Yes, yes. I know. <Initiate landing.>

<Error.>

No, no, no, no, no, no, no.

I ping Mission Control and tweak my avatar, trying to get the look right while I wait. The screens come into view and a young guy in a UASA uniform sits in front of me.

"I'm ready to land and start my analysis of the surface," I say. "I need you to resend me the ship's landing authorization."

"Resend?" he asks. "Um. Can you give me a minute? It's 2:00 a.m."

"Yes, of course."

Dr. Najim shows up an hour later wearing another one of her business skirts. She sits ironing-board straight with her legs together and her hands folded in her lap. "You've changed your avatar."

The old one didn't feel right anymore. "I needed a change."

"You've changed your gender. And your race."

"Well, I'm not any gender or any race now, am I?"

"How do you feel about this change?"

"It's just a picture." Honestly this new one isn't right either, but I wouldn't tell her that.

"I can't help but notice that you've changed yourself to a white male. I feel there's some significance to that." When I don't answer she says, "I hear you requested landing authorizations?"

"Yes. I've had enough waiting, I want to get down to the surface." *And out of this damn capsule*, I refrain from saying.

"I understand," she says. "But let's get a few of these kinks worked out first. We don't want to risk unintentional damage in case anything goes wrong due to your"—She rethinks her word choice—"processing problem."

"Then *help* me with my problem. What's wrong with me? Some hitch during boot-up? I was fine one second, I switched off for space flight, and woke up feeling like I'd been buried alive. Why am I suddenly afraid of being in space when I've loved it my whole life?"

She sighs. "This development is unprecedented. The rare issues with the other uploads were immediately evident, not weeks after. Your initial testing looked great, that's the reason you were selected."

"Listen," I say. "You've got colonists on their way who need to know if they've got a safe place to land. What you need is a *probe on the ground*, you need me down there."

Dr. Najim nods, but before she has a chance to say something I cut in.

"You can't give me this responsibility," I say and am not sure why I said it.

"But you just said you want to go down there."

"I'm not talking about that responsibility. I'm talking about the other one."

"What other one?"

"I don't know!"

I restart.

<Unidentified Error detected.>

When the video feed comes back Dr. Najim still sits in the same place. I wasn't gone long.

"Natasha Washington might help," I say. "I want to talk to her."

"That's you," she says as if I didn't know that.

"No, the other one. The human one who used to be me. She's alive right? Is she senile?"

Dr. Najim shakes her head. "Oh no, I'm not supposed to talk to you about your other self. That was one of the foundational rules of uploading. It's best that two distinct individuals are formed."

She seems to think it over.

"Listen," she says, lowering her voice. "I will tell you that she's alive and she's not senile, but there's no way you're talking to her."

"She could help me figure out what's wrong," I say. "She's me." *But sane.*

I sat on our neighbor's couch, playing a game on my phone while the baby slept upstairs. I slipped into my least favorite memory on purpose this time. There's something distinctly wrong with it, I just can't figure out what.

"Baby Sophia is up there right now." Matthew James stood at the foot of the stairs in his favorite airplane shirt. "Can we go check on her? I can't go up there by myself."

My phone screen showed I'd hit a new high score so I smiled and checked my watch. Sophia's parents would be home soon.

Matthew James ran to me. "Go up there and check on her," he yelled. "How are you supposed to take care of me if you can't take care of one little baby?"

I ignored him. The hand gripping my phantom throat squeezes like a vise-grip while the thirteen-year-old me continued breathing normally.

Her parents arrived home carrying the whiff of Chinese-food takeout. Sophia's dad paid me while her mom went up to check on her. Matthew James slammed his hands over his ears as Sophia's mother screamed.

"She's not breathing! She's not breathing!"

Another day in orbit, stuck in the capsule with my sensors going off as if I'm being crawled on by a thousand ants. I'm trying to figure out the piece I'm missing by playing through a memory, one where I'm an adult for once. I was accepting my degree in an outdoor graduation and the cherry blossoms were in full bloom. I looked out over the crowd at my smiling family—Mom, Dad, and ten-year-old

Matthew James. As the shadows draw in, something clicks in my brain, something important that's just out of reach. A ping from the Beacon brings me out of the memory.

It's like a whack to the head. My processors fire warnings. A quick sweep of the data packet tells me not to download it.

It's from Mission Control. I know what this means: a remote wipe and reload.

They decided to wipe me clean and upload the probe with some kind of AI to finish their job. They're trying to get rid of me. It's a risky move, one that could leave them with a hunk of metal and nothing else. I'm equipped for attacks like this. Of course I am, couldn't have a terrorist organization or rival government hijacking the mission's most important resource.

When my head clears I send them a single message: "It's not going to work, assholes."

I cut off communication and scramble for clues on how to fix myself. If they try that again and I have a malfunction they could get through my defenses. Cutting off the Beacon relay is an option—they can't wipe my processors clean and load the probe with AI if the Beacon shuts off.

Hours later, when I'm confident I'll hold for now, I reconnect to the Beacon and send a message.

"Let me talk to the human Natasha. Get her there today or I'm cutting off communication permanently."

They're fast, I'll give them that. Two hours later I watch my former self, now eighty-six, walk into Mission Control. Her hair has gone white and she's shrunk in her old age, but she still walks tall. She sits down with a huff, looks up at my avatar and raises an eyebrow.

"Why do you look like that?" Her voice sounds deep and crackly, as if she's smoked the last fifty years of her life. "You sure you're me?"

"The avatar is there so you have someone to talk to," I say.

"Well, I know that. It just doesn't look like any face I'd have wanted."

That shouldn't sting. I shouldn't care what she thinks. "I need to ask you about the night Sophia died."

Her brows furrow and her face blanches. "You really must be screwed in the head. I haven't thought about her in fifty years."

What a load of bull. "It doesn't bother you?"

"Nope."

"Tell me, have you had any children?"

She shakes her head, looks away and waves her hand dismissively. "Nothing to do with Sophia."

"No kids, fine. Ever had a dog? Or a cat? A fish? Been responsible for any living thing but yourself?"

The other Natasha's shoulders sag.

"If you could just help me understand why things happened like they did," I say. "The night Sophia died, why didn't we go check on her?"

"She died of SIDS," the old Natasha says, raising her voice. "Did you expect us to check on her every two minutes?"

"But when we were downstairs Matthew James told us to—"

"What? Who the hell is Matthew James?"

I study her face for signs she's not serious. Maybe she's senile after all. "Matthew James. Our ten-year-old brother." As I hear it I realize "brother" doesn't fit.

She looks up at me on the screen and I can practically see the wheels turning in her head. "Matthew James. Matthew James." Finally, she smiles. "Matthew James Whitaker!"

My nonexistent gut wrenches.

She fumbles on reading glasses and types into the palm of her hand. When she's found what she's looking for, she leans on the console to pull herself to her feet and reads, "Matthew James Whitaker, son of lead computer scientist Michael Whitaker. Died of cancer at age eleven." She peers at me over her glasses. "Six months after your departure."

On the recording, Whitaker sits in front of the camera, tears streaming down his deeply lined face. Uniformed officers stand on each side of him and Commander Cook stands with his back to the camera, arms folded.

"It worked," Whitaker says, unable to conceal a smile.

It all happened within a matter of hours after Natasha and I talked. Ninety-year-old Dr. Michael Whitaker was arrested for treason for sabotaging the mission. The other Natasha made sure they sent me the footage of Whitaker's confession upon his arrest. I watched as he broke into tears when he explained how the week before takeoff to Alpha Centauri he'd sneaked his lab equipment home to his young son for the scans. How after I was shut off he added the additional upload to the probe, figuring all he had to do was avoid being caught for the few hours before takeoff and then it'd be too late to do anything about it.

I study his face on the video and see how after all these years the wounds of his child's death haven't left him. He looks at the camera, seemingly at me. His voice falters as he says, "I gave him the stars."

I get a ping from Mission Control and pause the video.

My visual feed kicks in and Commander Cook and Dr. Najim stand behind the other Natasha, who sits in one of the leather chairs. All three smile.

"We have good news," Commander Cook says. "We think we can fix you without a complete wipe."

I send a wary smile to my androgynous avatar.

He puts a hand on the elderly Natasha's shoulder, as if he wants the next bit of information coming from her.

She clears her throat. "Your mind-construct wasn't designed for an additional upload. It doesn't know where *you* end and *it* begins."

I nod.

She smiles reassuringly. "The computer scientists believe they can restore you from your backup. You'll have no memory past prepping for takeoff, but I think you'll be happy to have these dark days behind you." She leans forward. "If you give Mission Control access, they can scrub the unauthorized upload."

She just called the consciousness of a little boy an unauthorized upload, and recommends I let them kill him so I don't have to deal with him anymore. I study her face, trying to picture me being her. I can't do it. I update my avatar back to my old self, the young version with the beautiful brown braids. Cook, Najim, and the old Natasha brighten, obviously thinking I'm on board with the proposal. My avatar gives the three of them a disgusted look.

And flips them the bird.

This time I seek out the shadows. Instead of darkness, I end up in sunlight. The airfield is as it was the day we visited, same light breeze, same roaring jets, but it's not my memory. My parents are gone and

Matthew James stands by himself, his white-blond hair falling into his eyes and a toy airplane clutched to his chest.

He squints at me in the bright sunlight and smiles. For the first time I see he has dimples. "You came," he says.

He seems shorter now because I'm at my full adult height. I feel like myself again.

"Can I talk to you?" I ask.

He nods and an airplane flies overhead. He looks up and grins back at me, cocking his head toward the plane and raising his eyebrows in delight.

"Do you know who I am?"

"You're Natasha," he says, his voice stronger than I'd expect from a little kid. "My dad wanted you to take care of me."

"I guess you could say that."

"Are we trapped up in space?"

"No. We're exactly where we're supposed to be."

"I don't like little places."

"It's not little here," I say, squinting up at the sky.

"But we aren't here," he says. "This isn't real."

"You're a smart kid." I study him for a moment as he watches the takeoffs. "Big fan of airplanes, huh?"

He nods. "And flying. When I get big enough Dad says he'll take me hang-gliding." He doesn't give me a chance to respond before he frowns and tosses his toy plane to his feet. "I heard that old lady. I know I'm dead."

"You're no more dead than me." I reach out my hand. "Want to help me explore Goldilocks?"

The metal shell that has encapsulated us for decades creaks open and a slit of light expands to the entire brilliant blue sky. Our six-foot-tall robotic probe uncurls and we stand upright. The tingly itching of our sensors fades away to processing the real input of a cool sixteen-degree-Celsius breeze with the warmth of Alpha Centauri B warming our gray synthetic skin. My processors translate the chemicals to smells as they were trained to do back home—earthy dirt, grassy and something pungent-sweet I can't place, but that my chemical analysis translates as carbon-rich. The rolling landscape is filled with high grass swaying in the wind like a purple ocean.

We didn't need Mission Control's authorization to land the ship, but they gave it to us anyway. Now that I know Matthew James is there, the extra noise in my processes make sense. He's less scared now, which helps our underlying feeling of panic, but it doesn't make up for everything. We spent two days getting to know each other and teaching our mind-construct how to deal with two uploads. At our processing speeds we had the malfunctions under control within hours.

We reach down and collect a sample of the candy-colored grass to analyze later.

Back at Mission Control, Commander Cook watches us explore our alien world, brow furrowed. "Remember your protocol, sample collection should wait until after all your systems are online."

"They're online already," I tell him. My avatar—back to her old self—stands beside the Matthew James avatar on the Mission Control screen.

His blond hair falls into his avatar's eyes just as it did in life. "We're the pinnacle of scientific advancement for our time," he says, borrowing a line from a marketing video in my memory banks.

Cook almost cracks a smile.

A month after our landing we walk over squishy orange moss to the edge of a four-thousand-foot cliff and see the ocean far in the distance. Below us is a valley of plant-covered rock formations filled with fins and spires like a massive purple castle.

One part of us imagines that exploring it will be like a giant jungle maze with imaginary pirates and dragons, while the other is already working on a theory that it'll provide a shelter base for a human settlement, perhaps even a city one day.

"Valley survey commencing," I tell Mission Control and Matthew James's excitement zings through us as he realizes the plan.

Mission Control pipes in. "But, how—? No, no, no, no, no. Your flight ability is for emergency use only. Find another way down."

We leap and extend our sails, catching an updraft. Forty-two thousand useless sensors light up so it *almost* feels like the wind is hitting real skin. The "oh-man-this-is-so-blasting-awesome" part of us gets guidance from the "let's-be-sure-we-land-safe" part.

And we fly.

—◆—

K.B. Rylander spends way too much time thinking up odd questions and tracking down the answers. When she's not writing, you can find her sipping fine bourbon or playing Lego with her kids, though hopefully not at the same time. She writes science fiction, fantasy, and young adult fiction, works in the beer and whiskey industry, speaks a decent amount of Swedish, is terrible at Scrabble, but plays a mean game of chess.

DEAR AMMI

by Aimee Ogden

Two people fighting over the same piece of asteroid real estate isn't new in science fiction, but the women in Aimee's story "Dear Ammi" bring the struggle into stark focus, with a seldom seen degree of gritty realism. Their reasons for being on that rock are as ancient as humanity and while they seem quite different in the beginning, they soon learn they are more similar than they thought.

NICO LOVED THE DARKNESS best of all, and the darkness loved her back.

For most of her fellow miners, the ones chattering over the short-range comm when their asteroids passed within range, getting back to their Pods at the end of the day's work was a relief. To Nico, it was a chore. The Pod was bright, while the only lights in the Digger were its twin headlamps and the dim glow of the console and the occasional flicker from the ion shield that wrapped her Pod and the active dig site in a protective shell. The Pod had three rooms (four if you counted the airlock); the Digger was as big as the Pod, of course, but it fit so snugly around Nico's body that it hardly seemed to be there at all. And the soft machine hum of the Pod wasn't enough to replace the constant roar of the Digger, the comforting white noise of Nico's day.

Lights flickered on as the airlock constricted behind Nico's back.

Already it was overwhelmingly bright, overwhelmingly silent in the Pod. Nico's eyes narrowed, her shoulders hunched. She pulled off her helmet and turned to put it in its locker.

A gauntleted fist clipped her on the chin.

Thanks to the asteroid's microgravity, she went sailing gently across the Pod instead of landing a sprawling heap at her attacker's feet. She scrambled up—too fast. Her feet left the ground and her head crashed into the ceiling. Doing the attacker's work for him—no good. She scrabbled at the floor plate when she came back down, and prized up one of the panels just as the attacker came at her a second time. The panel connected solidly with the stranger's faceplate. Nico's arm reverberated with the impact, and the intruder sailed gently across the Pod.

"Fuck," said the attacker, in a high clear voice, just as she settled onto the ground. Not a man, a woman. Young—early twenties, if she wasn't modded. "You cracked my faceplate, kutti!"

"Zio!" Nico shouted. "Send an SOS to Alpha Outpost!" The intruder's foot lanced out between Nico's feet, and then it was Nico's turn to drift gently to the floor with her feet over her head.

The AI pinged softly. "I'm sorry, Nico, but communication with the Outpost is unavailable right now."

"What?" The intruder was on Nico again before she settled, driving her into the wall at full force. All the wind blasted out of Nico's lungs in one great huff, and this time when she floated down to the floor she did it while whooping for breath. Zio repeated his polite error message.

"Can it, Corps Bore. I disabled the communications array on my way in." The intruder wrenched Nico's arms, still encased in her vac suit, behind her back. The movement made it even harder for Nico to catch her breath, but the intruder didn't seem to pay much mind as she secured Nico's arms together with a stretch of silver tape. Nico strained against the bonds, but found her arms thoroughly leashed to the wall behind her with one last length of tape.

"There we go," said the intruder, coming around in front of Nico. Nico guessed at accent; English, probably, or Australian at the outside. Dark skinned, but ashy—people got that way after a long time in space. An old make of helmet, now with a spider-web crack covering one side of the faceplate. The vac suit itself comprised at least three different models: the green gauntlets of a Chinese military uniform (with bonus brass knuckles added on), the once-white pants of some Engineering Corps castoffs, the torso and arms some sort of nameless civilian gray. A thick layer of sealant had been painted around the wrists of the suit, where the incompatible gauntlets and bodysuit wouldn't join together without help. "How you feeling, kutti? Got your wind back yet?"

"You Indy fuck-bucket," Nico spat. Inside her splintered helmet, the girl grinned. She had grass-green bangs hanging over one eye; the rest of her black hair was buzzed short like Nico's. Four studs decorated the cartilage in the ear that Nico could see, all of them thoroughly blooded—that was why the Corps of Engineers had a piercing ban. Her grassy fringe of bangs didn't quite conceal the star tattoo over her left eye. There was nothing military about her: She was sheer vac-suited chaos. "How did you get in here?"

The intruder laughed. "Are you kidding? Corps computers are so bug riddled it's not even funny." She shuffled across the Pod and into Nico's storage unit. "Actually, yeah, it's pretty funny. My name's Madhuja—what'll I call you? Besides kutti, I mean."

"Fuck you."

"Okay, Junior Technician Nicola Ramírez." Madhuja leaned back into the central part of the Pod, waving one of Nico's storage boxes in both hands. "You know your name and rank are stamped on, like, everything here—right?"

Nico lunged toward her, but only bounced at the end of her leash. "Get out of my stuff!" Could she get the tape closer to the multitool on her belt? Maybe she could cut through the tape yet.

"Relax, kutti, I'm not eating your Twinkies." Nico strained to see around the door into storage, but couldn't get far enough. Indies often carried splodes with them; was Madhuja booby-trapping the place for after she'd made whatever getaway she had planned? "Not yet, anyway. You hungry? Need me to fetch you some nosh?"

"I don't need anything from you, Leech. I know what you are."

A storage bin banged into place. "Yeah, because I told you. I'm Madhuja, ta-fuckin'-da."

"Where did you crash your offloader?"

A sudden stillness from the storage room. Sure, there were others this far out: the Kuiper research stations, the gas miners passing back and forth from Earth to Saturn and Uranus, even civilian mining operatives. Accidents happened to them too, but they wouldn't have showed up on Nico's doorstep covered in mismatched uniforms and piercings. The Independents, though . . . A ridiculous name for such an organization. There was nothing "independent" about them. Their short-range offloaders cruised the belt for sites already opened by Corps engineers or civilian ones, then swooped in to poach while miners were off duty. Not technically illegal, not with the sorry state of asteroid-belt claims. But a pain in the ass anyway. Nico had never been targeted by Leeches before, but the Corps had only redeployed her Pod here three weeks ago, after she'd depleted her last site. Leeches loved fresh sites.

"Yeah," said Nico, into the silence. "That's what I thought."

"Aw. You think I'm shite? That cuts real deep, kutti." Madhuja emerged from the storage unit with a medikit in hand and plopped into Nico's chair. She popped off her busted helmet and kicked it across the floor; it drifted gently to a rest beside Nico's bedroll. The entire rest of her spacesuit followed; Madhuja shimmied out of it like a caterpillar that had changed its mind and squirmed back out of the cocoon. It too floated across the room and came to an unsettling rest draped across Nico's bed with its arms and legs akimbo.

Meanwhile, Madhuja rooted through the tubes and pockets of the medikit. "Oh, come on," said Nico. She couldn't get the tape down to the multitool, but she thought she could saw it against the rough edge of the belt itself. "Offloaders don't come equipped with their own medikits?"

"Offloaders that belong to rich fuckers, maybe." Underneath her vac suit, Madhuja was much skinnier than Nico would have guessed. Nico could almost have counted her ribs through her ratty tank top; she could see the tiny red bruises across both shoulders that must have been the result of the offloader crash. Despite her state of dress, Madhuja had sweat beading her upper lip—what did she have to be nervous about? She had Nico dead to rights. "I look rich to you, kutti?"

"What you look like is a skeleton." The tape found the rough patch on the belt, and Nico felt it begin to give way—but painfully slowly. "Maybe you *should* have eaten my Twinkies."

"Yeah?" Madhuja had shaken out a cocktail of painkillers into the palm of her hand. "I think I found something here that runs more to my tastes." She tossed them into her mouth, and swallowed them dry, though her face contorted with the effort. "And that I won't puke right back up."

Nausea? Nico could use that. Maybe she wouldn't even have to fight the Leech, just let the concussion work itself out. "You hit your head in the crash?"

Madhuja pulled a moue. "Aww, you worried about me, kutti?" She patted her waist and swung her hips from side to side. "Just maintaining my girlish figure."

"Have you ever seen puke in microgravity? I don't need that flying around my house."

Madhuja crammed the rest of the medikit into a space in the console. "This? This isn't a home, it's a barracks. A tiny, shitty barracks." She jerked a thumb at the door. "My offloader? It wasn't any bigger than this, but it was my home, mate." She pursed her lips, then stood. "Speaking of which . . . hey, computer, how do we pack this thing up and get out of here?"

"Unknown request," said Zio. Sometimes Nico thought she heard just an edge of sarcasm in that tinny voice. Just wishful thinking, probably, but she liked it. "Unauthorized recipient. Nico?"

"Absolutely do not pack up the Pod, Zio. We're staying put." Until Outpost Security gets here to take out the trash, she didn't add out loud. Where did this stupid Leech get the idea that she deserved Nico's Pod for the wonderful achievement of pulverizing her own vessel? Only an Indy could be so selfish. Nico had heard of them before she enlisted—she'd gone to school with a boy who'd run off to join the Indies for whatever riches and glory lay on the other side of a career of looting. But her mother had raised her right, and when there wasn't enough at home for Nico to justify staying there any longer, she'd found an honest way to make a living. To send money home for Mamá and the boys, even. And all this so someone else could just swoop in and take it the easy way?

No. No way in hell, not while people were counting on Nico. Outpost Command and her family both. She found new vigor as she rubbed her wrist against her belt.

"What the fuck ever," Madhuja said. She got down on hands and knees with a grunt, and began crawling beneath the computer console, the screened one where Nico could watch videos from Earth or pick up visual communication from Outpost: updates, new training, fresh orders. "There's always a manual option. I'll figure it out."

There was a manual option, but it was biometrically linked to Nico. Of course, if Madhuja had hacked the door, she might well do the same again. Unless Nico stopped her.

Nico paused in sawing at the tape as Madhuja backed out from under the console and stood. She staggered once, and caught herself on the back of Nico's chair. Nico watched through lidded eyes as she swayed and steadied herself. "Feeling okay?" she asked.

"Don't get your hopes up, kutti." Madhuja turned to her. Her lips were cracked, though not bleeding. Her offloader must not have had the conditioned air that Nico's pod did. Good, Nico thought. She wished a lot worse than chapped lips on Madhuja.

"It's not hope. It's happening." Nico's hands were working again. How much longer? "I've seen concussions before. I just have to wait you out."

"Yeah?" said Madhuja. Her voice brittle suddenly, like the spider-webbed glass in her faceplate. From behind her back, she produced a gun. Not one of the fancy flechette guns that the armed Corps guards carried, just an old-fashioned handgun. One leveled at Nico's forehead. "And what if I get tired of you waiting for me to drop? If I just plug two bullets in you right now?"

"My brothers," said Nico, and her breath caught in her throat before she could finish the thought.

She stared at Madhuja, at the fingers wrapped around the gray gun, at the steady wrist, the straight arm. Madhuja, in turn, stared at her. Finally the gun dropped, made a soft sound against her thigh. "Fuck," she said, then flopped into Nico's chair. "It's not a concussion, kutti, I promise. Just a touch of leukemia, nothing to get your knickers bunched over."

The word punched Nico in the chest. The ashy skin, the little bruises. The fatigue. Blood cancer. "You're sick?" she asked, inanely. Her hands started working at the tape again, because they didn't know what else to do.

"Terminal," agreed Madhuja. Microgravity amplified her swagger as she pushed up out of Nico's chair and resumed her search, this time in the space where Nico's bedroll was. "You think I come out here for my health? No ion shield on an offloader, kutti.

Live hard, die young . . ." She upended the bedroll, which drifted across the Pod like a lumpy magic carpet. "And send some fuckin' money home before you do."

Behind Nico, the tape snapped.

Madhuja spun, one hand going for the gun. Nico brought her hands up, a pointless defensive gesture. Or one of surrender, she wasn't quite sure.

And the entire Pod shuddered.

"Shit!" Fatigue or not, Madhuja cleared the Pod in one great leap and landed beside the console. "Where's the camera? I got to see what's out there. Gimme it!"

Nico barely kept her footing in the wake of the tremors. Too much was happening for her to think, and it had been so long since she'd had to think at all. Wake up, check on the Pod and the Digger, go out and dig, come home, watch a movie, go to sleep. Should she prevent Madhuja from looking outside, keep her one step farther from what she wanted? Should she ignore whatever the hell had sent aftershocks through the asteroid under her feet? She made a choice. "Zio," she said, and braced her free hand against the wall. "Show us."

The monitor flickered to life, briefly flashing on the romantic drama Nico had paused last night at lights-out, before a starfield darkened the screen. The camera on the outside of the Pod tracked automatically, and centered and zoomed on a particular section of the field. All Nico saw at first was stars, but Madhuja's grunt of recognition made her approach for a closer look. There was a small flash of light from the center of the field—just before the deck tilted under her feet once more. This time, she hung on to the console to keep from pitching forward. Now she could see the dark, blocky shape where the light-flash had originated. "What is *that*?"

"That," said Madhuja, with grim satisfaction, "is a Viper." She shrugged when Nico gaped at her. Vipers were Indy enforcer ships, meant to blast their way through blockades or provide the firepower for fast raids on Corps outposts. What was one doing shooting at Nico's Pod? "Hey, good news is there's only one. Other one must have busted up in the thicket. Ha!"

Nico grasped the console with both hands. She could feel tears in her eyes, and blinked furiously to clear them. She wasn't going to let Madhuja see her crying like a baby miner on her first rock. "You brought Vipers here? You're going to get me killed!" A thought struck her. "Turn the comm array back on and we can signal the Outpost for help."

"Nah," said Madhuja, and elbowed Nico out of the way to spin the console over to herself. "First of all, I didn't actually disable your comm. I just crashed into it. Sorry!" She held up a hand and started talking faster to forestall Nico's outrage. One finger jabbed in the direction of the Viper; the patch of blocked starlight had grown larger on the screen. "Second, it's not like your pals at the outpost are getting here in time to save our sorry asses from that thing. And third off, the shelling is just them trying to scare us. They're not gonna blow atmo on us, though. If I'm dead I can't tell 'em where I sold that platinum lode I poached, right?" She squinted at the screen, her tongue protruding between her teeth. "They'll force their way into the airlock. This is going down with guns, not missiles."

"Is that supposed to make me feel better?" Nico asked, and her voice cracked on the last word.

Madhuja looked up from the screen. Nico expected a sarcastic retort, some dire predictions about firing a sidearm in a pressurized Pod. But Madhuja's brows drew in tight together, and she asked, "You got family back on Earth, Nicola?"

Madhuja's words from earlier echoed back to Nico. She broke eye contact, glared at the screen. "You think I'm out here for my health?"

Madhuja ducked her head, huffed a laugh. "Okay, yeah, stupid question. Little sister? Brother? Got a mom and dad yet?"

"Just my mom." Nico dragged her arm across her eyes. "And two younger brothers. They're in high school right now."

"Uh-huh. And Mama Ramírez wants them to grow up to be big strong Corps Bores just like Big Sis, I bet?"

Nico thought of Alex's underage drinking citation and the time Anthony had been planning to hold up a convenience store. He hadn't gotten caught, except by Mamá. Mamá hadn't told Nico, but Alex had let it slip in the vid message he'd sent at Nico's last birthday. "Probably wouldn't be the worst thing that could happen to them." Madhuja snorted. "What about you?"

"One sister. Just a kid still. But so smart, I mean, shit." Madhuja's shoulders pulled back, stretched wide under the weight of the pride they carried. "I'm not stupid or anything, but her? She'll *be* someone, you know? Like, a rocket scientist or a doctor." A laugh. "Cure leukemia or some shit, I don't know."

"Why aren't you in the Corps?" The question burst past Nico's lips. There was health care, maybe not the kind that cured cancer, but better than no ion shield and people shooting at you all the time. "A couple of years without piercings would've killed you?" Those were the wrong words, and Nico knew it as soon as they'd flown out of her mouth. Back home, at the recruiting station, she'd seen a half dozen other teachers' kids lined up. None of the school board's broods were out here carving up space rocks. But at least there'd been the option.

Madhuja's mouth twisted, but her voice was soft. "Ha, no, kutti, I know what kind of death's got my name on it." Madhuja mimed blowing her own brains out with one finger. "Didn't even try for admission. Your guys don't send recruiters to my side of the pond, you know." Her voice hardened. "Besides, only a couple of years to make some money, you got to go big. The Indies are my lottery ticket, kutti—you know how expensive med school is?"

"No." There had never been bigger dreams on Nico's radar than a Pod, a tour of duty, a pension.

A noisy exhalation from Madhuja. She jerked her head at the screen, where Nico could now make out some of the features of the approaching Viper in the dim starlight, the cold brightness of the so-distant sun. "Not long now. Listen, kutti, you stash yourself in storage, okay? It's me they're after, right, and you didn't nick anything—" Nico palmed her handgun again. "And you're not even armed. So, you go be a good little turtle, all right?"

Madhuja added a shove with her free hand, but Nico didn't move. For one thing, there wasn't much power behind the one-handed shove. For another, she was paralyzed by the vapor of an idea. If she moved, it would drift away like smoke. "You do all the maintenance on your own offloader," she said, and Madhuja grimaced.

"What the hell, kutti, you need a mechanics lesson *now*?"

"No," said Nico, and looked back at the screen. "But if you could divert some power from, I don't know, the lights in here, maybe the life support too, do you think you could amp up the ion shield enough to fuck with their computers when they come across?"

Madhuja stared at her, lips twisting. Nico flushed. "Shut up, okay? It was just a stupid idea."

"No," said Madhuja, "*you* shut up. I'm thinking." Her jaw worked, and she squinted into the empty space over Nico's shoulder. "They'll survive a landing at that height. Especially if they get their system back online before impact. But it'll fuck them up good, no lie." She slapped Nico on the shoulder. "Not bad for a Corps Bore. You gonna open up system access for me or what?"

Nico stayed out of Madhuja's way while she worked. She could do the bare minimum to keep her Pod and Digger up and running, but Corps miners just weren't expected to have the same level of down-and-dirty engineering knowledge that kept Indies alive. Her equipment was good, and for anything short of a catastrophic breach, Outpost wasn't too far away. Of course, catastrophes happened out here sometimes too. Just not often. Madhuja's Indy lottery ticket had long odds and a high cost to play, but a big payoff; Nico's ticket was a much surer bet that would never make her rich. Just comfortable, and safe. Safe enough.

She followed Madhuja's advice to get back into her helmet and seal up her vac suit; Madhuja did the same while waiting for her jury-rigged setup to reboot. "What are we going to do if they survive the crash and come in guns blazing?" Nico asked, and Madhuja grunted as she settled her spider-web-cracked helmet onto her shoulders and activated the seal. It held atmo, and they both breathed a sigh of relief.

"Kutti, anyone ever told you that you worry too much?"

They were both standing in front of the console when the Viper came across the ion shield. A faint blue glimmer ran down the length of the Viper when it hit—a discharge of static electricity, a gift from the ion shield to the Viper's hull. The engines stayed lit, but the controlled descent faltered. The heavier bow end of the ship, where the fuel tank lay beneath the ship's belly, pitched downward, caught in the light gravity field afforded by the asteroid. Madhuja sucked her teeth. "Maybe we'll get lucky and they'll blow on impact."

"I'll never be able to repair the comm array if it goes up in flames," said Nico.

"You'll never be able to repair it if you get a bullet between the eyes, kutti." The dim light of the screen waved on Madhuja's ashy face. Nico looked away.

They both felt the shudder of impact through the floor of the Pod.

There were no aftershocks though, no ex post facto explosion. Nico looked to Madhuja for instruction, but Madhuja just stared at the screen. "Fuck," she said, not angrily. Just tired. "Okay, kutti, hang tight. I'll be right back."

"What?" Nico cried, but Madhuja had flung herself across the Pod and into the airlock. It had already contracted by the time Nico could follow her—she banged one fist on the inner door and shouted for Madhuja. But of course, there was no response; the inside of the airlock would be full of vacuum by now.

And what to do when it finished cycling? She could follow Madhuja through the lock if she had to, but what then? Was this all some elaborate setup on the Leeches' part, to somehow enlist Nico's Pod in signaling a pickup? Crashing a friendly ship seemed a long way to go for a lift, but Nico had no idea what passed for common courtesy in Indy circles. She pushed off from the airlock and made her way back to the console to check out the outside video display, just in time to watch a small vac-suited figure pick its way out over the rocky landscape toward the Viper's landing site. By the time Madhuja reached the Viper, she was hardly more than a gray speck on the stream, and Nico watched the ship's airlock absorb her like a dark sponge.

Then nothing. Nico paced the length of the Pod—not nearly long enough to make for good pacing—while trying to think. Had Madhuja turned herself in to the Indies to spare Nico's life? Was she with them, planning an assault against the Pod? What could there be in Nico's little home worth selling her out for? Should Nico be planning a rescue mission, or a guerrilla attack?

She thought of her mother, and her two idiot brothers. How was she supposed to do right by them? And what would Mamá say now?

"Hey, kutti," chirped the short-range in Nico's suit, making her heart skip a beat. Madhuja's voice was out of breath, but clear as day.

"Madhuja?" Nico fumbled to open the channel on her end. "You all right over there?"

"I'm alive, right? I'm on the Viper's comm, not quite as shiny as your stuff, but beggars and choosers. I put a few bullets in the, what was it, Indy fuck-buckets?" Her laugh crackled the comm channel. "Coast is clear if you care to tag along. Or if you just want to loot their galley, I figure I owe you before I fix this thing up and take her out of here. For letting me crash at your place, you know."

"I'll be right there," said Nico, and the airlock was already cycling.

Madhuja closed the channel while Nico bounced over the rocky terrain toward the Viper—attending to the damage the ship had taken in its landing. But the airlock opened at Nico's request, and she ducked into the long, low corridor that ran up the core of the ship to the cockpit at the front. A body lay just inside the airlock, a bullet hole in the side of its helmet; another was crumpled at the foot of the ladder up into the pit. Nico shuddered.

The ship had vented its atmosphere, according to the readout in her suit; she left her helmet on as she stomped down the corridor and pulled herself up the waiting ladder. "Madhuja!" she called, pinging for an open channel, as she bounced up the last step into the dome. Madhuja was sitting in the pilot's chair, her back to Nico. She didn't react, her hands still on the console as Nico wriggled into the small space. "Hey, Madhuja, what are you looking at?"

Nico bent over Madhuja's shoulder to peek at the console. Nothing there, the screen was asleep. She looked back at Madhuja, whose face was not just ashy but icy white, whose faceplate was no longer laced with fine spider-web cracks but blown out completely.

The comm array on the Viper was still functional, short-range and long-range alike. Nico radioed the Outpost for assistance to recover the Viper wreck and to repair her own comm array. Madhuja's body she cleared away herself, and her Digger cut a deep, wide grave in the asteroid face. Far from the mineral deposits Nico was here to mine: Even in death Madhuja would never be surrounded by riches.

She left the plateless helmet on the floor next to her bed. She thought she should remember, that someone should. The Pod was still quiet and dark, but sometimes the helmet whispered its guilt when Nico tried to sleep. She still didn't move it, and after a few nights it kept quiet after lights-out.

It was three days after the crash and two days before the garrison arrived from the Outpost that Nico remembered Madhuja's time in storage.

She found what she was looking for in the box of freeze-dried potatoes and peas, and beamed it over to Zio right away. It wasn't video, like she'd expected, just raw text. Not in English, nor any alphabet Nico recognized, or knew how to pronounce. But Zio translated it for her automatically: *Dear Ammi, if you're reading this I'm already dead . . .*

At the end, two strings of numbers. A bank account and routing number? The message didn't say. Nico wondered how much ill-gotten Indy wealth lay hidden behind those digits. She wondered how many years of college it would pay for, whether it could manage the down payment for a better house, one out in the suburbs where the air was still clean. Cleaner.

She wondered how old Madhuja's sister was now.

Not fair, she thought, not fair. Not fair to plug away on this asteroid, and the next one, and the next one while an answer like this fell through her hands. So much money. Thirty pieces of silver, or thereabouts. Good job, Nico, you deserve it for committing manslaughter.

But there was nothing fair about burial in an asteroid field, either. Only a piece of Viper wreckage to mark the place. Nothing just about suffocating fast instead of dying slow. Indy fuck-bucket, Nico thought. Damn Leech. Thief, burglar, swindler, crook.

"Zio," she said aloud, before she could change her mind. She turned her back on the console. "I've got a packet for Earth. Priority one, okay?"

Aimee Ogden is a former science teacher and software tester; now she writes about sad astronauts and angry princesses. She lives in Wisconsin with an old dog, three-year-old twins, and a very patient husband. Her stories have also appeared in *Apex, Shimmer, Cast of Wonders, The Sockdolager,* and *Daily Science Fiction.*

CITIZEN-ASTRONAUT

by David D. Levine

Unlike most of our contest winners, David has actually been to Mars! Well, actually he spent two weeks at the Mars Desert Research Station in 2010 and participated in a simulated Mars mission and the experience added a lot of realism to his story "Citizen-Astronaut." On a real Mars mission the crew will be too far from Earth to get help, and even advice on the radio will often be impractical due to the time lag, so, as during his time in the Utah desert, David says improvised solutions will be common. And those distant astronauts will not want their decisions second-guessed or ruled on by committee, so might not exactly share all the details. In some cases, like in this story, that could lead to unfortunate mistakes.

I WAS TRYING TO FIX my kitchen garbage disposal when my phone trilled. I put it on speaker. "Gary Shu," I said, wiping my hands on a rag.

"Mr. Shu, this is Nnamdi Okonkwo from UNSA." A low voice, cultured.

"UNSA? Really?" Why would anyone from the UN Space Agency be calling *me*? I was just a second-string newsblogger.

"Really. This concerns your application for the Citizen-Astronaut Program."

187

"Oh, that." I'd made it as far as the semifinals, but when the finalists had been announced my name hadn't been on the list. That had been over a year ago. I picked up my screwdriver and resumed poking at the clog. "What about it?"

"You have probably heard the terrible news about Kim Yeun-ja."

"Yeah." She was the Korean painter who'd been selected as the first Citizen-Astronaut. Two weeks ago, less than two months before her scheduled launch, she'd broken her neck on a recreational hike in the Alps. She'd recover, but she wouldn't be up for a trip to Mars any time soon. A tragic story, and an excellent hook for a fundraising call. I kept trying to pry the whatever-it-was out of the disposal's blades.

"You are probably also aware of the difficulties we've been having with funding and public opinion." We'd had people on Mars continuously for over eight years now. The initial discoveries of water and life—frozen, subsurface water and fossils of microscopic, long-extinct life—had been newsworthy, but after that interest had declined steadily. And with declining public interest came a declining willingness by the UN's various governments to fund the ongoing mission.

"Uh-huh," I said, squinting down the disposal's throat. By now I was just waiting for the pitch so I could hang up on the guy in good conscience. "So what's the purpose of this call?"

"My superiors have decided that the loss of Ms. Kim provides an opportunity for us to . . . reprioritize the Citizen-Astronaut Program. Rather than call on Ms. Kim's backup, we have been instructed to bring in someone who is in a better position to influence public opinion. Someone such as yourself."

The screwdriver clattered to the floor. "Guh?" I managed.

"Can you come to Geneva right away?"

"Uh?" I swallowed. "Uh, for how long?"

He chuckled. "In Geneva? Thirty-seven days. But after that it might be quite a bit longer . . ."

Thirty-seven days? I checked my phone's calendar.

Thirty-seven days was the time until the Kasei 18 spacecraft launched for Mars.

The sixty-five-day voyage to Mars was about as exciting as a long bus trip, bracketed by the thundering, shuddering terrors of launch and aerobraking. Though I did what I could to make the trip interesting to my viewers, my ratings dropped steadily the whole time. I was handicapped by limited bandwidth—I couldn't embed even a single Spin or Jumbo3D frame in my reports, and was reduced to plain text and flat, still images—and by the fact that every day was the same. Although we were going almost two hundred thousand kilometers per hour, from inside the ship there was no way to tell we were moving at all.

But as I lay on my back after touchdown, heart pounding and sweat pooling in the small of my space-suited back, I knew everything had changed. I was *on Mars*! I couldn't wait to step out of the lander, to see the endless red desert spread out before me, to feel the dry, lifeless dust crunch under my boots.

The exit protocol was one of the things we'd had plenty of time to negotiate during the long trip out. The commander of our craft, the American-born Flemish climatologist Lynne Ann Morse, had graciously ceded her commander's prerogative to me as Citizen-Astronaut. I would be the first one out of the lander: the sixty-seventh person to set foot on Mars.

But before I could even unstrap myself, the hatch clanged open and Nam Dae-jung's scratched helmet poked in. I recognized his face immediately—he was one of the three members of the current crew who would be staying on, and with our arrival he was now commander of Expedition 18. A Korean geochemist, he was a small man, built like a fireplug, and his face was just about as red as one. "Get your butts out here," he shouted. "We've got a leak."

We four new arrivals got ourselves unstrapped and tumbled out of the hatch as quickly as we could, bouncing and stumbling in our haste. We immediately saw the problem: A pipe on the lander's underside had split open, and a white jet of steam and ice crystals was spewing out into the thin Martian atmosphere. Frost was already building up around the gap. I activated the camera in my helmet and began snapping pictures of the dramatic scene for my blog. Finally some excitement!

"That's just water," said Kabir Abuja, our Nigerian engineer, and scuttled to the back of the lander where the main valve panel was located. A moment later the stream of vapor cut off.

Kabir, Lynne Ann, and Dae-jung ducked under the lander to inspect the damage. I joined them, mindful of the descent engine's bell-shaped nozzle, which was still nearly red hot.

I saw a dusty red streak leading up to the damaged pipe. "Look at that," I said, pointing. "Looks like a rock got kicked up by the descent engine." I took pictures of that too.

"Easily repaired," said Kabir, and started backing out of the confined space. "It's only water anyway. No shortage of that." Even through his faceplate I could see the confident smile that almost never left his dark handsome face.

We'd brought a stock of liquid hydrogen and a cunning little chemical plant that would combine it with carbon dioxide from Mars's atmosphere to produce the methane rocket fuel we'd eventually use to leave the planet. This chemical process threw off water as a byproduct, some of which was cracked into oxygen and more hydrogen.

"Don't be so sure," said Dae-jung.

We all looked at him. My breath was loud in my helmet, which was beginning to fog up.

Dae-jung looked right back at us, his flat face defiant. "We've been having some plumbing problems."

Lynne Ann stepped up to him, their faceplates practically touching. "There was nothing about that in the daily reports."

Dae-jung turned away from her. "There are things we don't tell Mission Control. Come on now, let's get you unloaded. We've only got a few hours of daylight left."

While Kabir and Suma Handini, the current crew's Pakistani engineer, set up the insulated hoses to pipe our hydrogen into the habitat's buried tanks, the rest of us set up a bucket brigade to transfer the tonnes of food and other supplies from the lander's cargo bay. Our lander had set down right between the current crew's four-person lander and the two-person emergency ascent vehicle, less than fifty meters from the hab, and the boxes and canisters weighed only a third what they would on Earth, but their mass was unchanged so it was still a lot of work to move them around. By the time we got everything shifted, my space-adapted muscles were screaming with fatigue. "Why do we have to get all this stuff inside so quickly anyway?" I asked Li Huang, the current crew's Chinese climatologist, as we struggled with a case of dehydrated meats. "It was fine in hard vacuum for the last two months."

"They used to leave everything in the landers," he said, "to save space in the hab. But a couple of expeditions ago a lander fell over right after landing, and all the supplies were inaccessible until they could get it jacked up again."

"The lander fell *over*?!"

"Subsidence under the landing pad, I think it was."

That hadn't been in the official reports either.

We got everything shifted inside, took off and stowed our suits, and gathered in the wardroom. This half-circular room, eight meters in diameter, took up half of Deck 2 of the cylindrical hab. The largest enclosed space on Mars, it would serve as our meeting room, work room, dining room, and living room. It had one long table and with ten people seated around it we were all bumping elbows. We knew we'd have to get used to the crowding, though, as it wasn't going to change for the next 107 days.

Each new ship from Earth brought four new crew. The usual procedure was that four of the old crew would depart almost immediately, leaving a crew of six: four new crew members, and two experienced ones to provide continuity. But the inexorable mathematics of orbital mechanics dictated that on this particular rotation the old crew could not depart until 107 days after the new crew had arrived. This 107-day period, long for a turnaround but short for an expedition, was my personal territory—I had arrived with the new crew and would be departing with the old crew. Until then, ten people would have to share a space designed for six.

The ten of us introduced ourselves around the table—purely for etiquette's sake, of course, as we were all familiar with each other's dossiers. When it came to me, I told them how much I looked forward to posting my first blog from the surface of Mars, and showed off some of the exciting photos I'd gotten after the landing.

"You can't post those," Dae-jung said.

I stared at him. "Doesn't the habitat have at least as much communications bandwidth as the ship?"

"Not bandwidth," he said, raising one finger. "Politics. We don't let the public know about small problems that don't seriously impact the mission." All of the current crew nodded their heads in agreement.

I wasn't happy about the situation, but rather than provoke a conflict in my first day on Mars, I acquiesced. That night I posted a blog about our aerobraking, descent, and landing, emphasizing the noise and vibration; it wasn't bad, but I really felt that it lacked something.

It wasn't until hours later, lying on my hard narrow bunk with a gluey rehydrated meal in my belly, that I realized I had no idea who had wound up being the sixty-seventh person to set foot on Mars.

The next day, once we had breakfasted and unpacked our few personal items into our tiny, Spartan quarters, we found out we had a lot to learn.

It turned out that all the training we had received before departure, and the manuals we had read on the trip out, were almost completely worthless. Just about every system in the habitat, from the surface suits to the sinks, had been repaired, modified, or updated. "Do not under any circumstances touch this button," Dae-jung said, pointing to the toilet's FLUSH button, which was crossed with an X of tape. He and the four new kids—as he called us—were all crammed into the habitat's one tiny bathroom. "We don't flush urine at all, and when it's time to flush feces you wash it down with one liter of gray water." On a shelf glued to the wall stood a scarred plastic pitcher, above which a tap hand-labeled GRAY WATER protruded from a hole that looked like it had been melted through the plastic wall with a soldering iron.

"What happens if we push the button?" Lynne Ann asked, quite reasonably.

"We call it the Blue Spew. And whoever pushes the button has to clean up the mess."

Kabir looked dubious. "So why don't you just disconnect it?"

Dae-jung gave a little smirk and pulled a panel off of the wall, revealing a disordered nest of variously colored wires, conduits, and pipes. It didn't look a thing like the tidy pictures in the training manuals. "The last time we tried it, we lost power in the kitchen for half a week. Best to leave well enough alone."

Despite the close quarters and hassles of the hab, I was excited by actually being on Mars after the boring months of travel. Just about every day I got to put on my surface suit and tromp around on the surface of Mars—*Mars!* Lifeless and airless though it might be, it had a desolate beauty to it; the low-gravity mineral formations were spectacular and their colors changed from hour to hour as the sun passed across the sky. We'd brought a supply of new weather balloons, ultralight hydrogen-filled spheres that carried tiny instrument packages high into Mars's thin atmosphere, and they brought back more great pictures and interesting scientific data. I supplemented the limited number of photographs I could post each day with text: moments of personal drama and exciting new findings in biology, climatology, paleontology, and geology. My blog's ratings started to climb.

You might think that science is inherently dull, but personally I was fascinated by the question of why Mars's climate had changed from hospitable to inhospitable all those millions of years ago. I agreed with Secretary-General Zirinowski, who'd declared over twenty years ago that only through study of our dead sister planet could we find a way to reverse the climate change that was threatening to kill our own. I was thrilled by the opportunity to share my enthusiasm with the public, and I think that passion came through in my blog.

We new kids made a lot of mistakes in our first few weeks in the habitat, though. Lynne Ann forgot to plug in her backpack after her first EVA, so the battery ran down overnight and she couldn't go out at all the next day. (We called our outings EVAs because the hab was, technically, a vehicle—the first crewed vehicle to land on Mars, in fact—even though it wasn't going anywhere anymore.) Audra Miskinis, our Lithuanian paleobiologist, was the first of us to do a Blue Spew, but all four of us made the same mistake at least once in the first two weeks. Even Kabir the engineer managed to mess up, damaging the pressurized rover's gearbox the first time he tried to shift it into reverse.

I managed not to break any of the hab's systems, but the error I made was much worse.

The day Kabir stripped the rover's gears, I was riding in the shotgun seat. When the horrendous grinding noise came vibrating through the rover's frame, we looked at each other in horror, but it soon became clear what had happened—the exact same kind of boneheaded mistake any teenaged driver might make with the family car. The necessary parts were just steps away in the hab, Kabir and I worked together to repair the damage, and by dinner that day the rover was again ready to go and we were both laughing our heads off at the whole incident. It made such a good story that I led off with it in my daily blog that evening, and I was still chuckling about it when my head hit the pillow.

Nobody was laughing the next morning, though. While we'd slept, my humorous blog story had turned into a political scandal. A US senator, one who'd been opposed to the Kasei program since its inception, had seized on the incident as yet another example of waste and mismanagement, with a racial slur for Kabir thrown in for good measure. Mission Control had managed to blunt the public-relations damage, but they were none too pleased with Kabir for breaking the rover or with me for mentioning it in my post.

Dae-jung's face was dark as a storm cloud when he came thundering into my narrow little room. "Give me one good reason not to shut you out of the network right now," he said through clenched teeth.

I looked him straight in the eye. "I was just doing my job!" I said. "I'm here to represent the average citizen and increase public interest in the mission. All I did was report a minor incident in a humorous way."

He didn't back down. "I *told* you there are things we don't share with Mission Control, never mind blabbing it all over the public nets! Your little blog has undone *years* of careful political maneuvering in the UNSA Council."

"It's not my fault some senator used my blog to grind his own well-worn axe!"

"It's your fault for not *thinking!*" He slammed his fist against the cracked plastic wall. "*Everything* we do is being analyzed by people who want to shoot us down, and we can't hand them any ammunition!"

I had to look away. He was right—I'd been foolish to forget about how many political enemies the program had. "I'll be more careful in the future."

"You'll be more than careful," Dae-jung said. "From now on, you will not mention *anything* in your blog that could cast this program in a negative light."

"Now wait just a—"

"I will review your blogs before they are posted."

"You can't do that!"

He straightened, and even though he was at least ten centimeters shorter, he managed to look down his nose at me. "I am the commander of this expedition," he said. "You will obey my orders or you will be subject to discipline."

"I'll go over your head!"

In reply he gave me a smug little grin. "I'm sure Mission Control will give your protests the full attention they deserve."

I matched his grin with a level stare, jaw clenched and breathing hard through my nose. But he had the authority, he had the administrative passwords, and I was as certain as he was that in case of a dispute our superiors would side with him. They were already upset with me, and insubordination wouldn't help my case. "All right," I said after I had gotten my temper under control, "I'll let you review my blogs. *For a while.*"

"We will see," was all he said. He shut the door behind himself, leaving me seething in my narrow little stall like an angry bull with no rider.

I came back to my quarters after a grueling geological EVA to find a blinking video-message indicator on my display. Even though I had red dust caked in every crease of my body, I played it right away—it wasn't often anyone back home cared enough to spend the money on sending a video all the way to Mars.

It was my agent. "I'll get right to the point," she said. "The syndicate isn't happy."

Of course they weren't. Dae-jung insisted that anything negative, controversial, or unprofessional—in other words, anything of interest to the average viewer—be removed from my blogs, and that the scientific content be accurate and complete. Thanks to his careful editing, my blogs had turned into the same snooze-inducing stream of technical bafflegab that all the non-Citizen Astronauts had produced before I'd come along. After almost two months of this, my ratings were in the toilet.

"They're giving you three weeks. If your ratings don't improve substantially by the fifteenth of next month, they're moving you off the front page."

I sighed and put my head in my hands. They couldn't drop me completely—I had a contract through the end of my mission—but if my blog didn't appear on the syndicate's front page my already-puny ratings would vanish off the bottom of the chart. I'd come home to a tiny paycheck and a smoking hole where my career used to be. I'd have to start over from scratch.

I sent my agent a text message reminding her of the censorship I was facing—not that it should be a surprise to her; I'd kept her in the loop all along—and promising that I'd do everything I could to make my blog more interesting. But after I'd sent the message I found myself sitting and staring disconsolately at the blank screen.

I'd said I would do everything I could. But I'd already tried everything I could think of, including arguing with both Dae-jung and Mission Control, and nothing had helped.

Just then came a knock on the door. It was Kabir. "Hey, can you give me a hand with something here?"

I was still grimy and exhausted from my EVA, as well as depressed, but I knew Kabir wouldn't ask for help unless he really needed it. "Yeah, sure," I said.

It was the electrical system again, of course.

The small nuclear plant on the other side of Bathtub Ridge provided more than enough power for our needs. But the omnipresent dust, ultraviolet light, and extreme temperatures made insulation crack, switches short, fuses blow, and backup batteries fail, adding up to a rickety mess that could barely meet our needs on a good day.

And today was not looking to be one of the good days. We'd lost power in half of Deck 2 and none of the usual tricks had brought it back.

Kabir's legs protruded from an access panel in the ceiling of Deck 1. "Try again," came his muffled voice.

I flipped the circuit breaker. It immediately tripped again. "Nope."

Kabir cursed and squirmed around, still looking for the short circuit. While he searched, I peered at the tangle of conduits leading upwards from the panel. I was trying to figure out where the problem wire came from and where it went, but they were all the same color and it was almost impossible to trace each one visually. "Hang on," I said.

"Mmph?"

I ran my eyes along the wire again. "That wire you're looking at isn't even connected to anything. It just loops around."

Kabir pulled his upper torso out of the access panel. His hair was filthy with red dust. "So where's the short?"

"I don't know, but . . ." If *that* wire was just a dead loop, then the short had to be on *this* one. I followed it away from the panel, peering closely as it snaked along where the wall met the floor.

Then something caught at the back of my throat. "Huh." I closed my eyes and sniffed.

Yep. Burnt insulation.

"Here it is."

"You're kidding."

"No. Look." I pulled the conduit away from the wall, revealing a blackened spot and exposed wires.

"How the hell . . . ?"

I smiled and tapped my nose.

Kabir shook his head in admiration.

Now that we'd found the short, fixing it only took about ten more minutes. Everyone cheered as the lights and fans came back on.

But what we'd learned disturbed me. "If that whole conduit is just a dead loop," I said, pointing, "that means the main and backup power systems are both routed through the main panel. Single point of failure."

Kabir shrugged. "Dae-jung told me the secondary panel blew out a couple years ago and they had to rewire it. But the systems are still completely separate . . . they're just in the same place."

I sighed. Just another one of those things we didn't tell Mission Control about. "It'll have to do, I guess. Let's get everything closed up."

After we finished, everyone who happened to be in the wardroom when we reported our achievement toasted us with tea, heated up with the newly restored power.

"Gary's got the Magic Nose," Kabir said.

I waved a hand dismissively. "I was the super of my apartment building for a few years in grad school. I didn't get a lot of sleep, but the rent was cheap. I never dreamed I'd be using those same skills on Mars!"

Just then Dae-jung came in, and we told him we'd fixed the electrical failure. He humphed and nodded. "Good work."

I decided to press my advantage, small though it was. "So can I blog about it?"

He stared at me across the scuffed plastic table, while Suma and Kabir and the others looked on. Finally he blinked. "Very well. But you must emphasize the solution, not the problem, and I will still review your work before submission."

"Of course," I said, and tried to be glad of the small victory. It wasn't much, but it was a small note of human interest that I could use to leaven the usual scientific blah-blah-blah.

It helped, but not as much as I'd hoped. Three weeks went by— twenty-one days, twenty-four-and-a-half hours each, filled with clambering over rocks in my sweaty space suit, sifting through endless samples looking for microfossils, and constant battles with balky, malfunctioning equipment—and though I emphasized the positive enough to get some of the interesting bits past Dae-jung, my ratings remained less than stellar.

At least I'd been able to make myself useful. After the incident of the Magic Nose I'd gradually taken over more and more of the small repair and maintenance tasks that took up so much of Kabir and Suma's time, leaving them free to perform some major system upgrades that had been put off for far too long. It wasn't how I'd planned to spend my time on Mars, but I found it more satisfying than working on blogs that I knew were going to get edited into mush and then ignored by most of my potential audience.

On Monday night, washing dishes after yet another bland rehydrated meal, I reflected that when I woke up I would probably find my blog pulled from the front page and my ratings reduced to the low single digits. "I'm going out for a walk," I said to Suma and Audra after I'd dried and put away the last plate.

Technically, we weren't supposed to go out on EVA alone, for safety's sake. But that rule had been relaxed to the point that you could go solo as long as you didn't get out of sight of the hab. I suited up, got Suma to check me out, and cycled out to the surface.

The thing about being on the surface of Mars is that it's *quiet*. I'd grown accustomed to the many sounds of the hab, from the whir of fans to the hammering thud of the water pump; in fact, I'd gotten to the point that I noticed immediately if the sound changed, indicating that something wasn't working the way it should. But out on the surface, even with the echo of my breath and the soft clack of valves in my helmet, I felt something relax in my neck and jaw and I realized just how badly I'd needed to get away from the constant barrage of noise.

It was dark out there, too. I climbed a slight rise a couple hundred meters from the hab, switched off my headlamp, and looked up at stars scattered thick as salt spilled on a dark tablecloth. Twinkling just slightly in the thin atmosphere, they burned bright against a background blacker than any on Earth. Even through my scuffed faceplate they were awe-inspiring.

Then, as I turned back to the hab, it struck me hard that the few dim lights that shone from its windows were the only lights on the entire planet. We were alone here, entirely alone, and farther from home than any human beings had ever been before.

That's when I saw the flash.

It was brief and silent, but quite bright, and for a moment afterwards I couldn't see anything at all. But then the stars gradually reappeared, and I realized what I was seeing . . . or, more to the point, what I wasn't seeing.

The hab's lights had gone out. There was nothing but blackness below the horizon.

"Hello?" I called. Suma was on comms duty.

No response came on the radio.

I switched to channel 8. "This is Gary, on EVA, to anyone in the hab. Do you copy?"

Nothing. Not even static. Digital comms give you perfection or nothing at all.

I stood blinking into the endless dark. Heart pounding. Waiting.

Communications on channel 8 were automatically routed to the main speakers. Everyone in the hab—every single human being on Mars—should have heard my call. If no one was responding . . .

I switched on my headlamp and headed down the slope toward the hab, moving in a tiny rust-colored ellipse of illuminated soil. My breath was very loud in my helmet and I had to remind myself to take it slow and careful. Tripping and cracking my helmet would only make the problem worse. Whatever it was.

When I got close enough to illuminate the hab with my headlamp, I couldn't see any damage. The lights were still out, but as I walked around to the side where the main airlock was I could see flashlights moving around inside. That simultaneously reassured me and deepened my fears—some people at least were still alive, but what kind of failure could knock out both the primary and backup power systems?

Then the answer appeared around the curve of the hull.

A big elliptical hole, two or three meters long and maybe half a meter wide, slashed diagonally across the hab's skin and part of the airlock door, ending in a fresh one-meter crater in the dirt. Meteorite strike.

Jets of gas spewed silently in several directions from the edges of the gash, showing where the meteorite's grazing path had cut through pipes carrying water, air, and other fluids and gases. Nothing came out of the gaping void in the middle of the hole, though, indicating that whatever compartments the damage had breached had already lost all their air.

Fighting down panic, I forced myself to focus on the problem at hand. Which compartments were behind the damaged sections of wall? The main airlock, of course, and the EVA prep room next to it. What was on the other side of the prep room's back wall?

Aw, crap. The engineering workroom.

No wonder the power was out. The damage cut right through the main power panel. Where the main and secondary systems came together.

Single point of failure.

As I tried to visualize the Deck 1 floor plan, I realized the problem was even worse than I'd thought. If the EVA prep room and engineering workroom had both lost pressure, anyone left alive inside would be cut off from both the main airlock and the engineering airlock—and those were where the space suits were stored.

The two upper decks were equipped with survival balls, airtight spheres that could keep one or two people alive for a few days. But once you crawled into one of those you were dependent on someone in a full-service space suit to fix the problem or haul you to safety.

And that came down to me.

I realized I was hyperventilating. I adjusted my air mix and bent down, hands on knees, until I got my breathing under control.

Okay. Priority one was to assess the situation. Did that. Priority two was to ensure my own safety, then that of others. Priority three was to prevent further damage, then initiate repairs.

I was in no immediate danger. My suit had power, air, and water for almost seven hours, though heavy physical activity would reduce that. How about the rest of the crew?

I peered up at the windows in Decks 2 and 3. Flashlights still moved there. At least two, maybe three, maybe more.

There were handheld radios in the same emergency kits as the flashlights. I called all the handheld frequencies but got no response. Why?

After I gave up on that, I stepped back and waved, but got no reaction—probably nobody was looking out the window at the moment. Even throwing small rocks at the windows didn't prompt a response.

Well, they'd be okay for a few hours at least. Even if there were nine survivors and they were restricted to the top deck, that was still over a hundred cubic meters of air. Without power that air would get cold and stale pretty quickly, but the gouts of steam from the meteorite scar had slowed and stopped—they weren't losing any more of it.

The situation was stable, but it wouldn't improve by itself. After one more radio call—still no response—I headed back to the hab to see what I could do.

The main airlock's outer door was too damaged to open.

The gash made by the meteorite was too narrow and ragged to risk slipping through.

The engineering airlock door, around the back of the hab, appeared undamaged but wouldn't open. I hauled at the handle but it simply refused to budge. I peered through the small porthole in the outer door with my headlamp. Nobody was in the airlock that I could see.

I stopped to think. If both airlock doors had been closed at the time of impact, and the engineering workroom was open to Mars's near-vacuum, then the engineering airlock would be an island of air between the vacuums of the exterior and the interior. That air was doing nobody any good, and preventing me from opening the door.

I pried open the emergency manual depressurization panel and opened the valve I found there. Air jetted out—I regretted the loss but couldn't think of an alternative—and soon the pressure was equalized; I was able to open the door with no problem.

A long, hard look through the porthole in the inner door showed nothing moving inside the hab. There wasn't any visible damage, though papers and other lightweight objects were scattered everywhere. After a reflexive check to make sure the outer door was shut—probably pointless, but by now it was a deeply ingrained habit—I tried the inner door. The handle moved easily, indicating no pressure differential, but the door itself met some kind of resistance.

I pushed against the resistance and felt something fall away with a soft thud that reverberated through my feet. With a sense of dread I pushed the door the rest of the way open and stepped through.

Oh God. It was Suma. She'd made it as far as the airlock door. Now she lay still, eyes open and blood-red, dark skin peppered with red blotches.

"I'm sorry," I said aloud. The sound of my own shaking voice in my helmet made hot tears spring to my eyes, but I blinked hard and tried to sniff them back. I had no way to wipe my eyes.

I checked out the rest of the lower deck as quickly as I could. All the airtight doors had sprung shut as the pressure dropped, but with the hole slashing across so many compartments there was no air on either side of any of them. The main power panel was as badly damaged as I'd feared. And in the EVA prep room I found Audra halfway into her suit. She'd managed to get the helmet on her head and the air turned on full, but it hadn't been enough.

Damn. Damn, damn, damn.

The only good news was that all eight remaining suits were in their racks and appeared undamaged.

Okay. Time to head upstairs.

The airtight hatch at the top of the ladder was sealed and wouldn't budge. That was good news—it meant there was pressure on the other side. But there was no window in that hatch and I still had no radio communication with the survivors for reasons unknown. I tried pounding on the hatch but got no response; even when I pressed the top of my helmet against the hatch I heard nothing. That didn't mean too much, though. The hatch was heavily padded on both sides—I myself had bashed my elbows and knees against it many times and welcomed the padding—so the sound might not be audible.

How to get them out, or get the suits to them, with no airlock? How to even let them know I was here and trying to help?

I clung to the ladder, breathing hard. The indicator on my wrist said I had enough air for another four hours at this rate. Damn.

Okay. Think, think.

From the top of the ladder I looked down, passing my headlamp beam over scattered papers and equipment and . . . oh God, Suma's body. I swallowed. Think. From the bottom of the ladder it was just ten or twelve steps to the engineering airlock and its emergency suits. Not far, but too far to walk in vacuum, and donning the suits would take much too long.

But still . . . it wasn't far to walk. In fact, it wasn't a very large space at all.

If I could force open the hatch, air would flood down from the upper deck. Shared between the upper and lower decks it would thin out dramatically, but might still support life, at least long enough to get to the suits and don them.

The claustrophobic tightness of the hab might save us all.

I scanned my headlamp around the space, considering my plan . . . but no, damn it, it wouldn't work. There was still a huge hole in the wall behind the damaged power panel.

I climbed down the ladder and examined the hole. It was about one and a half square meters all told, with ragged edges of torn metal and plastic. Heavy power cables and conduits crossed the gap, blocking easy access. Some of them might still be live.

How to seal it? Even temporarily?

We had expanding foam for small holes. This was far beyond what that could cover.

But we also had something else that expanded . . .

I let myself out through the engineering airlock and ran to the rover. The box still held six weather balloons. I grabbed three, just in case, put them in my thigh pockets, and ran back inside.

I put one of the folded packages on the floor about two meters from the damaged power panel and pulled the inflation tab. It inflated rapidly, and in less than a minute it had nearly filled the space, bulging out tautly between floor and ceiling.

It wasn't a clean seal by any means. The taut plastic film was tough, but far from immune to punctures. The balloon was full of potentially explosive hydrogen.

It would have to do.

I went to the EVA prep room and hauled all eight suits to the base of the ladder.

There was just one more thing to do.

I went back outside and flung a few rocks at the windows, then inflated another weather balloon. As it rose gently into the black sky I played a flashlight beam across it, hoping someone inside would notice.

It worked. A flashlight from one of the Deck 2 windows caught me in the eyes. Behind it I saw a waving hand. Still nothing on the radio, though. At least they knew I was here.

I ran back inside. I checked that the balloon was still in place. I made absolutely sure that every airtight door on the lower deck was closed and sealed. I climbed the ladder.

And then I put my shoulder against the hatch and pushed.

A hundred kilopascals of air pressure pushed back. It was like lifting a car. It was impossible. It didn't budge at all.

I pushed harder.

The plastic and metal of my suit's hard torso creaked as I put every bit of my strength into the effort. The edge of the neck ring bit painfully into my shoulder. I found myself grunting "Nnnnngh . . ." through gritted teeth.

I kept pushing.

A jet of air hissed across my helmet, letting me know I'd managed to open the hatch by just a crack. I was elated, but the pressure didn't let up at all. I kept pushing.

And then, just as I feared my trembling legs and back would give out altogether, I heard/felt a scraping noise in the hatch. I looked up and saw the scratched metal tip of a pry bar probing at the gap.

I took a deep breath, gathered my strength, and *heaved*.

The pry bar made it through the gap, caught, and began levering the hatch upward. The jet of air turned into a hard wind, then a wash like a waterfall as the press of the hatch on my shoulder lessened and then evaporated. The hatch swung back with a clang, revealing Kabir's smiling face.

I clung, shivering, to the ladder rungs. It was all I could do to just stay in one place as the air rushed past me. Soon everyone would be safe.

The flow slowed . . . slowed . . . and then, with a *whump*, it sped up again.

I looked down.

The weather balloon was gone. Only a few scraps of torn plastic fluttered in the gap where the air was rapidly escaping. The sharp edges of the hole had punctured the balloon.

I looked up. There were Kabir and Lynne Ann, hair whipping around their heads as they moved to close the hatch again.

If that hatch closed it would shut off all hope. I didn't have the strength to push it open again.

But I had one last weather balloon in my pocket.

I pulled the tab and, as the package began to inflate, lobbed it underhand toward the hole in the wall.

The growing wad of plastic and gas struck the hole and stuck. It inflated for a moment, like a kid blowing bubble gum . . . then suddenly deflated. It had been punctured.

But this time it was only half-inflated. The plastic was not stretched taut under pressure. It didn't tear.

The punctured balloon caught in the hole . . . and stuck like a glob of gum. It bellied out, away from me, growing more and more taut as the air from the upper deck filled the lower deck.

But it held. For now.

"Come on!" I shouted, clambering down the ladder, waving my arm to reinforce the words they probably couldn't hear through my helmet. "Get in your suits! Hurry!"

Down the ladder they came, Kabir and Lynne Ann and all the rest. I counted them as they passed me, joining the mob scrambling to find and don all the pieces of their suits in the crowded space. Four. Five. Six.

Only six. "Where's Dae-jung?" I asked Kabir over radio as soon as he sealed his helmet.

"Still upstairs," he gasped. "Fell down the ladder when the lights went out. Broke his leg."

We made a bucket brigade, passing Dae-jung's helmet and torso and boots and all the rest up onto Deck 2. It wasn't easy getting him into the suit with a broken leg, and it must have hurt like hell, but though his eyes clenched tight shut and his skin was pale and sweaty he didn't make a sound.

I dogged down his helmet and turned on his backpack for him. As soon as the suit's cool air hit his face, his eyes opened.

"Thank you," he said.

It took nearly three days to get the hole repaired and the pressure restored and the power back on. When we finally contacted Mission Control they tried to maintain their usual bureaucratic detachment but, reading between the lines, you could tell how frantic they'd been during the days of silence.

There were a lot of lessons to be learned. One, reroute the power systems to avoid a single point of failure. Two, store emergency suits on all decks. Three, deploy analog radios as a backup. Digital radios were great, but the hab's metal structure had blocked enough of the signal that they'd refused to communicate at all; the more primitive analog radios would provide at least some communication in situations of weak signal.

We buried our dead. We worked hard, eighteen and twenty hours a day, getting the hab functioning and stable. And we started to think about what we were going to do next.

Our launch window for return would open in ten days. We'd lost two people, including our most experienced engineer, and a lot of air and water and other resources. Even worse, public confidence in the whole mission had been shaken by the incident. Mission Control strongly recommended we use both landers to abandon the station and return all eight of us home. They'd try again soon with a more robust hab.

But we knew that "soon" for UNSA almost certainly meant "next decade" and might mean "never."

Defying Mission Control's recommendation, we decided we'd stay on Mars until the next crew arrived in six months, then reassess the hab's status. Mission Control didn't like it, but there was nothing they could do about it.

We knew we were taking a risk, but Kasei 19 was already on the launch pad, its crew trained and ready. If we managed to fix the hab and do good science under these circumstances, it would be a public relations triumph. Mission Control would have no choice but to continue the program.

But we couldn't all stay. Dae-jung's leg was too badly broken for him to work at all. He'd need surgery to walk again, the sooner the better. And getting the population of the hab down would make our narrowed resource margins a lot more comfortable.

In the end my own decision wasn't as hard as you might think.

"I'm staying," I blogged, "because I can't leave now. There's a lot of work to be done to get the hab back in full working order . . . more than Kabir could possibly do alone. I'm not a professional engineer but I know I can do the work. And humanity *needs* this program to succeed. We've made some amazing discoveries already, but there's far more to be learned from Mars. That's why Lynne Ann and Huang are staying as well—to keep the science going. Two engineers and two scientists isn't a full crew, but it's enough to keep the dream alive."

After that post my ratings shot through the roof.

Which was nice, but it wasn't really important anymore.

The four of us stood and saluted as the lander rose silently into the salmon-colored sky. But we returned to the hab before its vapor trail had cleared.

We had a lot to do.

David D. Levine is the author of the Andre Norton Award-winning novel *Arabella of Mars* (Tor, 2016), its sequel *Arabella and the Battle of Venus* (Tor, 2017), and over fifty SF and fantasy stories. His story "Tk'Tk'Tk" won the Hugo, and he has been shortlisted for awards including the Hugo, Nebula, Campbell, and Sturgeon. His stories have appeared in *Asimov's, Analog, The Magazine of Fantasy & Science Fiction, Tor.com*, numerous Year's Best anthologies, and his award-winning collection *Space Magic*.

GEMINI XVII

by Brad R. Torgersen

Many people may not know that McDonnell (who built the Mercury and Gemini spacecraft) designer Jim Chamberlin had a plan for getting astronauts to the moon using the Gemini capsule design. If something had happened to block or stall funding for additional Apollo development, it's possible that NASA could have (as a fallback) gone with a hybrid Gemini design, using an Agena mated to a Centaur stage for translunar injection and a single-man lunar lander. These plans obviously never got much beyond the back-of-the-envelope stage. But if the Bay of Pigs had been successful, and Kennedy had been forced to commit America to two land wars (Vietnam and Cuba) . . . well, there you have the seeds for a story. Throw in the Russian N-1 rocket (which might have worked, but didn't) plus two unlikely allies, a Russian cosmonaut and an American astronaut, being forced to work together to avert disaster, and you've got Brad's thriller wrapped in a science fiction setting wrapped in an alternate history.

VIC WAS OUTSIDE for twenty minutes when his maneuvering pack burst.

No warning. The damned thing just blew.

With the clamshell doors on the Gemini capsule hanging wide open, I saw it all: Vic floating against the gorgeous backdrop of the

Indian Ocean, clutching the drum-shaped pack to his chest—like an oversized accordion, his gloved fingers and thumbs occasionally touching the jet triggers on the opposed handles—then poof. The unit went up. I'm not sure if Vic ever knew what happened. There was an instant where I thought I saw a surprised expression on his face through the remains of his visor and pressure helmet, then the entire Gemini-Chiron assembly got physically yanked as Vic's suit reached the limit of its umbilical, which snapped taut.

I instinctively reached for the stick.

By the time I got things stabilized, Houston was screaming at me for a status report. All I could do was reel Vic back to the spacecraft, his body now limp in his deflated pressure suit. Getting him into his seat without his assistance was impossible, so I stood up in the hatch and turned him over. The explosion had shredded him. His exposed tissue was puffy and shot through with darkly engorged veins and arteries. The flight surgeon had always wondered what space-vacuum death would look like. I got lots of pictures, then sat back down in the capsule and spent several minutes trying very hard not to cry.

Losing a friend so suddenly was bad enough. But there were ramifications to this that went far beyond the mission.

Rob Lawrence would have understood.

Too bad he died when his F-104 went in at Edwards. The front-seater under Rob's tutelage had made a rookie mistake, or so I'd heard from the other instructors.

Now there was only me. I could still remember the President—in a wheelchair since that nut put a bullet in his spine and killed Governor Connally back in '63—shaking my hand and telling me how important I was to the program. He didn't say it at the time, but I think I was his way of extending black Americans a symbolic olive branch after Watts.

The only brown face in Group 3, tacked on two years late, as a replacement for Ted Freeman when he died.

Not that I was unused to that kind of isolation. Dr. King's dream was still a long, long ways from fruition. Inside NASA, people knew me. And the press had given me a degree of national exposure which embarrassed—Malachi Washington, the first Negro Astronaut!

But all blacks look alike to many white eyes, and I didn't have to go very far from Houston or the Cape to be treated like just another nigger. Same for my wife Cheney and our two daughters, which galled me to no end. Cheney's father was a prominent businessman in Chicago. She was educated. And I'd be damned if I expected her or the girls to put up with that shit, just so that we could all be close to my work.

So, they stayed close to her parents, with me being gone for months at a time. Not too different from when I was flying the F-8 off carrier decks for the Navy.

Vic's body floated lifelessly outside the hatch. I considered what might happen now. With Vic gone, they'd order me to abort. Then the questions would begin. And the blame. Oh, maybe not from the other pilots. Neil and Mike and Ed. Even Al and the original Seven were cool. They knew the score.

It was the whisper campaign in the bureaucracy that I feared. They'd maroon me on the ground, like poor Deke. Only worse. Deke didn't have the added pressure and expectation that came with being black. My failure was black America's failure. And how in the hell was I going to look Vic's wife Alice in the eye? She'd admitted before we went up that she had a funny feeling about this mission.

I kept my voice calm as I relayed information back and forth to the ground. I was shocked when Director Kraft himself got on the horn.

"We'll proceed," my boss told me in no uncertain terms.

"Sir?"

"Mal, the CIA liaison says the Soviets sent up one of their N1 boosters an hour ago. You know what that means."

"Yessir," I said. Kruschev wasn't kidding around. We'd known for months that the Russians were rushing to get a capsule to the moon before we did. Only, none of us thought they'd be ready to go *before* Gemini 17 had already splashed down.

I considered my dead friend. "What about Vic?"

"Since you can't get him back onboard, and since I really don't think you'd want to be sitting next to his body for the next eight days, you'll just have to cut Astronaut Hemshaw loose."

"Jesus. Does Alice know?"

"Not yet. We'll tell her."

"With just me to run the show, we'll have to chop a lot out of the itinerary."

"Agreed. Look, Mal, under better circumstances I'd order an abort. But with that Russian mission on the way, and how things are going with the two wars, and Congress chopping at our budget—"

"I get the picture," I said.

And it was true. In more ways than one.

So, three hours after the accident, I uncoupled Vic from the spacecraft and sent his body drifting slowly towards the Earth, and eventual reentry—a fiery end, like the Norse of old. I sent my copilot a mental farewell, closed his door, then mine, and set about trying to figure out how to get to the moon and back with just one man to watch all the instruments and flip all the switches.

By spacecraft standards, Gemini was an old horse. And if Kennedy's first Vice President had had his way, Gemini would have been just a pit stop en route to Apollo. But with the U.S. military heavily committed to Cuba and Vietnam, neither Congress nor the Senate were in any mood to green-light yet another expensive NASA development project. Johnson was forced to be satisfied with ops remaining in Houston, while McDonnell kept its coveted contract. They flew the first Gemini-Chiron flights not long after dispensing with the Agena series, so that by 1967 things were ramping up for the first manned American reconnaissance of lunar space.

Technically, Chiron was the wedding of Agena hardware to the more robust Centaur booster stage. Launched separately on Titan II rockets, the Gemini docked in low Earth orbit with the Chiron and used the Chiron's engines to break out of and insert into both Earth and lunar trajectories. And once McDonnell and Grumman ironed out their dispute over the proposed lunar lander design, Chiron would essentially be four separate spacecraft in one.

In the last eighteen months, I'd done nothing but eat, drink, and sleep Gemini-Chiron. If the President had been determined to keep his promise to land a man on the moon by the end of the decade, I'd been determined to be that man. Or at least one of the men. All other considerations aside.

The seat next to me was painfully empty, such that I found myself actually shying away from it, as much as the too-cramped confines of the capsule would allow. If this had been one of the actual landing flights planned for later in the year, I'd have had no choice but to abort, because without one man to stay in orbit while the other took the lander down to the surface, there would be no point.

But for this first circumlunar trip, one man would have to do, and there was plenty to keep me occupied in spite of how much Kraft and Co. sliced out of the schedule.

Still, Vic's absence was ever-presently painful, such that I quickly grew to hate it. We'd trained together—relentlessly—in preparation for this historic flight. In spite of watching the Soviet Union roll ahead with its mighty super-booster. In spite of Dr. Von Braun's forced retirement, on account of the absentee trial at the Hague. In spite of seeing the posted names of friends who had been killed or gone missing over the skies of Havana and Hanoi. Nothing had distracted us, and together we had made the circumlunar flight our co-religion.

By the time I slid into lunar orbit, the entire thing had begun to seem profoundly, stupidly empty. Vic was dead. They'd make him a hero no matter what happened now. Without him here to share the sweetness of victory, I took little comfort in the realization of our dream. Whether I myself got back to Earth or not, the headlines in the papers would continue to be crowded with news from the Long War against Communism, of which the Battle for the Moon was just that—a single battle. Symbolic, yes. Grand. But ultimately of little importance to the men scraping and fighting in the mud-filled ditches.

My orders called for me to take pictures, so I took them.

My orders also called for telemetry, so I took it, and sent it.

I was on my sixth circuit around the dayside, and getting ready for the breakout burn that would put me on course back to Earth, when the feeds to the Chiron died. At first puzzled, I reset the breakers, only to watch them barber-pole again. Then a third time. By the fourth try I was flipping the switches back and forth with such panic that I almost broke them clean out of the panel.

Without the bell-bottomed rockets on the Chiron, there was no way I'd be breaking lunar orbit now.

Hollowly, I reported my situation back to Houston, who had no doubt already become appraised of the situation via the Gemini's computer.

It took almost a quarter of an orbit before anyone on the ground had the nerve to respond. By which time I was screaming incoherent obscenities within the claustrophobic confines of the cabin.

"You'll have to go check it outside" was their only suggestion.

As if I didn't already have the cabin depressurized.

Vic's malfunctioning thruster pack had done more damage than I'd first noticed. There were pieces of it embedded in the Chiron down near the collar where the nose of the Gemini committed adultery with the business end of the booster. I couldn't see it, but I guessed that under the cowling some of those pieces had chewed partway into the wiring. Why the connection hadn't failed before now, I could not be sure. Suffice to say that there was absolutely no way of effecting a repair.

While the mission controllers on Earth went politely apeshit, I allowed myself to drift away from the joined space vehicles and examine the limb of the moon as I flew once again towards the nightside. How long had that gray, cratered landscape been waiting for the first person from Earth to see it up close? Mountains and valleys, great heaping plains of what looked like soft putty . . . Vic would have given a gonad to see this view, especially from outside the spacecraft. I hoped—somewhat vainly—that where Vic was, he was vicariously enjoying the show.

The nightside was black like no other blackness I've ever experienced. The stars away from the moon were bright, fixed, and perfect; silent suns all raging mightily in the far-off depths of the Milky Way. When I was a teenager, I used to sit out in the country at my uncle's place, just he and I and the humid Mississippi air. Not a city light for fifty miles. And never had we ever gotten a night sky as perfect or as magnificent as this.

I felt my throat close up as dawn on the far limb greeted me, and I orbited back into radio contact.

The monkey house in Houston could offer me little, save for additional promises that they were "Working the problem."

Bullshit. More likely they were working how to best couch the news to the rest of the nation that the circumlunar flight—had they even yet allowed it to get out that one astronaut had already died—was now a total disaster. Doubtless Kennedy would not take kindly to such news. He needed something positive for the American people, as he prepared to hand the country over to his old rival, Nixon.

Jack wanted his administration to go out on a high note, so that hopefully in four years Bobby could latch on to that legacy—following Nixon's anticipated implosion under the weight of the two wars Jack had begun—and reclaim the throne for the family.

With me dead and the Gemini program badly stalled as a result, the President's second term was set to close on a decidedly sour note.

Especially since there was a Soviet capsule orbiting somewhere in lunar space. The Communists would be happily trumpeting about their victory while my corpse slowly freeze-dried.

Radio with the ground failed thirteen minutes into my ninth orbit. More leftovers from Vic's accident. Under normal circumstances, it would have been a perfect time for me to shit a brick. But I was all out of bricks, and could only muster a weak laugh, followed by silence as I continued to drift and stare at the implacable stars.

I saw the light moving. Perhaps a third of an orbit ahead of me. I hadn't seen it before, but upon closer visual inspection, I guessed that it was at a higher altitude, with less velocity. I floated and waited quietly, watching through two more orbits as the light drew nearer. I found I didn't at all miss the constant clucking from Houston. The silence of the radio had matched the silence of the cosmos.

One of the hand cameras had a telescopic lens. I fished it out of the Gemini and aimed it at the light. What initially seemed like a single object resolved into two, separate objects: another Chiron, and something I'd only ever seen in grainy black-and-white photos during security briefings.

The Soviet L3 was in big trouble. Panels had been blown off along one side of the booster assembly, with wires and plumbing strung out into space like the innards of a disemboweled man.

Apparently my mission wasn't the only one to have had technical difficulties.

The Chiron was a derelict from the test flights. GCBV-7003 and GCBV-7004. The first had conducted remote operations and thruster tests, before being deorbited over the Pacific. The second had been fired via radio to test the booster's ability to break Earth orbit and maneuver in translunar space. GCBV-7004 had actually reached lunar insertion before Earth lost contact with it.

The Russians were hijacking my only hope of getting home.

I reeled myself back to the hatch and crammed myself down into

my seat, hands and fingers moving almost too quickly for my thinking
to catch up with them. Neither needing nor caring about the checklist,
I closed the door, did a quick decouple via rote memory, and slowly
pulled the Gemini free of its wounded—and useless—Chiron booster.
In Earth orbit the Gemini would not have had enough onboard fuel to
jump the necessary distance. In the weaker lunar gravity, I hoped the
odds would be a little more in my favor. Using the Gemini's onboard
computer and radar, I locked on to the approaching light—which gave
solid pingbacks, to my relief—then set about some back-of-the-
envelope calculating, based on relative velocity and distance.

How the Russians might feel about my arrival was something I'd
deal with when I got there.

Whatever moroseness I'd been feeling about Vic's death, it had
been overcome with a single, maniacal drive to get home: kiss my wife,
see my kids, breathe fresh air that didn't come from a can. I forgot
about what had gone wrong to that point and made rendezvousing
with the defunct Chiron my sole goal in the universe.

How the Russians might feel about my arrival was something I'd
deal with when I got there.

I didn't realize I was sweating profusely until the pooled, salty
liquid began to creep from my face into the corners of my eyes. I
mopped at my face with a towel and blinked furiously, not daring to
take my eyes off the instruments as I thrusted, the fuel dwindling
down to near-zero and the Chiron—which had originally brought me
here—drifting away to become a small light unto itself.

GCBV-7004 looked relatively undamaged as I neared it.

My thruster fuel was past the point of being dangerously low.

The bozo package—a collection of radio and computer equipment
taken from the Gemini assembly line and cobbled together into a
"brain" for the unmanned Chiron—was resting solidly in GCBV-
7004's docking collar. With no way to radio the Chiron and order an
automated jettison, I put my helmet back on and depressurized for
yet another EVA.

When I popped my torso out to take a look, there was a similarly-
garbed figure sitting astride the bozo package, staring directly at me.

For a fleeting moment I wished for a weapon.

The figure waved at me. Stupidly, I waved back, and wanted to yell
for the intruder to get his ass off United States property.

Just meters apart, the figure and I considered one another for a
moment.

I raised my visor. Then he raised his.

"Holy shit . . ."

It took us a few minutes to get our radios synced. Her name was Raisa Zaslavskaya. I think she was even more surprised to see a brown face than I was to see a woman. Whatever unease we might have had between us—as competitors in the Long War—seemed a small thing compared to the unease we now felt over gender and ethnicity.

"Amerikanyetz," she said, "where is your copilot?"

Her English was far superior to my Russian.

"Dead," I said matter-of-factly. "Yours?"

"Da. Same."

"Is your spacecraft capable of Earth return flight?"

"Nyet."

"Mine is, but only if you haven't damaged the Chiron."

"I have not touched. Hope to salvage."

"Then it seems we've both got the same objective."

"Da."

Long silence. Too long.

"Have you had any success understanding American equipment?"

Pregnant pause. "Nyet."

"Let me help you."

"My government will not sanction it," she said.

"Do either of us have a choice?"

Another pregnant pause. "Nyet."

"Then listen to me, because this is what we have to do . . ."

Getting the bozo package off was easy. It was finding a way to get her into the Gemini that was hard. The Russian suit's umbilical wouldn't mate with the Gemini's life support system, and neither the Russian flight nor mine had packed the newer, backpack-independent models that we'd be using for eventual lunar landing. Unnecessary mass on a circumlunar mission—a decision made on the ground, which now proved maddening.

I held up a roll of duct tape between us as we hovered in the open doors of my spacecraft.

"How long can you hold your breath?"

"Long enough," Raisa said, her eyes fearful but determined.

Brad R. Torgersen

I then held up the end of the umbilical that Vic had been using during the accident. If we couldn't get her hose to work with the Gemini, we'd have to hope we could get the Gemini's hose to work with the Russian suit. Again, the couplers wouldn't mate, but if we could get a solid seal, and oxygen flowing, that would be all we'd need. The trick would be getting both her and me back into the Gemini and closing the hatches, then repressurizing without the jury-rigged connection failing.

I spent many minutes fumbling with the tape in my clumsy, suited hands, eventually stretching out several long strips, which I stuck to the hatchway of the Gemini. Then I held the hose ready while Raisa reached down and grasped the umbilical that led back to her damaged capsule, her hands visibly shaking.

"We'll count down," I said.

"Da. Chyetirye, tri, dva, *adeen!*"

She rotated, then ripped her hose free, squinting her eyes shut in the process.

The Russian hose shot away, bleeding air like a jet. I jammed the Gemini's hose into the now-vacated orifice on Raisa's suit and frantically began to wind duct tape around the connection. Her face was bright red and her head shook as I worked. Cursing, I ducked down into the Gemini and valved the feed. Vic's hose rippled like a snake come to life, and for a moment I thought the rigged connection would burst free. But the duct tape held, and Raisa's eyes popped open, her gasps audible over the radio.

"Da . . . da! I breathe!"

"No time to waste," I said, beginning to guide her floating body down into the right-hand seat. She let me do most of the work, as the cramped interior of the Gemini was unforgiving. Twice we stopped and I wrapped extra tape around the connection between her hose and suit—which was clearly leaking heavily—before she was finally down tight and we could try to close the hatch.

The door thumped onto the top of her helmet, inches from a solid seal.

We tried again, and again.

She screamed and pried at the CCCP-stenciled visor cowling that covered the top of her helmet, eventually ripping it free and spinning it into space.

The hatch closed.

I clambered down into my own seat as quickly as I could, listening to the hyperventilating going on next to me through the radio, then slammed my hatch shut and started the repressurization cycle.

To her credit, Cosmonaut Zaslavskaya waited until I gave her a thumbs-up before breaking the seal on her helmet and lifting the face bowl. Her cheeks were coated with sweat and there was evidence of hemorrhaging below the skin. But she gave me the first smile I'd seen her make since we first met, and this brought a smile to my face as well.

I set to work guiding the near-depleted Gemini into docking alignment with GCBV-7004. Two of the Chiron's fuel cells had been exhausted, but the third worked, and now it provided power to the Chiron's onboard systems as I nosed the Gemini into dock. If ever I had resented all the hundreds of times I'd practiced the maneuver in simulation, I was grateful now for the effort. The talkbacks barber-poled for a few agonizing seconds, then snapped to normal as the Gemini and Chiron linked up.

I relaxed in my seat and flipped open my own face bowl, exhaling loudly and closing my eyes in relief.

"Washington," my new copilot said.

"Malachi," I interrupted. "My name is Malachi."

"Malachi. Da. All is good?"

"Yes," I said, feeling it for the first time in many days. "All is good."

The GCBV-7004 was in surprisingly good shape for having been stranded in lunar orbit for almost nine months. Most importantly, the main engine responded to control input, though the main radio antenna was dead—a problem which had apparently been related to more than just the bozo package, and afflicted my original craft too. I made a mental note to have them inspect the radios on all the other Chirons when I got back. Until then, we'd be out of long-range radio contact.

I turned to inform the Russian woman, and found Raisa was already using Vic's flight manual and mechanical pencil, furiously scribbling notes across the blank pages, some of them in Cyrillic and some in identifiable numerals. Her mouth made silent words as she worked, and for a few minutes she seemed utterly unaware of my existence. Eventually she put her pencil in her lap and pursed her lips.

"No radio. Without assistance from ground, it will be very difficult to return."

"That much is certain," I said, frowning.

"I am unfamiliar with this design, so I will not be much help."

"I could teach you," I said.

"Your government would *allow* this?"

"My government isn't exactly in a position to stop me," I said.

She seemed bewildered. "In my country, is serious mistake to give away technology secrets."

"In mine too, but right now, I am guessing they'll be willing to make an exception."

"Mine would not be so willing," she said, chewing a lip.

"Then it's a good thing we'll be picked up by a U.S. Navy carrier."

Her eyes became fearful. "I am to be prisoner," she said.

"No, I don't think so. Consider yourself . . . my guest."

Her eyes strayed out the forward window, to the lost L3.

"Will be disgrace, in Moscow. Many repercussions. Myself included."

"The accident—" I motioned out the window "—was your fault?"

"Nyet. Valves. Terrible design. They would not listen to me when I told them so."

"Why?"

"I am a woman. The engineers are men."

She said it as if it were *ipso facto.* Then she pointed to my face and said, "White engineers listen to you?"

I stopped short. As a matter of fact, they *did.*

Well, most of them anyway. Some of the older ones who were Von Braun's holdouts still thought of me as *untermensch,* but they tended to keep their opinions to themselves and weren't part of the bigger picture anymore. The younger ones, the whiz kids, they were a little more hip. Many of them had gone to integrated schools. We didn't exactly have lunch together, but they'd shake my hand and give me the same respect due all the other Astronauts.

"If you knew there was a problem, whatever possessed you to launch in the first place? If an Astronaut suspected there was a glitch beforehand, he'd never let the countdown proceed."

"Is not so easy for Cosmonaut. Politics in Star City. Designer Korolev and comrades under great pressure to deliver results. Cosmonauts follow orders, not give them."

"Clearly, we've got some things to talk about," I said.

"Da."

I began warming up the Chiron's reaction thrusters, so as to get some distance between ourselves and the wrecked L3.

"Anything you want to say before we go?"

"Nyet," Raisa said, her voice turned bitter.

"Okay then, hold on. The Chiron's engines can provide quite a kick."

Zaslavskaya was a quick study. Our first day out from lunar orbit, I ran her through a crash course on the entire cockpit, during which she asked many questions. Often my language grew so technical or abstract as to require us to break concepts down to simply worded English, but she seemed to get the drift, and was openly admiring of the Gemini—especially the craftsmanship that went into its construction.

"How do you get workers to produce such equipment?"

"McDonnell hires good people," I said, "and pays well from what I've been told. Of course, NASA wouldn't have awarded them the contract if they had a reputation for shoddy work."

"Other design bureaus make spacecraft?"

"McDonnell isn't a bureau, it's a company. And yes, others make spacecraft. North American was in the running to produce the ship that would go to the moon. Grumman is still going to build the lander."

"And they all make workers build quality parts?"

"They have to in order to remain competitive with each other, though I have to admit we're always kicking them in the butt for the things that still get missed. Like whatever killed Vic."

"Will company be punished for your copilot's death?"

"No, but the accident will be thoroughly investigated, so that they can find out what happened and be sure it doesn't happen again. NASA can't overlook something as serious as an Astronaut's death. The public wouldn't stand for it."

Raisa's eyes grew hard. "When Vasily died, they did nothing."

"Who?"

"Husband."

I stared at her. "I'm sorry."

"I was sorry. All Cosmonauts sorry. Vasily become Hero of Soviet People, but problem left in place to kill other men."

"Just how many Cosmonauts have died?"

"You do not know?"

"Star City doesn't exactly broadcast it every time something goes wrong."

She grunted, shaking her head in disgust. "Moon booster kill two crews alone. No time allowed for investigation. Had to win against the Americans."

"They must have fixed *some* of the problems."

"And leave others untouched! Then Cosmonauts get blamed when things go wrong. Always."

This time I was the one who grunted and shook his head. I knew that game myself, all too well. And was reminded of just how awkward the mission review would be, assuming I survived to see it. First black Astronaut, loses his copilot and almost his whole ship, comes back with a Russian woman in tow.

"If it's as dangerous as all that," I said to her, "why don't you try and get out of the Cosmonaut corps?"

"Would be disgrace. Too many men already doubting the few women at Star City. Terashkova says we all fly, or die in process. Example to men. Courage. Would you leave NASA, even if launches fail?"

"No," I admitted. I probably wouldn't.

I asked the next question that seemed logical. "Was your copilot a woman?"

"Nyet. Male. Young. Soviet Air Force. Chauvinist. I would have had another, if they had allowed me to pick. But copilot had father in Politburo. No choice for me."

"What will happen to you when we get back?"

"I do not know. Will likely not launch ever again. Maybe worse."

"You wouldn't have to go back. You could stay in the States."

Her eyes grew large. "Not serious."

"Sure I'm serious."

"And be traitor to people? Never!"

"What have you got going for you back at Star City? Nothing good, it sounds like."

"Amerikanyetz, be quiet."

Her tone was exactly the same one my wife used on me whenever I'd said something that really pissed her off.

Not wanting to add insult to injury, I did as I was told.

Day two was an exercise in excruciating silence. Beyond basic *das* and *nyets* the Cosmonaut didn't have much to say to me. I ran her through some ad hoc drills on operating some of the Gemini's systems—especially those related to reentry—and she took a boatload of notes. Otherwise, my every attempt at chatty talk was met with a glare and a mouth sealed so tight, it became a harsh, thin line.

Day three, and the Earth had grown large again in the windows. The Chiron's radio was still out, but we'd soon be getting something from Gemini's onboard systems. We had no idea if we were coming in too quickly, at the wrong angle . . . Her math confirmed mine, which confirmed hers, and we hoped that we weren't just fooling ourselves. Or at least I assumed that we both hoped. She still didn't talk to me, and by the end of the day I was beginning to greatly look forward to kicking her ass out of my spacecraft and dealing with someone who didn't constantly look at me with suppressed hostility.

Some time, during the quiet dozing that passes for sleep on space missions, I heard her finally speak.

"I am sorry."

"Hmm?"

"Is not your fault. Would be dead now without your help."

I yawned and rubbed a hand over my eyes, feeling the stubble on my face.

"I simply see no outcome that is desirable," she said, eyes cast down to the control panel in front of her.

"You'd be treated well," I said. "I don't know what you get told back in Star City, but whatever you think is going to happen to you in the States, it's not. Probably the President will want you under wraps for awhile, maybe debrief you a bit, but myself and the other guys, we'd stick up for you and make sure you got a fair shake. Even citizenship, if you want it."

"You make it all sound easy, Malachi. Is not easy. I would be betrayer of Soviet people. But more important to me, I still would not fly."

"Sounds to me like you're grounded either way, so what's the use in trying to go back to Russia?"

She looked up suddenly, an intense twinkle in her gaze.

"If landed in Russia—Black Sea—I could claim *you* as prisoner. You would be returned to your country, eventually. Like your spy pilot Powers. But I could retain flight status with Terashkova's support."

"And the Soviet Air Force gets to pick apart the Gemini," I said ironically.

"Da."

"What makes you think I see any advantage to that scenario?"

"Eh?"

"Why would I do that for you? I already saved your life. It's you who owe me, not the other way around."

"American selfishness," Raisa snapped.

"Bullshit," I said. "You're not the only one with her ass in a crack."

"What does that mean?"

"It means that the first black Astronaut is *not* losing his ship to the Soviet Union!"

We were both shocked by my sudden outburst.

"Look," I said. "Back home, I'm like this big glaring signpost. What happens with me—what happens with this mission—it's very important to a great many people. Dr. King, he pulled me aside and told me that the eyes of every colored man, woman, and child would be on the stars while I am up here. If I fail—if this mission fails—it will fuck up a lot of things. For more than just me."

I could still remember the earnestness in Dr. King's expression. He got shot dead a few weeks later.

Raisa's eyes blinked once.

I drew a deep breath, collected myself, and continued.

"I don't know what it's like for a woman in Russia," I said, "but you have no idea what it's like to be a black man in America. No idea at all."

"Perhaps," she said.

"Perhaps my ass!"

"Amerikanyetz—Malachi—you are Christian, yes?"

"My parents are," I said. Cheney and I hadn't been to church since we lived in Chicago.

"Do you know my name? What it means to me?"

"I don't understand," I admitted.

"Jewish," she said. "Mother and father. Both sent to the gulag by Comrade Stalin."

I'd heard of the gulag and that the Communists weren't especially friendly with Jews. But the look on Raisa's face told me I clearly didn't know the half of it.

"What happened to them?"

"Dead. Like all sent to Siberia. I was spared because I was sent to live with a step uncle, who was good Party member. The NKVD could not touch him, and he made sure I got into school. I even kept my name, though I have had to be careful. The Jew in Russia is the 'nigger' of Soviet Union."

I wanted to tell her to go to hell—I hated hearing that word come off white lips.

But what could I say? It wasn't like I could refute her.

"So you see, Amerikanyetz. Is not so easy for *either* of us. What shall we do?"

I stared at her for a long time, then turned away and looked back out the window at the growing disc of the Earth. From this altitude, it was amazing to see the globe as a whole—one giant ball, slowly spinning. No borders and no obvious signs even that humans lived there at all. Just giant blue oceans and vast white clouds, with mottled green and brown land masses, all crumpled together.

When the Mediterranean came into view, I sat up a little.

"Zaslavskaya," I said. "Are there a lot of Russian Jews in Israel?"

"I know cousins and friends of Papa who fled south after the Great War."

"Think you could figure out the math necessary to put us down somewhere near the Eastern Med?"

Raisa's eyebrow arched at me.

"What is this thinking, Malachi?"

"Houston will never buy off on it. We'll have to make it look like an accident."

"We need *some* contact with ground, to confirm telemetry and trajectory."

"Yes, but once we get our bearings, could we figure out an alternate trajectory on our own?"

Raisa looked at Vic's book, now filled with her scribbling. "I was top of class, mathematics. Helped earn me slot with female Cosmonaut group."

"Let's hope so. Because once I cut radio to NASA, it's all on us to get down where we want."

We got ourselves straightened out on the fourth and final day. Had to burn a lot on the Chiron's engines to square up for a Pacific splashdown with the carrier *Hornet*. Told Houston all about what had happened in lunar orbit—save for the discovery of the L3 and my new copilot. It would be better for both of us if they didn't know—at least until after the boats from Tel Aviv picked us up. If they picked us up. We'd have no way of contacting anyone once we went radio silent— not without giving the game away. We'd have to assume that NASA would contact the Israelis and request assistance, once it was obvious where we might splash down. I made sure to throw in plenty of warnings about continued faults on the radio, and squelched the signal a few times for emphasis, to make it sound good.

Meanwhile, Raisa's hands were a blur as she worked it all out by pencil. Her muttering was almost like a monk's chanting as she went over and over her formulas, verifying and reverifying her work. When she could, she used the Gemini's computer—another piece of American technology for which she'd shown great fondness—and before I broke contact with Houston we had one final heart-to-heart about whether or not we could go through with it.

"Da," she said firmly. "It will work, Malachi."

"Good, 'cause I don't want us coming down somewhere we don't want to be. The Gemini is a watercraft. It's never been landed on the ground while a man was in it. And I don't even want to think about what might happen if we screw up and come in over Libya or Egypt or some place like that."

"Da, agreed. Would be bad for both of us."

"That is a bona fide fact, lady."

She stuck out her hand, without gloves. Her nails were trimmed to the quick, like a man's, and her grip was strong. Yet the feel of her much-smaller fingers, and my brown mitt wrapped around hers, like a boxer's, I was suddenly hit again by how odd it was being in orbit with a woman.

I killed the radio.

Per expectation, Houston began screaming.

Raisa and I ran the math again and again, concluding that it was as good as we both could make it, then we began the subtle, slow burn to slow us up and alter the deorbit just enough to bring us down shorter than NASA planned.

Saying farewell to the Chiron, we decoupled and set it free. It had served us well.

Reentry was as hellish as Vic had said it would be. He'd been up on a Gemini mission before, during one of the Agena tests, and hadn't been lying when he said that it felt like an elephant was standing on your chest. Outside the window the atmosphere had turned to flame, the friction causing a constant roar on the spacecraft's heat shield. Raisa's hands were balls of iron and her eyes were closed tightly as she spat unintelligible things to me in Russian. Prayers? Pleading? For all I knew she was singing, "Mary had a little lamb, little lamb, little lamb . . ."

It was only a handful of minutes, to get from orbit to parachute deployment, but it felt like an eternity, during which we were fully blind and absolutely trusting our edumacated guesstimations.

When the chutes momentarily hesitated to deploy, I sent forth a stream of cursing, figuring that Vic's accident had dealt us an unseen yet fatal blow. But when those orange-and-white stripes bloomed outside the window, and I felt our rapid fall to Earth cushioned gently by the rush of air into the fabric, I yelled with unrestrained glee and both Raisa and I clapped our gloved hands together and grinned at one another through the bowls of our helmets.

Radio was back, and I quickly scanned the bands that I knew we ought to be hearing, if there was anyone out there trying to talk to us.

A guttural language spat through static, and I looked at my partner, not sure whether to be happy or worried.

"Arabic?"

"No, Hebrew," she said, nodding confidently.

I cleared my throat experimentally, then set our radio to broadcast.

"Mayday, mayday, mayday, this is Gemini Seventeen, broadcasting to all who can hear me . . . I say again, mayday, mayday,

mayday, this is Gemini Seventeen, broadcasting. Assistance requested . . ."

Pickup went better than I could have hoped. The Israeli Air Force and Navy were waiting for us, though we'd landed well outside their nominal jurisdiction, in international waters. With the doors on the Gemini hanging open, we bobbed in the swells of the Med and enjoyed the miracle of warm, salty, fresh air, not a patch of land in sight. Compared to the *Hornet,* the Israeli Navy boat was a toy, but with IAF jets zooming overhead I felt curiously relaxed as the Israelis drew near and sent divers into the water. They brought a raft, which we happily fell into, and at once were barraged with questions by two frogsuited men speaking thickly accented English.

They had expected one Astronaut, which told me that they'd been briefed by NASA, insofar as the events I'd been willing to divulge. The fact that Raisa was so clearly a Russian *and* a woman was cause for much excitement, which continued all the way to the boat, all the way back to port, and all the way to a secured debriefing at an IAF lockdown facility in Tel Aviv, where my last glimpse of Raisa was as she was herded down a hallway opposite from me, each of us still in our space undergarments and exchanging worried but grateful glances.

She waved stupidly, and I waved back, and then she was gone.

Forty-eight hours later, I was getting off a U.S. Air Force plane in California, greeted by a pack of NASA officials who towed similar packs of military personnel and reporters. I kept my trap shut on the way from the plane to the waiting motorcade, bulbs flashing and popping and questions being screamed. Based on what I was being asked, it didn't seem as if the mission was being considered such a failure after all. Not in the press anyway, which is perhaps what mattered most. For all concerned.

Ten years and a lifetime later, I was still at NASA. Vic's death was hard on everyone, especially his family, but nobody blamed Astronaut Malachi Washington. It was a miracle I'd come down at all, just myself in a damaged ship—and no, they hadn't gotten word about Raisa, not from the Israelis and certainly not from me. Which was fine. So far as I was concerned, this was one of those things that had happened in

space, and was best kept in space. I'd made it back, I'd kissed my wife
and kids, and life had gone on its merry way, hallelujah.

Nixon did get elected, and the USA did put men on the moon—
before the Soviets, though they eventually got there too.

With the USSR working on a moon base, NASA had to work on a
moon base too.

And with more flights going up from the Cape than ever before,
there was plenty of work to go around. For all of us. So I stuck with it.
Got on three flights. One of which culminated in my being able to
spend a few days strolling around Mare Nectaris, as mission
commander. Cheney and the kids and I were on TV a few times. I got
to write and publish a book about my experience on Gemini 17, and
dedicated it to Vic and used the royalties to help set up a memorial
fund for Vic's kids.

The Kennedy clan never did unseat Nixon, though there was
muffled, unsubstantiated talk about some kind of scandal involving
tapes and a hotel.

Cheney and I laughed pretty hard when Nixon's successor—a
Republican best known as a B-movie actor—was elected in 1976. The
old man was roundly hated by Jesse Jackson and the other civil rights
crusaders from the Dr. King days. But Mr. Reagan seemed nice
enough, and was all about celebrating the sacrifices of the veterans
from the Vietnam and Cuban wars, many of whom had been my
friends. So I thought well of Reagan. Especially after he assigned me
as chief test pilot for his shuttle program that would be servicing the
Skylab projects, One through Six.

I was doing face time at one of NASA's combined NATO goodwill
junkets in Germany when I heard a familiar voice say,
"Amerikanyetz."

I stopped dead in my tracks and turned around, my foam cup
halfway to my mouth as she walked across the carpeted auditorium
towards me. She was all business in those high heels, and a tinge of
gray had touched her hair. But she smiled at me, an Israeli government
group following her obediently, like a pack of puppies.

"Colonel Zaslavskaya," said one of her aides, "this is Mr.
Washington, formerly of the—"

"—United States Navy," she said, extending a hand to me. I shook
it, and suddenly the decade between us evaporated.

"NASA test-pilot corps, at your service, ma'am," I said, not quite believing.

"Gentlemen," Raisa said to her entourage, "would you excuse us?"

The Israelis gave us room, going off to mingle with the many Houston and Cape eggheads who had come with me on this trip.

"You never told anyone the truth," she whispered.

"Seemed better that way," I said. "You're still using the name, I see."

"The Israelis treated me like a queen after we parted company. Made me an instant officer in the IAF. Said I was their key to keeping up with the rest of the West in space."

"What are you doing here?"

"What do you think, lump-head? I am here about your shuttle."

"Oh."

"Did they not tell you that your Reagan White House has requested that an Israeli pilot be sent, for the Skylab missions? As a show of solidarity with Israel?"

"No, they didn't tell me that. Raisa . . . you don't think the Soviets will care? I mean, I think they'd recognize one of their own, once the photographers and the newspapers got wind of this decision."

"I am Israeli citizen now. Cosmonaut Zaslavskaya . . . she is dead. If the Soviets do want to complain, what can they do? Go to war for me? Their economy is stressed to the point of breaking, and they are being eaten alive in Afghanistan. I think I am a low priority for the Politburo."

I smiled at her. Genuinely, and with great enthusiasm.

"So," I said, rubbing hands eagerly together, "you're going up with us on the shuttle."

"Only if you approve, I am told."

"I think I might be convinced to allow it, but under one condition."

"And that is?"

"Dinner. Just the two of us. Tonight."

"What about your wife?"

"Cheney will be thrilled to find out what's happened to you. I told her all about you when I got back the first time."

"A partner in silence, she is?"

"Yes. But she'll want to know everything. And so will I."

"It is a *date*, Amerikanyetz. If so, you must tell me all about walking on the moon."

"It was gray and it was flat."

She slugged me so hard in the chest I coughed and spilled my coffee.

"Sorry," I said, laughing. "I'll tell you all about it. I promise."

⟢⟡⟢

Brad R. Torgersen is a multi-award nominated, multi-award winning science fiction writer who has published prominently in the pages of *Analog Science Fiction and Fact*—the English language's oldest, most widely circulated science fiction magazine—as well as *Orson Scott Card's InterGalactic Medicine Show*, *Galaxy's Edge*, and many different anthologies. His novels are published by Baen Books. A healthcare tech worker by day, he is also a Chief Warrant Officer in the United States Army Reserve on the weekend, and writes sci-fi at night. Married for twenty-four years, he lives with his wife and daughter in the Intermountain West.

SCRAMBLE

by Martin L. Shoemaker

Throughout his programming career, Martin took occasional stabs at writing fiction, but nothing came of it. Then, in the Spring of 2010, he wrote what he thought could be the first chapter of a novel. He shared it with his brother-in-law, an avid reader who said, "That's not a chapter, that's a story. Send it out." Martin's writing career has taken off from there. This is that story. If you enjoy it and Martin's other work, thank his brother-in-law, Mark "Buck" Buckowing.

AUDIO-VIDEO RECORD from Tycho Traffic Investigation, Incident Report from the crash of the Transport Reynolds . . .

   LOGFILE: REYNOLDS/PsgCbn/AVRec/2062:04:13:01:23:12

   LOCATION: Passenger Cabin, Lunar Transport Reynolds, *en route from Neper Crater to Tycho.*

   "Everyone, please strap in!"

   "Steward Abraham—the explosion, his head—"

   "Mr. Zhou, he'll have to wait until Captain Hardigan has us safely on the regolith. Now please strap in, so I can deploy the safety cushions."

   "But why did the Captain seal the hatch?"

   "Standard Lunar emergency protocol, Miss Drew: seal the cabins to isolate leaks."

   "Will we make it to Tycho?"

"I'm sorry. Captain Hardigan has already contacted Tycho Traffic Control, and Tycho Rescue is on the way. They're the best Rescue service on Luna. Now please, raise your arms to make room for the safety cushions."

"How long—"

"Martha, brace for impact! Hard!"

The crashes, of course, are the worst.

Not that there are good accidents. Sure, it's good when we can pull them all through, but that's still not *good*. You feel like a million L when you pull off that miracle save; but if some guy has to have one of the worst days of *his* life just so *you* can feel like a hero . . . No, you can keep your million L. Even the good days ain't so good; and the bad days . . . Well, the bad days make me wonder why I don't just quit.

Industrial accidents are bad, but they're usually quick and clean. Either a guy survives, or he buys it in one shot. But a crash is tension and stress for an extended stretch, too long for adrenaline to keep you pumped. You start with a rush, but you always end exhausted, persisting on little more than the support of your squaddies and the knowledge that if you stop, somebody dies. I'll take a quiet Duty Watch any day.

Unfortunately, today wouldn't be a quiet Duty Watch. Doc, Liza, Adam, and I were in our couches in the *Jacob Evans*, playing cards on our suit comps. Cap and Mari were in the front, running diagnostics for the third time this Watch. Cap's a pain, running sims and drills to the point of obsession; but the Corporation of Tycho Under has given us top performance awards two years running, so he knows what he's doing.

The routine was interrupted in the worst way: the sound of umbilicals snapping away, and an alert on our suit comps and the main consoles. "Scramble! All squads scramble! Transport *Reynolds* inbound from Neper is off Traffic, repeat, off Traffic. Nav beacon has cut out. Pilot reports mechanical failure, attempting soft landing. No further communications. Scramble! All squads . . ."

Cap's training paid off: Before the second "scramble," we had helmets snapped to. Mari had the engines from idle to warm-up before the second "off Traffic." Six green lights showed us all strapped in for launch before the alert repeated.

Cap cut off the alert. "Pad Control, Third. Clear?"

"Third, Pad. Clear. You're Go." Patty Hayes, our Pad Controller, drilled as much as Cap. Between Patty's crew and ours, we had the ribbon for fastest launch three quarters running. They're aiming for one full year, and I'll bet we earned it today. Before Cap could say "Launch," Mari had already pushed the command, and the *Jake* hopped. There was a quick jolt of G forces as we set off on a ballistic arc calculated by Traffic. Mari would take us out of ballistic when I told her where to head.

LOGFILE: REYNOLDS/PsgCbn/AVRec/2062:05:24:01:23:54
LOGFILE INTERRUPTED. UNEXPLAINED INTERFERENCE.
ATTEMPTING RESYNCHRONIZATION.

Why would a squad *want* Outer Watch? Why would you want this job? It ain't the money, that's for sure. There are people getting rich in Tycho Under, but we ain't them. I'll bet their job is safer *and* less stressful than ours.

The stress starts with the flight out, and it's worse with a search. Even with nav beacons and sat recon, there's a lot of Lunar surface out there. Sometimes a nav beacon's damaged in the crash. Sometimes there're no recon eyes in good viewing position for as long as thirty minutes. Thirty minutes is a *long* time in Rescue. So if we don't have a beacon or an eye in position when a crash is called in, they scramble every squad and send us in the general direction.

As per drill, Cap depressurized as soon as all helmets had snapped to. Before long, the cabin was in vacuum. We didn't want to waste seconds depressurizing later.

"Ron, it's a search."

"Got it, Cap." That's what "off Traffic" means: no nav beacon, no sat recon, start searching! Sometimes Cap is a little *too* pushy. I know my job, damn it! They call me "Scout" because the brass are too stuffy to say what we say: G3, General Gopher and Grunt. Everyone else in a squad is a specialist: Commander, Pilot, Doctor, Programmer, Engineer. I'm the utility guy, the one who pitches in where anyone else needs a hand. I like it: I learn a little of everything, and it might even set me up for a command of my own someday.

But my one "specialist" duty is scouting for lost vessels and survivors, and I'm good at it. Even Cap admits that when quarterly review comes around; but in between, he pushes like I'm a green recruit who can't see a live drive flame in front of my nose.

I had already pulled open a split screen on my couch comp: radar signature and stats for Nashville-class transports; Tycho Traffic's track for the *Reynolds*; flight plots for the other hoppers; and maps of the likely landing zone.

The record track didn't make a lot of sense. I'll never be half the pilot Mari is, but I've logged enough flight hours to know how vessels usually behave. The *Reynolds* was off course and getting farther off *before* the nav beacon cut off. And the last seconds of the record track made even less sense: The beacon diverted suddenly and sharply veered east-northeast of its course, fast enough to give me the shudders. With acceleration that severe, anyone not strapped in at that divert point was probably lost already. Even those strapped in would have restraint injuries at a minimum. What was wrong with that ship?

I pushed my audio to the Scout Circuit. "Scout One, Scout Three. Check that track?"

"Three, One. Checked. Damnedest thing, Ron. Hope you packed extra splints. Breaks aplenty."

We didn't use actual splints, of course. Instant casts predated the Lunar Era. "One, Three. What's the search strategy, Mack?"

"Three, One. Two, Four, Five, and Six got off the Pad slow. We almost had you this time, Ron. Tell Mari Tim wants double or nothing on the next scramble. I'm having the slugs cover the near edges of the projected cone from that last track. Want to join us at the divert point and scout forward from there?"

"One, Three. Hold please." Mack made sense; but that cockeyed track still bothered me. "Liza, can you prep a Q&D?"

"Sure. Specs?" Liza's a perfectionist by nature. She *hates* Quick and Dirty sims. She wants to plan and prep and get everything exactly right before she tells it to run. But she's also the best Q&D *artiste* I've ever worked with, and no-nonsense on a scramble. Time during a scramble is too scarce for perfection.

"Assume a mass—small, but larger than a Nashville nav beacon." I pushed the Nashville specs over to her couch comp. "Assume some system failure propelled that mass away from the *Reynolds* at the divert point. Can you get a sim that matches this track from there?" I pushed over the track data as well.

Liza went to work, talking to the comp and keying in code simultaneously.

"Three, One. What's the word, Ron?"

"One, Three. Trying to make sense of that track." I looked over at Liza. She had a frown on her face, but she looked at me and nodded. "One, Three. Mack, I think maybe somehow the *Reynolds* ejected her nav beacon. Believe the track record from the divert point forward is a bogie."

Cap looked at me in his overhead mirror. "You sure, Ron?"

Before I could answer, Liza jumped in. "Ninety-three percent, Cap. I'm pushing the sim to all channels now."

Cap opened the Command Circuit. "All Squads, Command Three. Please confirm receipt of sim. High probability track record is that of a separated nav beacon."

Confirmations came in, and Mack returned in my ear. "Three, One. Nice eye, Ron. Liza have a projection for the rest of *Reynolds*?"

I looked at Liza. She was already waving for my attention, so I pulled her into Scout Circuit. "All Scouts, Prog Three. Revising sim with new projected zones based on how many pieces the *Reynolds* is in." I was proud of her. Liza's good, but she's the most squeamish of the squad. Translated from cold jargon, she had just said: *whether they might be alive, or strewn dead across the surface.* And with only a small tremor in her voice. I pushed her back out before she had the chance to say more. I didn't want to risk her voice cracking on an open circuit.

"All Scouts, Scout One. Cover projected zones indicated in the pop I'm pushing out now. Scout Three, you get the Good News Zone." That's Scout slang for the zone with the highest chance of survivors. I must've done well in Mack's eyes. He always gives the harshest peer reviews I've ever experienced, but for today, I had his endorsement.

Matching orders were coming in to Cap on Command Circuit as Liza turned toward the Good News Zone. Good news? We could still hope.

LOGFILE: REYNOLDS/PsgCbn/AVRec/2062:05:24:01:24:26
"Aaah . . . Aaah, owww . . ."
"Everyone . . . please remain calm . . . .Please . . . don't remove . . .

238 ・ Martin L. Shoemaker

your straps yet. . . . We've tumbled and landed . . . upside down . . . . If you fall, you could get . . . further injuries . . . ."

"My arm!"

"I'll help . . . . Give me a second . . . . Now . . . . Please, give me the safety cushions . . . . Young lady, please . . . let go of the cushion. I want to put them down so . . . there's a soft landing if anyone . . . falls.

"Now Mr. Zhou . . . . No, he's unconscious. Mr. Reed, you look OK. Do you think you can unstrap and lower yourself down? I can help you, and the cushions . . . . Can you make it?"

"I'll try, Mrs. Abraham. Let me . . . . OK, I'm coming down now. Slowly . . ."

"I've got you . . . . OWWWWWWWWWW! I'm sorry . . . . Dropped . . ."

"The cushions worked, I'm OK . . . . Mrs. Abraham? Are you all right?"

"I'm . . . all right . . . . Just need to . . . rest a second. My side . . . Can you unstrap the others and lower them down?"

"Some of them are . . ."

"I know. We have enough to deal with. Please, let's not discuss casualties yet. Just . . . just lay them in the rear. You'll find blankets in the cupboard, so you can cover . . . cover . . . Help me up, please. I need to get the first-aid-kit."

Liza had simmed a large ellipse of high-probability landing sites. (Never say "crash site." Never, *ever* say "crash site" if you don't have to. Not until you see a crash, and you just can't avoid the words any longer. Until then, always assume a safe landing at a *landing* site. Superstition? Fine, then it's *our* superstition.)

Now find the *Reynolds*. I could choose the obvious strategies: start from the center of the ellipse, and spiral out; or start from the edge, and spiral in. But both were time consuming, and seconds are precious. So while we flew, I tried to devise a better strategy.

Pilot reports mechanical failure, attempting soft landing. OK, go with that. Doc taught me his strategy in card games: When your cards aren't obviously winning cards or obviously losing, play as if the *other* cards are *exactly* what you need to win with *your* cards. The thinking is: You're stuck with the cards you have; if you can't win, it doesn't matter how you play; but if you *can* win, you *must* play a specific way to do so. This is how I approach a search: Assume the best, and start from there.

So assume the pilot maintained some control over the ship. What were his goals?

Ground the Reynolds *as close to Tycho Under, to Rescue, as he possibly could.*

Get her down as softly as he could.

Make her as easily discoverable as he could.

Bring her down someplace where the Second Quarter sun wouldn't cook the passengers if they had to evac.

The sun helped in the visibility goal, hurt in the shelter goal. Sometimes there are no good answers, only least bad.

How would he—assuming a he, I hadn't checked the crew roster—prioritize these goals? Soft first? If they didn't survive the landing, the rest wouldn't matter. I cut out almost thirty percent of the ellipse, because it was in an ejecta ray from Tycho's formation. That ray would be filled with rocks large and small that could tear a hull to shreds in even a soft crash.

Close, visible, or sheltered? If he's worried about close, he won't worry about sheltered. Or would he? If he's *really* considering an evac, he might also worry about how far his passengers and crew might have to walk midmonth. A shorter walk might be the way he'd bet.

"Ron, I need a course." Mari had followed a general approach vector. I could see from the main comp that we were nearing the ellipse. We would need a specific vector ASAP.

There was a choice that was close *and* sheltered, but risked being not soft: If he landed very *near* the ejecta ray, near also to the closest rim of the ellipse, then if need be they could use the shadows of the large rocks for shelter. It was a classic trick from Lunar Survival School: manual thermal control. When your suit gets hot, duck behind rocks for a while, let it cool off. With practice, you can make maybe fifteen percent normal progress that way. That's better than zero, and could be the difference that keeps you alive.

A quick pull from *Reynolds*'s records: Captain Neil Hardigan was a high-scoring graduate of Lunar Survival School, and top rated on Nashville class. He knew the tricks, he had the skills. "Mari, bring us in on the nearest edge, and skirt along the ejecta ray here." I traced out a rough course and pushed it to her nav comp. "Low and slow.

All eyes, you know the drill." All couch comps shifted to camera-eye view as Mari brought us low.

LOGFILE: REYNOLDS/PsgCbn/AVRec/2062:05:24:01:29:31

"They're all down. I've covered . . . . How are the injuries? I've had first-aid training. Can I help?"

"Hmmm . . . . Air is holding. I don't hear leaks. But . . . . You'll help more if you make sure we're sealed."

"But you—"

"I have a job to do. And I . . . need your help. I'm moving slow, and we need to seal the cabin. Have you ever applied seal strips?"

"No."

"It's not hard. There's a roll in the cupboard. Our air seems to be holding, but there's no sense . . . no sense skimping on strips. Tape every joint, every corner, any place plates meet the frame. Lay down a strip, touch it with . . . this activator, press the button, and you're done. If you hear a leak, strip it immediately, and call me over."

"Strip, activator, repeat. Got it."

"I'll be . . . I'll keep working on the injured."

Adam spotted the *Reynolds.* "Camera five." We all pulled five to focus. "It's bad. She's on her top, half in shadow of that big boulder. The tail's pointed toward Tycho, so the pilot cabin's near that smaller boulder." From Adam's description, I found the *Reynolds.* There was a large, crumpled dent in the exposed underbelly of the pilot cabin, roughly the shape of the small boulder.

"All Scouts, Scout Three. Confirmed sighting. Converge Beacon Three." Mari was already on course to the clearest spot, a little beyond the *Reynolds.* A hopper's a rough ride. They're meant for speed and maneuverability, not comfort, and Mari knows how to make one dance. From spotting to contact lights in under eight seconds: even Neil and Buzz might've balked at that approach. Mari cut the main engine, and the *Jacob Evans* was down.

"CTU Rescue, Command One. Supply drones converge Beacon Three." Often a search burned more fuel than a hopper could spare for the return flight. Sometimes we need more supplies than we can carry. The AI-piloted supply drones aren't built for search or first response, and they're uglier than sin; but when they home in with supplies just as you're running low on null plasma or jump juice, they're the prettiest things you've ever seen.

As we hit regolith, the big side doors cycled open and we unstrapped. We dropped out to the lith, closely followed by our swarm of scan bots.

This was the start of A1, Assess. Adam briefed us. "Nashville class is an older transport, all function, no style. Flight frame's solid and reliable. Shell is standard civilian-grade hull tiles in the stock configuration: flight cabin, passenger cabin, pressurized cargo cabin, and unpressurized cargo deck." Hull tiles are an ingenious design, stronger in their joins than in their middles: If there's going to be a hull stress break, it's far more likely to be in the middle than at a join—and the core within that middle is vacuum resin, an epoxy that bubbles up through cracks, then hardens to a rigid seal when it hits vacuum.

"Ron, I've found an attachment point for the Ear on the flight cabin. Let me know when the Pinger's attached." I felt sorry for Adam: when he looked in through the port to the flight cabin, he said nothing. That crumple was where Hardigan would've been. If there were good news to report there, Adam would've been all over the circuits with it. The crumple was also where the nav beacon should've been, or at least the explanation for its ejection.

But that wasn't my concern now: I needed to get the Pinger to the other end, ASAP, so I could feed Adam some pings. I leaped up on top of the *Reynolds* and bounded across.

"Ron, be careful . . ."

"Yes, Cap." On a smaller vessel, I might've just leaped over in one bounce; but Nashvilles are pretty long. Cap was right, I couldn't risk a spill. First rule of the Academy: "Don't add to the casualty list."

I was about to leap down, when I heard something.

LOGFILE: REYNOLDS/PsgCbn/AVRec/2062:05:24:01:38:54
"All right, Miss Drew, just a little needle prick . . . . I know, it hurts, but it's in now. You've . . . lost some blood, so you need some null plasma. I'll just tape this down, so the needle will stay in."
"I need to get out of here!"
"Please relax . . . . We can't leave. We're waiting for Rescue."
"You have emergency suits, right? Where's . . . where . . . wh . . ."

"What happened?"

"Oh, Mr. Reed . . . . I added a sedative to her IV, so she doesn't injure herself further."

"Mrs. Abraham, I've used up the seal strips. Are there more?"

"In the cupboard. But I think we're good for now. I checked the pressure gauge, we're holding."

"I can probably work the radio. Should I call for help?"

"No radio . . . . Antenna's on the roof. Was on the roof. Gone . . . Crushed now."

"Steward! I hear something on the roof!"

"Shh! Everyone, quiet for a moment. Listen . . ."

Thump . . . Thump . . .

"Someone's up there! Everyone, strike the walls! Find something solid, and hit it with something!"

Newcomers to Luna have an understandable misconception: that the surface is quiet, due to the vacuum. Actually, you bring your noise with you: suit noises, comm chatter, comp feeds, your own breathing. And air isn't the only way to conduct sound. It'll conduct through any good rigid object, including parts of a suit. Even the boots: our boots are pretty rigid, for pressure and for traction on the regolith. I heard, and also felt, a slight thumping beneath my feet. "Cap, thumping inside. Someone heard me."

Cap relayed the good news as I leaped down. That meant I was likely wasting my time. The Pinger and the Ear form an acoustic hull integrity tester, and the hull was probably intact if there were survivors. Still, I attached and activated the Pinger.

LOGFILE: REYNOLDS/PsgCbn/AVRec/2062:05:24:01:40:17

Weeoweoweee . . . Weeoweoweee . . .

"Good news, everyone! Tycho Rescue is here!"

"What's that sound?"

Weeoweoweee . . . Weeoweoweee . . .

"They call it a Pinger. It's sending coded . . . acoustics through the hull. At the other end of the ship, they've attached an Ear."

Weeoweoweee . . . Weeoweoweee . . .

"It's receiving pings and measuring how they propagate . . . through the hull. They compare the results against the acoustic signature from

our last maintenance review. The Ear filters these echoes into a 3D model of our flight frame, hull . . . contents . . . ."

Weeoweoweee . . . Weeoweoweee . . .

The Ear pushed its model to Liza's suit comp. She integrated the acoustic model and the visual model from the darting scan bots into a sim of the crash site.

There, I'd thought it, at last: *crash site.* Hardigan had done an admirable job, given what I could see. The *Reynolds* would never fly again; but the ship wasn't a total loss, and there were survivors. Of course, I was sure Hardigan wasn't among them.

Liza pushed her model to our suit comps, and confirmed my suspicions. "Sim fit is ninety-seven percent. Some glitch in the cooling system blew a chunk right out of the flight cabin, took the nav beacon, long range comm, and part of the guidance system with it. Captain Hardigan must've been suited, since he survived to seal the cabins. Then with crippled guidance, he brought the *Reynolds* down here. He would've made it, if he had cleared that boulder. The sim says he could have, but would've probably ripped the bottom out of the passenger cabin. He took it himself. Sim and acoustics say his lower half was crushed." She swallowed, a dry, painful sound. "Probably instant."

LOGFILE: REYNOLDS/PsgCbn/AVRec/2062:05:24:01:41:58
"Where are they?"
". . . working. Protocol for our safety, Four A's. Assess, Atmosphere, Access . . . Assist. If they don't follow protocol, we could . . . lose our air."

"Cap, problem here." Adam pushed the structural model into the common view. "Flight frame is intact, but seriously twisted."

"Any join breaks?"

"Weak spots, no breaks." I was already ahead of Adam. I was working my way around the hull, applying seal strips from my roll wherever the model showed a weakness. The scan bots helped, laser pinpointing the weakest areas. Apply a strip, then apply the activator to dissolve the seal granules, little carbon bubbles with vacuum resin within. You wouldn't want to fly in a vessel patched together with seal strips, but you wouldn't have to worry about losing air. This was A2,

Atmosphere. "If they can't breathe, you can't save 'em" is the second rule at Rescue Academy.

"But that's not the problem," Adam continued. "It's the airlocks. This ship has three: in the nose, the side, and the roof."

"And the nose is gone, and she's flat on her roof. Let me guess: the frame is too twisted to open the side lock?"

"You got it, Cap. Impact with the boulder and then the tumble stressed it too much. We *might* get it open; we'd never close it again."

"Where's the best access?"

"Bottom—well, topside now. Least chance we'll injure someone."

"Ron, how's the stripping?"

"Still about a dozen joins to hit. One or two could use a second strip."

"Keep on that. We'll unship the lock. But take a moment to establish comm, if you can. Tell 'em we're coming in through the top, and to stand clear. Don't want to drop anything on them."

Cap, Doc, and Adam went back to the *Jake* to unship the rear airlock. Rescue hoppers are modified so the rear lock is removable. We can fix it to a hull, seal strip it good and tight, and *voila!* Instant airlock! It's massive, but nothing three strong men can't handle in Lunar G.

Meanwhile, I checked the broadband comm scanner. No signal, other than us and our data bands. I pulled the Pinger from my belt again, and hooked it to my comm line. The Pinger's a multiuse device: It can ping, but it can also serve as a conduction speaker to project into a vessel. And it also gives me at least a muffled listen into the interior. I affixed it to a join where the model showed a good hull contact.

LOGFILE: REYNOLDS/PsgCbn/AVRec/2062:05:24:01:43:26
"Anyone inside Reynolds, *this is CTU Rescue Three. If you can hear my voice, strike something solid three times."*

"Everyone . . . quiet . . ."

Clang, clang, clang!

"Reynolds, we're beginning rescue efforts. More squads are en route. Do you need medical assistance? Strike once for yes, twice for no."

Clang!

"How many injured?"

Clang, clang, clang, clang!

"How many able?"
Clang! Clang!

Six survivors, four injured. We never ask the last question: *How many dead?* It only depresses or even panics the survivors. Their departure log told the tale: Captain Hardigan, one steward, fourteen passengers. Ten dead already.

"Have you begun first aid?" *Clang!* This person was good. I checked the log again. "Is this Abraham?" *Clang!* Martha Abraham, ship's steward. The odds for the survivors just went up. Abraham was fully rated on emergency protocols, first aid, and Lunar survival. "Martha, I'm Ron Ward. Have you sealed your joins?" *Clang!* I could stop stripping. Her internal seals would hold far better than mine. "Fantastic! Martha, we're rigging a lock in the deck center, aft of the thruster assembly. You read?" *Clang!* "OK, get your passengers clear so we don't drop anything on them." *Clang!* "Martha, I've gotta help with the lock. You're going to be all right." *Clang!* I hoped she believed it. I was starting to.

LOGFILE: REYNOLDS/PsgCbn/AVRec/2062:05:24:01:45:18
"All right . . . . Rescue is here. Mr. Reed, please help . . . keep everyone in the front . . . ."

"Cap, ship's steward has stripped the seals internally and started first aid. I can help with the lock."

"Negative. We've got it. Bounce topside, help us lift from there."

As I returned topside, I saw the *Alex Evans* landing a safe distance away. Rescue One had arrived. In the distance, I saw nose jets from the other hoppers. It was about to get crowded here. Nothing wrong with that. Six Doctors for four injured is much better odds than just Doc and me. I'm a fair field medic, but not even close to an M.D. We Scouts could run null plasma to the docs, carry wounded, and otherwise play G3s, while the Doctors did the critical work.

I looked down, and the lock was hullside, waiting for me. I crouched down and grabbed hold. "Got it." Then, just like a drill, my squaddies took turns bouncing up to join me while the others held the lock up. As soon as we were more up than down, we hoisted the lock up and over.

Cap and Doc bounced up as Adam directed us to place the lock. Again just like a drill, Adam and Doc crouched down and we placed it over them, so they could start work inside as it pressurized. We fixed it to the flight frame with mag clamps as Adam directed; and then I spread a liberal helping of seal strips all around the joins. Before I got halfway around, I ran into Mack laying strips from the other side, under guidance from his Engineer, Matt Winter. "Howdy, Mack."

"Howdy, Ron. Seals look good. I'm pressurizing."

As soon as there was enough air pressure to confirm the seals, Adam set to work on the hull plates. This was A3, Access, sometimes the trickiest part.

LOGFILE: REYNOLDS/PsgCbn/AVRec/2062:05:24:01:47:50
"What's that noise?"

"They're grinding the hull plates . . . . Plates are attached with molecular adhesive, doesn't want to let go."

"So they're cutting through the plates?"

"No . . . . Vacuum resin in the plates is a sticky mess. Worse when you hit vacuum . . . . Whole suit goes rigid. So they'll remove plates at joins . . . . Just takes time . . . ."

Adam and Doc were hard at work on the joins. I watched on the lock's cam as they worked. Adam picked out and ground cuts into the joins, and then Doc applied solvent. Working their way around, they soon had one plate free, enough for a slim hand to snake through and shake Doc's gloved hand. No, they weren't shaking . . .

LOGFILE: REYNOLDS/PsgCbn/AVRec/2062:05:24:01:48:37
"Steward Abraham, Dr. Jones."

"Good to . . . see you, Doctor. We need more null plasma . . ."

"Martha, you sound weak."

"Doctor, please . . . Null plasma. Still have passengers in shock."

"All right, here's my aid pack. We'll have more when the lock is working."

"God blessed—" Adam was working the third plate, which would give them enough room for Access in suits; but he held up his grinder.

On the camera, I could see that the grind shaft had snapped clear off. "Adam, we've got Matt's kit here. You need another grind wheel?"

Doc cut in as he started shedding his suit. "Negative. I don't want to waste time on a pressure cycle. People are in bad shape down there. Adam, unsuit, we can squeeze in through the gap." I was sure Doc's lanky frame would fit, but Adam would have a tight squeeze. Adam's a moose. I've never been Downside, so I've never seen an actual moose; but if they're as large as Adam, they must be impressive. "Once we're in, we pull in our gear, and Ron can fold down the lock doors and let Matt and the other Doctors in." The pressure doors on those portable locks are panels that fold up against the side walls, then down to seal the lock. They're not fancy like a modern passenger lock, just functional and reliable.

"Good call, Doc." Adam pulled off his helmet and started stripping off his suit.

LOGFILE: REYNOLDS/PsgCbn/AVRec/2062:05:24:01:48:37
"I've got you, Doctor."
"Thank you, Mr . . . . ?"
"Reed, Johann Reed."
"Adam, hand down my pack, and then join us. Johann, my backpack unfolds into a stretcher capsule, which we'll likely need. Can you help Adam assemble it?"
"Doctor, here."
"Martha?"
"Mr. Zhou is the worst. Compound . . . fracture and . . ."
"Martha, let me—"
"COMPOUND FRACTURE AND multiple lacerations from flying debris. Suspect also internal injuries from . . . restraining harness. I've given three . . . four units of null plasma. Pressure's up, but sinking again. Shock . . ."
"Yes, I expect he's in shock, too. I'll take care of him, you should lie down."
"Other passengers need me. I'll be over here. Be fine . . ."
"Okayyyy . . . . Adam, Johann . . . If you're done with the stretcher, Martha could use some help with the other passengers. Don't let her exert herself."

◈ ◈ ◈

The other Doctors queued up with Matt to enter the lock. Doc was already deep into A4, Assist. He was pushing reports out on the Doctor Circuit for opinions: *compound fracture, lacerations, restraint-induced internal injuries, shock; concussion, multiple fractures, possible internal injuries, shock; concussion, possible hematoma; multiple lacerations, sedated to prevent further injuries; internal injuries, likely severe, shock.*

"Pressure zero. Let's go!" Matt opened the outer lock door, and he and the Doctors climbed in. It would be a tight fit: He could remove more plates in there, but all I could see on the lock's cam was Doctors' legs. Some of them unsuited to crawl through while Matt worked.

I hate these strange, idle moments you get at odd times in a rescue. There's literally nothing I can do for a while, even though every impulse in me is screaming at me to *do something!* Third rule of the Academy: "Hurry kills." Those idle-tense moments are when I most wonder why I took this job. Just when my adrenaline is pumping hardest, I sit and wonder and plan for the unforeseen; but I can't *do* anything. Fight-or-flight panic kicks in, and *I hate it!*

Matt pulled up the third tile, and the remaining Doctors dropped inside. Matt dropped in their packs as we Scouts queued up to help our Docs.

LOGFILE: REYNOLDS/PsgCbn/AVRec/2062:05:24:01:52:34
"Jones, where we at?"
"Compound fracture and lacerations are bandaged up, and I've stabilized BPs. The steward did a fantastic job."
"The steward? Really?"
"Uh-huh. Ultrasound confirms concussions and hematoma, so I've started fluids and null plasma and analgesics."
"And the internal case?"
"Now that you're here, I'll take care of her."

Doc came across the All-Hands Circuit. "Scouts, hold back. Matt, can you help us lift? Stretcher capsule coming out."

If Doc had a patient, *I* had a patient. My chief duty on the lith is Doc's corpsman. I shouldered aside Mack and the other Scouts, leaped up on top of the lock, and checked the indicators. "Cap, depressurizing at fifteen percent." I looked at Cap, and he nodded: We could spare that much air. I keyed the override, and the lock opened with a brief white puff as moisture in the air sublimated.

I reached down, and Matt and Doc were ready: They had the stretcher poles right where I expected them. I pulled up and hand-over-hand pulled out the stretcher capsule, a large plastic bubble stretched between two poles. A comp on the side hooked to cables and hoses that snaked into the form strapped to the base. I tried not to look too closely: Too much red, and I would get a close look all too soon.

Mack helped me steady the stretcher as Doc bounced out. "Cap, emergency evac here. Spleen, liver, maybe more. Can you spare the *Jake*?"

"Plenty of rides home here. Go!"

Doc nodded. "Mari, prep the table." We dropped down to the regolith, and the Scouts passed us down the stretcher. Then we set off in a long lope designed to cover ground quickly without losing control or jolting the patient too much.

"Operate here, or do we evac?"

"Both, I fear; but let's plan on evac." Spleen was pretty serious for a field operation. Doc wouldn't consider it if the patient had good odds of reaching CTU. I didn't look forward to this trip.

The big doors of the *Jake* were all sealed already, save for port aft, the door where we bring in patients. Mari had stayed on board, prepping the hopper for a quick departure. Too often, we need every spare second in getting the injured to the hospital.

We reached the big door in short time, and lifted the stretcher through. Mari closed and sealed the door, and we clamped the stretcher capsule to the table. The umbilicals hooked in automatically, and the med comp lit up with a body scan and readings. As the cabin pressurized, we strapped into our couches. Mari didn't wait for us to inform her: She pushed the launch as soon as we had three greens.

As soon as the initial thrust lifted, Mari called back, "Quick or smooth, Doc?"

"Let me check." He pulled the table diagnostics. "Damn. Smooth, Mari. Ron, masks and gloves. She can't wait."

For the first time, I looked closely at our patient; and all I could say under my breath was, "Liar." Martha Abraham wasn't on the able list, not even close. I pulled Doc's log. She had to know she had internal injuries: Maybe not spleen specifically, but she must have been in one hellish amount of pain. Yet she had struggled to stay conscious, treated the injured, comforted them and assured them that Tycho Rescue would find them soon. Then she communicated with me and took supplies from Doc and applied more treatment. It wasn't until all the Doctors were inside that she would let Doc look at her. Strong woman, Martha.

Now Doc was saying without saying: She wouldn't survive the trip without emergency surgery. The ride settled enough for us to unstrap. We stripped off our gloves and helmets; then as Doc popped the stretcher and looked over Martha, I got out the sterile packs. I opened a set of bath gloves and offered them to Doc. He thrust his hands in, then yanked them out, as sterile as modern science could manage. Then I put his sterile op gloves on, careful to only touch the removable grips. Same with his mask. When I pulled the grips off, Doc was *clean*. Before I could ask, Mari hit the autopilot long enough to help me with my gloves and mask. If Madhu weren't such a good friend and Helen weren't my wife, I could go for Mari. She can practically read my mind.

The autoclave and the supply locker were both already open and ready. I started handing Doc whatever he needed: scalpels, clamps, scissors, sponges, and far too much null plasma. Three times I had to adjust the anesthetic on the stretcher. Whether from pain or the ride or just stubbornness, Martha kept struggling up from sleep. Finally Doc adjusted it. Not that he didn't trust me, but this was delicate: Too much would kill her, and not enough would let her struggle and kill herself. While I held an incision open for him, he tweaked some levels up, others down, until Martha settled down. Then he picked the scalpel back up and resumed work.

And so we passed the trip back. It seemed to take a Lunar day or more; ship's clock read twenty-three minutes when Mari said, "Approach, Doc. Do we circle, or do we land? I have clearance for Watson Pad." Watson Medical Labs is the finest hospital on Luna, and also the top-rated ER.

"Two minutes, then land." He didn't tell her to have a team ready. They know their jobs. "Another plasma, then let's start packing this. Surgical tape. No sense in sutures, they'll have to open her right up again." I slapped another unit of plasma into the stretcher as Doc pumped some drug into her IV. Then we closed her up as best we could, and strapped in.

Right on schedule, Mari took us down. Not many pilots outside of Rescue are certified to land at Watson: The pad is right next to the emergency room, with a dome that can be extended over a ship for fast evac. One slip in landing could be a disaster *and* shut down a big part of the disaster-relief mechanism. Mari made no slips. We landed, and didn't wait for pressure: We had Martha's stretcher sealed and mobile again, ready to go. The big doors opened, and the suited emergency team lifted her onto a gurney. They left on a run, Doc keeping pace and filling them in with her latest stats.

That left Mari to taxi the *Jake* back out, and me with nothing to do. The adrenaline rush was over, the stress was gone, and the exhaustion wasted no time settling in. I hustled to get inside the lock so they could clear the dome; but that was the last hustle I had left for today. I shuffled down Under and to the tram to the Rescue offices. On automatic pilot, I found my desk and started my incident report. That's boring work; but after a crash, boring is all the energy I can muster.

I was reviewing the model, trying to make sense of how the nav beacon and comm unit were lost (T.I. will probably ground all the Nashvilles for a cooling system overhaul, since that was the likely cause), when the *Reynolds*'s AV record logs came in on the Rescue net. Reviewing logs takes even less energy than paperwork does; so I switched on the log player, scrolled to the beginning, and watched the camera-eye view from inside the *Reynolds*.

LOGFILE: REYNOLDS/PsgCbn/AVRec/2062:05:24:01:54:10
"Can you believe that steward?"
"Not sure I could've held up like she did. Transport Academy can take pride in their first-aid classes. I don't think any of these patients would've lived if she hadn't been here."
"And the pain she must've had! The shock!"
"Uh-huh. Jones has his work cut out for him."
"Do you think she'll make it?"
" . . . "

And there's my why, always the same why. I could walk away from this whole business. But Martha Abraham's out there because her passengers need her. And Martha needs me, they all need me. What choice do I have?

I was reopening the paperwork when a pop announced the news of the successful rescue of the *Reynolds*. The squads were inbound with survivors.

About the time I realized I had reread the same hull specs for the fourth time and still didn't know what they said, there was another pop: the announcement of the Lovell Medal for Command in Service to Crew, Vessel, and Mission, awarded to Captain Neil Hardigan, Pilot *Reynolds*; and to Lieutenant Martha Abraham, First Steward. Both awards: posthumous.

I shut down my desk comp and set course for the Old Town Tavern and the largest whiskey they would serve me. Needed or not, I'm done.

For tonight. Tomorrow is another day in Rescue.

⇐⇒

Martin L. Shoemaker is a programmer who writes on the side... or maybe it's the other way around. Programming pays the bills, but his second-place story in the Jim Baen Memorial Writing Contest earned him lunch with Buzz Aldrin. Programming never did that! His *Clarkesworld* story "Today I Am Paul" received the Washington Science Fiction Society's Small Press Award, and was also nominated for a Nebula. It has been reprinted in *Year's Best Science Fiction: Thirty-third Annual Edition* (edited by Gardner Dozois), *The Best Science Fiction of the Year: Volume One* (edited by Neil Clarke), *The Year's Best Science Fiction and Fantasy 2016* (edited by Rich Horton), and *The Year's Top Ten Tales of Science Fiction 8* (edited by Allan Kaster). It has been translated into French, Hebrew, Czech, Polish, German, and Chinese. Others of his stories have appeared in *Analog, Galaxy's Edge, Digital Science Fiction, Forever Magazine*, and *Writers of the Future Volume 31*. His novella "Murder on the Aldrin Express" was reprinted in *Year's Best Science Fiction Thirty-First Annual Collection* and in *Year's Top Short SF Novels 4*. His novelette "Racing to Mars" received the Analog Analytical Laboratory Award. You can learn more about Martin's fiction at http://Shoemaker.Space.

BALANCE

by Marina J. Lostetter

Marina's story "Balance" is actually an excerpt from her debut novel,
Noumenon, *that is now available through HarperCollins. The novel
is an an epic space adventure starring an empathetic AI, alien
megastructures, and generations upon generations of clones. "Balance"
is just a small, but important, snapshot from that journey, told through
the eyes of an eight-year-old boy coming to grips with death and his place
in this vast human endeavor.*

"HELLOOOOO," said Jamal in his small, singsong voice. "Convoy
computer, helloooo." The eight-year-old bounced a soccer ball on his
knee in front of the access panel. He was supposed to be in class.

"Hello, Jamal," said the ship's AI.

"Do I get a new baby brother today?"

"My records indicate that your parents will jointly travel to
Hippocrates during their lunch hour to retrieve the next available,
fully-gestated clone."

The boy tossed his ball at the panel and deftly caught it on the
rebound. "But is it a brother?" Computers could be so dumb. He'd
make them smarter when he grew up.

"The next available clone is that of Nakamura Akane. Her original
earned a doctorate in engineering and ship design from the university
of—"

"A sister?" Jamal kicked the ball down the hallway. "You're giving me a sister?" He knocked his forehead against the wall and scrunched his eyes shut in frustration. "Why, computer? What did I ever do to you?"

"I am not in control of the growth patterns. And I had no influence over when your parents submitted their request."

"Mr. Kaeden?"

"Ah, great," Jamal grumbled. Through the hall came Dr. Seal, his teacher, carrying the scuffed soccer ball. "You had to tattle on me, too?"

"I do not tattle," said the AI. "Dr. Seal inquired as to your location. You are here. I related such."

"Not cool, man. Not cool."

"The temperature is seventy-one degrees Fahrenheit, twenty-one point seven degrees Celsius."

"No, cool, like neat, or awesome, or stellar."

"Those words are not synonyms."

"Mr. Kaeden," Dr. Seal reiterated, standing over the boy. "You are supposed to be in class."

"You are too," he mumbled.

"Jamal will have to cohabitate with a sibling soon," the computer explained. "The fact that he was not consulted on its gender seems to have caused him distress."

"I'm getting a sister," Jamal said with a pout.

"Sisters are people too," said Dr. Seal as he took Jamal by the hand and led him away from the access panel.

Nobody understood. The other kids just made fun of the poopy diapers in his future, and all the grown-ups either waved aside the problem or seemed mad that he was mad.

"But it's a girl," he tried to explain.

The botanist that had come to give a lecture on their classroom air garden scrunched up her face. "I'm a girl."

His ears turned from dark chocolate to strawberry chocolate. He didn't mean . . . Ugh. "Yeah, whatever," he mumbled. "You're not a sister." *Even if you are, you're not* my *sister.*

When class finally got out he knew where he'd have to go to find a sympathetic ear. If anybody in the convoy could understand, it would be Diego.

When he arrived at his family's quarters he was surprised to see his aðon and pabbi—mother and father—there by themselves. No baby. His hopes rose for a moment. Maybe they'd changed their minds. Maybe they weren't going to get a baby after all.

His pabbi kicked that fantasy out from under him. "We thought you'd like to come," he explained. "We rescheduled for tomorrow and excused you from class."

"We didn't want you to feel left out," said his aðon from the bedroom. She was changing out of her work jumper.

Well wasn't that just . . . He didn't feel left out, but he wanted to be left out. If he never had to see his sister it would be too soon. They were making a big, fat, ugly mistake. Why'd they want to go and ruin their perfect family with a sister, huh? Weren't the three of them enough?

He dropped his pack in the entryway and slumped over to the dining table. "Can I go visit Diego when he gets off work?" he asked after he sat down, picking at his fingers and swinging his feet.

"Sure," said Pabbi. "As long as he says it's okay. If he's busy you come right home."

Diego was Jamal's afi's—his granddad's—best friend. Jamal would never say so out loud, but he liked Diego better than Afi. Afi only liked old-people things, and more importantly, only things right in front of him. He had no imagination.

Diego, though . . . Diego knew how to dream while still awake.

Jamal impatiently watched the minutes tick away. Diego's shift was officially over at 1600, which meant he should be back at his cabin no later than 1630. As soon as the last minute rolled over, Jamal was out the door and down the hall to the nearest lift.

He had to wait a whole 'nother five minutes before Diego got there. Jamal sat in front of the old man's door, knees up to his chin, feet squirming in his shoes.

"Que pasa?" Diego squinted at Jamal when he got close. "Someone have a bad day?" He was dressed in the corn yellow of most foodstuff workers. His ruddy wrinkles made him look like he'd been basking in the sun all day, though he hadn't been anywhere near the artificial Sol of a communal garden.

Jamal shrugged, suddenly aware that his complaint might come off as whiny. "How was your day?" he asked politely. Something about being around Diego always made him feel more polite.

"Fine. Figured how to make the soy processing more efficient. My original designed the system, you know. I just made it better." Diego opened the door. "I was going to watch a movie this evening," he said as the lights came on. "You might find it amusing. Coming in?"

Diego's quarters didn't have as many rooms as Jamal's. He'd said it was because he didn't need them. "Only one of me. Can't take up a family cabin anymore. Wouldn't be right."

The place smelled like beans and cheese. Diego checked his slow cooker in the kitchenette, then came back to the main sitting and sleeping area. "How's the new baby? Problems already? If you liked it you wouldn't be here."

"No baby yet," said Jamal, crossing his arms. "They're gonna take me with when they get her."

"Ah. That's nice."

"No, it's not."

"Oh?"

Jamal shrugged. "Decided I don't want a sib. 'Specially a sister." Diego laughed lightly and Jamal took immediate offense. "You too? You don't get it. Why doesn't anyone get it?"

"I'm not laughing at you, amigo. I'm enjoying the simplicity of your problem, not that it is a problem."

"What do you mean?"

"We've figured out how to live in space and investigate cosmic phenomena up close. But we still haven't figured out how to make a new brother appreciate his sister. I had a sister, you know."

"You did? But, you were born on Earth. Was it another clone?"

The old man shook his head and gestured for Jamal to have a seat. "Nope. My sister was born the old-fashioned way. She did not accompany me on the mission."

"What's 'the old-fashioned way'?"

Diego's face went blank for a moment, then he waved the question aside. "Never you mind. My point is, I felt the same as you, or at least similar, when I was told I'd be sharing my parents with a girl. Anita. Oh, I hated the idea. I considered running away and abandoning my duties if my mother went through with this whole giving birth thing."

Jamal gasped. Abandoning your duty was about the lowest thing a convoy member could do. The thought of it made him sick inside. "You did?"

"Considered, I said, considered. I didn't, of course. I stuck it out. The baby was born, came home, and then . . . guess what?"

Jamal pursed his lips. "What?"

"I was just as upset with the baby there as I was when she hadn't been around yet. But I got over it, eventually. You'll learn to like being a big brother. You'll get excited when she learns to walk, and talk. But you should never hold her gender against her."

"Why not?"

"Why would you hold anything against someone that they can't help? You know what that's called? Prejudice."

"Sounds stupid."

"It is stupid. Very stupid. But, there was a time and place where your friend Lewis might not have liked you because of the color of your skin, and where someone like my late wife might never have looked twice at a man who spoke a different language than she did."

"Everyone on board speaks the same language."

"I'll give you that. What I'm saying is we're explorers, Jamal. Astronauts. You'd understand how wonderful that is if you'd been born on Earth . . . Point is, if we can't leave all that other bull pucky behind us, well, what's it all for? And how do we honor our unique position in humanity's history?"

"Through loyalty, efficiency, and dedication," Jamal recited.

"Yes, but also through understanding. Living in a convoy means we're rubbing elbows left and right. We have to look at what ties us together. As soon as we start disliking each other for our little differences it'll all go to pot. There's nowhere to run, you see? You're stuck with everyone on board. Might as well be nice to them, might as well appreciate them. So, don't be mad that you've got a sister. Don't be blinded by that thing you call 'stupid.'"

"Yeah, alright," Jamal conceded. "I'll try 'n' like her. Can I not like her if she's annoying?"

Diego considered for a moment. "Yes. But I still suggest you try."

"So what's the movie you were gonna watch?"

"It's old, I have to warn you."

Oh no. Not like Afi old, he hoped.

"It's about space travel. Before they'd had much space travel." Diego dimmed the lights and accessed the computer.

Before they'd had much space travel? Jamal couldn't even imagine such a time. "Like a million years ago?"

"No, not quite," Diego chuckled. "You sit right there. This is the best of the series—classic lines in this one. You'll like it; there's a bold captain, a first officer with pointy ears, and a villain you'll love to hate."

"That was awesome!" Jamal said when the credits rolled. "They were so—weird. They really thought you could chop people into tiny little bits and send them through space? And get a person on the other side, not a pile of guts?"

Diego nodded as though he weren't really listening. "Glad you enjoyed it. Better run along home. Your parents will probably want to head down to the mess soon."

Jamal prepared to leave. Diego stopped him just before he went out the door. "Jamal, do you know what your sister's serial number is?"

"Er . . . No."

"It's her production number. It's how we keep track of how many babies are being born. Can you ask your padre—your pabbi for me?"

What'd he want that for? "Okay," he said slowly. "I'll ask."

"Don't forget. It's important."

"Okay. I won't forget."

Hippocrates loomed before their shuttle, the second biggest ship in the convoy. It looked . . . intimidating. Especially with all of its arms sticking out all over the place. Pabbi explained that the 'arms' were umbilicals; they could dock with the other ships during emergencies.

The ship reminded Jamal of a dead bug. Or the prickly shell of a nut. Maybe a sea creature—they had an aquarium on *Eden*. Sea urchins were supposedly high in protein. How much protein did he need every day? Well, he was only four foot eleven, so . . .

He tried to keep up the wandering train of thought. He wanted his mind to stay away from the pending sister-assault for as long as possible. Figures and calculations for calorie intake swarmed through his brain.

Diego had made him feel a little better about the idea of having a sister, but not much.

Other shuttles zipped by outside, white and silvery against the blackness of space. Light from external LEDs bounced off hulls and windows, producing a glare that kept all natural starlight at bay. The ships and shuttles were bright objects in a dark cocoon. When Jamal touched one corner of the shuttle side-shield, graphics popped up to label the hidden nebulae and galaxies and systems. But even the star charts couldn't hold his attention for long.

His thoughts shifted. The classroom butterflies would be free of their cocoons soon. Then the class would take a trip to *Mira*'s communal garden and release the bugs. Butterflies helped pollinate the plants. Plants were a good source of fiber . . .

The spiny ship swelled before the shuttle and soon blotted out the rest of the convoy. Near its bottom a bay door opened, ready to gulp up their little shuttle—and Jamal's dreams of being an only child.

His family was greeted inside by a lady who wore a sea-foam-green jumpsuit wrapped in a white smock. A paper mask, held on by bands around her ears, rested awkwardly beneath her chin; she looked like she had a bulbous, snowy beard.

"Hello," she said warmly, "I'm Sailuk Okpik. You're here to pick up an infant who's come to term?" His parents indicated they had. "This way," she directed.

Jamal had visited *Hippocrates* only once, on an interconvoy field trip. His yearly physicals, mental checkups, and even his broken leg had all been attended to in *Mira*'s med bay. But there were a few things done on *Hippocrates* that took place on no other ship: cloning, for one. Jamal had never been to the growing rooms or the birthing chambers before.

The kids told all types of stories about the spooky tubes. About the half-grown babies with their guts hanging out, and the two-headed flukes they had to discard in secret. Some said the accidental deformities got ground up and put in kids' lunches. Others said they grew them to adults and had them work in secret. Still others said the doctors tried to kill the mistakes, but that they lived and formed their own society in the ships' walls. There they lurked, watching, waiting, ready to strangle healthy crewmembers in their sleep whenever they got their chance.

Jamal didn't believe those stories. Not really.

"Would you like a full tour?" asked Sailuk. "You probably took it when you picked up your son, but some second-timers like to see it

again. Though, I have to warn you, some children don't react well."
She turned her round face towards Jamal. "Do you scare easy?"

"I don't know," said his aðon, "The fetus tanks were a bit much for
me when I first saw them, and I was twelve."

"I think he can handle it," said his pabbi. "What do you think,
Jamal? Are you up for learning where babies come from?"

"Is it gross?" he asked, turning to Sailuk.

"Sure is," she said frankly.

What would the other kids say, if they found out he'd gone all
wimpyfied? "I can take it," he said, puffing out his chest.

"Are you sure?" Moms could be so stuffy sometimes.

"Yes, Aðon," he said in a tone that conveyed how tiresome her
question was. "I'm not a baby."

That settled that.

A wide lift at the end of a long hall took them to the very top deck
level. When the doors opened Jamal was immediately surprised by
the lighting. Instead of a cold white, everything was bathed in pinkish-
purple.

"The lighting helps protect the babies' skin," said Sailuk. "In most
fetal stages it can't handle the rays included in our normal lighting.
Most of the convoy lights were developed to mimic actual sunlight as
closely as possible, to prevent problems like seasonal affective
disorder. But these lights screen out anything that would be harmful
to the undeveloped infant. They work like an old-fashioned dark room
for developing photographs—or, of course, a mother's womb."

The first room they went into was bright again. White, normal
light.

"Here we do the actual cloning. It's slightly different than
traditional Earth cloning, in that instead of using DNA from the
original, we build DNA identical to the original and then insert it into
a healthy ovum. So over here"—she led them to the left— "you can
see Anatoly analyzing a newly formed molecule chain to make sure it
is identical to the original pattern."

A man in a clean room bent over a microscope and manipulated
something on the slide before him.

This was boring so far. Not scary. If Jamal wanted to watch people
play with molecules he could just go back to class.

Sailuk ran them through the rest of the first stages, using weird,

gibberish words like *histone* and *zygote*. Jamal didn't understand how
goats had anything to do with making babies.

They moved on to another purple room. This one was lined with
tubes behind a glass window. In each tube sat one worm, suspended
in some strange, snot-like solution. Jamal and his parents had entered
a viewing cubicle.

"Those are babies," his aðon said. "They're only a few weeks old."

"Ew," he said curtly. "But they don't look anything like a baby.
Look, this one has legs and a tail." It was more like a smooth, rubbery
lizard than a human. "Ach, this one has big glassy eyeballs, too." No
way these were people.

On they went, through more rooms with viewing cubicles, and he
began to see the connection. The more the worms came to look like
the thing with legs, the more the thing with legs came to look like a
salamander, the more the salamander came to look like a wrinkly
naked thing . . . the more creeped out Jamal got.

Babies weren't just annoying, they were freaky. Like aliens. And
here they were displayed in jars like specimens of dead animals. The
whole thing felt . . . unnatural.

"What's 'the old-fashioned way'?" he asked suddenly.

His parents stopped scrutinizing a tube that held a baby with head
stubble. "What?"

"Diego said his sister was born the old-fashioned way, but he
wouldn't say what that was."

The adults shared a look. "People used to be born and die a little
different than on board," said his mother. "I suppose that's the way
they still do it on Earth. It was messier, and less efficient."

"Moms carried the babies in their bellies," Pabbi said, patting
Aðon's stomach.

"Uh . . ." was all Jamal could say. That would be even weirder than
all this. "Oh, and he wanted me to ask what the baby's number is."

His parents eyeballed each other again. What was all this look-
passing and eyebrow-raising about?

"He must be close," said Pabbi. "I wonder how many more he
has."

"Far fewer than your dad," said Aðon.

Annoyingly, they let the matter drop without explaining their
cryptic chatter to Jamal.

Finally, the bulk of the freak show was over. Time to get the baby and head home.

"We'd like to attend the birthing," insisted Pabbi. "We were there for Jamal's first breath. We'd like to be there for Akane's."

"We're going to watch her come out of the tube and get all cleaned up," Jamal's aðon said to him, overly perky. "Look, there she is." They entered one last room, this one with normal light again. One tube occupied the space, surrounded by four technicians. This baby looked like the ones in the previous room—you know, actually like a baby. Like a real little person instead of a funky slimy thing. She had hair and eyelashes and fingernails and everything.

Two of the technicians held the tube in place while the other two unhooked it from its wires and apparatuses. Eventually they popped the top off and tipped it over. The baby came spilling out onto a thick, foam-looking pad that sucked up most of the liquid.

A man came at the baby with a hose, the tip of which looked like the plastic vacuum the dentist used. The man pushed it up the baby's nose and in her mouth and soon she was crying. A hoarse, squeaky cry that didn't sound anything like the crying Jamal had expected.

She looked a lot smaller now that she was out of the tube, wiggling and naked on a table under the lights. She looked vulnerable.

Jamal felt a pang of protectiveness. "Can't they get her a blanket or something?"

"They will," Sailuk assured him. "They have to clean her up first."

After the baby was prepped and swaddled, Sailuk went into the room to retrieve her.

When the crying Akane was brought before her new family, Sailuk asked, "Who would like to hold her first?"

Jamal tentatively raised his hand. "Can I?"

"Not so bad as you feared, eh?" asked Diego, packing a trowel and a small shovel in his bag.

"No, guess not. She's kind of nice. Except when she cries while I'm trying to sleep."

"Did you get the number?" he asked casually, opening the door to his quarters and ushering Jamal out. They were going to work in *Mira*'s communal garden.

"Oh, yeah, here." Jamal pulled a small 'flex-sheet out of his pocket. "She's S8-F94-3-16008."

"Five more until I get my notice," Diego said.

"Huh?"

"I'll tell you about it when we get to the garden. I'll feel more comfortable with some dirt under my nails."

The artificial sun sat high overhead, and the cows mooed in a bored sort of way. The weather-planners were pretending it was hot today. The thermostat must have read at least thirty-one degrees Celsius. Luckily a large part of the garden sat in the shade of a big tree. A few butterflies flitted by, and Jamal thought he recognized one from his classroom.

The air smelled sweet here. But he was pretty sure the scent wasn't emanating from the flowers or the grass—it was one more illusion. They pumped in the smell to make the space seem bigger and more open than it was.

Diego dug right in. Only a few minutes passed before his hands, forearms, and boots were caked with enriched soil. "That's better. Get a bit of this mud on you, it's nice and cool." He drew a dirty line down the arch of Jamal's nose. "Good war paint," he said with a wink.

Getting into the spirit, Jamal put a dirty handprint on Diego's cheek. "Looks like I whacked you one."

"Let me return the favor." Jamal's face now sported two handprints that mirrored each other. The dirt might as well have been face paint, and the handprints butterfly wings. "Can't forget to wash that off before you go home. Otherwise your madre will have my hide. With a new baby to think about she doesn't need to be giving you extra baths as well."

"What were you saying before?" Jamal asked, looking over a bowl of seeds they'd picked up at the entrance to the field. "About Akane's number?"

"I should probably make you ask your parents," said Diego. He dug a small hole and gestured for Jamal to sprinkle in a few seeds. "But that would be for their sake, not yours. Jamal, I'm going to retire soon."

The smile slumped off the boy's face. "What?" He stood up straight. "Why?"

No. No. No. Diego wasn't old enough to retire. Only really old people retired. And it wasn't something you talked about. It just happened, they disappeared one day. Said good-bye and left for . . . somewhere.

"What does Akane's number have to do with that?" he added.

"Sit back down so we can talk about this rationally," Diego ordered, patting the ground.

Jamal narrowed his eyes. Anything Diego said from this moment on would be held under the highest scrutiny. Sick people retired, frail people retired, incapable people retired—Diego was none of those things.

"You're eight. You're big enough to understand about retirement. On Earth I learned about it a whole lot sooner than eight. And we didn't have that nice euphemism for it. We just called it what it was."

No one ever said, but Jamal wasn't stupid. He knew where retirees went. He knew. He just didn't like to think about it. If no one ever talked about the truth, if everyone always glossed over the facts, why couldn't he? "I do understand," he said.

"Then sit down. You know I'm going to die, but you don't understand the how or why of it. So let me tell you."

Jamal finally sat and said in a small voice, "Did the doctors find something?"

"No. Nothing like that. I'm as healthy as a, as one of those bovines over there. But my number is about to come up, quite literally. You see, everything on the convoy's got to balance. All that's ever here is all there ever will be. Even if we find an asteroid to mine, we can only carry so much. We're a closed environment. We have to scrimp and save and control and manage. So, we have to pick and choose when it comes to some things. Where do we put our resources?"

Jamal picked at a strand of grass and it gave him a thin cut—it didn't bleed but it smarted. What did this mumbo jumbo about management have to do with Diego dying?

"Are you listening?"

"Yes," Jamal mumbled.

"To conserve our resources, birthing can never get out of synch with dying. We can't have more babies born than people who die. So, everyone on board has numbers. Two numbers—a number that corresponds to their birth and one that corresponds to their death. When the 16,013th baby of the third generation is born, I'll get my notice. It'll let me know that after another three clones are brought to term I'll be scheduled for official retirement. They'll set a date, and I'll go over to *Hippocrates* and they'll—"

Jamal's hands flew to his ears. "Shut up. I don't want to hear about it. I don't want to know how they'll kill you."

"Oh, stop it now." Diego pried Jamal's hands from his head.

Fire and water surged inside Jamal's brain. His face grew hot and swollen. "But why? You're still a perfectly good person. There's nothing wrong with you. Retirement is for people who have problems that can't be reversed."

"Yes, I know. And a lot of people go that way. They get some sort of terminal or chronic problem and never see their end-number. But I'm lucky, Jamal. I got to live my full life."

"It's all Akane's fault," Jamal realized. "If parents stopped asking for babies then they wouldn't have to kill you. It's not fair! Why grow a new person when you have to kill a perfectly good person to get it? It's not right!"

"Now don't go blaming your parents or your sister. Babies can't be blamed for anything."

"This is stupid." The boy stood and pulled at his hair. "You have to fight, you can't let them take you."

"They're not carrying me away kicking and screaming. This is how things work. This is how they're supposed to be. The old die off, leaving resources for the young. We just make it a little neater and a little tidier. The exact same thing happens on Earth. It's a natural cycle."

"That's bull—"

"Watch your language."

"I won't let this happen. They can take the baby *back*."

"Now you're just being childish. Listen to me. I'm okay with this. I knew it was coming. I'm happy to give my resources over. It makes me proud to do so. I'm helping the mission. I'm assuring the convoy remains balanced and healthy. To prolong my life after retirement age would be selfish. Wrong. Disloyal." He pushed himself up and took Jamal by the shoulders. "I would be abandoning my responsibilities. It would be the worst thing I could do, you know that."

Jamal threw his arms around Diego's waist. "I don't want you to go. I don't want them to take you away."

"I know, boy. But it's for you and your generation. I die so you can live."

Jamal put on a brave face—even if it was wet and puffy—when he went home. No amount of reassurance from Diego could convince him the old man's retirement was a good thing, though. No one *wanted* to die.

Why would they want to exchange Diego—he'd just fixed that bean processor or something, hadn't he?—for a useless baby. How did that make any sense?

This was wrong. He might only be eight, but there was no way he would sit by while they hauled off his favorite person in all of space.

That night he lay wide awake while Akane cried out in the communal space. His parents were trying to soothe her, but she just wouldn't shut up.

Since he couldn't sleep he worked on a plan. Diego wasn't going anywhere without a fight.

The next day was group-play day. Not really school, and not really a day off. Someone—someone's grandma, if he remembered right—called it daycare. If your mom and dad didn't have the day off when you did, you went to group-play.

Several halls merged to form the communal play space. It wasn't a room, and it wasn't a passage either. It was a strange space on *Mira*, meant for mingling but rarely used by anyone other than children. Chairs and tables popped out from cubbies in the walls. Hidden closets held extra dishes and celebratory items. The area could be turned into a fort with a few reappropriated bed sheets and a little squinting.

When Jamal saw that the group-play guardian's back was turned, it was time to initiate Plan Diego. He shoved his hands in his pockets and sidestepped down the hall, away from the communal area. He found an access panel and dropped to his knees. From his pocket he produced a screwdriver taken from his parent's emergency tool kit.

Carefully, Jamal unscrewed the fasteners that secured the panel, then crawled inside. There were all kinds of rumors about the access tunnels. Sure, sure, the wrongly grown freaks were supposed to live in them, but that wasn't all. Alligators, giant bugs, ghosts, and even alien egg sacs were supposed to call the convoy ducts home.

Several times he had to stop and fight off the willies—especially when the motion-sensing work lights failed to flick on as fast as he'd hoped.

Cramped, dusty, and sweltering, the tunnels were not the stuff of playtime fantasy. It was slow going, pulling himself up flimsy ladders, shuffling through tight shafts, and squeezing around awkward corners. No one was meant to travel from one end of the ship to the other this way, but that was the idea. If someone found Jamal wandering the hallways they'd stop him, turn him around, and escort his butt right back to daycare.

Twenty minutes later he kicked his way out of another access panel. Only a moment passed before he regained his bearings and confirmed he was where he wanted to be: outside AI's main server room.

He pounded ferociously on the door.

"Yeah, just a sec," came a man's voice from inside. A moment later the door slid to the side, revealing a tall, well-built, middle-aged black man.

"I need your help," Jamal said.

The man considered the boy for a second longer before realizing, "Hey, you're my replacement, aren't you?"

There were two primary clones for each job—cycle mates. Clone A would be in charge while Clone B apprenticed—all while another Clone A was educated and another Clone B was born. The staggered growth was meant to add some normalcy—so that no one was forced into the surreal situation of having to train a genetic mirror of themselves. Subsequently, no fewer than two versions of a clone were alive at any one time.

Jamal seeking out his predecessor was unusual, but not unprecedented. It was natural to be curious about your genetic twin. But cornering them at their place of work was discouraged, because it was rude. Young Jamal was acutely—though not fully—aware of this when the older Jamal invited him into the server room. The space was dark. Ghostly lights formed rows and columns down the sides of the big, black servers, which in turn had been laid out in the room on a grid.

"Something tells me you shouldn't be here, little man," said the older clone. He sat down at his work station near the rear of the room. He swiveled his chair to face Jamal, and did not offer the boy a seat.

Jamal realized for the first time why it was important to have "the third" slapped on the end of his name. "I need your help, uh, sir. It's important. Something terrible is happening on board, and we've got to stop it."

"What? And you came to me because you thought, heck, I'm you and I'll understand your problem immediately through, what, a mind-meld? Do they not explain what a clone is to you kids?"

That wasn't it at all. "You're not me," Jamal said, indignant. "I came here because you've got access to I.C.C. I want to change some records and you can do it best."

Older Jamal considered this for a moment. He nodded once. "Okay. Spill."

Jamal explained, went on and on about Diego's multitude of virtues, then presented his solution. "I just want you to change the babies' numbers. Make it so fifty—no, a hundred babies have to be born before Diego retires. Or, you know, just change Diego's other number—his death number."

"I cannot allow tampering with the convoy's inventory system," said I.C.C.

"What it said." Older Jamal sniffed and wiped his nose on his eggplant-colored jumpsuit sleeve.

"Inventory?" said Jamal. "You mean like when we have to count all of our quarter's spoons and forks and stuff to make sure it's all there? You do that with people?"

"Of course. What did you think the numbers were for?" The computer sounded confused, though its inflections were even.

"Look, kid," said Older Jamal. A work cap sat on his terminal. He picked it up and twirled it between his hands. "You've got to face it. We're all spoons, okay? If you want a brand new spoon, you have to get rid of the bent one. Get it?"

"But there's nothing wrong with this spoon," Jamal insisted. "And he's not a spoon, he's a person. He's my friend."

"Yeah, well, we all lose friends. This is just how things work. We're all on a timetable, all set up to rotate. You were born at the precise time you needed to be so that you could replace me when I start to get slow. It'll be the same for the Jamal after you. It's part of life. I suggest you accept it and run back to school."

"But why is it a part of life?"

"Because some guy back on Earth looked at all the numbers and decided this way was best for the mission."

Jamal squeezed the screwdriver in his pocket, looking for something to hold onto. Something to use as a touchstone. His whole world seemed to be sliding off its blocks. "Is it?"

Older Jamal placed his cap on his head. "Is it what?"

"Best?" Jamal turned toward a blinking red light and camera lens mounted in the back of the room. "Is it, I.C.C.?"

"I do not currently have a holistic comprehension of the idea: best. Please clarify."

His little hands did a dance in the air as he tried to explain. "Best, you know, the, uh goodest way to do stuff. Like, brushing your teeth is better than not brushing your teeth, otherwise you've got to see the dentist with the drill."

"I think the word he's looking for," said Older Jamal, repositioning himself in front of a monitor at his work station, "is efficient. Is our current grow-and-recycle system the most efficient use of personnel in accordance with the mission?"

"It is a system in which the fail-safes create inefficiencies, but ensure the greatest chance of overall success," responded I.C.C. in its cold, mechanical way.

Older Jamal shrugged, "There you have it."

There you have what? "I don't understand."

The computer began again, "The system is reliant on—"

"Let me put it in laymen's terms, I.C.C." Older Jamal waved a hand in dismissal. I.C.C. thanked him, and it almost sounded relieved. Jamal knew it wasn't used to answering to a child. "Look, little man. Sure, our system isn't the best in the sense that we don't squeeze every last drop of productivity out of a person before they croak. We work them 'til death, but we don't work them *to* death. Come here."

Flicking a finger at the boy, he simultaneously stiff-armed 'flex-sheets, a half-eaten sandwich, and a coffee cup aside on his console. With a sliver of trepidation, Jamal came forward and let the man pick him up and place him on the now-clean surface.

Jamal looked his older, biological twin in the eye. The expression he found was stern, but not unkind. There were flecks of gray in the hair nearest the man's temples, and Jamal found himself wondering just how many years into his future he was looking.

"Everything in service to the mission, correct?" the man asked.

"Yes," Jamal agreed.

"And what is that mission?"

"To make it to the interstellar anomaly, designation LQ Pyx, and discover . . . discover whatever we can."

"Who has to make it?"

Twisting his lips, Jamal thought for a moment before answering. "We do."

"Who do? You and me? No, kid. It's not a who, it's a what. The convoy. Everything we do is in service to the convoy, and it's the convoy's mission to get to the star and figure out if we're really seeing what we think we're seeing: a giant, artificial construct. Whether it's a Dyson sphere or not doesn't matter. What matters is the life—the intelligence, greater than ours. Where did they come from? Where are they now? Why haven't they contacted us? Huh? Inquiring minds want to know. You and I, we'll never get to see the answers. But the convoy will." He patted Jamal's head. "We're just parts. Cogs in a machine. Pieces in I.C.C.'s system. You've got to decide you're okay with that, or be miserable. It is what it is. Life's always been what it is. It's whether you accept that or not that makes it good or bad, right or wrong, upsetting or not."

Jamal sighed. Why was everyone he talked to so . . . what was the word for it? It was a good word, he'd just learned it . . . *rational*. That was it. They were like the computer. Didn't they ever listen to their feelings instead of their brains? Or was that what being grown-up was all about: learning to be logical?

But wasn't ignoring your feelings illogical? Why was his gut so insistent if he was supposed to ignore it?

"What if there's a better way?" he asked.

"A bunch of bigwigged, scientific mucky-mucks back on Earth couldn't figure out a better way, but sure, you're what, nine? I have complete faith that a nine-year-old can figure out a better way."

"I know what sarcasm is."

"Good."

Jamal pouted. "Why don't we just try my way? An experiment with Diego, to see if maybe I'm right and this is wrong."

Red and blue lights began flashing down one of the server rows, and Older Jamal went to check on them. "Think it's best if you went home now, kid," he called.

I.C.C. opened the server room door.

"That's it? Just no?"

Older Jamal sniffed again, loud enough to be heard over the humming of the servers. "Just no. Believe me kid, they thought of everything when it came to the mission. If you want to change the system you'll have to shirk the mission."

Again, Jamal felt sick at the idea. The convoy was his home, the mission filled him with pride and wonder. They were explorers, boldly going . . . somewhere. He was proud to be a part of it.

But not proud of how they were going about it.

He went back to daycare the same way he'd come, and wasn't surprised to find that none of the adults had realized he was missing.

Nothing he did or said seemed to matter to anyone.

The day came far too soon. Jamal had racked his brain for weeks, trying to find a suitable solution, and at every turn Diego tried to discourage him.

"You don't have to defend me, boy. Someone died for all of us. Someone died so your pabbi could be born, someone died so you could be born."

That just made him more upset.

"I want to come with you, over to *Hippocrates*," Jamal declared that morning. His parents had excused him from class so that he could say his good-byes.

"Your Afi is coming with me. I don't want you there, Jamal. It'd be too hard." He was packing a bag. It was tradition to pack up your quarters before you retired. The most important things went in a black duffle bag, to be handed out to your loved ones as mementos. This the retiree would keep with them until the end. Everything else went back into surplus. Supplies to be used again, by someone new.

Bleary-eyed, Jamal hugged Diego around the middle and refused to let go for a full three minutes.

"I know it's hard. You cry if you want to, let it all out. I'll miss you, too. But you've got to know I'm doing the right thing. It's for the greater good."

Jamal wanted to puke on the greater good. The greater good could get sucked out an airlock for all he cared.

"Now, I'm going to take a nice, soothing bath before I go. Would you mind putting my bag by the door on your way out?" He kissed Jamal on the top of the head, said one last goodbye, and went to his bathroom with a smile on his face.

Desiring nothing more than to run down the hall wailing, Jamal took a deep breath and retrieved the bag from the table. He couldn't deny Diego his last request.

The bag was heavy. Way too heavy for Jamal to lift. He had to drag it all the way across the room. And then it hit him. It was heavy like a person—a small person. Like a Jamal-sized person.

He would go to *Hippocrates* after all, and stop this terrible mistake.

Few sounds came through the fabric ungarbled. Light was totally absent, and the tight space forced him into the fetal position. It was a deadly combination of comfort and sensory deprivation that lead to an impromptu nap.

There was no telling how much time had passed before a jarring woke him. Someone had picked up the bag. Afi, if his ears weren't lying. It must be time to go.

Hold still, he told himself. If he'd stayed asleep he probably wouldn't have had anything to worry about.

He could tell when they'd entered the shuttle bay, and again when they'd boarded a shuttle. He was thrown unceremoniously into an empty seat, and it took all of his willpower not to let out an *oomph*.

What would he actually do once they arrived? He hadn't thought that far ahead. Surely he would make a grand speech. Something like in the movies, where the hero dashes in and convinces everyone he's right through the power of words.

But what then? If Diego said he didn't want to retire would everyone else just let it happen?

He never got a chance to find out. He never even got to make his speech, grand or otherwise.

He was picked up and plopped down several more times before he decided they'd reached the end of the line. This was it, the place he was supposed to be. Time to make his grand entrance.

Jamal deftly unzipped himself, jumped up, and cried, "Stop!"

Everyone stared. There were five other people in the pristine, white room—but none of them were Afi or Diego.

Nearby stood a door, and without missing a beat Jamal threw it open. On the other side lay a glass cubicle—an observation station, like all the clone-growing rooms had.

A place from which to watch someone retire, should you feel the need.

On the other side of the pane, Diego reclined in a dentist's chair. On one side was a lady wearing one of those medical masks and a hair net, and on the other sat Afi, holding Diego's hand. They'd wrapped Diego in a long, white fluffy robe that folded down around his feet. He'd been swaddled, like Akane. His eyes were closed.

Clear plastic tubing stuck out of Diego's right arm and extended up to a bag of foggy, slightly blue liquid. The lady pumped something into the bag with a needle, and the solution turned pale yellow.

"No!" shouted Jamal. He banged on the glass with both fists. "Stop it! Stopit stopit stopit!"

Diego's eyes flew open as Afi and the technician's heads both snapped in Jamal's direction.

"Please," Jamal pleaded. "Please don't take him away." His vision blurred, and he had to take huge gulps of air as his lungs stuttered. "Please." His voice cracked and he turned away.

As he hid his face there was a commotion on the other side of the glass. Furniture squeaked across the floor, metal rattled, three voices argued and one yelped. When Jamal looked up and rubbed his eyes, Diego stood before him, palms pressed to the window.

"It's okay, Jamal. You have to let me go. It's time for you to learn new things and meet new people. You can't hang around an old fool forever." Diego sounded muffled, but the words were clear. So was the meaning.

"I don't want to let you go." He knew how selfish it sounded. He pressed his palm against the glass as if pressing it to Diego's hand.

"Go back out that door, now," said Diego. "It's time to say goodbye." With that he returned to the chair, lay back down, and shut his eyes.

❖ ❖ ❖

Jamal had never been in more trouble in his life. Apparently hitching a ride to the retirement wing was almost as bad as abandoning the mission. Almost.

No one cared about his excuses. No one cared he'd done it for a noble cause. All they cared about was teaching him never to do it again. They gave him a week to grieve, then enacted his penalty.

As punishment they made him clean the access ducts without the aid of bots. Ironically, the same ducts he'd high-jacked as a short cut to the server room.

Gleaming before him now was a plate that read:

> *Here interned are the ashes of Dr. Leonard McCloud.*
> *May the convoy carry him in death*
> *to the stars he only dreamed of in life.*

It marked the final resting place of some guy from Earth—some guy who had helped build the mission, but never saw it launch. *Guess there really are dead people in the walls,* Jamal thought.

Viscous cleaning solution ran down through the words, obscuring them. He mopped the orange-scented cleaner up with a rag.

There would be no plaques for Diego. Spoons only get remembered by other spoons.

"I.C.C.?"

"Yes, Jamal?"

The boy rubbed a hand across his eyes. The fumes stung. "Does it hurt when you die?"

"I have not experienced death, and do not have enough information to extrapolate—"

A burning rimmed his eyes. What strong cleaner.

No, he couldn't fool himself. He wasn't crying because of the chemicals. "That's not what I meant," he said. "Never mind."

A stiff silence followed. Jamal continued to polish the nameplate long after it was clean.

Though he was angry at Diego for leaving, Jamal realized he was also proud of the old man. He'd done something he believed in, no matter the personal cost. He'd done it for Jamal and Akane and all the other children. That could be good—should be good. But Jamal knew it was okay to be sad, too.

Akane. Diego was gone, and Akane was here. *She is cute*, Jamal admitted to himself. And *gurgley*.

That day, before he'd gone off to attend to his punishment, she'd grabbed his finger for the first time. She'd held it and smiled, and he had smiled, too.

He didn't want her to go back to *Hippocrates* anymore, or to disappear altogether. He didn't even want her to be a boy. Now he just wanted to be a good big brother. Like Diego had been for Anita.

"Diego . . . he was your friend?" I.C.C. eventually asked. It was a cautious question, asked microseconds slower than usual questions from the AI.

"Yes," Jamal croaked.

"I don't comprehend what that means."

Wiping the snot from his nose, Jamal cleared his throat. "I know," he said, and patted the wall as if I.C.C. could feel the gesture. "I'll teach you."

Marina J. Lostetter's original short fiction has appeared in venues such as *Lightspeed*, *Orson Scott Card's InterGalactic Medicine Show*, and *Flash Fiction Online*. Originally from Oregon, she now lives in Arkansas with her husband, Alex. Her debut novel, *Noumenon*, is an epic space adventure starring an empathetic AI, alien megastructures, and generations upon generations of clones. Marina tweets as @MarinaLostetter and her official website can be found at www.lostetter.net.

TO LOSE THE STARS

by Jennifer Brozek

Jennifer said the space mining companies in her story are based on real firms like Planetary Resources, whose HQ is in nearby Redmond, WA; Barrick Gold Corporation, the Canadian gold mining company; and Vale, the Brazilian mining company. Extrapolating the futures of these companies, with their many successes and failures, added a great deal of realism to this powerful story of a lone miner who is forced to make a decision between what she wants and what is right.

THE LAST THING Theresa expected to find more than two hundred million klicks from Earth was a corpse. When *Nevitt*, the oldest of her prospector machine HUBs reported the find, she thought the HUB had finally blown its last logic circuit. Especially since *Copernicus* and *Hypatia*'s swarms were reporting the normal: thousands of asteroids within the designated field of search. Some promising. Most not.

But here was a corpse.

From where Theresa sat in the control center of her survey and exploration ship, she could tell precious little about the dead person on the large hunk of rock in her little corner of the asteroid belt between Jupiter and Mars. It was suited up in an older, bulkier style of EVA suit. It was covered with the dust of who knows how many years and was slumped over on its side, partially facedown. She

277

couldn't see any of the suit's patches well enough to get a sense of who the corpse once was or who they had worked for.

Part of her wanted to send *Nevitt* in closer. The other part of her wanted to run screaming. A dead body in the middle of space was a warning. It could be nothing else. There was something dangerous here. Even if that danger was a stupid adventurer who got careless and then got dead. Not only that, if she figured out who the person was, the burden of responsibility fell upon her shoulders.

Instead, Theresa ordered *Nevitt* to ignore the anomaly and release its survey swarm. She had a job to do and time was getting short. This was her second-to-last scheduled stop before her authorized expedition terminated. Either she found what she—and her client— wanted or she went home empty-handed. Again. It would be nice to find something before the tail end of the expedition.

The corpse could wait. It'd been waiting there for a long time. Besides, if it was actually someone and this section of the belt proved rich, the claim, technically, had already been staked. Though, not officially. Otherwise, the company wouldn't have sent her to these coordinates. If the area was just as fruitless as the previous five sites, she could leave the corpse in peace, enjoying its private burial in space.

Theresa yawned and stretched as an insistent binging woke her from her nap. She unhooked herself from her sleep bag and grumbled, "Yeah, yeah, yeah. You're worse than a cat." Floating through the small ship from her personal pod and into the command center, she flipped off the alarm that declared her little army of prospector survey machines had touched down on all of the asteroids over twenty meters in length, their respective HUBs had analyzed the samples, and had the all-important survey report ready for her discerning eye.

Copernicus reported in first. Sixty percent trash, thirty percent promising material, and ten percent unknown. Theresa rubbed her eyes and opened the details on the report. She had programmed her three HUBs to report in worst to best. The fact that thirty percent was promising gave her pause. This was better than everything else she'd surveyed in the last six months.

Gold, palladium, silicon, nickel, and good old frozen water. All of it was in demand by the company, the space station, and Earth. She tapped her leg with a smile. "Promising indeed."

Hypatia's report made Theresa sit back and suck in a breath. Forty-four percent trash, fifty-three percent promising material, and three percent unknown. The detailed report included platinum, iron, and industrial-grade diamond in the mix. For a second, Theresa wondered why she couldn't breathe. Then she realized that she'd been holding her breath while she read *Hypatia*'s details. She let it out with a soft, "*Dios mio.*"

Her hand shook and her heart hammered as she pulled up *Nevitt*'s report. Twenty-four percent trash, seventy-one percent promising material, and five percent unknown. Gold, gold, and more gold. On that kilometer-long, kilometer-and-a-half wide rock where the corpse was, most of it was gold held together by quartz and frozen dirt. All of the surrounding asteroids claimed the same. "*Ave María.* I found it."

Theresa pushed herself up out of her seat in a rush and gave a cry of victory as she traversed her small ship down to her personal pod. A sumersault sent her to the observation bubble where she could see three survey HUBs attached to the side of the ship. "You beautiful machines, we did it! We're rich!" Even at one percent, her portion of the find, Theresa couldn't calculate just how rich she was, but it was a lot.

More than she'd ever dreamed.

Not only would she have enough to afford another prospecting run, she would have enough to live in style while she was at the space station on her mandatory acclimation tour. Hell, she *and* Matias would live in style. She could afford to share with her best guy.

Her eye drifted away from the prospector HUBs to look into the black behind them at the pinpricks of light. This beauty, this space, these stars were still hers. She stared at them for a long time, thinking nothing, and basking in the joy of a found treasure.

Turning over again, Theresa returned to the control module, dreaming champagne and pure-air dreams. She settled into her seat again to reread the reports and to make sure they had not made a mistake. After a moment's thought, she sent *Copernicus* and his swarm out to redo *Nevitt*'s section. Just to be sure.

Hypatia, she sent to look at the corpse once more.

Watching the computer screen with an odd lump in her stomach, Theresa read the delayed text message from her client, Larissa Perez from the Barrick-Vale Mining and Exploration Corporation. She answered after some hesitation.

Larissa: Well, Miss Ibarra, almost last stop. What do you have for us?

Theresa: Nothing concrete yet. Looks promising.

Larissa: How promising?

Theresa paused again, reluctant to admit what she knew. There was the corpse to consider. Now that she was certain of a real find, she had to deal with the body. She had to figure out what to do.

Theresa: I don't know.

Larissa: This is important. Our next scheduled freelancer isn't for another 20 months. Holding it for you. You're one of our best. If you fail, we'll need to schedule sooner.

Theresa: I know. I know. I just need to be sure.

Larissa: How promising?

Theresa could feel her client's impatience and knew that the above wasn't an idle threat. The corporation needed resources and needed them yesterday. The sooner they knew they needed to ramp up a mining expedition, the better.

Theresa: Promising enough. Will contact if I get confirmation.

Larissa: That will have to do.

Larissa: Sending you a video from Matias. He spent a lot on this one. Enjoy it.

Theresa: I will. He's a good one.

An hour after Larissa logged off, the promised video finished loading and Theresa was able to view it. Her brief wonder at why Matias had sent a video message, instead of the usual letter, became immediately clear as the screen came to life with her lover's face.

"Happy anniversary, *amorcita*! Two years since we crashed into each other in the hallway. I'll bet you forgot, all alone out there in the black." Matias, a handsome, swarthy man in his midthirties, held a bouquet of daisies up to the screen. She could see the gray above his ears showing more than it had the last time she'd seen him. Even so, he was the youngest lover she'd taken. It was almost a scandal amongst her surveyor peers. She touched the screen, murmuring, "You're right, *mi cielo*. I'd forgotten."

"I have to keep this short, but I wanted you to know I was thinking of you and I haven't run off with the neighbor. I miss you so much, *bonita*. But soon, you'll be home and we'll be together again. After that only one more survey, and then . . ." Matias gave the screen his most endearing come-hither look. "And then, we will *talk* about things, you and I. I wanted you to know that I'm thinking of you and am still waiting for you."

Matias waved the bouquet of daisies at the screen. "*Te amo*, Theresa. Until next time. A longer letter is coming."

Theresa turned off the screen as Matias froze with the daisies obscuring his smile. Her own smile was gone as well. She had forgotten, until that moment, that this was her penultimate survey expedition. During the next one, she would turn fifty. Then, she would be considered too old to make the nine-to-twelve-month solo journey into space.

Floating from her seat, Theresa headed to the observation dome. She stared out the window at the stars for a moment before focusing her eyes on her own reflection. She wasn't a beauty by any conventional standard, but she was a handsome woman with short hair that stuck out in all directions and faint laugh lines around her eyes. The lack of gravity gave her the artificial youth of a full face. Without gravity to hold you down, the wrinkles she knew were there disappeared. In contrast to the perceived youth, her hair had gone to iron, speckled through with its original black.

"I don't feel old."

The protest echoed thousands upon thousands of laments, railing at the encroachment of age. She may not feel old, but the regulations would not bend. Under the age of fifty and you were qualified for solo expeditions. Over the age of fifty and you weren't. More than one surveyor fought the system and lost. Too many young and immortal kids were willing to take to the stars for a pittance. To do her job for less money up front.

And dear Matias had reminded her of this. One more survey expedition was all she had left. Officially. She knew he wanted to marry her, despite the fact that she'd told him there would be no such commitments while she was in space most of the time. She'd encouraged him to leave her. Instead, he'd hung on with hope in his heart. Matias was waiting until she was grounded to propose, not realizing the grounding might kill her.

The binging alarm of *Copernicus*'s waiting report pulled Theresa from her melancholy. There was still work to be done. And a corpse to deal with.

Theresa took a breath and entered into full VR mode with *Hypatia*. *Hypatia* was her newest survey HUB. She'd bought the technological marvel after *Hadfield* was crunched between two erratic, fast moving asteroids. It was partially her own fault for not being fast enough and partially the mechanical failure of a thruster. It hurt, financially, but wasn't surprising. Most survey expeditions lost at least one HUB and one-third of their swarm to the vagaries of space. A survey expedition that didn't was lucky.

Hypatia had all of the cutting-edge survey innovations Theresa could afford at the time, including the virtual reality set up that made it feel as if she were the HUB and not just piloting it. Every movement of woman and machine synched up. She'd trained for months in a simulator for this moment. Because, sometimes, you have to get your virtual hands dirty to be sure of a find.

She'd never trained to move a body.

Centering herself, Theresa moved *Hypatia*'s arms out and grabbed the body by the shoulder and head. She heaved it left, pushing it back into its original sitting position. At first it wouldn't cooperate, flopping back over. Theresa swore softly, then maneuvered herself back into position and pulled the corpse upright again. She overcompensated in hopes that the body would balance itself.

This time, though, she didn't let go. Again, it started to slump over. Dead weight on a rock with even the tiniest bit of gravity was still dead weight and uncooperative. Finally, Theresa decided to let gravity do her work. She pulled the body over until it was laying on its back, then moved away. The body stayed put. Theresa counted this as a victory. She noted that something was slung around the body's neck that wasn't part of the suit.

Unfortunately, the suit was still covered with the dust of ages and told her nothing of the person inside. Though, something pinged on the edge of her awareness. Now that the body was laid out, its silhouette was vaguely familiar. The front helm reflected her own mechanical image back at her. Cleaning it would do no good. Not that she really wanted to see a frozen, desiccated skull grinning at her.

Theresa activated *Hypatia*'s blowers and blew the space dust off of the body's chest. With that, she realized she'd just solved one of the greatest mysteries of the last century.

Hiroshi Nevitt, the Godfather of all freelance surveyors.

Hiroshi Nevitt, the first solo surveyor and the golden boy of the first inner-system mining company, Planetary Resources and Exploration.

Hiroshi Nevitt, the man who disappeared without a trace and the reason there were no more preprogrammed survey ships.

Hiroshi Nevitt, the reason that the age of fifty was the expiration date for all solo surveyors.

Theresa stared at the Planetary Resources and Exploration patch just below the emblazoned "NEVITT" on the body's upper left chest. A thousand questions collided in her brain all at once. Beyond how, why, and what happened, she wondered what the hell she should do now. She reached out *Hypatia*'s grabber and caught hold of the thing slung around Hiroshi's neck and pulled it to her. It was surprisingly heavy for its size and thumped to Hiroshi's chest when she let go. A quick cleaning revealed it to be a plaque of gold, and another mystery became clear.

Two weeks before Hiroshi left on his ill-fated final trip, he'd emptied his savings and bought a kilo of gold bullion. No one knew about it until his survey ship automatically returned to the station without him and he was declared dead. His family screamed foul play and theft. It was just another added twist of weirdness to a ship that came into port without its master.

Of course, Planetáry Resources and Exploration was vilified by the media. Its preplanned automatic survey ship had left the face of space exploration to die a horrible death, alone, in the blackness of space. Some called it murder. Nothing could be proven, of course. But that was the end of Planetary Resources and Exploration's space mining dominance. The public turned its back on the North American company and funded new, less tainted, companies to go to the stars.

In essence, Hiroshi Nevitt's disappearance allowed Barrick-Vale to grow in prominence and allowed her, a poor but brilliant Brazilian girl, to become a premiere surveyor from South America.

Now, as she gazed at the pounded gold plaque with its crudely made but even writing, Theresa knew exactly what had happened. Perhaps not Hiroshi's thoughts, but the emotions he felt and why he did what he did. The plaque itself told the story better than anyone else could.

HIROSHI NEVITT
1997—2047
I WILL NOT LOSE THE STARS

Theresa's memory was fuzzy, but she remembered Hiroshi's final solo survey run was to be his last. He had been getting up in age and Planetary Resources and Exploration wanted to send younger, newly qualified surveyors. They wanted to set Hiroshi up on a media circuit as a recruiter to the "Space is Our Future" cause. She guessed he had agreed because she remembered seeing the ads for the upcoming "Talks with Hiroshi" back when she was a teen. He had inspired her to become the woman she was today.

It seemed that Hiroshi had other ideas. From the declaration on his golden gravestone, Hiroshi liked the idea of being permanently grounded as much as she did. Theresa wondered what he thought as he pounded the gold bullion flat, then pounded in the letters that made up his epitaph. She wondered what he felt as he hung the plaque around his neck, watched his survey ship fly away without him, and listened to the suit's oxygen alarm sound in his ears as he gazed at the stars he refused to leave.

Theresa returned *Hypatia* to her outside loading dock and pulled back into her own body. She had a decision to make: Go home a hero or go home rich.

Despite Hiroshi's death, the fact that he was here, in this part of the asteroid belt so rich in the resources that her client needed, was claim enough for the courts. Hiroshi worked for Planetary Resources and Exploration. Technically, this find was theirs. Oh, Theresa knew she would be a hero to the world if she brought home Hiroshi's body. But the mining claim would go to the rival company and she didn't have a contract with them. Her client would be pissed and she would be poor.

Certainly, the media circus *could* make her rich, but she'd need to stay stationside, then planetside, to take advantage of it. An endless parade of well-paid talk shows, perhaps a book or a movie deal. While she was the golden girl to the world, she'd be nothing, a failure, to the mining companies that could send her back into space. Also, play the media game too long, and fifty would come quick.

Theresa floated in her chair, watching the stars go by. She was a responsible woman. She couldn't just knock Hiroshi's body off his chosen deathbed. Pulling up the image of the plaque, she read it over and over again. "I will not lose the stars," she quoted. "What would you want now, now that you're dead and gone? Do I take you home to be immortalized even more than you already are? Do I do my duty and lose the stars for you or do I do my duty to the corporation?"

Theresa bowed her head, hearing the voices of her family, especially her grandmother, telling her to do the righteous thing, to give the man a proper burial with full rites. She also heard the voices of her peers, encouraging her to keep what she'd found and let the dead keep their own secrets. But Hiroshi Nevitt was a hero to the world. His disappearance had shocked everyone and could have killed the space community if the Isolationists had had their way. Bringing Hiroshi home would silence the conspiracy of an alien menace just waiting to conquer one and all.

Theresa raised her head and decided.

Inside the cargo bay where the HUBs, their swarms, and their samples lived when the survey and exploration ship was on the move, Theresa stood in her little-used EVA suit. Made from the latest and greatest she could afford, the suit moved with relative ease. It was slimmer and far more user-friendly than the suit Hiroshi Nevitt wore. *Hypatia* still held Hiroshi's body to keep it from floating haphazardly in the cargo bay.

Theresa drifted over to *Hypatia* and Hiroshi. She eyed the kilo of gold floating around Hiroshi's neck. She wouldn't take it. She wouldn't steal from the dead. But there was an attraction to holding that much gold, that much worth, just once. Hooking a foot into one of the floor bars, she reached out and touched the plaque, then grasped it in both hands. She couldn't feel its true weight, but the substance of it still impressed her. Running a hand over the stamped letters, she delighted in their impressions. "You're going home," Theresa told the body. "We're both going to be famous whether we like it or not. Earth needs its heroes."

She let go of the plaque and watched it float to the end of its tether. A flash of black against the gold on the back of the plaque caught Theresa's attention as she turned away. Turning back, she flipped the plaque up and discovered Hiroshi had written on it in something that looked like black marker. Theresa spun herself until she was upside down to the body but right side up to the writing and read. It took a moment to decipher Hiroshi's handwriting amongst the raised stamp marks.

"*The stars are my home. I am finally home.*"

Theresa felt like she'd been punched in the gut. She didn't know when this had been written—before or after the creation of the epitaph—but it hit her in the core of her being. Hiroshi Nevitt had committed suicide rather than return to Earth. Who was she to say that Earth needed Hiroshi more than he needed the stars?

❖ ❖ ❖

Theresa: Good news, Mrs. Perez. The find is confirmed. Sending data now.

Larissa: How good? I get to "keep my job" good, I "get promoted" good, or I "get to retire" good?

Theresa smirked at the screen, hearing her boss's voice in her head. Larissa, as her handler and direct employer in the company, got a bonus every time one of her freelance surveyors found something worth sending the mining team out for. It was in her own interest to hire the best.

Theresa: One of the latter two. Look at Prospector Hub 3's report first. It's the best of the lot.

There was a much longer pause than normal. It was expected. Not only did Larissa need time to read the report, she needed to go through the due diligence of looking at the rest of the reports to get an overall impression of the claim. Theresa had scrubbed all of the records of finding Hiroshi Nevitt's body from the report.

Larissa: Good job, Miss Ibarra. The first of your advance bonuses will be in your account by the time you return to the station.

Theresa: Thank you.

Larissa: I owe you a drink for this one. Let's hope your last stop of this survey trip is as fruitful.

Theresa: Let's hope. Transitioning to final stop in two hours. I should reach it in three days. Will ping you then.

Larissa: Acknowledged. I've just sent your email. Enjoy!

Technically, Theresa could leave now. But she had one last duty to perform. She shifted her focus to the control center and to *Nevitt*. The HUB had its namesake carefully strapped to it and was waiting for its orders. Theresa took a breath and sent the preprogrammed command. She watched as *Nevitt* took off on a path perpendicular to the solar system's ecliptic plane, ensuring—at least for a while—Hiroshi's final rest would not be disturbed again. After the initial burn, the HUB was programmed to hit its thrusters once every thirty-six hours until it ran out of fuel. It would go a long, long way before it lost power and started to drift. Switching her view screen to *Nevitt*'s point of view, Theresa bowed her head for a moment.

"From the stars we came, to the stars I commend you. May their light ever shine bright in the blackness of space. May you always know your path. May you always find home." She paused in her cobbled together final prayer. "May you never lose the stars, Hiroshi. May you ever know their beauty."

She stopped then and just watched the HUB head out with its precious cargo to parts unknown. She would watch until she lost the signal. Then she would head to her final survey spot of this trip. In the meantime, she would read words of love from Matias and contemplate her richness in wealth and soul. Theresa knew she had done the right thing by sending Hiroshi back to the stars.

But now she had to think about her own future. The next trip would be her official last. Perhaps she would have enough money to come back again. It was likely with this recent find. She would know before her next—her last—company survey trip. Then, she would make her own decisions. One thing was certain; she, like Hiroshi, would do everything she could to keep the stars she loved so much.

Jennifer Brozek is a Hugo Award finalist and a multiple Bram Stoker Award finalist. She has worked in the publishing industry since 2004. With the number of edited anthologies, novels, RPG books, and nonfiction books under her belt, Jennifer is often considered a Renaissance woman, but she prefers to be known as a wordslinger and optimist. When she is not writing her heart out, she is gallivanting around the Pacific Northwest in its wonderfully mercurial weather. Read more about her at www.jenniferbrozek.com or follow her on Twitter: @JenniferBrozek.

CYLINDERS

by Ronald D. Ferguson

Ron is working on a novel called The Prometheus Proposal, *which investigates the problems and politics plaguing the first starship project that plans to send only the "dead and unborn" to another star system. His tense and touching thriller "Cylinders" takes place at the very beginning of that project, thirty years before the ship is built.*

"I'VE HAD ENOUGH ADVICE from you, Jerry," Rachael Watanabe says when I follow her from the weightlessness of the Red Cylinder into the open axis of the rotating Green Cylinder. "Today, I am fourteen, and I'm going by zip line to celebrate my birthday."

Despite my advice—everything I suggest seems to make her angry—we don't take a transition-ring elevator. Instead, we crawl along the webbing that surrounds the axis entrance to the Green Cylinder. In less than a minute, we are on the zip-line platform. The platform rotates with the cylinder, but at this distance from the axis, the created gravity is negligible.

Rachael arranges a harness about her shoulders and legs. She reaches for the next zip-line trolley. This is my last chance to dissuade her.

"Your mother would not approve, Rachael. There are other ways to celebrate."

"I want to see the Earth, Jerry. I haven't seen the Earth for a year. The best view is from the central dome in the Green Cylinder base."

"Take the elevator to the surface. Walk two kilometers—"

"You might look like my father, Jerry, but you're not him. I don't have to do what you say." Rachael fumbles with the trolley connection. "You're not even human."

"Mostly true." I step forward with the intention of helping her hook up. "However—"

Her harness clicks into the trolley. She engages the power and the trolley pulls her along the zip line out and over the farmland a kilometer below.

I must protect her. Having no other option, I connect to the next trolley. A moment later, I accelerate along the zip line. At the halfway point to where the Green Cylinder surface meets the opposing base, apparent gravity and our velocity increase sufficiently for the trolley to switch to regenerative braking.

A minute later, a bright flash illuminates our destination. Have the solar reflectors malfunctioned?

The atmosphere alarm buzzes three times followed by a continuing blast on the horn. The warning indicates that at least one window has blown out.

The solar reflectors are programmed to shut over any broken window, but the bright light must have been an explosion. How many windows broke? The reflectors should close to stop the air loss and seal the leak, but what if they are damaged or malfunction?

I search actionable decision branches.

How close does the zip line come to the broken windows? If the reflectors don't close before we reach our destination, how will Rachael breathe? Will the vacuum suck her into space?

Suspended from the zip line, I can do little except review the decision tree. Despite my instructions to protect her, I am helpless. We must ride fate to our destination.

She is a hundred meters ahead of me. I increase my volume to maximum. "Don't unsnap your harness when you arrive." I'm not sure Rachael hears or listens. Maybe I shouldn't offer her advice: It only aggravates her stubbornness.

Ahead, the zip line terminates fifty meters from the window strip. Tomato plants bend towards two broken windows, and a cone of swirling air and debris targets each. Slowly, the high-pitched shriek of escaping air mellows to an angry swoosh, but as the continuing horn blast indicates, the reflectors have yet to complete the seal.

The broken windows lie less than two hundred meters beyond the boundary between the window strip and the agricultural strip. They are easy to see because of the cylinder's curvature. The window strip on the other side of the agriculture strip is higher but a kilometer away, too far away to distinguish individual windows. On the cylinder surface two kilometers overhead, another window strip separates the two remaining agricultural strips.

Rachael alights on the platform at the end of the run. Before I can stop her, she shrugs off her harness and skips knee-deep through the fluttering plants towards the window strip. Her blouse flaps in the unusual wind blowing toward the broken windows. She stumbles and momentarily goes airborne because of the light gravity.

I don't wait until I reach the platform. Ten meters from the surface, I undo my harness and allow my tangential velocity to carry me into the tomatoes. Taking advantage of the small speed difference between me and the cylinder, I hit the surface running.

She plants her feet and skids through some plants. I grab her arm and pull her back. The wind diminishes to a breeze by the time I've dragged her back to the landing platform. The horn stops, announcing that the reflectors completed the seal of the fractured glass. Rachael's blouse ceases its flutter, and the danger appears to be past. I release her arm but stand at ready.

In the distance, an emergency crew and security specialists converge on the damaged section of windows.

"Don't tell Mom about this." Rachael glares at me. "The fail-safes worked perfectly."

"Very well. I will not mention what happened unless asked, but you should tell your mother."

"Why? She already worries too much."

"Because the flash of light suggests an explosion broke the windows. Sabotage. The security guards will question you as a witness. You are a minor. They will follow up with an interview of your mother. You should tell her before they do."

"She'll ground me for not listening to you."

"Taking the elevators was only a suggestion. You are correct that the zip line is more efficient than walking the length of the agricultural strip even with the cylinder surface gravity at twenty-eight percent of Earth's. The window blowout was unpredictable and not your fault."

"Thank you." Her smile is not quite a smirk. I am unsure whether she has manipulated me again.

"After we talk to security, we'll take an elevator to the observation dome. You can still see the Earth for your birthday."

"No. My birthday is ruined." The expression clouding her face is a familiar pout. "I want to go home, Jerry."

"We must wait for security to interview us before you go back to your mother's apartment."

"I don't mean the apartment. I want to go home to Earth. I miss my friends. I miss my Dad."

Her eyes glisten. I don't respond because her father is dead. The videos of him stored in me hint at his memories. I can replay them for her, but reminding her of that never comforts her.

Two security officers approach us.

She shrugs. "We may as well go back to the apartment when this is over."

A flash of light illuminates the middle of the overhead window strip. The atmosphere alarm sounds again. Another explosion. Another rupture.

"Yes," I say. "Returning to the Blue Cylinder is a good idea."

Rachael seems more amiable, less tense, after we enter the Blue Cylinder. Although the Green and Blue Cylinders have opposite angular velocities at thirty revolutions per hour, the surface gravity generated in the two-kilometer-long, one-kilometer-radius Green Cylinder is half that of the two-kilometer-radius, one-kilometer-long Blue Cylinder. The non-rotating Red Cylinder joins the other two, produces no gravity, and serves as a shuttle dock.

I suspect Rachael would not enjoy returning to full Earth gravity after living on L5 Station Oh for the past year. Humans are sensitive to such things.

When we enter the apartment, Rachael's mother, Jane, sits at the dining table having tea with a young man only five or six years older than Rachael. The man pushes his tea aside and stands.

"Dr. Katz." Jane nods at Rachael. "This is my daughter, Rachael. Rachael, meet Dr. Daniel Katz."

"Please, call me Dan." He extends his hand. "Your mother is allowing me to do postdoctoral work with her this next year."

Rachael hesitates before smiling and shaking his hand.

"And this"—Jane gestures at me—"is Jerry."

"Jerry is operational?" Dan's eyes widen. "Everyone in graduate school followed your work on Jerry. Except for the facial detail, he looks like any other android."

"Thank you, Dr. Katz." I extend my hand. "Jane says I am a work in progress."

"Outstanding." Dan smiles and shakes my hand. "Call me Dan, Jerry. I hope that you and I will spend many informative hours together."

"I am at your service, Dan."

"You didn't take your phone with you, Rachael." Jane doesn't look angry or worried. Perhaps she hasn't heard about the window sabotage in the Green Cylinder.

"It's my birthday." Rachael sticks out her lower lip. "I didn't want to be disturbed. Do I smell cookies?"

"Birthday cookies in the kitchen. Help yourself but save room for lunch." Rachael's brow furrows. "Sean Jeffords called you three times this morning. I'm tired of telling him you aren't available."

"I'll call him back." Holding three cookies, Rachael returns from the kitchen. "I left my phone in my room. May I be excused?"

"Of course." Jane waits until Rachael is out of the room before she continues. "How was your time with Rachael, Jerry?"

Shrugging is called for, but my shoulders aren't designed for it. "I try to please her, but everything I do irritates her."

"Maybe you try too hard to please her. How did she behave during the security alert?"

"You know about the broken windows?"

"Everyone knows," Jane says. "The director made the announcement by phone broadcast and over the intercom. The safety features worked flawlessly, but it must have been a distraction. I assumed that's why you returned early. I thought perhaps Rachael was upset."

"Not that I could tell. Sabotage is always intended to disrupt, but she took it quite well even after the second set of windows exploded. Perhaps she doesn't understand the danger."

"Sabotage?" Now Jane looks puzzled, worried. "The Director didn't mention sabotage. I want you to watch her more closely, Jerry."

"Of course, but she will not like it. Her behavior is a mystery to me."

"She's a fourteen-year-old girl." Jane sighs as if her comment is an explanation and returns to her chair. "We should finish our tea, Dan. Sit. Sit. You, too, Jerry. No, join us at the table."

"Thank you." I take the chair across from Dan.

Dan glances about as if unsure what to say. Perhaps the sabotage unsettled him. I decide not to mention the windows again unless Jane brings it up.

Dan sips from his cup. "Excellent tea, Dr. Watanabe. I usually prefer coffee, but this . . ."

"Call me Jane. Save the doctor and ma'am stuff for formal situations. Now, how did a PhD in biology get interested in cybernetics?"

Dan seems relieved to discuss something other than sabotage and Rachael, but I will have to spend more time with him to be certain that I properly read his face.

"I had a masters in cybernetics first. That's always been my major interest. Biology is an extension of my interest in cybernetics, not the other way around. Also, I've been writing computer programs since I was seven—"

"And you started college when you were twelve? Precocious."

"That's why I have no social skills. Anyway, the overlap between creating smarter AI machines and understanding systems that can achieve goals is . . . well, I don't mean to ramble on. Too much enthusiasm, I'm afraid, and of course, no social skills."

"Cybernetics and AI. That explains your dissertation."

Dan tilts his head. "You read my dissertation?"

"Yes." Jane sets her tea on the table. "I read it while I was completing Jerry. The method you used to thin slice and scan a cat's brain to generate a 3D model to digitally emulate a particular feline cortex fascinates me. Quite innovative and a novel approach for generating goal strategies in an AI. That's why I contacted you."

"The method wasn't as successful as I had hoped." Dan sets his tea aside and leans towards Jane. "What does modeling the synaptic connections of a cat have to do with Jerry?"

Interesting. The discussion is about me. Perhaps they will question me later. I compare their conversation with my Gerald Watanabe videos, but that doesn't help to make sense of everything they say. I store their conversation in Verbal Markup Language. Later, I will review the conversation word by word and compare it with information from the station library. Most humans don't do that even with technological assistance available.

"Some people think my approach for instilling my late husband's memories into Jerry shows promise. I do not. First, I had no good way to collect his memories. Installing available video recordings is a poor substitute for actual experience and also is difficult for Jerry to reliably index and access. Second, too many filters stand between the memories of a deceased human and the creation of an AI emulation. The method you describe in your dissertation is more complex than what I did, but I believe it has a better promise for creating an AI based on the memories of a specific person, memories that can help the AI formulate strategies and accomplish goals."

"You want to try my AI approach for emulating cat brains but using human memories?" Dan laughs.

"What's funny?"

"I applied for admission to medical school next year as preparation for the same attempt."

"You can't come with me," Rachael says.

I don't know why she says that. She knows I must follow her if I am to protect her. I am also unsure how to read her grin and the tilt of her head. Is she being derisive or devious?

"We still have another hour of scheduled interaction time together. Your mother suggested you might try to deceive me."

"And when the hour is done, you will still follow me about like a puppy." She purses her lips. "Don't you remember what happened when you followed me into the girls' dressing room? The girls thought you were a man. We don't want a repeat of that."

"I endeavor to stay in the background like an old piece of furniture." I am unsure why I attempted a simile. I'm not good with similes. Perhaps I quoted Gerald Watanabe. "Your mother thinks it important that I spend time near you to keep you safe."

"Important for you, not for me. Nevertheless, you cannot come."

"Why?"

"School work. Sean and I are assigned to have sex in the biology lab. Sex involves two people, but no observers and especially no androids."

None of my video recordings from Gerald Watanabe include sex instruction. I consider my next action, but I find no alternative except to wait for more information.

Rachael shrugs. "Why don't you access the station library. Look up *sex* and *teenagers*. You'll see that I'm right."

The request is reasonable, and I access the station library. The amount of information is enormous and poorly indexed. I struggle to extract a consensus from the information tsunami hash-tagged *sex* and *teenagers*.

Rachael taps her foot and rolls her eyes while I review the data. Without waiting for me to finish, she giggles, hugs me, and walks away. I am unaccustomed to hugging and unable to decipher her actions.

Moments later, I interrupt my attempt to understand *sex* and *teenagers* to return to my imperative to keep Rachael safe. She's gone. To find her, I track her phone. The phone reports that she is still near me, but I do not see her. After ten minutes of failure and having no alternative, I return to Jane's lab. Returning to the lab after losing Rachael has become a familiar pattern for me.

Jane and Dan are reviewing the computer screen on Jane's desk when I enter. I wait just inside the door. My batteries are low, but I don't want to intrude.

Dan shakes his head. "What I did for the cat was inadequate. Creating a digital object to emulate a single neuron-synaptic bundle requires significant computer memory. I refined the design to improve memory usage, but that was too late for my dissertation. I should have used ten times as much memory to model the one billion neurons and ten trillion synapses in a cat's brain, but money was short. I also couldn't afford the latest in massive parallel processing, and so my cat was slow-witted, incredibly dumb, and shallow of memory."

"But the program reacted like a cat." Jane drummed her fingers on the tabletop, her jaw firmly set. "Determined money can solve the equipment problem. That won't slow us here. Scientists first attempted emulating a cat brain seventy years ago, but your cat works better. The neurons you designed have complex branches rather than a single-point representation. You emulated more than six types of synapses, not just one. I could go on, but what sets your work apart for me is that you used a particular dead cat's brain to preconfigure the neuron-synaptic layout in the digital cortex. I'm convinced that's what's missing from Jerry, why his learning feels more like rote repetition rather than the formation of new data paths. Current AI technology is very good at creating smart androids but not so good at emulating real people."

"A real person's behavior is not always smart," Dan says. "My approach isn't easy. A human brain takes twenty to twenty-five times as much memory as a cat. Besides, my method requires a freshly frozen and thinly sectioned brain to construct a 3D model of the synaptic structure."

"I understand. My late husband, Gerald Watanabe . . . I wanted his personality as the model for Jerry. Modeling the android to look like Gerald was easy, but I didn't have a viable approach to instill Gerald's memories much less emulate his personality."

"Your late husband? I am sorry for your loss."

"Three years ago. He died from a glioblastoma tumor a few weeks after being diagnosed, but he had many brain scans including those that yield 3D images. I have copies of two of those scans. That's why I thought you could help."

Dan rubs his chin. "I'm not sure that 3D image scans are detailed enough . . . ."

"And . . . and he donated his body to science. I have his brain stored at 77 Kelvin."

"There will be ischemic damage."

"Damn it, Dan. Don't be so negative. Do you want to try this or not?"

"Of course, I want to try it, but even if we succeed, you've got to understand that the emulation simply produces an AI with thought patterns based on the topology of your husband's brain. It won't be your husband."

"Yes, but your emulation reproduced behavior that the cat learned before it died. Jerry can replay the videos of Gerald that I stored in him, but he can't reconstruct any of Gerald's experiences or memories."

"I don't know—"

"Please, Dan. I'm doing this for Rachael. I don't want my daughter to forget her father, and I hope that this will be better than what I tried with Jerry."

"The videos may be good for calibration, if we can correlate them to some of the memory structures. I don't have great confidence in 3D holograms or sections from a damaged brain, but perhaps we can learn a lot in the attempt. This will be very expensive, Jane. Who's going to pay?"

"I'll introduce you to the money man in a video conference after lunch."

"Okay then. I'm ready. Let's do it."

Jane smiles and touches Dan's hand. "Thank you."

They stand. I take that as my cue to go to my charging station. I wonder whether I should tell Jane that I've misplaced her daughter again. Probably, she's already guessed that because I arrived early and alone.

When I face the charging station to engage the power connector, Jane asks, "Jerry, why is Rachael's phone taped to your back?"

Jane and Dan have finished lunch by the time my charge is complete. No one has given me instructions, so I don't leave my charging station.

The screen on Jane's desk clears, and the introductions begin.

"Dr. McLeod," Jane says. "It's good to see you. This is Daniel Katz, the young scientist I told you about."

Despite a new, gray mustache, I recognize sixty-seven-year-old Dr. Alastair McLeod from a five-year-old corporate photo. His hair is thinner now and his ears larger, but the face metrics match. Dr. McLeod owns the majority share of McLeod Enterprises, controls the L5 Station Oh, and is the richest man in the solar system.

"Jane, you look well." Dr. McLeod's voice is gruff. "Dan, I'm pleased to meet you. I hate to be curt, but I only have ten minutes."

"Yes, sir," Jane says. "I'll be quick. Did you have a chance to read our proposal?"

Dan glances at Jane. He looks surprised. Was it the phrase "our proposal"?

"No," Dr. McLeod says. "Brief me."

"All the popular approaches to implant a dead human's memories and personality into an AI have had little success. Dan's method of emulating a cat's brain shows more promise because it alters the thinking strategy of the AI based on the neuron-synaptic structure of the selected subject, but the implementation will be very expensive, requiring massive parallel processing and thousands of terabytes of memory to create a digital cortex based on a human's synaptic connections."

"I understand," McLeod says. "Unfortunately, mass production of qubit memory and quantum processors is several years away. You'll have to be satisfied with the technology currently available."

"That much memory won't fit inside Jerry's shell," Dan says. "We'll be limited to a large box to house the digital cortex."

"Is he always this negative?" McLeod asks.

Jane looks away and bites a smile from her lips.

Dan leans forward. "I don't want to give unrealistic expect—"

"Son, I know a bit about applying science. We do the research now, then when the technology catches up, we will be ready for a better implementation. What do you think is feasible in this first iteration?"

"Realistically, I would be surprised if we can salvage more than five percent of Gerald Watanabe's memory structure to embed in the machine memory. However, that means we don't need a complete digital cortex for our first attempt. We can build a limited module, one that will fit into Jerry's shell while we run parallel research on the full-sized digital cortex in a big box."

"I like this boy, Jane." McLeod smiles. "Send me the budget, and I'll approve it."

"Yes, sir."

"Uh, Dr. McLeod." Dan says. "Generic AI design is well standardized and very effective. Can I ask why you are interested in constructing an AI with memories from a specific person? My approach requires that the person be dead before emulation. I guarantee that the process will not grant immortality to the person who provides the memory structures."

"I'm not interested in immortality, Dan. Are you familiar with the Prometheus Proposal?"

"No, sir."

"You should be. The purpose of the L5 Station Oh is for research to support Prometheus. Everything we do there is related to Prometheus, and that includes AIs who can emulate specific humans. Become familiar with Prometheus before we talk again. Decide whether what we propose is worth the cost and dangers before you commit. Good to meet you, Dan. And Jane, always good to see you. Keep me informed."

A logo from McLeod Enterprises replaces Alastair McLeod's face on the screen. Jane congratulates Dan. He still looks puzzled.

Anticipating that Dan might ask my help, I resolve to learn about the Prometheus Proposal. I access the station library. Researching the Prometheus Proposal takes very little time. Many articles recount Alastair McLeod's unwavering support for the proposal as well as the opposition from competitors like Nixon Liu of Sol Bio Systems. Among the vocal moral critics is psychologist-turned-video-evangelist, Stanley Stanton.

The briefest summary of the Prometheus Proposal was given by Alastair McLeod to a Senate Committee during his bid to lease the L5 Lagrange point that trails the Moon.

McLeod's response to Senator Johnson's inquiry about the essence of the Prometheus Proposal was succinct. "We don't have the technology to take ourselves to the stars, and so, instead, we shall send the dead and the unborn."

"Does he have to come with us?" Sean Jeffords asks Rachael, but he looks at me.

"He always lurks about. Just ignore him." Rachael pulls herself along the safety line that leads into the zero-gravity gymnastics room. "I want you to teach me the free-fall sumersault. Come on. Ignore Jerry. It's not like we're on a date."

Sean frowns and says nothing.

"Anyway, my Mom limits my required interaction with Jerry to two hours each day. She wants him to learn from me. I guess I owe it to my Dad's memory to make an effort."

"I still don't get it." Sean releases the safety line and pushes into the ten-meter cube. All six walls of the cube are padded and a safety rope drifts from each corner. "He's just a robot made to look human."

Sean rolls into a ball, rotates, and plants his feet firmly against the wall. He pushes off towards the opposing wall and executes a half twist.

Rachael glares at me when I follow her into the cube.

"Stay out of the way," she says. "Your two hours are up, and I need to improve my zero-gravity skills."

Sean pivots against the far wall padding, grabs a rope, and coils his legs against the wall.

"Of course," I say. "Education is very important, but please observe the safety guidelines posted on the gymnasium door."

"I know how to follow instructions." Rachael seems angry. Again.

"Instructions?" Perhaps I should change the subject.

Sean uncoils his legs and sails towards us while executing a sumersault.

"Did you learn much from having sex with Sean in the biology lab? I couldn't find detailed instructions for coitus in the station library, or I would have sent them to you. The videos they had were difficult to decipher."

"What!" Sean loses control and crashes into the adjacent wall. The pad absorbs most of his momentum.

"Can you be quiet for the next hour?" Rachael grits her teeth and grabs my arm. "No more talk about sex or the biology lab."

"Certainly. If that is what you require."

"What did he say about us?" Sean demands.

"Nothing. Jerry is easily confused." Rachael squints and gives me a two-handed push towards the door. Newton's Third Law applies, and she drifts away from the safety line. Does she notice?

"I apologize for the confusion," I say. Still angry? I attempt to mollify her. "My assignment is to keep you safe and remind you of your father, Gerald Watanabe."

"You're not doing very well." Now, Rachael floats a full meter from the door. "I thought you were going to be quiet, Jerry. Wait in the corridor. I'll tell you when I'm ready to go."

"As you wish." I reposition myself just outside the door so that I can watch and listen.

"He wants to keep you safe?" Sean flexes his fingers as if he injured them bouncing against the wall. "What about me?"

Rachael waves her arms. "Sean, I can't reach the safety rope." Her efforts to swim in the air rotate her a quarter turn out of alignment with the door.

"Eventually, you'll drift into a wall." Sean continues to massage his hand.

"Eventually? Are you serious? Help me get back."

I stick my head in the door. "Would you like me to get you a safety rope?"

"No!" the two simultaneously shout.

Sean traverses to the nearest corner and gathers the attached rope. He snakes the line out to Rachael. She hauls herself to him.

"I don't like your robot." Sean nods at me. Resentment fills his voice. "Is he going to watch?"

Determination sets Rachael's jaw. "Not after I shut the door."

Dan closes my abdominal access panel. He lowers the laboratory lights to normal brightness.

"That finishes the installation of memory and processors for the limited digital cortex," he says. "As soon as we have a good synaptic model in the computer, we'll upload a reduced configuration into your memory. How does it feel so far?"

"I feel fine." Feel? I have no tactile sensors inside my abdomen. Apparently, he wants polite conversation. News is a common topic for such conversation. "Did you get the news? They caught the saboteur that blew out the windows in the Green Cylinder. He was an engineer with the solar-reflector maintenance crew."

"Do you think there may have been more than one?"

"Sir?" I don't understand his question. "Only one saboteur was identified. No saboteurs were reported among the remainder of the window maintenance crew."

"From what I've read, the Prometheus Proposal has many enemies. This station is key to the development of the technology needed for Prometheus to succeed. Do you have an opinion whether there might be other saboteurs?"

"Opinion? Is that about things somewhere between fiction and fact?"

"Use fuzzy logic, Jerry. Your opinion comes from your analysis of what is likely true when the evidence is insufficient to support a fact."

"Fuzzy logic. I understand. What measure?"

"Some folks form an opinion with less than a twenty percent chance of being correct, especially when high emotional content accompanies their evidence."

"I have no chemical support for emotions."

"Noted. Having an opinion is more difficult when there are numerous alternatives. Fortunately, this situation has only two: more saboteurs or not. Set the decision metric to sixty percent. That is a good place to start. Review empirical information about other saboteurs as relevant to the question of whether there are more saboteurs, calculate the probabilities of the two alternatives and use the sixty percent cutoff to select your opinion. 'No opinion' is an acceptable conclusion if neither alternative rises to the level of the cutoff. Can you do that?"

"I already have. Based on the amount of opposition to the Prometheus Proposal and the number of people espousing violence, my opinion is that there is at least one more saboteur onboard, most likely another maintenance technician although perhaps not in the window crew."

"Excellent." Dan smiles. "The same opinion as mine. Did that feel different from your usual thought process?"

"I'm not sure." Again he uses the word feel. "I don't review my thought processes while thinking."

"I've redirected your data input circuits through the new digital cortex. The parallel processors will compare the structure of the new data, identify similar structures in the digital cortex and use those to strengthen the synaptic connections. Now your memories will be stored two ways, your original process for raw data and by the strengthening of emulated synapses in the digital cortex. Based on that you may be able to review your thought processes when the digital cortex gains more experience."

"I don't understand."

"You don't need to at this stage. Each day we will update the software for the digital cortex in an attempt to make it behave like the brain of Gerald Watanabe. If you notice any changes in the way you think, please tell me."

"Will this help me carry out my assignment of protecting Rachael and connecting her with her father?"

"That's why we are doing this, Jerry."

❖ ❖ ❖

After several weeks of daily updates from Dan, I notice no changes in the way I process data. However, someone starts a fire in the zygote research lab and one of the lab technicians is killed by smoke inhalation. More sabotage.

Dan compliments me on my opinion about more saboteurs, but Jane has harsh words.

"No matter how idealistically motivated, eventually sabotage causes a death, and then the saboteurs become terrorists, and killing gets easier."

One evening while performing my usual watch duty while Jane is at the lab, I pretend I'm a piece of furniture at the back wall of the darkened living room. Rachael and Sean sit on the sofa.

"Don't do that," Rachael says.

"Why not?" Sean asks. "You're my girlfriend."

"I'm not your girlfriend. We're just friends."

"Then why did you let me kiss you?"

"Curiosity. I wanted to see if I liked it."

"Did you?"

"Not enough to want to be your girlfriend. Stop it, Sean. I told you not to do that."

Rachael needs protection. I step from the shadows. Usually my voice sounds exactly like Gerald Watanabe's, but I up the volume of my recording of Jane clearing her throat to get their attention before I speak. "It's time for you to go home, Sean."

"Who's going to make me?" Sean says. "You, robot? I don't have to do what a machine says."

I turn up the room lights. "If you do not leave, I will carry you from the apartment."

His face flushes with anger.

"You don't dare hurt me." Sean stands. "My father is an electrical engineer. He'll disassemble you and use your pieces for spare parts."

"No one will be hurt unless you struggle, in which case you are far more likely to sustain damage than I am." I step towards him.

He retreats to the door, pauses to glare at me, and then points at Rachael. "All right for you, Rachael. You had your chance. You'll be sorry." He slams the door when he leaves.

Rachael stands and clasps her hands. I try to read her face. A faint smile is on her lips, but a glimmer of a tear is in her eye.

"May I be of service, Rachael?" I move to her side.

She sighs deeply and leans her head against my shoulder. Jane would hug her, but I am unsure what Rachael expects from me.

"We think we know someone, but we can never really know anyone can we, Jerry?"

I parse the sentence repeatedly, but the meaning eludes me. "Can I get you a glass of water?"

"No thank you, Jerry. I'm going to my room. G'night."

"Jerry?"

Are my eyes closed? I never close my eyes, not even while recharging. Why hadn't I seen Rachael approach? An afterimage of a little girl on a carousel fades away. When did memories start fading from my consciousness?

"Yes, Rachael." I check my battery: fully charged.

"I want to see the Earth."

"Aren't you and Sean going to the Green Cylinder this week? You can see it then."

"We were, but he's still mad at me. I'm the one who should be mad. He sent me a message telling me not to go to the Green Cylinder without him and especially don't go today. He can't tell me what to do, Jerry."

I recognize her stubborn streak. "Is that why you want to go today, because Sean told you not to?"

"Mom says I can go to the observation dome in the Green Cylinder if you come with me."

"Of course I will go with you." I disconnect from my charging station. How long ago had we first attempted to visit the observation dome to see the Earth? Seventeen weeks and three days since her fourteenth birthday. "Did you bring water and a snack?"

"I have everything I need." She pats her waist pack. "Can we go now?"

I glance at the status screen for the lab. Jane and Dan are listed as unavailable except for emergencies. Their calendars indicate a budget meeting. Rachael has no reason to lie to me about her mother's permission.

"Yes. Let's go."

We take an elevator to the Blue Cylinder transition ring. By the time the elevator reaches the cylinder axis, we are effectively weightless. We enter the Red Cylinder.

"You should call Jane when we get to the observation dome," I say. "She will be out of her meeting by then."

"I left my phone at home."

"How can you forget your phone so often? How will people track you?"

Rachael smiles and pushes into the central corridor. Clearly, she wants to try her navigation skill in zero gravity. I follow more sedately, keeping within reach of the safety rails in case I need to subdue her enthusiasm, but the few people in the main corridor pose little risk for a clumsy collision.

An information panel flashes a message above one of the port corridors. A Moon shuttle is docking at the port. Disembarkation begins in ten minutes, and unloading cargo starts in thirty.

Rachael touches a wall and pushes off again. At this rate, we will traverse to the Green Cylinder transition ring before the passengers crowd into the Red Cylinder main corridor.

Moments later, Rachael drags her foot along the wall to slow her approach to the transition ring. She smiles as if she is pleased with her zero-gee skills. She should be. Her maneuvers are much better than our last trip to the Green Cylinder.

"Shall we take the zip line?" I ask so that she does not think that I want to control the trip.

"We can take the elevator." Rachael smiles. "I don't mind walking today."

She grabs the safety rail and propels herself until she is well ahead of me. At the next junction, she grabs the rail and pivots into the corridor that leads to the elevators.

Voices. She must have met someone. Their conversation grows louder while I approach the elevator corridor. Sean: his voice is distinctive. He sounds angry. I pause in the main corridor. Humans often need privacy to resolve their disagreements.

"What are you doing here?" Sean asks. "I told you to stay away."

"I'm going to the observation dome to see the Earth," Rachael says. "And I don't care what you say."

"Well, you can't use the elevators. They are all closed. Take the zip line."

"All closed? How can they all be closed?"

"Electrical problems. My Dad is fixing them. He told me to stand watch. Where's your robo-guardian? He's one of the bad guys, you know. Your Mom too."

"What bad guys?"

"The ones planning to send unborn babies to the stars. No Moms. No Dads. They can't do it without robots to raise the kids, but robots know nothing about raising humans. They might as well kill the babies here."

"I don't know what you're talking about."

"Sure you do. Old Man McLeod pays for your Mom's research. She's helping to build robots to raise the kids. She's helping to kill the babies."

"You're crazy, Sean. Dr. McLeod pays all the salaries here, including your Dad's. If my Mom is guilty, so is your Dad."

"That's not true!" Sean shouts. "You better go home now, Rachael."

Rachael drifts into the main corridor. Sean follows her. Their eyes are locked. Apparently, the reconciliation is not proceeding smoothly.

Anger distorts Sean's face. At first, I don't recognize the unfamiliar expression on Rachael's face, then I realize that it is fear. Now, Sean is between Rachael and me.

"That is enough, Sean," I say. "Rachael, you should go. I will handle this."

Relief spreads across Rachael's face. She grabs the safety rail and retreats towards the Green Cylinder transition ring.

Sean twists his head and glares at me. He has a pry bar in his hand. He faces me, releases the safety rail, and takes a two-handed grip on the pry bar.

I approach in the hope of calming him.

He screams, "Dad! Help!" and swings the bar at me. The action causes him to rotate and spoils his aim.

I grab the misdirected bar and jerk it from his hands. The force of the blow breaks my thumb. I throw the bar aside and use my free hand to shove Sean back down the elevator corridor. The reaction bounces me against the opposite wall. Sean tumbles and misses the safety rail in the corridor.

I don't wait to see whether he stabilizes. I grab the safety rail and follow Rachael to the transition ring. She is frantically tapping icons on a communication panel when I arrive. To her right, the status panel shows all elevators as out of order.

"Communications don't work," she says. "I can't get security to answer."

"Security?" No communication? I check for wireless connections. That doesn't work either.

"Maybe someone disabled communications," Rachael says. "Why?"

I form an opinion. "Sean Jeffords and his father must be saboteurs."

"Not Sean. That makes no sense. He's just a kid, not much older than me."

"His father is not a kid. He's an electrical engineer. Wireless repeaters aren't working. Likely he sabotaged the emergency panels so that no one could alert security. "

"Alert security to what?" Her eyes widen. "He's working on the elevators. Is he going to blow them up?"

"I don't know. Look at the elevator status diagram. The icon indicates that Elevator A is underway. Maybe it is not sabotage. Perhaps Mr. Jeffords has repaired the elevator. My opinion that they are saboteurs could be wrong."

"They're escaping," Rachael says. "I should have brought my phone."

"The only way off the station is through the shuttle ports in the Red Cylinder, not by descent to the Green Cylinder surface."

The Elevator A icon turns red indicating a malfunction, but no alarm sounds. The elevator does not grind to an emergency stop. Instead, it picks up speed. The safety features don't slow it.

Releasing an elevator to crash full speed into its destination will destroy it as effectively as a bomb. The icon for Elevator B lights but the elevator doesn't move. Not yet. Apparently, sabotaging an elevator takes longer than a communications panel.

"We've got to warn someone," Rachael says.

"How? No communications."

"They can't have disabled all the panels. I know. Let's take the zip line to the opposite cylinder base. Maybe the panels there still work."

No better strategy comes to me. I could travel faster alone, but I won't leave Rachael near Sean. "Yes. We should go."

We work our way into the open axis of the Green Cylinder and descend the webbing to the nearest zip line platform. When we reach the platform, its rotation isn't enough to provide significant weight.

I'm helping Rachael put on her harness, when a powerful shove against my back knocks us from the platform. I keep my grip on Rachael while we drift into the void. A kilometer below us the boundary between farmland and window slowly rotates. We no longer rotate with it.

On the zip-line platform, a large man gives an angry grunt and retreats up the webbing to the Red Cylinder opening.

Sean waits for the man at the opening. He yells, "I told you you'd be sorry, Rachael, you and your tin man." His voice cracks almost as if he is crying.

The man and boy disappear into the Red Cylinder corridor.

"How will we get back, Jerry?" Rachael seems calm. Apparently she doesn't recognize the danger.

We are weightless, in free fall, but now the thirty rotations per hour of the zip-line platform about the cylinder axis is obvious. I analyze our velocity, both from the push and from the linear velocity imparted by the rotating platform: just over one meter per second but the largest component is perpendicular to the cylinder axis and towards the cylinder surface. I must protect Rachael. How?

"We can't get back," I say. "We have no way to alter our current trajectory."

Rachael wraps her arms about me. She presses her face against my chest. I am unsure how to respond. Rachael needs her mother, but I am the only one here. I put an arm around her.

"If I had brought my phone, I could call Mom. How long before someone sees us and gets help?"

"We can't wait for rescue, Rachael. Eventually, our current velocity will take us to the cylinder surface. We are not moving very fast, but the relative velocity of the cylinder surface is more than one-hundred-fifty kilometers per hour. We will not survive the collision."

"Oh." Her voice is faint. She tightens her grip. "Will we die, Jerry?"

"That is my opinion."

"I'm afraid." She is silent for seventeen seconds before she speaks again. "I wish I could say goodbye to my Mom."

"I understand." I tilt her head against my chest. Tears streak her face. A strategy germinates. "Do not worry. I may have a way to return you to the Red Cylinder. From there, you must sneak past Sean and his father and go to the port where the shuttle just docked. Even if the panels there are down, the shuttle crew can send a message to security by radio."

"This is like when I was stranded away from the walls in the zero-gee gym, isn't it?" She looks into my eyes. "How can you get us to the Red Cylinder? We have nothing to grab. No one to throw us a safety line. How . . . ?"

"Newton's Third Law. But I cannot return us. Just you."

"I don't know anything . . . ."

Her face blurs and becomes the face of an eleven-year-old girl standing beside my bed. The little girl says, "Please don't go. I'll miss you, Daddy."

". . . about Newton—"

"What?" My mind clears the little girl's image. Who was she? She looked like a younger version of Rachael.

Rachael trembles. "I said, 'I don't know anything about Newton.'"

"Third Law. Every action has an equal and opposite reaction." I stroke her hair before I realize what I am doing.

Rachael needs more. What can I do? I am an android, not someone who knows how to give her the reassurance she needs.

Is that my opinion? Sometimes you are not what you think; you are what you do. I must do whatever helps Rachael. The strategy coalesces.

"Don't worry, Pumpkin. Do exactly what I tell you. Everything will be all right."

Her eyes widen. "Pumpkin?"

"We are going to play cannonball, Rachael."

"Like my dad played swimming-pool cannonball with me when I was little?"

"Yes. You know how. Just a minor change. Grab my hands. Roll into a ball and place the bottom of your feet against the bottom of mine. Feet to feet. Stay coiled. Hold tight."

"I will."

My thumb is useless for gripping, and so we hook our fingers together. "That's good. See the opening into the Red Cylinder? We're aiming you for that. It doesn't matter if you miss a little. There's lots of webbing all about. Just grab hold, don't let go. Then pull yourself along the cylinder base until you enter the Red Cylinder. You know what to do when you get inside."

She nods. "But what about you, Jerry?"

"I will count to three." I estimate the rotation relative to the axis. "When I say three, we release hands and push as hard as we can with our legs."

"What about you, Jerry? How will you get back?"

"My purpose is to keep you safe."

"And help me remember my father. I know."

"Exactly. Ready? I'm going to count."

On three, we release hands and push. Rachael sails towards the Red Cylinder opening.

Her trip back takes much longer than our trip out. At last, she grabs the netting and hauls herself to the Red Cylinder. She waves to me . . .

Another image replaces her: A very young girl in a yellow dress with a purple bow in her hair waves while I drive away. I am sure it is Rachael as a child. She speaks, but I can barely hear her words.

"I love you, Daddy. I'm missing you bunches and bunches."

By the time the image fades, Rachael has disappeared into the Red Cylinder corridor.

Pushing Rachael to safety has increased my velocity. My timeframe to destruction is accelerated. I'll reach the surface in about sixteen minutes.

Peculiar thoughts. Did I malfunction? The images of Rachael as a child must be from the digital cortex Dan installed. Dan should know about this change in my thought process. I rotate so that my feet face the cylinder surface. I don't expect that will let me survive when I hit, but perhaps some of my memory won't be too badly damaged. In my most secure memory location, I record a separate audio message congratulating Dan for his success with the digital cortex.

At six minutes from the surface, an alarm sounds. Rachael must have reached the shuttle port. She is safe. Soon security will arrive to stop the saboteurs.

I say aloud, "That's my girl," but upon analysis, I don't know why.

I'm confused by my responses. Is doing something without knowing why one of the things that distinguishes a human from a machine?

The cylinder surface gives the illusion of acceleration while it quickly passes beneath me. I am not fooled, my velocity is unchanged. At thirty seconds to impact, a peculiar feeling—that's what Dan would call it—invades me. Comparisons with my catalog of human emotions persuade me that the feeling most resembles melancholy.

I regret nothing. I don't understand the purpose of regret. What's past is past. The future is tenuous. My thoughts are always in the present, have always been about what happens now, but somehow Gerald Watanabe's synaptic structures influence my thoughts . . .

Now, for the brief time until impact, my present feels empty because I will never see Rachael Watanabe again.

⚬⬥⚬

Ronald D. Ferguson writes full time after years of teaching college mathematics. He lives with his wife Layne and a rescue dog named Cash not far from the shadow of the Alamo.